THE WAVE

A Novel in the Time of Global Warming

Gunilla Caulfield

Copyright © 2010 Gunilla Caulfield
All rights reserved.

ISBN: 1439272816
ISBN-13: 9781439272817

Cover photo by Mark Kanegis

Also by Gunilla Caulfield:

"The Bookseller and Other Stories"

∽

"Murder on Bearskin Neck"
(An Annie Quitnot mystery)

DEDICATION

This book is for my children and grandchildren. In fact, for all children and grandchildren, for they are the future.

And for Al Gore.

CHAPTER 1

When the great ice shelf broke off, the earth, deep in its core, heaved a sigh of relief. It shifted its mantle and brought forth a great tremor, which followed the iceberg and gave it more power, creating a massive wave that rolled along surely but secretly under the surface of the ocean.

CHAPTER 2

President Albion was addressing a group of state governors at an annual fundraiser. Governor Seamans of Nevada had just finished a short speech, and Albion was at the podium thanking him, adding a few joking asides audible enough to draw laughter from the group.

The president then turned to the business at hand. It was 2050, local elections were coming up, and it was time to pay one's dues to the party. The conservatives were firmly in command and had everything well in hand so far, but one should never take anything for granted.

Tax cuts, incentives for big business to combat foreign imports, education, and crime control—the agenda never varied. The governors listened intently, noting down programs of interest to their state as the president outlined his objectives. The pork barrel was passed around every year, and some were better at grabbing the slippery thing than others.

Smatterings of applause interrupted the speech regularly, and each time the president pretended to be surprised and pleased, always repeating his last sentence in case the ovation had caused anyone to miss it. He had begun to expand on the subject of possible new subsidies for industry when Press Secretary McPherson appeared at his side with a folded message. The president, slightly irritated at the interruption, unfolded the paper and glanced at it. He stepped down from the podium while reading the message, and the governors started chatting and taking the opportunity to press down a few mouthfuls of dry chicken and barely cooked greens while they waited.

As usual, the food had been cold when it hit the table, and the wine hadn't been much help. Fortunately, stronger beverages had preceded the dinner, which had been delayed in order for the president to attend a funeral service for a retired general.

The noise in the room masked the conversation between the president and the press secretary. McPherson was pale, and the president, as anyone would have seen had they bothered to look at him, was in a state of shock.

The door to the left of the podium, through which McPherson had entered earlier, opened again and two guards appeared. McPherson was forcibly steering President Albion toward the door, handing him over to the guards before making his own way back to the podium. He cleared his throat into the microphone, and when the noise continued unabated, banged his hand on the podium until the crowd quieted down.

"Ladies and gentlemen, I apologize on behalf of the president. President Albion has unfortunately been called away on a matter that requires his immediate attention. He told me he trusts you will understand and that you have his full support in the programs that have been outlined. He asked me to request that Governor Haskins take over the podium in his absence, and that you continue the evening as planned. If he is able to, the president has promised to return later. Thank you. Governor Haskins, if you would be so kind?"

Haskins made his way to the podium, swaying slightly, his face flushed with importance, augmented by drink to a pink sheen. He whispered a question to McPherson, who only shook his head in response before hurrying after the president.

Haskins' drawl followed the press secretary out into the corridor. McPherson could already hear the hoverjet that had been quickly enlisted to serve as Air Force One, and walked faster.

When he got outside the door, the small group that had gathered there was starting down the path. The president was in the center, surrounded by uniforms. He kept looking back and when McPherson finally appeared, Albion waved him on impatiently.

"Pete, where's my wife?"

"She's safe, sir. She's gone ahead," McPherson said.

"When we get aboard, you're going to have to fill me in, Pete…"

"I'm not going, sir."

"What do you mean? Of course you are. I need you with me."

Albion looked a little unnerved, and McPherson forced a smile to calm him down.

"Sir, all the seats are accounted for. Everyone is aboard except for you. The rest of us are coming later, separately. Hurry, please. You'll be fully briefed by General McClellan." McPherson smiled again, and gently put his hand on the president's elbow to urge him on. Pete steadied the president as they ran, bent down now to avoid the downdraft. At the bottom of the steps, Albion turned around.

"Make sure to bring Evie, Pete. Tell them I said so."

McPherson nodded and looked the president in the eye. "Thank you, Mr. President. Goodbye, sir…and take care."

The door was barely closed before the jet lifted vertically with a great roar. McPherson started back up the path to join the others. None of them knew what he knew, and he would not tell them. Nor would he tell Evie, his girlfriend, if he ever saw her again.

He had also lied to the president about his wife. Mrs. Albion had not gone ahead. She had gone off for a drive earlier in the day, as she often insisted on doing, and had not returned.

CHAPTER 3

President Albion barely made it into his seat before the hoverjet took off. General McClellan occupied the seat in the center and Albion quickly scanned the members of his cabinet, seated next to the general and in the seats behind them, who had been selected to fly with him. He was glad to see Senator Steinfeld, but missed Senators Halkey and Price. Maybe they had been out of town.

The jet veered suddenly and Albion tried strapping on his seatbelt, but the buckle was jamming. He shook his head in disgust and turned to McClellan.

"Joe, I need a complete briefing here. Magnitude, timeframe, the whole thing."

"Well, sir, I'll tell you all I know, which isn't a hell of a lot. Some sort of tsunami caused by an earthquake, so far as we can tell. Major wall of water, it seems—although the individual tremors weren't that high on the scale, which is why the urgency of the warning is puzzling. We'll know more in a few minutes. I'm expecting an ESAT report anytime now."

While the general was still speaking, a sheaf of papers was put in his hands. After he scanned the pages, he handed them to Albion, without the thought occurring to either of them that the president should have been the first to read them. The report was couched in scientific language and accompanied by a number of graphs, but the message was clear.

"Mr. President, I'm afraid it's not good news. If this report is correct, it appears that a major tsunami maybe headed for our shores. *All* our shores, it seems, although I don't quite understand that."

"God." The president didn't bother to look at the papers. McClellan was well versed in reading these reports, and Albion would have to trust him. They sat in silence, as though speaking about it would make the thing real.

"What has been done in terms of evacuation?" the president asked finally.

McClellan only blinked.

"Joe...broadcasts? What?"

"Nothing's been broadcast, sir," McClellan replied tersely.

"What the hell are you saying? No warnings? You mean people don't know this thing is coming?"

McClellan looked impatient, annoyed. "Sir, what good would it do? How could you even consider evacuating people from the entire coastline of the United States? Whole cities like New York, Washington, Los Angeles? Do you know what would happen if the news broke? People would be killing each other trying to get away. They would die, trapped in gridlock, colliding in the sky..."

"McClellan! *Shut up.* Please. This is unconscionable. Unthinkable. The people must be told. Even if only a few may save themselves, they must be given the opportunity. Not to let them try would be murder on a mass scale." The president was irate; his face flushed. His knuckles turned white as he grasped the armrests.

"Sir, with all due respect, we have already voted on the issue. All communication systems have been shut down."

"For God's sake, Joe, what have you done? You voted without me? You made this decision without me? And what about the cabinet? And the senators, congressmen? Are they safe? Were any of them notified? Was this a unilateral decision?"

"It was entirely within our rights, sir, under the emergency powers act."

"Rights? How can you talk about rights?" The president was getting up out of his seat, red-faced, trembling with rage. A scuffle ensued, with McClellan trying to force the president back into his seat and getting some help from Secretary of State Atkins.

The jet lurched slightly, and the pilot swore. The co-pilot squeezed through the door into the passenger section with a pained expression on his face. He looked at McClellan, who nodded vigorously. They had been expecting this, and now the president would need to be put down, temporarily. The co-pilot jabbed the needle into Albion's arm. The president slumped back in his seat, his head lolling.

"Close call, Sam. Thanks. Just couldn't handle the news, I guess. Should be out until we get there, right?"

"Sure, general. He'll be out for a couple of hours."

McClellan took a deep breath, sat down, and strapped himself back in. A shot of whisky right about now would have been just the thing. He was confident that they had made the right decision. For all they knew, the scientists might be wrong. Happened often enough. Then people would have gotten themselves killed for nothing.

In fact, that's likely the way it'll turn out, he thought. *This thing was just blown way out of proportion, will probably just amount to coastal flooding, severe beach erosion, that sort of thing. Houses lost maybe, and the drowning of people who acted stupidly.*

He looked over at Secretary of State Atkins, who sat staring out the window into the dusk. Atkins had been against shutting communications down. He had received the first inkling of the news in a communiqué from a European counterpart, and had immediately alerted McClellan, who had called the voting members of the cabinet for a videocon. All this had taken place while the president was at the memorial service. They had discussed the issue and voted on it within the space of less than five minutes. McClellan had suggested it would take too long to get the President in on the videocon. They knew there was no margin of time; it had to be immediate or someone would pick up the news, somewhere, broadcast it, and then panic would ensue.

SYSCOM had been shut down—the great system that managed the country's broadcast media as well as all other national and international communications systems, private and commercial, via the TELSAT links. Except the G-line, of course, the old government hotline. They had kept the G-line open, even though it was no longer considered absolutely secure. *It was quite easy*, McClellan thought. They had shut down SYSCOM in the past, called it a "systems upgrade" or "emergency preparedness testing," but of course they'd always broadcast a warning of the system shutdown ahead.

The only person who had any knowledge of the event—outside of the twelve people in the cabin and the lab workers who had forwarded the report and been assured that the matter was being handled—was McPherson. His information was now incomplete and limited to the earliest report; besides, he could be trusted. Extreme loyalty was unusual in people these days, but Pete had proven himself in the past.

Unfortunate that he had to be left behind, if it gets bad, the general thought. But the important thing was that they had complete containment.

The primary goal was to get the president out safely. Once they got to Camp David, they would make an effort to get as many senators and congressmen as possible airlifted out of Washington. Of the short list of people they had begun to call around the country using the G-line, no one had been informed about the nature of the emergency. It had been decided that the briefing should wait until they were in the safe room at the camp.

We did the right thing, he thought. If this did turn out to be major, they could control the scope of it—let the news out piecemeal to help control panic. If it turned out that the event was not serious, they could get the system back up and blame the downtime on precautions due to a possible natural event, which had fortunately been avoided.

McClellan stretched his long legs as far as they would go in the cramped space. He was a tall man and found flying in these small jets exhausting and uncomfortable. He looked at the president, who was now snoring.

What a softie. God, how I miss DeLong.

DeLong had been elected president two years before, a man in the prime of his life at forty-eight, exactly what had been intended when the age limit of running for president had been adjusted. No younger than forty-five and no older than sixty. You had to have paid your dues and proved your mettle before getting in, and you had to get out before you reached the age of vascular instability.

DeLong had been in excellent physical shape, an exercise fanatic who had started each day with a five-mile run on the treadmill. Two months into his presidency, he had collapsed on the floor of the rec room. Within an hour, he was dead. An undetected brain aneurysm, probably aggravated by strenuous exercise. *You never know, do you?* the general mused.

That's how Albion got to be president. He had been a last-minute choice for vice president, after a previous candidate had suddenly withdrawn when the media unearthed some unsavory details from his past. Albion had an immaculate record and was a moderate, which nicely balanced DeLong's right-wing stands. The voters liked that kind of balance. It made it seem as though everyone would get a fair shake. Of course, both parties were really just mirror images of each other these days, each with a right, a moderate, and a left. If candidates were not required to declare themselves Republican or Democrat, it would be hard to tell which party they belonged to.

DeLong, however, had in reality been as far right as you could get in the Republican Party, while Albion could pass for a moderate of either party. Because of his reputation as a fence-mender, and his willingness to quietly toe the party line, he had seemed ideal—a man who would be happy to stay in the background and who would not make waves. The only small snag had been the wife. *A poor choice*, McClellan thought. *Artistic, they said. More like a nutcase.*

She had improved her image (even in McClellan's eyes) by serving as a volunteer, doing art therapy with emotionally disturbed youth. Yet she had seemed depressed lately. *Didn't like life in the White House: appearing at parties, being the supportive wife*, he supposed. *Where is she, anyway?*

The jet lurched again and the president began to slide out of his seat. McClellan tried unsuccessfully to strap him in.

Just then, the co-pilot stuck his head out the cabin door. "Damn fog down below. We're trying to get above it, then we'll put her on auto. We'd sure like to contact ground control... Arch said to ask if we could break silence."

"Negative. Tell Archie *no*. Wait, I'll tell him myself." McClellan started to unbuckle his seatbelt. The jet suddenly turned its nose up sharply.

"Jeesus."

The pilot looked back at them briefly through the cabin doorway. Then the jet swerved to the left and they were on their side, starting to roll.

The hillside that received them was remote. The trees absorbed some of the sound of the crash. The fireball was brief and violent, and set the surrounding woods on fire. The pine trees crackled, and the flames flickered and glowed eerily through the fog like a distant lightning storm.

CHAPTER 4

The wind had started howling the day before and a whiteout had enveloped the great south polar continent. It wasn't really snowing; the wind just picked up the snow and whipped it around, reshaping it into new forms the way it does sand dunes in the desert. Considering the epic consequences it would have, the short, dry *cr-a-a-ack* seemed a surprisingly brief and insignificant warning. The weight of the ice shelf that broke off was tremendous and the speed with which it sank so swift that, moments after the event, in the great black silence that followed, it appeared as though nothing had happened.

Decades of global warming had altered the way the ice shelves grew and diminished seasonally. The water temperature, which had risen so slowly that only a few scientists took it seriously (and others could always be found to counter the claims that a disaster was sure to happen), had caused the underside of the ledges and shelves to melt. These had instead grown outward, like gigantic frilly petticoats floating on the water. The slight warming of the air above Antarctica had created fogs and mists, bringing the moisture that never before had hovered above the southernmost continent. This had resulted in actual precipitation, until then nearly unknown in this arid and frigid desert, where annual snowfall had amounted to no more than two inches per year, and had added to the weight of the ice shelves.

Years ago, in the last decades of the previous century, some scientists in the popular Greenpeace movement had predicted that the great Ross' Ice Shelf might break off, creating havoc and raising the level of the oceans by as much as thirty-five feet. They had been scoffed at then. They would never live to know that when it actually happened, they would be far below the mark. Some scientists had estimated that if all the ice in Antarctica were to melt, the ocean level would rise by 200 feet. Even these old prophets of doom would never have expected an event like this to take place in the deep of the Antarctic winter, but the change in climate had made the ice shelves treacherously unstable.

The current event was the result of continued global warming caused in great part by human mismanagement of the planet, and it included a chain of events that these earlier scientists may not have foreseen. Ocean levels had been slowly and steadily rising for over a century. The polluting miasma called the Brown Cloud had grown and traveled at its own speed across the continents. The hole in the ozone layer had widened. The deserts had spread. The rainforests had been cut down recklessly, both by greedy corporations and by local farmers starved for arable land. All the moisture that had previously been trapped in these areas had been absorbed into the atmosphere, and then returned to the earth's oceans in the form of rain. The ice cap at the North Pole had diminished rapidly and eventually melted away completely. The combined effect was an ocean level that had risen by ten feet in the past century instead of three, as had been predicted.

Early on, there was anxiety among many small island nations. In the 1980s, the Maldives had pleaded with the United Nations to come to their rescue. Their islands consisted of mere low, palm tree-covered humps surrounded by beaches, and the rising water level was becoming an imminent threat.

The world scientists and politicians argued for decades. In 2012 a strong typhoon was forecast, and the prudent left for the nearest mainland. Those that remained disappeared along with the islands. When the typhoon was over, the sun glittered cruelly across the unbroken water.

The same storm system had spelled the end for Bangladesh, where tragedy had struck before. This time the loss of life and land, sucked away by the water in great slurps, had been so great that those who survived had finally left, trading their life in the watery fields for poverty in squalid and overcrowded cities.

Venice had been another great loss. Many extravagant plans to save it had been drafted over the decades. One suggestion was to enclose the city in a giant moat, with locks to control the water level. Another was to move it inland, stone by stone. Yet another proposed to fill in the canals and the bay, making it a dry city, and encircling it with an enormous wall. Then the canals would be re-dug and lined, and only the old gondolas would be allowed on the water to preserve the image of the ancient city and keep the tourists coming.

While these great plans were being discussed, and with the astronomical cost estimates revised continually, the city slowly disintegrated. Frescoes that could not be removed in time were ravaged by mildew, and the great works by Veronese and Tiepolo were soon lost to mankind. Buildings were undermined and collapsing. Bridges fell, which made getting around by foot impossible. In the end, what was left of the city was hardly worth saving. It was finally abandoned, and the sea rushed in unimpeded, turning the city into a magnificent but ephemeral ruin. While these changes had taken place over a period of decades, the wave that was now making its way north would do its damage in the space of hours.

CHAPTER 5

Suzie's bright, cheerful voice filled the room.

"Welcome back, Ingrid! How was your day? Adam asked me to tell you he won't be home until tomorrow. He had to go to an important dinner. I have several other messages for you…"

"Shut up, Suzie." The screen went blank and Ingrid sank into her reading chair, the only piece of furniture in the apartment that she had personally selected.

We should have picked a male voice, she thought. It was her first thought every morning, when a more sensuous version of Suzie's voice insinuated itself into their bedroom to wake them up. At first she had felt a stab of jealousy at the sound of it. Later, after she and Adam had begun to drift apart, that feeling had been replaced by mere irritation. Suzie had been Adam's choice, as had nearly everything else in their life together recently. An evening all to herself sounded fine to Ingrid.

She walked over to the manual control pad on the wall and pressed '*messages.*' When alone, Ingrid preferred bypassing Suzie. The screen lit up again. Did it seem reluctant? Was Suzie sulking? Good.

"Ingrid, where are you? Has something happened to you? I have this awful feeling that something is wrong."

Ingrid sighed at the anxiety in her mother's voice. Greta was one of those people who seemed to have second sight.

Whenever Ingrid was in trouble, Greta would know, and a call would come from Sweden. However, this time her mother was wrong. At least, there was no *acute* problem, just the continuing downward spiral.

Ingrid watched the screen, waiting for the rest of the message. The image showed her mother's house, a still picture taken in apple blossom time. Her mother did not like to send her face on the videm.

Ingrid was born in Stockholm. Ted, her American father, had met her mother there while working for a company with a branch office in Sweden. When Ingrid was four, the branch closed and the family moved to the States. For the next eight years Greta tried to adjust to living in Boston. Ted's parents were loving and helpful, taking the edge off Greta's longing for her own family. One day, after she had finally begun to feel at home, Ted came home with an armful of flowers and a bottle of champagne.

"Guess what? We're moving to Chicago!"

Greta never made the move to Chicago. Instead, she returned to Sweden, taking Ingrid with her. They lived in a small house with a view of the Baltic, just outside Stockholm. Ingrid spent her teenage years going to school in Stockholm, doing most of her homework on the hour-long train ride so that she could have the late afternoon free to spend with her mother. As Ingrid got older, she and Greta were often taken for sisters, walking along the seashore with their long blond hair flying and pants rolled up to the knees. Most of her friends lived in the city, and Ingrid was reluctant to ask them home, preferring solitude or the company of her mother.

Ingrid spent summer vacations with her father in the States, while Greta remained behind in Sweden. Ingrid missed her mother then, and was happy when the visit came to an end and her father put her on the plane back home. When he remarried, Ingrid spent her annual visits with her American grandparents, who by then had retired to their summer home on Cape Ann. Her father would make the obligatory overnight stop at the island—always without his new wife, who was "not about to take on a teenager with an attitude." (Ingrid heard this description of herself the first time she met Jamie, through the thin wall of their adjoining bedrooms.) Ingrid didn't mind much, and when she went back to Sweden for the school year, it was her grandparents that she missed, not her father.

The summer after she finished college she came to stay with her grandparents as usual. *They are growing old,* she thought. What would she do when they were no longer there? Would she still come to the States? The year before she hadn't seen her father at all. He and Jamie had been on a cruise in the West Indies, and Ingrid had spent the summer on the Dogtown Moor with her grandfather, exploring the old cellar holes of early settlers.

Grandpa Josh, a professor of geology, was an ardent naturalist and never missed a chance to point out any alien flora: the heather that some immigrant had brought and planted near their home, the lilac bush, the paper mulberry, all still growing near the old homestead sites. The houses themselves were long gone, and it took an old hand to find the foundations—overgrown mounds of granite boulders fallen into what had once been the cellars.

Ingrid, by then a newly graduated young teacher, took every opportunity to collect information that she could use to inspire her students, and eagerly absorbed her grandfather's lectures on nature and history. She had done her student teaching at a public school in Stockholm, and was hoping to get some experience teaching at an American school. Her thirst for knowledge was both stimulating and gratifying to Grandpa Josh, who waxed poetic about the Dogtown settlers.

They had walked down the old Babson Boulder Trail, where Ingrid made a list of the inscriptions that had been carved into the rocks long ago. Roger Babson, a local eccentric and philanthropist who ran for president on the Prohibition ticket, had hired Finnish quarry workers during the Depression to carve mottos into the boulders that had been deposited as part of the glacial terminal moraine. Babson wrote, "My family says I'm defacing the boulders and disgracing the family with these inscriptions, but the work gives me a lot of satisfaction, fresh air, exercise and sunshine. I am really trying to write a simple book with words carved in stone instead of printed on paper."

Ingrid still remembered some of the mottos:
NEVER TRY/NEVER WIN
PROSPERITY FOLLOWS SERVICE
KEEP OUT OF DEBT
HELP MOTHER
IF WORK STOPS, VALUES DECAY
GET A JOB
TRUTH

That was also the fateful summer when she met Adam. She had duplicated her mother's mistake, she thought now, getting stuck in this place far from home. Although, to be fair, she had loved it here and had no regrets during the early years.

When her beloved grandfather died a few years after she and Adam were married, she was left with the responsibility to care for Grandmother Lil. Her father, who by then never left his lair, refused to take it on. Ingrid and her father exchanged videograms at Christmas, but she had not seen him for several years. In the last image, his face had seemed strangely lopsided, as though he'd had a stroke.

But that summer she had fallen passionately in love, dragging Adam with her to Cape Ann to meet her grandparents. Grandpa Josh walked them through the Dogtown woods to a place called, in what had seemed like a sign, Adam's Pines. In late August, among pines tall and straight as schooner masts, that was where Adam pulled the engagement ring out of his pocket and promptly dropped it, leaving them scratching through layers of fragrant pine needles. When they finally found it, they bound themselves together for that span of time young lovers so eagerly call *forever.* Her mother cried and refused to come to a wedding in the States, and Adam did the charitable thing and brought Ingrid home to Sweden to be married. Then he took Ingrid with him back to the States, and her mother cried twice as hard, since she had immediately become attached to Adam, too.

Greta had not set foot in the States since she moved back home. "Maybe when you give me a grandchild," she had said once. That was a sore point, which Ingrid now avoided contemplating.

Ingrid had not seen her mother's face for over five years, since Greta stopped appearing on the videm. Her voice was still the same, although her Swedish accent had become more pronounced and she often had to search for words. Ingrid spoke fluent Swedish, but Greta had insisted on the two of them speaking English.

Ingrid always thought of her mother the way she had last seen her on the screen. It had been on a summer's day, when Greta had just returned from a swim in the brackish water of

Lake Mälaren. She had sold the big house and moved into a cottage surrounded by an old orchard. Five minutes away was the beach, with fine, silvery-gray sand. The water in the lake was a lustrous green, colored by the abundant sea grass that shimmered softly in the slow current. On that day, in a larger than life image, her mother had aimed her smiling eyes at Ingrid. Her Nordic pale blond hair had been pinned on top of her head, leaving a few wet strands clinging to her cheeks. There had been goose bumps on her arms and shoulders, and Ingrid had remembered how cold the water could be there, even in summer.

Ingrid finished the last of her coffee and told Suzie to call her mother. The screen flickered slightly before showing an image of Greta's kitchen. *Well, she's finally changed her home screen, at least.* The kitchen looked neat and cozy, with its sunny birch furniture and cabinets. Ingrid imagined she could smell her mother's cooking. Fresh dill. Cardamom. The windows were open, and it was only when the wind ruffled the curtains that Ingrid realized it was a live image, not the usual still shot. Suddenly she heard her mother's voice.

"I'm coming...don't go away!"

Ingrid sat down in her chair, keeping her eyes on the screen. In a moment, Greta's face appeared, zooming up large and close, oversized, out of focus, as though she were trying to climb through the screen.

"Mamma, what's the matter? You're too close. I can't see you," Ingrid said.

Her mother stepped back a little, took a deep breath, and sat down. Ingrid was shocked at her appearance. First, there was the look of fear in her eyes. Then, the fact that her mother's hair had gone completely white and her face was creased with lines of age she had never before let her daughter see. Ingrid gripped the arms of her chair tightly. Was her mother ill?

"Oh, Ingrid, my dearest lilla flicka, if I could only be with you now!" Greta cried, wringing her hands.

"Why, what's happened, Mamma? Are you sick?" Now Ingrid had gotten up and was standing right in front of the screen, reaching out for her mother.

"Ingrid, jag kan inte se dej! *I can't see you...*"

The screen flickered again and her mother's voice was cut off and replaced by a loud scratchy noise, which ended abruptly. Then the screen went blank. In the silence that followed, Ingrid heard her neighbor's door slam. She looked out the window. Everything seemed normal.

"Suzie, call Mother again, please."

Nothing happened. No Suzie.

Ingrid tried the manual control, without success. Another system shutdown, obviously. That happened periodically. Then, without being prompted, the screen lit up. *ALL CONNECTIONS— INTERPERSONAL, NATIONAL, AND INTERNATIONAL— TEMPORARILY TERMINATED. SYSTEMS ARE BEING SERVICED. PLEASE REFRAIN FROM USING. AUTOMATIC UPDATES WILL KEEP YOU INFORMED. THANK YOU.* The same message was relayed by voice and then the screen went blank again.

Ingrid shook her head. *At least I'm rid of Suzie for a while.* She felt anxious about the cut-off conversation, but maybe it was nothing. Greta had always been independent and able to take care of herself.

Ingrid decided not to worry and instead went to cook herself a Swedish dinner and "think positive thoughts," a favorite expression of Greta's.

CHAPTER 6

The helo dropped the lone passenger off inside the compound before immediately lifting off again. The crew had had their hands full trying to airlift out-of-state senators and other bigwigs from far and wide to Camp David. This passenger was the last, and now they could go back to Fort Ritchie. They hoped they wouldn't be called later for stragglers or to return any of the people they had just delivered. Their bodies ached for a couple of beers and a bed.

As they rose over the ridges of the Catoctin Mountains, they ran into wisps of fog, which was denser down in the valley. The pilot noticed a faint glow in the distance—a campfire gone out of control, maybe. He would report it when they got back to base. They passed the final ridge that ran south of the fort, and landed just as the sun was setting.

Back at Camp David, at the old Eisenhower Heliport, their passenger was met at the pad by two uniformed men and escorted by foot up the wooded road. The latest arrival was a slight, elderly man, dressed in white. The fine silk of his suit, which seemed out of place on such an ascetic-looking figure, was creased from the cramped seating in the helo, and he pulled the thin, gray travel coat tightly around his slender body. A white head covering was in his pocket behind the handkerchief, carefully folded into a triangle.

The uniformed men took him to Laurel Lodge, where the president's men were assembled in the large meeting room. They all stood as he walked into the room, and he raised both hands high in greeting. *It won't be long now. I will miss this...miss these men, the intense discussions into the night.* He looked forward to the changes that were to take place in his life, returning to a life of simplicity he had long missed. Smiling, he took his seat beside Halkey.

"The president is not here yet?" he asked, turning to the senator.

"Guess not. Just arrived myself. Know what this is about?" Senator Halkey shook his head, and asked a question in return.

"No. I got the call just as I was leaving for San Francisco."

Halkey nodded and returned to an earlier conversation with Price, who was seated on his right. The man in white scanned the faces around the table. He had put on his small skullcap before entering the room, and tried fastidiously to smooth out his wrinkled attire. His hair gleamed white at the temples, and a little wisp of it stuck out from under the cap and rested on his forehead. His face was smooth and the expression generally kind. At the moment, he was calm and quiet. When inspired by a cause, however, he would radiate an almost propulsive energy that often made people take a step back to avoid being caught up in his vortex and forced into some "voluntary" assignment.

Under the suit he wore a white collarless shirt with small gold buttons, each etched with a tiny cross. The white handkerchief in his pocket had a thin edging of gold. If he had a weakness, it was his appearance. It was neither vanity nor a wish to draw attention to himself that was behind the image he presented to the world. It was hero worship. In the *baby seminary*, his heroes had been the saints and clerics of the past that he had seen depicted in books and paintings. Early on he had begun to emulate their looks as well as their deeds; in fact, he himself had composed the ensemble he was now wearing.

While waiting for something to happen, Sheedy sat idly watching the goings-on. As often these days, his thoughts turned to the past. Charles Sheedy had arrived at his position after a lifetime of devoting himself to serving God. His years in the Church had been rewarding. In the last decades, the Church had gained strength and become a guiding force in people's lives again. Before then, there had been a period when it seemed to have lost all its power over the people. In the history of this country, the separation of church and state had been the first serious blow. At some point, during the years of prosperity and material excess that followed the world wars, people had started searching for spiritual guidance again. There were some disastrous early results: esoteric cults, charismatics taking advantage of needy people who hungered for meaning in their lives. The New Age cults and movements had seemed to threaten the established religions, drawing people away from the traditional churches. But mainstream Americans eventually found these alternative religions to be unsatisfactory, even unpatriotic, bringing in foreign rituals and practices that included mysterious exercises and odd food habits.

Faith, Sheedy had always felt, was expressed simply by following a moral and ethical belief structure. Incense burning and meditation accompanied by electronic harp music could not replace this basic tenet. The Moral Majority movement had been one of the frontrunners when it came to getting religion back into mainstream life and into the political arena. The movement had not been successful in the end, but it had shown the way.

In Europe, the Vatican had begun to lose its hold. Italians wanted to get divorced and have abortions like the rest of the Europeans. The young people in Europe were turning their backs on God. In America, the tide had turned the other way. After a scandal involving sexual abuse that rocked the Church—indeed, brought it to its knees—had subsided, healing had finally been accomplished, and a new religious fervor gripped the nation. People again demanded prayer back in school, the banning of much literature both in schools and on the web, and stricter laws on pornography. Homosexuals, who had finally become accepted—and had, in some states, even been allowed to marry—had to go back into the closet. Minorities were again subtly repressed, women's rights curtailed.

Sheedy felt uneasy with some of these trends, and hoped to encourage more tolerance and understanding. He wished to end discrimination and to find better solutions—to the abortion issue, for instance.

The anti-abortion movement had finally achieved success. The movement had suffered early setbacks, especially after being infiltrated by vigilantes who took the law into their own hands. Nevertheless, the pro-life activists had persevered, and abortion was finally illegal in every state. Teenagers were seen through their pregnancies and cared for in religious institutions, only to be forced to give their babies up for adoption, being considered neither morally fit nor mature enough to keep them. They were simply used as brooding hens, supplying children for those unfortunate but *deserving* mothers who were unable to bear their own.

Reverence for life was selective, to Sheedy's great regret, as capital punishment had made a comeback and was now routinely mandated and carried out without delay. *Morality* was the new catchword; people became infatuated with the idea of it.

The role reversal was complete. Long ago, Europeans had fled religious persecution and come to America, a secular haven, where each sect and branch had been allowed its freedom, and religion and state were held separate. Now, the Europeans had gained this freedom—partly brought on by the great influx of Muslims earlier in the century—while Americans were clamoring for religion to become an integral part of government.

When it was discovered that Pope Clement had been conspiring with the Vatican librarian to sell off some priceless treasures to an Eastern country, the hierarchy had begun to crumble. It was found to be only the tip of the iceberg. The pope had intended to sell *all* the great collections of the Vatican—art works, books, and papers—except those of scholarly importance to theologians. With the riches, he had planned to feed and clothe the hungry and the poor of the world. *Heavens above,* people said, *what is the world coming to?*

The dust had finally settled after the librarian had been fired and sent to a retreat and the pope had suffered a stroke and died after two agonizing months. When the puff of white smoke announced "habemus papam," there was another great shock in store. The new pope was an American named Pope Amerigus, a name greeted in Europe with much ridicule and some hilarity. It indicated a further change. The cardinals had felt, nearly to a man, that the only chance for survival of the Church as a world power was to move its seat to America. People there took the Church seriously. In Europe, the word of God no longer carried any weight. Last but not least, the lion's share of new money into the Church came from America. American cardinals had swayed the majority and secured the vote.

The Vatican moved to St. Louis, Amerigus' home turf. Charles Sheedy—and many with him—had felt that Chicago would have been a better choice, but Amerigus had quickly settled the case when the City of St. Louis offered a large section of land along the river encompassing the Gateway Arch and the *pièce de resistance:* the Old Cathedral, the Basilica of St. Louis.

That had been almost forty years ago, and Sheedy had still been in the seminary at the time. He had made his way slowly through the ranks of the Church. Having been been a strong advocate for the people in his community, he had served on various local councils, and when the Church rescinded the rule that for many decades had kept the clergy out of the national political arena, he had thrown himself ardently into the fray. Fifteen years ago, he had been elected senator and gone to Washington.

He had slaved at it, tenaciously going after each goal on behalf of his people. He had commuted tirelessly, keeping himself strongly tied to his diocese, and, as a reward, found himself bishop. Then the step from bishop to archbishop and, almost unbelievably, the elevation to cardinal six years ago. Even while carrying out the duties of this demanding position, he continued serving in Washington.

Due to his selfless exertions, his close attention to every issue, and his seemingly endless energy, he had been appointed speaker of the house two years ago. Sometimes he had felt he should give up one of his callings, but he had never been able to choose which, and had decided that as long as he was able to cope, perhaps he was meant to do both.

The religious masses had sway in Washington. When they, as a group, put pressure on their representatives to adjust the school curriculum so that it would reflect the new moral vision, they were listened to. When they insisted that Americans had the right and responsibility to clean up the Internet so that their children would not become corrupted, a great filtering system was developed and installed. It was introduced first in schools and public libraries; later, through the various public servers, the whole Web as available to Americans had been purged of objectionable sites. Instead of the Worldwide Web ("www"), there was now the AMWEB.

The government was in control; all communications media were under central command. A board that included a large number of high ranking clergy regulated the public and private links alike.

When Amerigus died at the age of ninety-six, Pope Urban followed, an able caretaker who consolidated and finalized many of the vast changes that had taken place. He convened Vatican III, which solidified and strengthened Vatican II. Vatican III called for a faithful adherence to doctrine and staunchly blocked any attempt to move toward a liberation theology. When that pope succumbed to pneumonia two months ago, everyone felt the vacuum and scrambled to come up with someone capable of taking over the leadership. Cardinal Sheedy had made it to the short list.

Last month, the conclave had selected Cardinal Charles Joseph Sheedy, speaker of the house, as their next pope. The cardinal, now Pope Fidelis, had agreed to remain in Washington as speaker until a new one was appointed—as long as the selection process did not get too protracted—after which he would retire from all worldly positions and serve only God.

***

It was dark now at Camp David, and the people gathered there were getting impatient. Some were getting up from the large meeting room table with its straight-backed chairs and ambling over to the more comfortable conference room.

Halkey checked his watch and got up to stretch. He smiled at the pope, whom he still thought of as "Sheedy" and addressed as "Mr. Speaker," rather than "Your Holiness," which was the address most people were now using.

It is a matter of protocol, he thought. *If I were asking him to hear my confession, I would call him "Your Holiness."*

"Hope they're planning to feed us at some point," Halkey said. "Think I'll go and check on what's happening."

CHAPTER 7

The president was the only one who might have known where Ariana Albion had gone. No one else—not even Pete—knew that the first lady secretly kept a studio because, as Ariana had said, "Pete's first instinct would be to protect *me*, not my privacy."

Whenever she could get away, she would disappear through the backstreets of Washington and climb the stairs up to her attic. Through the one large window at the gable end of the building, she could see the Capitol in the distance, and in the foreground a jumble of rooftops. Right below the window was a courtyard with a great chestnut tree that she had painted once, on a winter's day, when the black skeleton of it had stood out in great contrast to the newfallen snow.

The attic was spacious, almost like the Soho studio she had rented in her student days, and her work lined the walls of the room. Additional canvases in various states of completion were stacked toward the back. The paintings were sizeable, most too large to fit on an easel, so she had made a tilting stand that she could adjust with a ratchet to hold them while she worked.

Albion had never been to see the studio—they both knew it would have led to the discovery of her hiding place—but Ariana often showed him photos of her work. Sometimes he felt the emptiness she left behind when she sneaked off. At the same time, he didn't begrudge her the time or the opportunity to pursue her own dreams. He felt regret at the clandestine way it had to be carried out, without ever putting pressure on her to tailor her work to better suit a judgmental society.

The reason for the secrecy lay in the nature of the paintings, and in the reaction they would draw from people who beheld them. The sheer scale of the canvases was imposing. Anyone walking in would be surrounded by monumental images, most of them dark and earthy in color.

The canvas she had recently been working on was on the stand, facing the great window. A line stretched sinuously from the top left corner toward the bottom right. Finely rendered shading covered the left side of the canvas to reveal with almost palpable intimacy the soft surface of a body. Without being explicit, the image seemed erotic, even at this early stage. Most of the canvases gathered around the studio were images of the human body, sometimes clothed, sometimes nude. There were outsized images of faces, of parts of the face, of limbs and curves of the body, of an ear surrounded by wavy hair. These were portraits of the president of the United States that would never hang in the White House. The reaction of any receptive viewer would be shock at the mere suggestivity, and the sensuousness of the images would leave most viewers stunned.

There were also paintings of other subjects, including some equally revealing self-portraits, but it was the paintings of her husband that had forced Ariana into hiding. Nudity would, even by itself, be seen as an inappropriate subject for a first lady. Landscapes, traditional watercolors of flowers in vases—these would be admired, and reproductions would be made for people to hang on their walls. Ariana Albion's intimate visions of her husband would cause an uproar.

Usually, when the first lady disappeared from the White House, the studio was where she went. Today, however, she had gone elsewhere.

***

Pete McPherson deserved his reputation as a loyal and trustworthy government employee. He always followed orders, carrying them out faithfully and, when necessary, with diplomatic tact.

Only, I was never asked to do anything that really went against my conscience before, he thought.

He unstrapped the wristcom and placed it on the desk. He would not need it again. Everything looked orderly. Not that it would matter, soon.

As he walked down the hall, he saw a reflection of himself in one of the great gilt mirrors that some ostentatious first lady had favored. He looked anxious and drawn. His black crew cut accentuated the pale skin, and his eyes seemed to have receded into their hollows. He was tall, and thinly built even though he worked out to put on some muscle. He tried relaxing his clenched jaws and straightened his back.

McPherson left the White House through the east wing door that led to the carpark. A fence with a gate and guardhouse surrounded the rows of freshly charged PTVs. These days, most people used the subway for transportation, but Pete wanted to avoid crowds. He didn't feel sure he could look anyone in the eye.

In hot weather, which was most of the time lately, the Personal Transport Vehicle—a small, lightweight, short-distance fuel cell car—was his best alternative. Since the ban on private cars in cities, PTV rentals had become so popular that most people—Pete being one—no longer missed owning a car. You could pick up a PTV on nearly any city block, drive to your destination, and drop it off at the nearest carpark.

In rural America and in the small outer suburbs that lay beyond the metropolitan sprawl, people were still attached to their private vehicles. The family station wagons of a hundred years ago had been transformed into sleek tanks, a second home with all the comforts of a small apartment.

Speed trains criss-crossing the country had in large part replaced air travel. It was more comfortable, safer, cheaper, and, most importantly, caused far less pollution. Another consideration was time. Travel between New York and Los Angeles was faster on the speed train, if one included time spent at airports. More frequent volcanic eruptions on all continents often caused havoc in air travel. Great ash clouds grounded the planes, sometimes for weeks, and frequently brought the industry to its knees.

Pete selected a vehicle, got in, and drove up to the gate. The guard nodded in recognition and Pete put his hand on the charge plate. When he heard the small click, he removed his hand and drove off.

There had been no point in staying at the White House. He would go and look for Evie, and then he would have to deal with keeping the news to himself. He had never lied to her before; he just didn't tell her everything. She had accepted this from the start, knowing it was part of his job. *But this is personal,* he thought. *This concerns our lives.*

However, he *had* just lied to the president. Was that in the line of duty? He had never done that before, nor kept anything from him. Lying was part of politics, of diplomacy—in fact, every branch of government had its own form of lying, couched in its own particular code. But when he told the president that Ariana was safe, that she'd gone ahead, that had been an outright, personal lie. He knew Albion would not have left without that assurance about his wife. And the safety of the president was paramount. But when he found out that Pete had lied to him, would Albion forgive him? Would he thank him for putting the country first? It didn't really matter now, did it? At least the president would be safe.

Pete drove toward Evie's house, hoping she would be home from work. He pulled in at the carpark a block away and clocked off the PTV. Then he walked up the worn steps to the entrance and pressed Evie's button. He grinned into the monitor and when the door opened, he hurried inside and ran up the stairs. Evie, her curly red hair like a halo, let him into her small apartment. She was padding around in her bare feet, which made her seem even more diminutive than her five-feet-two, and was wearing a silky green robe over her underwear. Pete followed her into the kitchenette.

"Pete, what are you doing here? Why aren't you at work? I wasn't expecting you, was I? I just came home and was thinking of grabbing a quick bite before I have to go back out. Would you like a veggie roll?"

Pete shook his head. "Not hungry, thanks. A glass of something cold, though, whatever you've got. Are you going out for the night?" He bit his tongue. *As though I have the right to check up on her.*

He certainly had no claim on Evie. Pete felt a twinge of regret that he had never come around to asking her the big question. He had felt that it was an awkward time to get married, and decided to wait until his tenure at the White House was over. Well, it wasn't important anymore.

"No, I promised to help Ariana set up her exhibition, and I'm supposed to meet her in half an hour…"

"Ariana! You know where she is?"

"Well, she may have gone in early to get started. I don't know. She's setting up a show for the kids."

"Evie, where is this place?"

"Around the corner. What's the matter, Pete? Is anything wrong?"

"Nothing to worry about. Can I go with you? I need to talk to Ariana."

"Sure. Let's go. Let me just go get some clothes on. I'll take this along and eat on the way." She went into the bedroom and came back out a moment later wearing slacks and a sleeveless top.

He took her hand outside, and she gave him a questioning look. Pete was never one to flaunt his feelings in public, and even holding hands was not routine with him. They walked at a quick pace to the old Masonic Hall, which today was set up like an auditorium facing a great stage. Ariana was standing on the stage, half in shadow. She was wearing a black dress, and her dark hair was tied back with a scarf that matched her bright red lipstick. She was pulling something that looked like a zebra across the stage, a great construction of wire and papier-mâché. When she saw them, she smiled.

"Boy, Evie, am I glad to see you've brought a helper. Some of these pieces are very awkward. Give us a hand, Pete."

"Ariana, I need to talk to you. Right now." Pete got up onto the stage, taking two steps at a time. Evie stayed below.

He took Ariana by the shoulders and spoke to her quietly but intently. "The president has gone to Camp David. He needs you to meet him there. It's urgent, Ariana. You must go immediately."

"What do you mean 'must' go? How do I go when he's gone without me? 'Here, plane, come to mama'?" Ariana waved her arms theatrically.

"This is serious, Ariana." Pete let go of her shoulders and stepped back.

"I don't suppose you can tell me about it. No? Okay, then. But these kids are going to be mighty disappointed." She gave Evie a pleading look. Pete caught it and made a rapid decision.

"Evie's coming with us. I'm driving you there. We can't wait for any other arrangement."

"Whatever you say, big boss. I don't suppose there's time to pack, either?"

"Sorry. You look just fine." He tried not to look at his watch. Then he remembered that he had left the wristcom at the White House.

"I won't in the morning, when I've slept in this."

Ariana locked the great double doors. Pete left the women at the gate of the carpark and went to find the attendant.

"Don't suppose you have any trekkers in?"

The attendant craned his neck, squinting toward the back of the lot, where the long-distance vehicles were kept.

"Let's have a look," he said.

They walked down the ramp. "Just this one, and it's a two-seater."

"It'll have to do, then," Pete said.

The attendant looked back toward the gate. "There's three of youse. Can't let you do it. You know the rules."

Pete sighed, pulling his FID card out of its clip and fishing some bills out of his pocket. Cash was a fairly useless commodity, normally, with all businesses and automats taking the card. Coins, of course, were no longer in use at all. But Pete always carried some bills for just this kind of occasion. "You can add a special clean-up to the charge," he said with a wink.

Working for the government, Pete was using his FID card. The citizens at large were issued, at birth, the CWWID card, short for "comprehensive world-wide ID," more commonly called the "quid." The quid card eliminated the need for any other card or paperwork, being a combination of ID card, charge card, passport, voter registration card, social security card, insurance card and any other function the bearer chose or needed to give it.

The attendant smiled. Nice way to make a few bucks without any sweat.

They put Ariana in the center, as though they automatically felt the need to protect the president's wife.

Why am I here? Evie thought. She was often invited along to the White House for special events and spent time helping Ariana with her projects, but she had never been to Camp David. She sensed that there was something serious going on.

Pete knew that Evie was puzzled and was relieved to have Ariana sitting between them. It gave him time to think. *Who am I doing this for? The President? Evie? Or for myself? Maybe it won't matter in the end.*

They drove in silence through the darkening city. It was a quiet night. All traffic except the PTVs went underground, and people did, too, preferring the well-lit and cheerful tunnels, air-conditioned and lined with boutiques and cafés, to the streets.

The subtropolis—the great underground city—was vast, several levels deep, with the underground transit and great vaulted archives at the lower levels. The prisons were located on the lowest level, far below the city streets. There, the inmates lived in separate, monitored cubicles, where they were supplied with food, clean laundry, and other necessities through narrow chutes. There was no personal communication or visitation between inmates, nor ever with the outside world, until the end of the sentence. The wall screen brought pre-selected programs of a religious or moral nature. The prisoners were not deemed deserving of free education or special training but were allowed to participate in certain work programs, such as testing the intelligibility of government surveys and forms.

The second level was devoted mainly to offices and the businesses that supplied or served the prisons, while the topmost level consisted of the subterranean walking streets, lined with malls, parks and gardens, chapels and restaurants. People entered the subtropolis through any subway station, hotel lobby, or public building. The flashing yellow arrow, which indicated the entrance to the underground, could be seen on every city block. Large elevators connected the levels—some even traveled horizontally—unless one preferred the rolling sidewalks or escalators. Gondolas traveled above many sections, a pleasant way to float above it all from one mall to the next.

Evie worked in a salon on the top level and loved the "climate," which was always spring-like. She could go from her place of work to the restaurants or shops in her short sleeves even in the middle of winter. The light was so similar to daylight that it was always a surprise to go outside into the evening darkness. The daylight was constant underground; during the day it was transported via fiber optics, and businesses ran in shifts, twenty-four hours a day. Heat was also easy to provide—just harvest and store the heat produced by a multitude of sources and pump it back out again.

It was a safer environment than the ground-level city, where most of the criminal element still roamed. Up there, getaways were easy. Down in the subtropolis, sections could quickly be sealed off until the criminal was apprehended. The homeless had been an early threat to the ambiance, but had soon retreated to their old haunts in the back alleys outside. Vagrants were simply not tolerated and would be picked up and hustled off to shelters, where they were forced to choose from long lists of menial jobs available around the city.

Most cities had begun building underground when they ran out of real estate up above. Then the land conservation people had picked up on the idea, and many sprawling towns were built underneath what remained of the nation's prairies and open lands. In this way, forests and parklands were preserved, making the "green" people happy. It made ecological sense, too, and saved vast amounts of energy.

The surface city seemed to go on forever. Pete turned the corner onto the ramp that brought them onto ERAD, the elevated radial highway that would take them above it all and speed them out of the metropolis. Soon they would be in the mountains. He was beginning to breathe easier. He thought of stopping to recharge the fuel cell at one of the many lots along the way, but decided that it would have to wait until later.

CHAPTER 8

The iceberg, which was the size of a small continent, remained submerged for a long time. The wave it had created, with additional help from the tremor, rolled on inexorably.

The weight of the massive wall of water, still hiding below the ocean surface, exerted pressure on the earth as it went along. There were rumblings from the overlapping plates, and great gushes of lava and steam were expelled through the fissures. The original tremor had had the further effect of breaking off shelves on the remaining sides of Antarctica—the Ronne, Riiser-Larsen, Fimbul, Amery, and Shackleton ice shelves— as though the continent wanted to balance itself and be rid of anything that wasn't solid rock. This also released the *ice rivers*, the fast-flowing sections of the glaciers that, lubricated by a thin layer of meltwater above the bedrock, now flowed unimpeded into the sea.

So it was that great arcs of waves, in syncopated harmony, started making their way up toward the equator, encircling the entire globe, each finding its separate trail in a different ocean.

CHAPTER 9

Ingrid went over to the music center and touched the pad. She let the menu scroll down. *Temple bells.* Right. She changed out of the suit she had worn to work and put on shorts and a thin, sleeveless top. She let down her blond hair, which she always wore in a spinsterly twist at school. In an effort to gain some authority over her unruly girls, she tried to look business-like—even unfeminine—using no make-up or jewelry. She didn't want them to focus on her as a woman, just on the subject she was teaching. Any distraction was deadly; she'd lose them right from the start.

She did some stretching exercises, but without much enthusiasm. Her body was limber, thin, and tall like her mother's. She looked younger than thirty-seven, without being proud of it. In fact, she no longer cared.

Her skin was light and burned instantly in the sun, and she had to cover up or wear radiation block. She had tried the sun pills, but they made her feel nauseous. Tanned skin was a fashion of the past, anyway. People were pale. In the cities they hardly ventured outside, but went to their destination via the tunnels. Children played in the underground parks, playgrounds, and swimming pools. Out here in the country, she could still see children playing outdoors during the day, but they were all on the pills and usually wore radiation-resistant clothing for added protection. There was talk of a new inoculation against the harmful rays, but it was still experimental.

Ingrid finished the exercises by touching her toes before grasping her ankles and touching her face to her knees. She had fine blond hair, nearly invisible, on her arms and legs. In resolute Swedish tradition, she refused to have her body hair removed. Adam used to refer to it as her "fur" and stroke it backwards, and she would hiss like a cat. But that was long ago. Her skin was lightly freckled, unlined except for fine crow's feet around the eyes. *Remnants from happier days, when I used to smile*, she thought, when she looked in the mirror.

Her eyes were an oddly light shade of aqua, like old swirly glass marbles, and slightly unsettling to look into. They radiated an unflinching sincerity, or maybe it was that wide-eyed Scandinavian innocence that covers up an unexpected determination, even hardness. Adam had referred to it as "the stubborn Swede look." It was one of her chief weapons against her students. They could not stare her down. If they tried, she would ignore the challenge and pointedly shift her focus to another student, the way cats do. The ultimate rejection. It made her feel ashamed sometimes, but in the animal world of the classroom, it was *eat or be eaten.*

The soft sound of bells enveloped her and she lay down on the floor, hoping for a short nap, pushing some cushions around to get comfortable. After a few minutes, she got up in disgust. The music left her unsatisfied. She wasn't listening to real temple bells, just a surrogate—a computer-created sound-alike. She searched idly for an alternative. She didn't enjoy contemporary music. Composers just generated a theme by formula, punched it in, and let it develop itself electronically. There was never any emotion behind it that you could feel.

Sometimes Ingrid would listen to old opera music, no matter how theatrical and sentimental. She would select Gigli, Björling, Callas, Pavarotti, Shiraz—their old voices reclaimed and made to sound as though they were alive, next to her, vibrating. Turning the volume up high, she would sit with her eyes closed until she was saturated and exhausted. Sometimes she had to replay an aria over and over before the release would come. The duet from *The Pearl Fishers* with Björling was one of her favorites, as was Shiraz's rendition of Strauss' *Vier letzte Lieder*. And, of course, some of the mad scenes with Callas. But right now she needed something calming, not stirring.

She went into the den. The floor in there was a massive sunken waterbed. The transparent plastic cover floated on the turquoise water, which was lit along the sides like a pool. On top of the cover were gel cushions of various sizes and shapes. She sank into the undulating softness and touched the panel on the side. The walls came to life. She selected one of her favorite scenes, a sunset in Tahiti (she imagined) with sandy beaches and palm trees, the fronds swaying softly in the breeze. Holographic birds flew above her head, making swooshing sounds. Even the ceiling became part of the scene, shifting slowly, in real time, from pink to purple and finally to midnight blue, stars appearing as the sun set. The sound of waves put her to sleep.

When she awoke, the virtual moon was up, reflecting in blue-black water. It was hot in the den. The air conditioning system needed to be serviced, she thought. She shuddered, unaccountably feeling cold despite the heat in the room.

Everything seemed to be going wrong. Her marriage was coming apart. *I still love Adam...or do I?* She shook her head in confusion. How could it have happened? Even work had lost its appeal. She had loved teaching in the beginning, but her position in a public school, where the classroom teacher was in effect only an aide to the virtual teacher, had left her feeling unfulfilled. The head teacher on the wall-sized screen was seen in every classroom of the country. Quizzes and tests, which the students took on their desk screen, were standardized and were corrected immediately and automatically. The classroom teacher was merely a facilitator. Ingrid had taken a personal interest in her students in the city school and tutored those who needed help, even though tutoring was available online in the afternoons for students lagging behind.

Homework had long since been abolished. Parents had become adamant on the issue, insisting that the school was responsible for educating the children, not the parents. In the classroom, each of the children sat at a flat computer desktop on legs. There were no desk lids to lift to find pencils and paper. Books were no longer handed out, which had cut the school budgets way down. The entire curriculum for each grade was covered on the desktop. Handwriting was no longer taught, and the students were unfamiliar with script writing. Texting on the flat keyboard was the only form of writing they knew, and they were all familiar with it, having used their own playcoms since early childhood.

The desk computers were controlled by the teacher. Students had access only to the subject on the screen, there was no switching to the Web or communicating with friends. Tests were standardized and arrived simultaneously to all classrooms in each area.

Required reading was channeled to each classroom desk top. While reading skills were still being taught, many students preferred to use the audio-book, and during study hours they could choose to read or listen to their compulsory material.

Those that chose to read turned on the *reading eye* detector, and the pages turned automatically when they got to the bottom of the page.

Ingrid had longed to have a more personal impact on her students, and not just act as facilitator, and had finally applied for her current position as a teacher at a girls' school in Bennington. It was a private school, and she would be the actual teacher for most of her classes, only lectures and tests being done, by law, electronically. When she was accepted, Adam had been happy for her. Available just five minutes out of town by shuttle was a commuterport with both air and speedrail facilities that he could use. Adam had still been a freshman lawyer when they moved to Bennington, working for the Legal Aid Society in Boston. He had been a very idealistic young man in those days. That was before he started working for Taney, Butler & McKenna.

Bennington was located in a lovely region, away from big-city noise and pollution. It was a wealthy community, and the town fathers had managed to keep the stately-looking center from being overdeveloped. Outside the town limits was another story. High-rise residences and office buildings took turns with shopping malls and entertainment megaplexes along the speedrail all the way to North Station in Boston.

From North Station, Adam walked to work; when the weather was bad, he took the shuttle bus. The Big Dig, the tunnel project that fifty years ago was to have solved the city's rush hour traffic, had instead caused miles of bumper-to-bumper jams, and soon afterward private cars had been prohibited in the city. In the city center, even the PTVs were banned. North and South Station had finally been connected, making continuous train service possible up and down the Eastern seaboard. Some years ago the city's tunnel systems had been reinforced (the tunnels were located below sea level and had been frequently closed due to leaks) and turned into walking streets and malls, as in other cities.

Ingrid and Adam had thought themselves fortunate when they located a home within the town of Bennington. The house was comfortable, with all possible conveniences. It was an old Victorian house with lovely gingerbread fretwork on the outside, but the interior had been modernized and simplified. The ceilings were still tall and graceful, decorated with plaster roses, and they had kept some of the elegant mahogany cabinetry to hide electronics and other utilities. The kitchen was a dream, with temperature-controlled countertops and built-in appliances that she could access with a remote from the classroom, in case her evening plans changed. The old free-standing refrigerator had been replaced by a wall of temperature-controlled compartments, some cool, some warm and dry, suited to various products.

In the beginning, she and Adam had spent long evenings in the kitchen together, chopping vegetables for Chinese food and baking bread. The pantry was always well stocked. It was refilled weekly when the delivery truck arrived with the items she had ordered online. She remembered wistfully how much fun it had been to shop in stores when she was a child, *real stores,* where you could touch the cucumbers and tomatoes and pick out just what you wanted.

Shopping online wasn't the same. The Click-and-Shop showed images of gorgeous-looking fruit, but when it arrived, it was flavorless. Meats were either chemically treated so that they would keep for weeks or freeze-dried. The treated meat lacked the texture of fresh meat, as well as having an odd taste, and the freeze-dried—even if you soaked it in milk to reconstitute and tenderize it—tended to be tough. Dairy products were also treated; milk and cream would last for weeks. Frozen foods were a thing of the past, being too prone to spoilage during the more and more frequent power failures. Food was either fresh, as most vegetables and fruit; dried; or treated to be used before a due date.

But there were no local food markets left to go to. The last remaining holdouts had closed years ago. Now there were only vast warehouse distributorships, connected to the Web, serving the area where you lived. In the cities, at least they still had delis. Some of them, if you were lucky, even cooked the food right in the store and you could smell it outside in the street, and see the meat turning on spits in the wall-sized ovens.

The best feature of the house, they had agreed, was the wrap-around porch where they could sit and enjoy the cool of the evening. It seemed a long time now since they had done that: sit in the old porch swing and talk about their future and children and trips they would like to take.

She remembered a night early on, when she had been sitting on the porch waiting for Adam to return from work. The setting sun had flecked the clapboard with orange, and her lids had felt heavy. She had nodded off before feeling herself being carried, still half-asleep, up the stairs. Adam had dropped her on the four-poster bed and rapidly and eagerly pulled her clothes off. Afterwards they had watched the last glorious golden glints slide down the bedroom wall before the sun set, followed by the evening chirp of spring peepers and raucous cawing from the flock of crows that often settled in the tall maple trees at dusk. At that moment, she had felt her life approaching fullness; the only lack she had felt was of children.

Despite moving away from the stresses of the city, things had not gone smoothly. She had come to dislike her job almost from the start. Used to brash inner-city kids, with their vile language and a disturbing amount of violence, she hadn't known what to expect. What she had found was a school full of vicious little brats, backstabbers, and snobs, who had no regard for anyone outside their small circle—least of all for their teachers. The teachers were cruelly harassed, sometimes even threatened with lawsuits accusing them of psychological abuse or sexual misdeeds, unless they allowed the student to make the grade.

Maybe the education experts were right. Maybe having a live teacher in the classroom was an outmoded idea. Distance learning from home had been the national aim. But not all mothers were capable of home schooling their children, even if they only needed to act as monitors. It had been tried and failed. Distance learning was already the norm for the college-level student, with the courses taken electronically. Famous teachers, long dead, taught many college classes, their erudite voices suffusing lushly carpeted studies and tenement walk-ups alike. The old ivy-covered university buildings were now much sought after as residences for the wealthy. Some of Ingrid's present students would, no doubt, end up living at Harvard, or Princeton, or Yale.

Ingrid sighed. She missed the city kids. They were outspoken, but they were honest. There was nothing wrong with their moral values; they were just a bit violent in defending them. She thought of them now and then with real regret and longing, remembering rough and dirty children with belligerent attitudes that often hid sensitive and touchy egos. Ingrid had tried unsuccessfully to muster the same kind of empathy for the Bennington girls—they were, after all, just children—but their blatant egotism and refusal to take on any challenges she offered them defeated her. She missed the city itself, she decided. It had been a while.

That's it. I'll go visit Mim. I'll just call her and tell her I'm on the way.

Suddenly energized, she switched off the ice hotel and went into the living room. She turned to Suzie, but found the system still down. *I'll go anyway. If she's not home, I might even drive out to the island.*

Her grandfather had left Ingrid the small stone house on Cape Ann in his will, with the stipulation that her grandmother could remain there until she died. Grandmother Lil, now a spry ninety-two-year-old, still lived in the house, with a nurse who was elderly herself but still able to clean and cook for the two of them. Ingrid knew she had been lucky to find Betsy. Ingrid and Adam had spent several summers with the two women, pointing the granite and helping keep her grandmother's roses alive.

Ingrid packed a few things and left a hand-written note on the bathroom mirror for Adam. She never left a message with Suzie if she could help it, even when Suzie was up and running, so Adam knew where to look.

Adam, I've gone to Boston to visit Mim. Love, Ingrid. She had hesitated momentarily at the word "love."

CHAPTER 10

The fire squad arrived at the scene. A report had been called in and the men found the blaze easily, and also the remains of the aircraft that had crashed high up on the hillside.

"No survivors here. Blown to smithereens, the whole thing. Just put out the fire and call in a tech squad. These poor suckers never knew what hit them, but I guess someone's gotta figure it out."

They trained the pressurized anti-oxygen on the burn site and remained until the final sizzle was silenced. Then they went down the hill toward Thurmont, where they reported the crash of the plane. When the news reached the chief, he paled. He closed the door and reached for the G-line pad and pressed his index finger on the red button.

"Reporting plane down. No survivors." He gave the location of the crash and the time the fire had been called in, and waited anxiously for a response, for some sort of reassurance. None came. The call was terminated and the chief was left standing, a sense of foreboding eating away at him.

Later, when the lights blinked, he could hear the emergency power system kick in. With SYSCOM down, he only had the G-line, and after his last call, a power glitch seemed too trivial to report. It would probably switch back shortly.

CHAPTER 11

The pope got up and walked out onto the front lawn. He studied the gardens that surrounded Laurel Lodge. Many of the first ladies had left their marks here. There were rock gardens, small waterfalls and fountains, and here and there little bronze signs telling short anecdotes from the past. The other lodges were scattered in the woods—Aspen Lodge, where the president would stay tonight, and Birch, Hickory, Dogwood, Poplar, Cedar, and Rosebud Lodges, where the rest of the staff and visitors would set up camp. The cabins and lodges were named after native trees, many of which graced the compound.

The pope was pleased that Eisenhower had changed the name of the compound itself from Shangri-La to Camp David. Shangri-La, which was what Roosevelt named it when he established it, was sort of unseemly, Fidelis thought, as though the place were some religious retreat where you would receive guidance from a lama, or, worse, hope to live forever and never meet your maker.

He looked around into the dusk, where some of the lodges were still visible among the trees. Hickory held the library; Chestnut used to house the old switchboard until the WHCA, the White House Communications Agency, got its own new site. Poplar was the office of the CO. Aspen Lodge was by tradition the president's abode. The entrance to this lodge was level with the path, which had provided easy access for FDR's wheelchair. To the west of it there was a lovely little man-made pond with a softly cascading waterfall. Two years ago, Sheedy had sat in one of the old oak seats beside it for a leisurely afternoon chat with DeLong. FDR had originally named the lodge The Bear's Den; years later, it had been the last lodge to receive the name of a tree, when it was changed to Aspen Lodge in honor of Mrs. Eisenhower—Mamie being a native of Colorado, where the state tree was the aspen.

There were four bedrooms and five fireplaces in Aspen, and a screened porch that was part of the living room. It was still furnished with some of the second-hand items that Roosevelt had taken from the White House storage. Nixon had built the swimming pool, and Nancy Reagan had enlarged the kitchen and made additions to the flower garden. President Carter had met with Begin and Sadat in the office in Aspen Lodge prior to the Camp David Accords of the previous century, and Rockwell had hosted financial discussions in the twenties between the U.S., the EU, and the African nations. The Rockwell discussions never came to much, in the perhaps too casual surroundings of the living room and porch. Most of the other lodges were just small guest cabins. Witch Hazel had once been called the Grace Tully Cabin after FDR's secretary, who had stayed there when she was at the camp. Had Lucy Mercer, the president's mistress, stayed there, too? The pope grimaced.

Further out, not visible from where he stood, was the bridle path. It ran along the perimeter of the camp and had been first cleared and used by the Kennedys. *What was the name of Caroline's horse? Macaroni, wasn't it?*

The path was later paved over by Nixon then restored by the Reagans, who were provided with horses by the National Park Service. After terrorists had tried to breach the outer fence twenty years ago, during the Baker administration, a no-man's land had been created, which had swallowed up the bridle path and a wide swath of forest surrounding it. The fence had quickly been replaced with a massive physical wall and sophisticated electronic security, and the patrol force had been strengthened.

On the grounds there were still acres of areas for recreational use—golf, fishing, tennis, swimming—although FDR's old Bear's Wallow was long gone. There were the barracks, which were the crew's living quarters, and there was, of course, Evergreen, the chapel. Underneath it all there was a complex road system with a maze of tunnels and caverns of various levels of security. Each building had its own entrance into the underground, and you could go, unseen, via the tunnels to any other location at Camp David, a fact that had been convenient on many diplomatic occasions.

The sun had set, but at this altitude the blue dusk was still luminous. Down below, mist hung over the valleys. It was dry up here, which was a relief after the humid heat of the city. The pope breathed deeply. He turned around at the sound of men running in his direction. They caught sight of him, and four of them immediately surrounded him.

"Sir, we must ask you to come inside. We have a message."

They led him back into the lodge, stopping just inside the door. There they stopped and turned to him, solemn-faced.

"The president's plane has gone down."

The pope waited for the rest. His hands were steady, but he clasped them behind his back just the same. The sound of his pulse seemed to him loud enough to be echoing out the door and rolling over the hillside.

"There were no survivors." Their faces were white, their cheeks taut.

"Sir, you are our new commander-in-chief. These men, or their replacements, will remain with you at all times." The young officer paused, as though waiting for directions. "Would you like us to have everyone assemble in the meeting room?"

"Thank you, yes... No, let us assemble at Evergreen. We will all need guidance."

CHAPTER 12

He could not see. His face felt wet and cold and hot at the same time. He struggled to get up, and each time he fell back down. Finally he dragged himself on hands and knees, ripping himself on the sharp twigs and vicious briar. He pulled himself along, toward what, he did not know. He realized he was not blind when he saw lights in the distance. In the trees, the mountain darkness had been total. There was a road down there. He worked his way down the hill, inch by inch. The lights were long gone before he made it down to the narrow roadway. Maybe someone else would come.

He tried to rest against a rock, but was afraid he might fall unconscious again. He made an effort to stand up. The pain in his head made him feel faint, and he fell across the road and lost consciousness.

A vehicle was coming up the hill. The headlights picked up the crumpled figure and came to a stop at the last moment. The driver cautiously opened his door and approached. When he knelt down he heard moaning and knew that in the pile of rags there was a human being, still alive. He shook him gently, but looked away at the sight of the face, which was bloody and soiled.

"Watch out…" the voice came with great effort, weak and trembling.

"It's going to be okay. I'll get you to a clinic," the driver said.

"The wave…the wave is coming." A mere whisper now.

"Okay, okay, got it. Don't worry now. Just relax."

He half-dragged the broken body over to the vehicle and managed to push him into the seat. The man groaned and lost consciousness again.

The driver knew there was an emergency station further on, beyond the summit and part way down the other side. There was no other traffic and he went as fast as he dared. The road curved crazily up here. It was an old road that led to the National Parklands, where people rented campsites. But it was late now, and the vacationers would all be snug in their tents.

When they got to the station, he ran inside for help. Two orderlies came back out with him, dragging a folding gurney between them.

"He's pretty bad. His face, especially. And I think he must have a concussion or something. He was raving about a wave."

The orderly snickered.

"A wave, huh? Up in the mountains? Drunk, probably. Or lit on drugs. He stinks, too. God, what a mess. Well, we'll make him happy."

As soon as they got inside they sanitized him, put him to bed, and got him tubed. His face was indeed a mess, but beyond picking loose bits of leaves and twigs off and taping a gaping cut, they had to leave it alone. Bones and burns they had to leave to the specialists. They were just techs—plugging in was about the limit. *Just keep 'em alive.*

The two orderlies went back out to the receiving area, where they had a card game going. They had just reheated their coffee for at least the third time, making it truly undrinkable, when the lights blinked and the emergency power switched on.

"Great. Go hit the resets, will ya? I'll call in and report." But the lines were dead. They'd have to sit tight.

CHAPTER 13

The small monitor on the dashboard of the PTV crackled to life. Images flickered across the screen.

Pete pulled off the road and adjusted the receiver. A face came into focus. Sheedy. Pete recognized the interior of the Evergreen chapel behind the pope. Sheedy had pulled a white robe over his suit, a white and gold miter was on his head *(Did he carry it in his suitcase?)*, and he was standing in the pulpit, eyes closed in private prayer. Suddenly he lifted his hands high in a gesture that was becoming his trademark, and opened his eyes to face the audience.

"My fellow Americans, brothers and sisters in Christ," he began. The camera zoomed out, showing the backs of those gathered in the chapel. *Where is the president?* Pete wondered. Maybe he was in the safe room with the cabinet members who were not present at the chapel.

"Our nation, in the past, has gone through times of trial. We have suffered terrible tragedy, and each time we have come through stronger than before. We have come upon such a time once more."

Is he going to announce the wave? Has McClellan been overruled? Where is McClellan anyway? Pete felt Evie's eyes on him, but forced himself not to look at her. Ariana was concentrating tensely on the screen.

"It is with the greatest and most profound feeling of sorrow that I must announce to you, my dear countrymen, the death of our beloved president."

A great, hoarse moan escaped Ariana's lips. Pete was stunned, disbelieving, trying to store the revelation away from his gut, and waiting for the pope to continue. He cast a quick glance at Evie, who was no longer looking at him. Evie's small, delicate hand wound itself around Ariana's neck—like the hand of a child, softly caressing and consoling—while Evie herself had started weeping quietly.

"The president was on his way to meet with us here at Camp David when his plane went down, killing all on board."

My God. More than half of the top leaders of this country had been on that plane. Then Pete's heart nearly stopped. *They don't know about the wave! None of them know. I am the only one left who knows.*

He reached for the wristcom and remembered again that he had left it behind. The PTV was provided with two-way access to SYSCOM, which obviously had been brought back up in order to broadcast the pope's message. But the outgoing line was dead. They were broadcasting only, no other traffic had been enabled.

Pete pulled back out onto the road. They had to get to Camp David.

God! The entire government in Washington, the senators and congressmen...the Pentagon... Had someone reached them before the plane went down?

They listened to the rest of the broadcast in silence, Pete driving furiously around the dark hairpin curves. He shook his head in disbelief when the speaker of the house, still wearing his papal robe, was sworn in as president of the United States of America. The broadcast ended with a brief statement: *Tomorrow will be a national day of mourning. Except for important bulletins, SYSCOM will remain shut down until further notice.*

CHAPTER 14

"Senator Birke…" The pope called out across the table, making himself heard over the bedlam. The senator got up, walked around the room, and pulled up a chair by the pope's side.

The pope continued speaking in a rather hushed voice audible only to Birke. "It appears we have no knowledge whatsoever of the purpose of the meeting we were called here for. There must have been an urgent reason. The secrecy, the shutting down of SYSCOM, all of this makes me quite worried. Is there no way of getting at the bottom of this?" The pope frowned, leaning toward Birke to make sure of being heard. "I think leaving SYSCOM down overnight can only be a good thing. It will give the people time to reflect on their mortality instead of getting caught up in a flurry of news and briefings and jamming the system with unnecessary communications." Birke snickered inwardly. *Reflect on their mortality. What crap.*

"But tomorrow," the pope continued, "we must turn SYSCOM back on and use it effectively in controlling the future of this country and the new administration. In the meanwhile, we must do all we can to understand what brought us here. I heard from Senator Presser that WIF was closed, allowing no international flights to land. Did anyone find this to be true at other airports? Have our borders been closed? Could we be under threat of attack from abroad? Do we have anyone here from the Pentagon?"

Birke shrugged. The news about the closing of WIF, the international airfield in Washington, didn't surprise him. It was always one of the first reactions to any perceived national emergency.

"McClellan was on the plane, so he's gone," Sheedy continued. "In our current situation, no communications system can be trusted. We won't even use the G-lines. We must use personnel only. Send someone back immediately with a pilot who can fly. I have no faith in instruments at a moment like this."

Birke nodded indulgently. *Paranoid old coot. He won't be easy to control. Not like Albion. Even DeLong had been manageable, as long as you made him think he made the decisions. That's why I wouldn't accept the VP nomination. No power. This is where I belong, right in the thick of it.*

The pope rose, looked around the table, and then faced Birke again.

"I'm retiring to Aspen Lodge. Once you've made the arrangements, why don't you join me there for an evening meal? They ought to be able to send something over for us. We can wait for news over there. In fact, why don't you plan on spending the night?"

Afraid of the dark, are you, Your Holiness? Birke thought, but nodded and went looking for a crack pilot, one of the old-time mavericks that still knew how to fly by the seat of his pants.

CHAPTER 15

"Please, Pete, could you pull over? I need some air." Ariana put her hand on his sleeve. Even in the faint light from the dashboard Pete could see that she was pale, her face tautly controlled.

They stopped at a pullout. When Pete turned the car off they were left in total darkness. Evie searched blindly through the glove compartment for the flashlight, until Pete turned on the overhead light.

"We won't be here long. I'll leave this on. Come on outside, Ariana."

Evie remained in the car, feeling that Ariana probably needed some time alone with Pete. She knew from the past that there was information that may be sensitive, and Ariana may not feel she could speak freely in front of Evie.

Ariana leaned on Pete for a few minutes, feeling weak. Then she straightened up and let go of him. "Thanks, Pete. God, I thought I was going to be sick. I can't believe this is happening. Why did he have to leave in such a hurry? What's going on? There must have been some sort of emergency or urgent reason for him to take off like that."

Her face crumpled, and she thought for a moment she was going to cry. But that had to wait. She had learned, during her time in the White House, to keep her emotions in tight control. And when that failed, she always made sure to be alone. But now she lost control, and a sob escaped her. "Then to have the plane crash... It seems an unlikely coincidence, don't you think?"

"I don't know, Ariana. Let's get going. Maybe we'll find out when we get there." Pete felt torn. Ariana's needs were immediate, but getting the information about the pending catastrophe to whoever was in charge must be considered more urgent.

"Why, Pete? Why do I have to go there? I don't want to see any of those people. There's no one there who's going to talk to me. They avoid me like the plague. Without Ben, I just couldn't stomach any of them, except maybe Phil Steinfeld."

And he's gone, too, Pete thought, but did not say.

"Where are we, anyway?" Ariana asked. "Do we have far to go?"

"We're past Frederick. We should be getting into Thurmont soon. Then we'll turn off onto the Hagerstown road. It won't be long, Ariana."

"Do we really have to go? I mean, why can't we go back to Washington? What good will it do to go up there now? They'll send Ben's body back to Washington, won't they? I want to be where he is, Pete." Ariana was beginning to tremble, and Pete was afraid she might get hysterical. Evie had stepped out of the car and was walking around to join them.

We can't go back, Pete thought. *I have to warn them.*

He could no longer make up for his lie to the president by bringing Ariana to him. But neither was he about to drive her back into the unimaginable disaster that was coming, and which they had just left behind.

"Why don't we continue on to Thurmont and I'll try to find out what's happening? Then we can decide what's best?"

Ariana nodded. They got back into the car and pulled out onto the road. Far in the distance, there was a sound as of thunder, a prolonged rolling, surging rumble.

"Sounds like we've got a storm coming. I hate those mountain lightning storms," Evie said, shivering.

CHAPTER 16

"Great weather for night flying. God, look at those stars."

Steve Provo had turned on the cabin communicator to keep his passengers informed of their progress. He lifted the helo through the mist and headed south, out of the mountains. The inky bowl of the sky joined the earth invisibly and would have been indistinguishable from it had it not been for the stars that came to an abrupt halt at the horizon. The moon was still low; soon, it would outshine the stars.

The cities and towns below provided a different kind of light, static and harsh in comparison to the gentle glimmer from space. Provo liked taking the little detour that would bring them over Hagerstown. They would continue down to the river valley then follow the river into the city. The Potomac ran like a winding ribbon across the countryside, now and then reflecting the rising moon.

"See that, sir? That's the battlefield of Antietam, on the other side of those loops in the river." He swung the helo lower, sweeping down close to the water.

"That's enough, Provo. Get us home. This is no time for sightseeing." Colonel Wheaton was rapping on the window in irritation. Senator Presser was in the seat behind them, staring gloomily out over the dark fields.

Provo pulled up and roared along the meandering river toward Washington. "Whatever you say."

The colonel had personally pulled Provo from his bunk in the barracks and waited for him to get dressed before dragging him to the heliport. He had been shoved into his seat and given his orders: *Take Wheaton and Presser to the Pentagon pad, wait for them, and bring them back.* What the rush was, he didn't know. There was always a rush. Everything was so damn important. All Provo cared about was flying. As usual, he'd stifle his feelings and keep his comments to himself to stay out of trouble. He took the helo higher to get a better view.

They passed Sharpsburg, Sandy Hook, and Brunswick. The lights on the ground were fast making the stars fade. Now they could see Washington in the distance. He inched up just a tad, hoping Wheaton wouldn't complain again, and looked down the coastline. You could tell where the ocean started from the brilliant outline of the land, as though the water was putting out a brush fire all along the edge.

He was looking south along the coast when he noticed that the water appeared to be winning its battle against the fire. The lights were going out, and darkness was advancing up the coastline.

CHAPTER 17

Ingrid got as far as Athol on the speedrail before getting hold of herself. She stepped off the train and went into the waiting area, where she bought coffee at a self-serve and sat down on a bench.

What was I thinking? I can't show up at Mim's this time of night. What if she has company? I haven't even talked to her for months. What if Jay moved back in?

Mim's boyfriend had put a damper on their friendship. Jay was possessive and didn't like Mim going anywhere without him, even just shopping or to a movie. Then Mim and Jay had had a fight and Jay had moved out, but the last time Ingrid talked to Mim on the videm she had seen Jay's sweatshirt draped over a chair in the background.

When she finished her coffee, she tried calling Mim on the wristcom, but the lights blinked an out-of-service message. Ingrid sighed. Adam was still in New York, so she couldn't reach him, either, to tell him of her change of plans. Well, there was Grandma Lil left. It would be a long haul, but she could rent a PTV and drive out to Cape Ann. She could sleep in the little guest cabin in back of the house, where she and Adam used to bunk in privacy in the days when their privacy had still seemed precious. In the morning, she would go visit with Grandma and call Adam.

***

The carpark adjoined the station. The attendant checked the fuel cell and removed a bag of trash from the passenger seat before clocking the vehicle out to her. He asked for her quid card and studied the hologram face on the screen.

"We've lost our connection. This will go into back-up," he informed her, before turning back to the screen. "You ought to get a new card. This doesn't look like you," he said. She leaned over and looked at the image on the screen. The picture was only a couple of years old, but it could have been ten. She had looked happy then. She had thought she was.

"Thanks. I will," she told him.

She slid the quid card back into its home clip at her waist before putting a hand on the charge screen. Then she picked up her bags and left.

After getting into the PTV, she turned onto the highway and drove toward the coast as fast as it would go, which never seemed fast enough. She opened the window wide, hoping the breeze would keep her awake. Near Gardner, after nodding off and nearly going off the road before being awakened by the loud warning beep, she pulled over and took a two-hour nap. When her wrist alarm went off, she continued eastward. There was hardly any traffic, since most people in this area used public transportation. It was cheaper, more comfortable, and faster. But she knew that at this time of night there wouldn't be a connection out to the island; the last Shore Bullet left Boston at eleven.

Soon she would be out of the hills and into familiar territory. She and Adam had spent a lot of time antiquing in this area, looking for unusual objects for their home and old books, which was Adam's special interest. She recognized the feeling of excitement she always got when she neared the seashore, like a nervous stomach. It was still over a hundred miles away, but she thought she could already smell the ocean.

CHAPTER 18

The mile high wall of water rose up in the air and seemed to hold there for an eternity, as though sizing up the enemy before unleashing its fury upon it. Then it relaxed and fell over the land, engulfing it, triumphantly forcing itself into bays and up rivers, flowing freely over lowlands, effortlessly smoothing every obstacle in its way. It carried the debris along, hoarding it like a treasure, and used it to scour the land clean.

The great ridges in mid-ocean buckled as the wall of water passed over them, trembling violently. Dikes and fissures erupted, spewing magma, gas, and steam, and shaping the wave like a plow that went driving toward the land on either side. Nothing could stop it. Everywhere the land had to adjust to accommodate the water.

CHAPTER 19

When they reached the outskirts of Thurmont, they were stunned by sirens and blinded by flashing lights lining the road. They were waved over and an officer stuck his face into the car, shining a light into Pete's face.

"Where are you coming from? Did you see it? Did you see the water?"

Pete shook his head. He felt nothing yet. Or, what he felt was *cold*. A simple fearful cold that chilled him to the bone.

So...it's come. We're too late, he thought dully.

As the truth sank in, he whitened and his hands began to tremble. He started to get out of the car, but the officer, only interested in eyewitness accounts, waved him on.

"What was he talking about, Pete? What water? A flood?" Ariana asked, looking more confused than concerned, too numb after the news about her husband to be worried about anything else. Pete shook his head as he pulled the car back out into the road.

"We'll stop again and I'll try to get some more information," he promised. He continued up the road until he saw a cluster of police cruisers pulled out onto a rest area. He drove in and found an open space.

"Wait here," he said to Evie, "don't leave the car. Stay with Ariana. I'll go and find out what's happened." Evie nodded, looking frightened.

***

When Pete came back, his jaw was clenched. There was nothing to go back to now. He would have to take Ariana to Camp David after all, and leave her there. Maybe Albion's body was there, too. Maybe they would have to bury him up there. Maybe, maybe. But first he had to explain what had happened, beyond the death of her husband and the others that had died with the president in the plane. He had to find a way to tell them of this larger event that would change not only *their* lives, but that of everyone living.

For a moment, he saw in his mind all those who had been trapped in the subtropolis: the workers and the shoppers, the elderly sitting on benches, watching the hustling world go by. He saw children playing in the parks on swing sets and in wading pools, screaming when they saw the crushing wave of water coming toward them. Then he saw them being swept away. He saw prisoners fighting for breath before drowning, far underground in their cells.

Furiously, he shrugged the visions off so that he could tell Evie and Ariana what had happened, steeling himself to keep his voice under control.

When he finished, Evie was sobbing uncontrollably and Ariana was now the one offering consolation—like an automaton, stroking Evie's hair until it gathered into static peaks. Evie's entire family had lived in the Washington area; her parents in their small brick house in Georgetown and her two brothers and their families in Annapolis and Fair Haven would all have been on the front line.

When Evie was worn out from crying and began to settle into a state of shocked calm, Ariana turned to Pete.

"We're not going to Camp David. Ben is gone, Pete. I'll never get him back. Maybe they'll think I went down with the plane too. I'd like to keep it that way. What has happened now is so colossal that nobody is going to care whether I turn up or not. I'm going to disappear. Just take me somewhere far away from here, where nobody expects me to be. Please, Pete…it'll be the last favor I ever ask of you." She put her hand on his, which was gripping the steering wheel tightly.

Evie started crying again and Pete made another quick decision. He pulled out into the roadway toward town.

"You'd better hunch down then, Ariana. Put your scarf around your hair or something. We'll head north, and when we get out of town to some quiet place, we'll stop and check the map. We'll pull over at the next recharge lot, and then we'll have to find a place to sleep."

Ariana gave his arm a hard squeeze, but he shrugged her off. He thought he was probably doing the right thing, but what would happen if someone found out?

CHAPTER 20

When it completed its round, the wave had changed the earth. Islands were plunged into the deep, continents reshaped and divided, salty inland seas created where once sweet rivers had flowed.

The crown jewels of the world, its coastal cities, were gone—the buildings wiped off their plinths as though they had been made of clay. Steel and granite was strewn along the shores, here and there sticking out of the ocean like grotesque trees.

The low-lying countries were inundated. Europa, the European States, was diminished by several member nations. Holland, where, since time immemorial, people had struggled with a system of dikes to preserve the land, was awash, along with Denmark and other large sections of the European coastline. What remained of Scandinavia was severed from the continent on the Russian side.

In the oceans of the world, entire island nations disappeared. In the Mediterranean, the lovely city on the Bosphorus called Istanbul received the final, crushing blow of the wave, and its minarets now lay at the bottom of the Black Sea, which had thus received its second great flood.

The United States, likewise, was unrecognizable. The tsunami caused a series of major earthquakes in the West. The plates groaned. The fault lines opened up and swallowed what they could. The western part of California separated from the mainland, as though a giant zipper had slit the land from the Gulf of California up through the San Joaquin Valley, and much of it was now part of the Pacific sea floor.

The great river gorges filled up far inland, the churning and roiling water reaching levels not seen since ancient times. When the water finally turned and started going back out, it caused great debris flows, torrents of rocks and boulders that widened the canyons and destroyed everything in their path. Vast areas of land subsided, creating valleys that resembled raw wounds.

The gulf coast had been sinking for centuries, and the wave rolled across it effortlessly. A large part of the central plains, which had been inundated by floods in the past, became a permanent sea, with the difference being that the water was not sweet, as in previous floods, but briny, having surged up in immense bores along the rivers from the Gulf of Mexico. The bores overwhelmed the levees and dams, sluiceways and locks of the great Mississippi-Missouri River system. It stirred up the highly erodible soils of the flood plain and made soup out of the silt and sediment that had been purposely trapped in deep, cold-water reservoirs. The returning water pushed the silt and eroded soil before it, like a glacier run amok, and, finally, running out of energy, dumped it in the form of a giant berm where the Thebes Gap had formerly constricted the flow of the Mississippi River. The inland sea had become landlocked. What remained of the great cities on the river—among them, St. Louis—rose out of the water like skeletal mangrove forests.

The coastlines were redrawn. Great archipelagos appeared. Rocky crags and islands formed the diminished outer limits of the country, and nowhere was a sandy stretch of beach to be seen. The Everglades, which over the last century had been so valiantly defended and preserved, would not be seen again until the earth went through another cycle, in another lifetime.

CHAPTER 21

She sat facing the sunset across the wide expanse of water. Another night was approaching.

Ingrid would always remember them, the nights of silence that followed in the wake of the wave. Gone was the constant hum, the white noise produced by a machine-driven civilization: the soft susurration of the electronically controlled climate, the slight buzz from the gigantic "daylight" system, the hydraulic, pneumatic, and electronic sounds that mingled with the human voices into the ever-present and somehow comforting ambiance of humanity.

Even in Bennington, such noises had been heard. Their house had a hum of its own, with its many electronic systems. She had felt she could walk through the school complex blindfolded and tell by the sound where she was, with all the electronic clicks and beeps. Cameras whirred as they turned to monitor her, P.A. systems followed her everywhere, and the announcements for the visually impaired let her know where she was at every junction.

Out here, there were not even trees to whisper in the wind. Her entire world was barren rock. This evening, the water was still, not the slightest little clucking wavelet brushed against the rocks. The air was cool, even with the granite radiating the residual heat of the sun. Summer had come to an end, and there were decisions to be made.

She got up and walked back up the hill, careful to keep her feet out of the crevices in the cliffs. Dusk was coming earlier, and she felt more anxious each evening. She crossed a small section of pavement, a remnant of one of the old roads on the island. The roads were gone, along with the houses, trees, plants, animals, and every grain of sand and soil. Birds still came, seagulls and eider ducks and mallards and even swans, but no songbirds, no warblers or towhees or mockingbirds or cardinals or chickadees. There was nothing for them to eat and no thickets for their nests. All that was left was solid ledge and monumental granite boulders.

Primeval time had returned. *It must have been like this after the Ice Age,* she thought, when the glacier retreated and left the great terminal moraine on the island, along with the *erratics,* the great lonely rocks that she and Grandpa Josh had come across in the woods in the old days. A few gigantic boulders still sat, like ancient steles, giving the island a druidic appearance. The smaller rocks from the moraine had been swept along by the wave, filling the gullies and crevices and quarries and probably the bottom of the ocean halfway up to Maine. If there was anything left of the towns on the island, it was underwater rubble.

The towns had been built at the water's edge, a circle of fishing villages, artists' colonies, and tourist Meccas. What remained of the island now was the high plateau—the area that had once been called Dogtown—and a few smaller craggy islets around it, the larger ones on the ocean side.

The sandy beaches that once had surrounded the island had long since become seasonal, the fragile dunes having been lost in the succession of storms and hurricanes that had raged more and more frequently. The barrier beaches, which had been the home to countless summer cabins, had been forcibly closed down as the sea level rose. The houses had been razed after the turn of the century. Every winter the storms sucked all the sand off the beaches, leaving them rocky and slimy with seaweed. And every spring the waves deposited the soft golden sand back on top of the rocks and pebbles.

There was a tale of a new public works director, who had been an "inlander" unfamiliar with that fact. Seeing the bare rocks in the spring, he had, to the great glee of the townsfolk, kindly ordered truckloads of sand to be dumped on the beaches "so the children will be able to play."

Now, many months after the wave, Ingrid was continuing to work on a project to map the area and to give names to the islands and straits, a task that had helped her keep her sanity in the early days after the disaster. She had known the island well, and when she came upon something that was still recognizable, it left her both angry and melancholy.

Cape Ann had been a large island, built sturdily out of granite, which accounted for the fact that there was something left of it. How many of the lovely islands that the world had recently lost had simply consisted of big sand reefs, covered with vegetation and ramshackle cities and towns? It made no difference, though. As long as people built their homes at the edge of the sea, they had been equally vulnerable. Now the island was small, fragile. What would happen in a hurricane?

The highest point on the new Dogtown was less than a hundred feet above sea level. Once there had been thousands of acres of woods, swamps, and moorland there, with reservoirs and water-filled quarries, and trails where people would pick blueberries and hunt for lady's slippers and black trumpets. Long ago, the early settlers had lived in the Dogtown section of the island, where she now stood. They had grazed their cattle on the

Commons, and raised herbs and vegetables around their humble cabins. In time they had moved down to the shore, leaving the old women (some of whom were witches, it was said) and the dogs to fend for themselves. Finally it had only been the dogs that lived up in Dogtown, giving the area its name.

Now Ingrid was nearing the place where she had constructed her shelter. She tried never to think of the day she arrived, but the memory kept coming back to her.

***

She had been driving through the hills near Gardner. Traffic had been slowing down, until all the cars slowly came to a standstill. No cars had been coming from the opposite direction. She had sat and waited briefly before going to investigate. She knew it wasn't supposed to be a good idea to get out of the car. Adam always reminded her to stay in her seat in an emergency, lock the doors, roll up the windows, and wait for help. But she had sensed that there was something different going on, something that required her to act on her own behalf instead of remaining inert and waiting for a rescue that may never come.

So she had joined the other drivers. Together, they had made their way on foot to the crest of the hill in the dark. They had seen the line of cars stretching for miles into the distance, ending far down in the valley at what looked like a lake, the moon reflecting across it. Beyond was only blackness. She remembered the screams and the shock. When she got closer, she had seen whole houses floating in the water, some tilting and sinking slowly, a flotilla of small Titanics...and cars, and bodies.

***

Abrupt pain brought her back to the present. She had jammed her foot between the rocks and she swore as she struggled to pull it out, praying at the same time that she hadn't twisted her ankle. She rubbed it and wiggled her foot gingerly back and forth, but there seemed to be no harm done.

Up ahead was the heap of granite she called home. She knew she was on her own property, even though the house was gone and, along with it, Grandmother Lil and her nurse, Betsy. The stone wall that had surrounded the property had been leveled and joined the rest of the rubble in Goose Cove and beyond.

She had spent two days criss-crossing what she was sure must once have been the upper end of Dennison Street, looking for anything she could recognize, little by little narrowing her search down until she had finally found it. In the backyard there had been a ledge that joined the vertical cliff face to form a seat. Ingrid remembered lying on the ledge as a child, soaking up the heat from the sun and reaching out to pick the blueberries that grew around the edges. Sometimes the berries would shrivel up from the heat of the rock and she would pick "blueberry raisins." Those were the happy days of childhood, when her parents' divorce was still in the future and her own life seemed to stretch on endlessly, like the sea. The days when the smell of dry grass and the screech of seagulls would lull her to sleep even on that hard granite ledge.

Finding the ledge, she had backtracked to where the house would have stood, and found a depression filled with large, jammed boulders. She had scrabbled desperately, trying to pry the stones away, until her fingers bled and her breathing came in short, sobbing spurts.

In the time since, she had painstakingly used poles and logs as levers and emptied the cellar. All the earth had been sucked away by the wave and the foundation was gone, but she had placed stones roughly in the way she remembered that the house had stood and filled the outside of these walls with rubble gathered at low tide. Then she had gone hunting along the shore and collected all the useful debris she could find, of which there was an unlimited supply, to build a flat roof over the cellar hole. This was her home. And soon the time would come to decide whether to try to survive the winter here, or go back ashore to the terrors that awaited there.

CHAPTER 22

The first chapter of his presidency had been an unimaginable nightmare, Pope Fidelis felt. Before taking office, only hours after Albion's death, he had rapidly considered how becoming president would affect his duties and responsibilities at the Vatican. At the end of that long night, after he had begun to comprehend the magnitude of the larger catastrophe that had befallen them, he had known there was no alternative and that, again, he had been chosen to lead from two offices simultaneously.

The government had been reduced to the group of people who had been assembled at Camp David and a small number of others. These others, who had arrived since that night, were the few senators and congressmen who had been spread out all over the country after a short recess. *The ones that had been remiss in their duty,* Fidelis thought, *to get back to Washington in a timely fashion.* The large majority—those with a sense of duty to their constituents, who had returned in time for the final debate and vote on the proposed new church tax—had drowned, without ever getting to cast that vote. The pope smiled grimly at the irony of it all.

Despite the great inroads the Church had made in the past half-century, there had still been enough votes, according to the pollsters, to defeat the tax. The funding would have meant security for all the small parishes and parochial schools still forced to depend on the old voucher system to survive. If the vote had been in the affirmative, it would have meant equal funding for the parochial schools. *Well, perhaps a new day has dawned*, Fidelis thought, then shrugged guiltily.

Wheaton and Presser had returned, white-faced, from their aborted flight to the Pentagon after the pilot, Provo, had first spotted the wave. They had been escorted directly to Aspen Lodge, where they had made their report. Presser had needed to leave the room twice before being able to control himself long enough to give his version. Provo had actually given the most detailed description, his language as graphic as the images it evoked.

Moments after their report, the pope had understood why they had all been ordered to Camp David, and had closed his eyes and clenched his fists in an involuntary gesture of despair. The president and McClellan had obviously known of the coming catastrophe and had been on the way to tell them—or were perhaps just trying to get out of harm's way. Why had the people not been warned? In all likelihood, no one outside of the passengers who had perished in that plane crash had been aware of what was coming. The wave, or as the pope would henceforth refer to it, *the deluge,* had been kept secret and arrived without warning. Whose decision had that been?

Pope Fidelis had decided he would set up an interim White House at Camp David. When Birke finally arrived at his lodge on that terrible evening, the pope had realized that he would have preferred spending the night alone, unencumbered by this power-greedy prattler who already seemed to have an agenda. He had listened to the hastily drawn plans of action suggested by Birke, who had seemed to be salivating excessively. As soon as the pope had detected a break in the torrent of words, he had excused himself, citing prayer and rest as a necessary next step.

Prayers had certainly been in order. In speaking to God, he had tried keeping his tone from becoming accusatory. He had not asked questions. He had not said, *"Why?"* or, *"Lord, where do I start?"* In the days to come, his own conscience would guide him.

It wasn't exactly that he didn't trust the Lord to give him proper guidance. The Lord, after all, had provided him with the understanding of people that he would now use to shape them, to help them conform to the rules of a new society, a new order. There simply was no time for introspection or to appeal to the Lord for answers. The Lord had guided and approved him; now He could test his mettle. Fidelis would not let Him down. When he opened his mouth, words would flow from it like bursts of flame.

During that long night, in the aftermath of global disaster and personal exaltation, Pope Fidelis had realized that in order to achieve success, he would have to continue to keep his two selves united in one form in his own mind. Outwardly, however, he would have to be two separate figures, one temporal, the other spiritual, each supporting the other, each reinforcing the power of the other. He did not then understand how this decision would eventually lead to his own destruction.

All his life he had balanced the sincere goodness that came from God with the daily reality of political demands, until they became as a tightly wound cable. Now, the cable would begin to fray. To Fidelis, it had all seemed so simple. He had thought naively that he could divide himself in two, and when the job was done, put himself together again. The spiritual entity would have to lead. The people would need Pope Fidelis first to see to their souls and to gather them into the house of the Lord.

Later, in the days and weeks that followed, President Sheedy would appear to restore order and see to their physical needs.

As he sat in the approaching dawn, Fidelis had made mental notes. He had to assess the extent of the destruction, which then he could only guess at. Provide food. Shelter. Medicine. Restore power and communication. A census would have to be taken as soon as possible. Orphanages had to be created. *There always had to be orphanages.*

He had felt sure that Wheaton would prove effective in delegating visits to all military bases in order to determine the status of the armed forces: manpower, machines, and weapons. On that night, Fidelis did not begin to consider the rest of the world. For a brief moment it intruded on his mind, but he pushed it away forcefully. Not yet. He had to accept his limitations. He would start here. However, in trying to cover every possible aspect of the days that lay ahead, he had made two major mistakes. He had thought he understood the scope of the event. And he had forgotten the dead.

CHAPTER 23

Global reaction to the approaching wave had set off a nightmare of its own. As the wave traveled along, terrifying and apocalyptic emergency response procedures in all countries had automatically been set in play. Missiles, some armed with devastating biological cartridges, had left their subterranean hideouts, aimed at both friend and foe, with the computers confused by the rapidly encroaching but unknown enemy. All over the world these weapons had wreaked their destruction, hitting major cities, military installations, and other targets of strategic importance. Those who were unaware of the wave thought, perhaps in their last moments, that another world war had begun. What they didn't know was that it had not been started by an enemy such as a dictator or a terrorist organization, but was the result of man's own hubris in thinking he could use and abuse the earth with abandon without adverse result.

Of course, it may have been that it was simply what was in store for the earth in nature's grand scheme of things all along, and man had no control over it. In any event, while the coastline was being altered and scoured clean, the interior was pocked with great craters where, formerly, cities had been, and a dusty layer of rubble covered the dead—though it was woefully inadequate to hide the stench. The survivors fled, taking only what they had in their pockets, streaking out in all directions, looking for food and shelter.

The problem with disposing of the dead was the worst along the coast. Smoke hung over the coastline for weeks. Fires were still being lit, but were fewer and smaller. At first they had tried to bury the dead, but there were simply too many. Millions of bloated bodies. They couldn't dig fast enough, and where the wave had passed, there was no earth left to dig. The cemeteries were gone, peeled away right down to the bedrock. Those who had slumbered there had found other resting places. People resorted to burning the bodies as fast as they could, using accelerants to ensure complete disintegration. The summer heat was relentless, and within a week they were forced to close off the entire coastline, allowing only military and emergency personnel onto a fifty-mile stretch that started at the new water line.

Unfortunately, needs were vast all over the country, which forced the troops to spread themselves too thin to deal with another major problem: looting. It seemed extraordinarily sickening that people would stoop so low. Large bands of looters and thieves, wearing masks to protect themselves from the stench, overran the regions that had been evacuated. These were the areas where the destruction and incipient epidemic had made it too dangerous to stay. It also happened to be the area where the new gentry had settled on large, pseudo-mansioned estates in order to live near the prevailing ocean breezes, surrounded by greenbelts and private lakes and miles of security fences. These residents had unceremoniously been forced to evacuate, leaving their homes and property behind unprotected.

The bands, roving the countryside and not ashamed to steal from dead bodies, caused the spreading of pestilence and disease that still ravaged the country in successive waves. There was no help to be had from the hospitals. Emergency triage and rescue centers had at first been organized in every large building and arena that could be converted for such use in order to take care of the original victims. When epidemic disease struck, the only measure left was large-scale quarantine. Areas were closed off, and people within them were left with no hope for care other than what they could provide for each other. Where there were not enough troops to patrol the areas, local militias were formed, and people trying to break out of quarantine were shot on sight.

It was a time of selfishness, of protecting one's own family and, ultimately, oneself. Shock turned to greed and suspicion. People competed fiercely for resources necessary to survive: food, water, and lodging.

The dead—well, they no longer needed anything, and their property was fair game. There was no time to mourn them. It was best to help oneself to whatever useful or potentially valuable items they had left behind, and move on.

CHAPTER 24

When the number of funeral pyres seemed to be subsiding, military planes went up and down the coastline sending out cascades of white powder. People living on the no-man's land, like Ingrid, were terrified. She cowered in her cellar. When she finally ventured out, the island and what she could see of the mainland looked like they had been dusted with snow. At least it hadn't killed her…yet. Maybe the chemical was safe.

She lay sleepless in her dark cellarhole, looking out at the stars for comfort. Visions from the recent past kept sweeping through her mind, obliterating the night sky with images of floating corpses and twisted wreckage.

***

Ingrid had spent the first hours after the flood in the PTV. After seeing the water, she had walked back to the car, got in, locked the doors carefully, and closed the windows, even though she knew it was like shutting the barn door after the horse was gone. She had been unable to walk away—to save herself from any further flooding, should it come, or even to join the people who gathered into billowing groups outside, some screaming or shouting, others standing silent. Behind her the line of cars extended up over the hill, and people were running back and forth past her. She dimly knew that life had changed forever. She had no concept of what had taken place—

what volcanic eruption, planetary collision, or other calamity might have befallen the earth. She only knew what she had seen with her own eyes. The ocean had risen and invaded the coast and whatever cities and towns that had been there, and when the water had receded, it was not to its familiar coastline.

She understood other things. Even if the water were now—or ever—to retreat to its original limit, it was too late for the people. Mim was gone. Adam, her husband and long-ago lover, was gone, too. She had tried to reach people on her wristcom many times since that day, but to no avail. The watch would tell time for years to come, but there was no access to videocom, messages, news, music, or any of the many other functions she now missed. She could set off the emergency alarm, all right, if someone tried to attack her, but there would be no one around to hear it.

***

Ingrid twisted in her makeshift bed, trying to conjure up memories of happier times in order to go back to sleep. How distant they seemed, the days when she had been rushing home to let down her hair, change into something flouncy, throw a meal together, set the table, and light the candles. Ingrid couldn't refrain from smiling at a memory in which she saw Adam coming home from work, running through the maples with the setting sun at his back, skipping like a child across the lawn, and bounding up the steps to join her on the porch swing.

"How was your day?" he'd asked without waiting for an answer. "Mine was nasty. It's so hot in town you wouldn't believe it. They shut down the Maggie because of cooling problems, so I had to postpone my trip until tomorrow. Want to come with me?"

"To Washington? You know I can't...they couldn't find a sub in time. Does that mean you won't be home by the weekend? I told Grandma we'd be out to see her. Just think about going for a swim down Plum Cove, or across the river at Wingaersheek Beach."

"Come on, don't torture me... I'll do my best—you go anyway. I'll join you there if I can. Right now I'm a lot more interested in our plans for the evening, my lovely."

"Are you hungry?"

"Eh, it can wait. I've got a better plan."

The plan hadn't varied much from day to day. On that particular night, Adam had seemed unusually relaxed, and after a brief but heated session in the bedroom, they had stayed up late into the night. After making plans for a visit to Sweden later in the year, they had gone for a long walk in the moonlight, and when they reached the fields on the outskirts of town, Adam had pulled her down onto the grass and made love to her again.

The day after, the Maggie—the magnetic levitation train (early on, people had balked at calling it the *Maglev,* which they thought made it sound like a Russian invention) had been back in service, and Adam had gone on his trip to Washington. When he returned, everything had changed, and life had never seemed as simple and joyful again.

Not long afterward, Ingrid had begun to think of her life as divided into segments. There was *Before Adam.* That segment was her childhood, when she was a no-nonsense kind of a girl and nothing anyone did or said would bother her. Even after the split-up of her parents, she was self-assured, positive, forward-looking—maybe even more so then. She remembered feeling happy: happy at home with her mother in Sweden, and happy at her grandparents' house in the States. Then, *With Adam Before*

Washington, came a different kind of happiness: the newlywed years. Smooth sailing mostly, with life still stretched out like the ocean on a summer day.

With Adam After Washington was neither a roller-coaster ride nor a steep slope, but a decline that was so gradual she could hardly tell she was going downhill until she got to the bottom. Now that she looked back, the years *After Washington* loomed like a mountain, casting a great shadow over her. Never again had they gone for moonlight walks or sat up all night talking. The trip to Sweden had not materialized. In time, she had stopped preparing dinner for two, since Adam rarely made it home until late, and by the time he got home she was often asleep.

As always, her thoughts returned to that night when the whole world had changed. Sitting motionless in the PTV, staring out into the dark, Ingrid had pushed her thoughts of Adam as far back into her mind as she could. People all around the world were gone. Her mother—oh, her mother was gone! Her mother must have known what was coming, Ingrid had realized with a sudden, painful cry, but had been cut off when she tried to warn her. Grandmother Lil was gone. But what if her dead body was trapped in that solid stone house with no one to bury it?

Ingrid had made her decision, which she knew even then was madness. In order to continue living, she would pursue one single goal at a time. The first one was to get to the island, if it was still there.

She had laughed dryly when she reached into the back seat of the PTV for her bags, packed only with a couple of changes of nice city clothes. Keeping the underwear, a sweater, and her Litkit with the rest of her usual junk in the large, zippered vinyl bag, she stuffed the city clothes and high heeled shoes into the other bag and left it on the back seat. Then she set out on foot to try to locate some food and whatever else she could find that might be useful.

There was far less panic than she had expected. It was as though people felt this was something that would quietly go away, the way damage after tornadoes and hurricanes always got cleaned up. Ingrid instinctively felt that it would not be so. *I'm like Mom. I have these "feelings." And I know this won't go away. Not in my lifetime.*

With the crammed bag on her shoulder, she began her long march to the coast. In that, she was alone, with everyone else moving—sometimes in large herds, like cattle—in the opposite direction to find a place inland to stay and wait comfortably for a return to normalcy. She had not looked back, except when she heard frightening sounds and saw what looked like comets streaking toward the earth, to land someplace far away over the horizon. She felt the earth tremble and thought maybe the end of the world was near, but nothing came of it, and she kept going.

It had taken her over a week to get to Mount Ann, where she was first able to look out over Cape Ann. *It looks like Sweden,* she thought, *like the skerries, but without the softening green.*

Spread out before her was a great, rocky archipelago, a myriad of craggy, barren little islands, where before had been forested mainland with lush green bays and marshes. At the end of the mainland had been the island of Cape Ann, connected to it by three bridges, one of them the Railroad Bridge. Fifty thousand people had inhabited Cape Ann, most of them in the villages that made up the city of Gloucester. The little town of Rockport, on the northern tip of the island, had been home to ten thousand. These numbers had tripled every summer when the tourists arrived. Over a hundred thousand people and their homes, parks, churches, and libraries had disappeared here in a flash, along with any familiar landmarks.

How will I find the island? Is it even there? Long before she had gotten to the seashore, she had known, in her rational mind, that there would be no house left and no grandmother trapped inside it. There were no houses standing anywhere within miles of the new coastline, even on the highest land. They had been swept away. There was debris everywhere—although less as she neared the ocean—and dead bodies. Sometimes the dead lay in clusters, even seeming to cling to each other. She had started out by frantically checking them, especially the children, for any sign of life, but soon realized the hopelessness of it.

On the first day she had collected any quid cards off the bodies, feeling it was her civic duty to turn these in so that the families would know. By the second day she had rushed past, turning her head grimly the other way. By then the great whale carcasses and heaps of dead fish and crustaceans had started to swell and reek, and she had pulled a t-shirt over her head like a balaclava, leaving only her eyes uncovered.

She did not know why she kept going. There was simply no other option. There was only plan one, and she could not deviate from it or she might perish. Could she have turned around? What if Adam had made it home from New York, after all? No. It was better this way. If he *was* alive, he would think she was dead, like Mim, and perhaps he would be relieved. She tried to keep her thoughts of him away, but they festered.

Adam had long since stopped needing her. She had no longer gone to the dinners he was invited to with his colleagues at the firm. She remembered how proudly he had once introduced her, how his eyes had searched for hers across the room while he was deep in conversation with some important client. She remembered the glint and surreptitious smile when his eyes had found hers, and the drive home to the intimacy of their bedroom. In recent times he hadn't even bothered to call and tell her of any change of plan or itinerary—the message left with Suzie had been a rare exception.

It was after Adam left the Legal Aid Society to join Taney, Butler & McKenna that Ingrid had begun to notice a change. It had started around the time of that trip to Washington. Adam's social conscience had always favored those who were down on their luck and in need of a passionate ally, and in the early days at the Legal Aid Society he had often discussed his most troubling cases with her. She had ached for him when he lost, and celebrated with him when he won.

At TB&M, things had been different. The firm worked on a lot of cases that reflected the current stringent religious and moral ethic as much as law, cases involving euthanasia, abortion, suicide. The list was always growing. The firm seemed to specialize in "search-and-destroy" law, vigorously going after and prosecuting *sinners* instead of *criminals,* she thought. Ingrid had grown increasingly uncomfortable. When she finally questioned her husband about it, he simply told her there was nothing to worry about.

Adam had risen steadily in the firm. After the trip to Washington, there had been a sudden and substantial increase in the salary he was bringing home. Ingrid had worried about it. Was he involved in something shady, even illegal? He seemed to have stopped agonizing over the firm's direction. Finally, he hadn't mentioned work at all. It wasn't long afterward, she thought now, that they stopped truly communicating.

Another truth, which she also now tried to face, was that her own teaching career had become something of an obsession with her. Ingrid had loved teaching from the outset. It had helped her open up, softened some of an aloofness that often kept her from making close friendships. When they moved to Bennington, she had been anxious to succeed—after all, *she* had caused them to leave everything behind to move and start over. When Adam started coming home later, she had begun to spend evenings correcting homework and making lesson plans. Even on the rare occasion when Adam was home, she often would not come to bed until he was asleep—maybe as a payback for the many nights she had spent alone in bed. When she became reluctant to go away for a weekend with him or even go into town and meet old friends for dinner, always citing some important school project or deadline, Adam had at first tried to hide his irritation. Later, he had often gone by himself, and she had simply told him to have a good time.

Adam's job at TB&M was soon taking all his time, which included weekends and frequent and extended trips to all parts of the country. Ingrid had remained preoccupied with her teaching, and so they had gone their separate ways in what they both seemed to accept as "comfortable togetherness." Neither of them appeared to need the other, and their sexual encounters became few and rudimentary, each of them turning the other way afterwards to fall asleep. If Ingrid was discontented, Adam didn't seem to notice. And if Adam needed her—as a representative wife, or as a warm and supportive companion—Ingrid, with surprising ease, withdrew to become the distant and self-absorbed girl she had been long ago.

Without realizing it, the two, who had once sworn eternal love to each other on that soft carpet of pine needles, had grown apart. What was it they had been afraid of? Why hadn't one of them tried to break down the wall, to communicate, to bring the other one back? Ingrid knew herself well enough to suspect that her pride might have stood in the way. Or fear of Adam rejecting her, as her father had effectively done before him. No, she would not torture herself with psychoanalysis. She was still the no-nonsense girl, something that could turn out to be either weakness or strength. It could make her hard and unfeeling, or it could make her resilient enough to bear the hardships to come. She intended to forge ahead, not get mired down in regrets about the past. She would not allow herself to be guilt-ridden about situations she had not purposely caused. Things happened in life, and she had just accepted and dealt with whatever realities were thrown at her.

The separation from Adam had been a long time coming, and the only thing Ingrid felt at that very moment, sitting in that PTV, staring out into that unbearably dark night, was relief. She would use her ability to distance herself from the difficult and the disagreeable and simply look forward. She would stick to her plan and do whatever could be done for Grandmother Lil, as there was no one else to do anything for. She never considered her father, even to wonder whether he might be alive.

Ingrid had torn across fields of rubble, skirted impassable stretches of rock and concrete trapped in gullies, and avoided twisted wreckage of steel that left her wondering about their origins. Had they been vehicles or buildings? She couldn't tell. The wave had transformed them beyond recognition. She followed roads whenever they appeared. They would show up for stretches, only to disappear into rivers, lakes, or bays, which she would ford or swim across, slinging the handles of her bag around her neck.

Once, swimming across a narrow, water-filled valley toward a road she had glimpsed on the other side, she bumped into a body. Her long blond hair got snagged on the cadaver's coat buttons and she started towing the body behind her. She didn't scream, only worked frantically to extricate herself from the unwanted cargo. Then she plunged forward until she felt solid ground beneath her. She tried standing up and walking in the water, but her legs trembled so badly that she had to give up. For a while, she just lay in the water, floating aimlessly. Finally, she calmed down and managed to paddle herself along until she reached the far side, where she crawled ashore and continued, stumbling ever eastward.

By the time she got to Mount Ann, there was nothing left beneath her feet but bedrock—the familiar granite: gray, buff, or rust-colored. All vegetation had been stripped off. Trees, bushes, grass—all were gone. Here and there gigantic trees had been caught in rocky clefts, trees that perhaps came from South America, she thought. Who could tell? Standing up on the hillside, looking out over the ledge at the sea with the sun setting behind her, a stark vision opened before her. She stared out over the vast stretch of bare cliffs that formed the new edge of the mainland. Out beyond a strait of water lay a startling and unfamiliar view of rocky islands. Only the horizon looked familiar: blue meeting blue.

Among all the islands, she did not see anything that looked like Cape Ann—once a richly forested green island, girt by granite shores and sandy beaches and thickly planted with small, wooden homes. *If it's still here, it will be the one furthest out.* In order to get to it, she would have to swim from island to island.

She started out that night, but darkness set in and she was forced to stay on the first island she reached, falling asleep on the still-warm rock. The following morning, she kept going, swimming from one island to the next. The water was remarkably clean, she thought. Most of the real debris had been deposited miles inland. The water reminded her of mulled cider with bits of cinnamon bark and other spices floating on top, as between the islands the sea was covered with a fine layer of shredded wood. All heavier particles had sunk to the bottom. She found herself coated with an oily substance after swimming across one stretch, but it was easily wiped off.

Eventually she reached an island, which—even though it appeared too ridiculously small and low—was larger and higher than the rest. She sensed it was Cape Ann even before she scrambled over cliffs and ledges for some time to reach the top, where she was able to look out over the unbroken sea. By then it was late in the afternoon, and she found a sheltered place where she went to sleep and slept until sunset. Screeching seagulls awakened her and she looked around in confusion until she remembered where she was, and then she cried.

How long ago was that? And how long would she be able to stay here?

CHAPTER 25

"Are we on?" These words, spoken by Pope Fidelis, had been the first heard from SYSCOM, nearly two days after the wave. There was a lot of static and no image to go with the sound. Nevertheless, wherever people heard these words—which was within a very small radius, indeed—they stopped to listen.

Fidelis did not know then—in fact, would not learn until much later—that the broadcast would only reach a tiny audience.

In countries all around the world, sophisticated systems, programmed to function even when every last human being was gone, had reacted to the catastrophe by releasing their rockets and missiles, like gigantic fireworks signaling the apocalypse. The U.S. defense system had managed to defeat some of them and prevent them from reaching their earthly targets. However, the multitude of U.S. satellites had not fared well and all but the antiquated MILSTAR, which apparently was not thought important enough to waste missiles on, were gone, as were, to be sure, those of other countries.

The fate of GALAXY II, the international space station, was unknown, and not enough had yet been known about the status of telecommunication capabilities. When Fidelis started speaking, he falsely assumed that Americans all around the country were listening.

"The Lord saw that the wickedness of man was great in the earth, and that every imagination of the thoughts of his heart was only evil continually. And the Lord was sorry that He had made man on the earth, and it grieved Him to His heart. So the Lord said, 'I will blot out man whom I have created from the face of the ground, man and beast and creeping things and birds of the air, for I am sorry that I have made them.'"

"But Noah found favor in the eyes of the Lord. Noah was a righteous man, blameless in his generation; Noah walked with God."

"And the Lord said, 'Behold, I will bring a flood of waters upon the earth, to destroy all flesh in which is the breath of life from under heaven; everything that is life on the earth shall die."

"And rain fell upon the earth forty days and forty nights. But God remembered Noah and all the beasts and all the cattle that were with him in the ark."

"And God said to Noah, 'Behold, I establish my covenant with you, that never again shall all flesh be cut off by the waters of a flood, and never again shall there be a flood to destroy the earth.' And God said, 'This is the sign of the covenant, which I make between me and you and every living creature that is with you, for all future generations: I set my bow in the cloud, and it shall be a sign of the covenant between me and the earth.'"

The pope's voice had strengthened as he spoke, and was now vibrating with power. The fact that there was no image to go with the voice was unsettling to those listening, and they stared blankly at their walls, expecting the screen to light up. The disembodied voice coming out of nowhere frightened them, as though God himself were speaking.

"But Noah's descendants broke their covenant with God. And when God saw this, saw that the wickedness of man was great in the earth again, and that man had broken the covenant, it grieved Him to His heart. And He sent His flood of waters upon the earth again. And this was the punishment for our sins."

"And when the days of weeping are past, we must make our own covenant with the Lord. We must cleanse ourselves of the wickedness, and the sins, and the evil thoughts in our hearts. We must purify our souls, and dedicate ourselves to the Lord. Only when we have done this will the Lord make a wind blow over the earth and the water subside."

Senator Davis shook his head in disbelief, then laughed dryly and turned to Birke, who looked pained.

"Seems to me God's the one who broke the covenant. Didn't He promise not to send another flood? *We* did what He told us, didn't we? *Be fruitful and multiply,* and all that. Now, maybe if we hadn't, we wouldn't be in this mess…"

"What the covenant states, if I remember exactly, is 'never again shall *all* flesh be cut off, and never again shall there be a flood to *destroy the earth…*' Well, *we* are still here, and so is at least *part* of the earth. God's no fool, you know. Do you really think He would write a contract He couldn't get out of?" Birke walked away, irritated. Religion could be a useful tool, but he had to deal with political realities now, and didn't want God to get in his way.

Prayer in small doses and encouragement to stand behind the leader suited him fine, but the pope would have to be toned down a bit.

CHAPTER 26

When they finally pulled in at a recharge lot on that first night Pete had discovered that no recharge was possible. All over the country, cars were stranded in the lots. Many more were stalled along highways and byways, having been driven as far as their fuel cells lasted.

SYSCOM had never fully come back up. The Government Information Channel, functioning on emergency backup power, had crackled to life a couple of times, first with the speech by Pope Fidelis and on the following day with the announcement of martial law.

Since that time, Pete, Evie, and Ariana had gone without news. Newspapers hadn't been published for decades—everyone had kept up with the news via SYSCOM—but they had begun to see handprinted broadsides, like remnants from colonial times, nailed to trees. News traveled as if by some unseen Pony Express. "WORLDWIDE TSUNAMI KILLS BILLIONS" had been the first headline. The story itself had been full of error and speculation, both in terms of the cause of the disaster and the damage in its wake. "PRESIDENT DEAD. POPE TAKES OFFICE," "MISSILES ATTACK NATION," "NATIONAL POWER GRID DOWN," and "CURFEW IN EFFECT" had followed. They had read every word, hungry for information, at the same time assuming that the countrywide power failure was being worked on day and night.

The part about the curfew they had read carefully and then disregarded. *"All citizens ordered to remain in their home area."* Well, their home area no longer existed. They were headed for whatever they could find to replace it.

"Utah or Vermont? I have never been to either." Evie shook her head while answering Pete's question.

"If you decide on Vermont, we can stay together until we get to Massachusetts," Ariana said. "I don't know why they all moved up there. I asked them, 'What's wrong with Brooklyn?'" She laughed, suddenly remembering something else. "That's what my brother Aren asked *me* years later, when I told him I was moving into the White House: 'What's wrong with Brooklyn?'"

Ariana was listlessly eating one of the bruised apples they had gleaned from an orchard. Food was becoming a problem, although they had not gone hungry yet. Early on, they had visited the handimarts that serviced the local campers. They were filled with row upon row of of automats, but even these marts were now closed down, having run out of products.

Pete and Evie were used to the "supsups," or *supplemental suppers,* hermetically sealed food in any shape and flavor they liked. Like most working people, they had frequently taken these instead of meals. Supsups were fortified with everything the human body needed except emotional satisfaction. Using up all their available cash reserves they had hoarded all the food they could find along with a box of Campfire Beef Jerky, which they treasured, and as much bottled water as they could comfortably carry. They shared the burdens and discarded anything they didn't need. Ariana had traded her high heels and dress for a sweat suit and sneakers somebody had left behind in a gym bag.

"Vermont it is, then," Pete determined. "Dad lives up in the hills, not far from Brattleboro. Mom moved back to Utah years ago. That's where she's from: Great Salt Lake. She left Dad; just said one day that she'd had enough, I never knew of what. Used to think maybe it was me. Then, about a year later, Dad came home and said, 'Meet my wife, Luce.' She's very nice. You'll like Luce."

Ariana and Evie both laughed, and Pete grinned and took Evie's hand, swinging it back and forth as they walked at a comfortable pace. Birds were singing in the shrubs and high trees, which here consisted mostly of beeches and maples and an occasional evergreen.

"I haven't seen Mom for years," he continued. "She's happy out there in Utah. Not my kind of country. I have to be within easy reach of the sea…or did, until now."

Pete turned to Evie. It felt strange to have these conversations, but somehow the trite and mundane helped keep them calm. There was only so much they could handle of the other stuff, but it was always there in the background and would pop up unannounced and silence them.

Well, at least they were safe up there on that winding, solitary road, away from the populated areas—away from what Pete knew was a nightmare after a few forays in search of food. There was carnage in every small town, where even ordinary people had begun to resort to violence to secure food and other supplies for themselves and their families—breaking into houses and looting indiscriminately, even from their own neighbors.

Without visible leadership to remind them of their patriotic duty—*to unite, to be compassionate and look out for each other, to work for the common good in the face of common disaster*—

the people had returned to the primitive mindset of the Stone Age and only looked out for themselves. In the years before the wave, they had been constantly exhorted by their political and cultural leaders, who had, uninvited, graced their living room walls. Those overpowering talking heads had coached them and shamed them and bribed them in turn in order to shape the direction of the nation. Now the nation drifted, a ship without a captain.

Pete put his arm around Evie's shoulder. She was looking pale and grew tired more easily than Ariana, who seemed instead to gain strength through physical exertion. Ariana had not cried since the night of her husband's death. They never knew where Albion's body had gone, or whether there had been a funeral. They had heard or seen no bulletins, and Ariana never brought it up. One night Pete had listened to her— she had been sitting apart from them and had apparently thought they were asleep—reciting softly to herself:

"Upon my bed by night
I sought him whom my soul loves;
I sought him but found him not;
I called him, but he gave no answer..."

The Songs of Solomon. It was her way of grieving, he thought, and left her alone, hoping it would give her some consolation. Evie was dealing with her own sorrow in silence, reserving her crying for the long, dark nights when they had rigged up their makeshift shelter and all snuggled together for comfort and warmth. Pete missed the privacy of Evie's bedroom, but felt bound to keep them all together within arm's reach. His hands would seek out Evie's body, but she gently pushed them away. He had to be content with tracing the features of her face and stealthy kisses in the dark.

The leaves were starting to turn, and nights were cool. One of the troubling things that occurred to Pete now and then was that they were going in the wrong direction. They occasionally met groups of people walking south, which seemed more logical with winter coming. What if power could not be restored and they had to face winter without food or shelter? That was unthinkable, and so they kept walking northward.

CHAPTER 27

Power had not been restored. In the early years, nuclear plants had been placed on the coastline in order to use the seawater for cooling. At the time of the wave, only a few of these old plants had been left, on the West Coast. The last one on the Eastern seaboard, which had been located in Seabrook, just up the coast from Cape Ann, had been laboriously dismantled thirty years before, after unmanageable leaks had been discovered. The remaining West Coast seaside plants were now a troubling thought. Had the flood emergency systems functioned, and would they hold underwater? They were antiquated, and certainly had not been designed to withstand an event of this magnitude. What if they had been compromised?

Many of the operating newer inland plants were also submerged, and missiles had struck a number of them. Radiation would affect vast areas and, without any effort at control or containment, would spread death and illness far into the future.

At the first sign of difficulty, as soon as the wave struck along the southern coast, the 347 operating nuclear plants automatically shut down. The power grid itself, its infrastructure totally dependent on computer command, would take time to restore. Breaks in the grid would have to be physically located before repairs could be attempted, and many power stations, lines, and junctions were now under masses of rubble, and some were under water in lakes or rivers.

To avoid mass electrocutions, every break would have to be discovered and repaired or isolated before the power could be turned back on. Small pocket areas that relied entirely on solar and self-generated power systems would be the first to regain limited power. However, as all energy, private or public, whether solar, wind, nuclear, or energy generated any other way, was by law connected to the national grid, people in the pocket areas had to begin by severing these connections and creating small loops of individual service areas, or even single units. Until then, even these potentially self-sustaining areas were without power.

Water and sewage were even larger and more urgent problems. For years the nation had depended on fresh water from desalinizing plants on the coast. The old system of water reservoirs had long ago become totally inadequate. In order to circumvent local water bans in those days, people had simply had private wells dug, which had led to unregulated use of water. This had lowered the general water table disastrously, in places causing land to subside and buildings to collapse. Leading from the desalinizing plants, a grid of water pipelines had been constructed that supplied the entire country, but not a single plant had survived the wave. People were forced to rely on reserves of locally stored water, which rapidly became exhausted.

Lakes and rivers were tainted with seawater, raw sewage, and, which seemed worst of all, dead bodies. Without power, the pumping stations and sewage treatment plants could not function, and sewage traveled freely through streams and waterways out to the ocean. When the tide came in, it brought dead bodies up the rivers, depositing them along the shores. Day after day the sea heaped the endless harvest back onto the land, unwilling to accept this foreign pollutant.

Before long, food would become a catastrophic problem. Many of the nation's growing regions were flooded with salt water, and the now-sterile fields would not produce again until the soil was restored, which would be a matter of years. Distribution was another problem, as mile-wide craters, new lakes, and widened rivers suddenly interrupted roads and speedrail tracks. Without a communications system, filling even the direst emergency needs was a logistical nightmare.

The Alaska oil fields had rapidly run out of oil, and the exploration along the West Coast had not yielded any great supply, but when new oil was discovered under the Blake Plateau off the coast of South Carolina, it had effectively taken the urgency out of the energy problem. The ecologically minded had trumpeted their fears on deaf ears. The country could depend on this new source of fuel to last at least a hundred years, it was estimated, and in the meantime the government could take its time to figure out a solution for the future—or, even better, leave it for the next generation to deal with.

The PTVs ran on fuel cells only, but most large private vehicles driven by the many people who lived outside the cities were still running on petroleum, the cheapest fuel now that OPEC no longer had a veritable monopoly. Planes still guzzled petroleum and caused pollution by spewing vast amounts of fuel into the air.

Landfills had long ago been outlawed and large incinerator plants with sophisticated filtering systems had taken their place. By incinerating the trash and garbage and using giant turbines to turn the heat into energy, enough power was created to supply much of the heat and electricity to major cities in the country.

The giant wave had ripped open all the undersea ocean wells on its travel around the globe, including the ones at the

Blake Plateau, where oil was still gushing out freely. A military fly-over had confirmed that the rigs were gone and that thick, undulating oil slicks covered large sections of the Atlantic. All stored fuel in the country was now reserved for military use. Airfields and roads were similarly restricted to military use, and all public and private transportation was prohibited.

Distribution of food and other necessities to the local food depots was handled by the National Guard. However, deliveries were often hijacked by large, angry mobs attacking the convoys as though they were robbing the stagecoaches of the old West. Due to lack of information, goods were also sent to locales that no longer existed, and were sometimes left to rot by newly created lakeshores.

CHAPTER 28

The dog came toward her running and barking, and jumped all over her, nearly knocking her down. She tried to fend him off, using the stick she always carried.

"Back, Cerberus, *stay, stay*," she shouted. The dog finally calmed down and was satisfied to trot behind her, nuzzling at the back of her legs at every opportunity. Ingrid laughed when instant reflexes buckled her knees, nearly making her fall.

"Come on, you silly dog. I should never have taken you in!"

The dog looked at her adoringly, the tip of his pink tongue sticking out of his black muzzle, and she bent and hugged him, lifting him up as though he were a child, and stroked the shiny black head.

He had recovered fully. Cerberus had been her first companion on the island. She had found him among the rocks on the landward side, half-drowned, his fur torn and one leg broken, in the days when bloated bodies were still floating around, going in and out with the tides. Finding something in the water that was still alive had thrilled her. She had fed him and given him water, set the leg, and kept him clean, although sometimes uncertain whether to wish for his recovery and the responsibility of feeding and caring for him. Now she could not imagine life without him. She realized how lonely she had been before he came.

It was with a great sense of shame that she had remembered Adam's dog, Brian Boru, a great furry mongrel with some Irish wolfhound in him. Boru had been lounging in Adam's favorite chair when she left, casting a long, lazy eye after her as she walked by him. She tried not to think about what might have happened to Boru since then. However, she tried to console herself that there was the automatic dogfood dispenser by the back door, and Boru had his own entryway that responded to his collar to let him in or out. Furthermore, Adam had always bragged about Boru's intelligence.

Cerberus was a great companion and followed her everywhere, except when he got whiff of some adventure lurking around the bend and would take off like a shot. That was how she had acquired her first human companion.

Cerberus had come home yelping and whining one day, and would not give up until she followed him. Ingrid had been unwilling to go, being in the middle of a book she was reading on Litkit. She enjoyed reading rather than listening, which she had been forced to do in bed so the light wouldn't keep Adam awake. She had avoided arguing with him at night. A sleepless night would mean losing the thin edge she had on the class and the students would walk all over her.

Her only regret was that she hadn't downloaded more books. But there had been no need to keep a number of books on the Litkit, since you could download any book ever written, instantly, as long as you paid the annual fee. However, Ingrid always liked to keep a "library" of books by some of her favorite authors on hand.

Public libraries had been closed years ago. She wondered dully what had happened to the world's recorded stock of literature. The Gutenberg Project had been a leader in archiving literature that could be downloaded, and later others had come along. What if nothing could be retrieved? She had tried to download books several times since she came to the island, but there was still no signal for any kind of communication. Well, as long as there was a sun in the sky, she could read and re-read the ones she had.

The first time she used Litkit after her arrival on the island she had seen that there was a note on it. Maybe it was just a list of books she had meant to download, but she had refused to open the note, afraid of what it might contain and what memories it might trigger. As usual, she had noticed it when she opened the Litkit, but had made an effort to shake it off.

Cerberus had barked again. She had tried shooing the dog away, but he barked persistently and danced around her as though mad until she put down her reading. She ran behind him as fast as she could, with the dog dancing and yapping impatiently whenever she lagged behind. They crossed the entire Dogtown Island and waded across to Lambkill, which was what she had named the next largest island on the seaward side. The islands were separated by a narrow strait, which had been partially filled with debris and boulders. She could walk across at low tide without getting her feet wet, but at high tide she had to swim.

When they reached the crest of Lambkill and looked down toward the water, she saw the old dory up on the rocks. She ran down the hill, which still held immense boulders jammed into the deeper crevices. The wave had not bothered to completely sweep away the glacial deposit from this once-massive leading edge of the terminal moraine.

The Lambkill hill had been named by the farmers in the old times. This had been where they had gone looking for their missing lambs, usually finding them dead—trapped between the stones with their legs broken. Ingrid was careful, there was no medical help to be had now, and hopped from ledge to ledge, following Cerberus.

I don't believe it! A boat! Oh, God, let it be in one piece! No more rafting for us, Cerbie, she thought.

It had not occurred to her that there might be someone in the boat. The man was slumped over the center seat, face down. She assumed that he was dead, but something in the dog's attitude made her go and gently turn the body over. His face, horribly blistered, made her shudder before she realized that he was looking at her through the small slits of squinting eyes. His reddish-brown hair had been bleached yellow by the sun and was stiff with salt. He tried to speak, but was too hoarse. She took out her water flask and tried to get a little into his mouth, spilling most of it on the scraggly blond beard and down his neck. He lay back exhausted, nearly unconscious, but still looking at her.

She looked back up over Lambkill and knew she would never manage to drag him across, ford the strait, and then continue across the entire Dogtown to her cellar. It was early afternoon, with the tide coming in. She looked in the dory, but found no oars there. The man had tied himself to the boat—to avoid falling overboard, she guessed—and she undid the rope and gauged the length to see if she might be able to walk along the shore and drag the boat behind her.

An hour later, the tide set the dory afloat and she started out, going northward, hoping the strait would be navigable by the time they got around the bend.

The man was delirious for three days. She fed him broth and soft crackers and tried to keep him clean. On the fourth day he suddenly started trying to clear his throat, waking her up just after sunrise. In the half-light from the hatch door, left open as usual so that she could fall asleep looking at the stars, she saw him try to get up, and smiled at the look of surprise on his face when his legs wouldn't carry him.

At that time she was still moving boulders around, creating a stone wall around "her property," and trying to turn the area around her cellar home into a yard. She thought of one of the original Dogtown settlers, Old Ruth, who had built most of the stone walls in Dogtown. Stone walls had separated the Commons area, where everybody's cattle had grazed, from the various homesteads. Old Ruth had also cleared fields for growing vegetables. Stone walls had erupted all across the woods, a testament to her industriousness.

The retreating glacier had left enough building material for a lifetime of work, but now the wave had easily licked the island's surface clean of boulders, except for those trapped in gullies and quarries, and the giant erratics. Ingrid had used up the supply of stones trapped in the cellar and scoured every crevice in the vicinity for enough stone to surround her yard.

When Ingrid got tired of building walls and returned to the cellar, the man was sitting outside, leaning against a rock. He had been watching her roll boulders and labor to raise them and wedge them together solidly. Ingrid went inside and stirred the embers of the fire in the corner. The makeshift chimney let the smoke out through a hole in the roof. She put a kettle half-filled with water over the fire. Water was a precious commodity, even though they were surrounded by it. After she had run out of what she brought with her, she had resorted to one of her grandfather's wilderness tricks and made her own distilled seawater, hanging a cup under the lid inside the kettle—a lucky beachcombing find—and letting the steam condense and drip into the cup. Then she had poured it back and forth to aerate it and make it palatable.

The thought of drinking the water that held the drowned had bothered her. She had tested the water in the quarries and pools, but they had all been emptied by the wave, the lovely, sweet water replaced with salty seawater. In the end she had scrubbed the salty crust off some areas of ledge nearby where puddles would form in the rain, and after every rain she gathered the water. *I am a water farmer,* she thought.

"What's your name?" he asked, hobbling inside and crumpling down on the bed she had made for him out of mounds of seaweed covered by an old tarp.

It was the first sensible speech she had heard from him. She hesitated for a moment. "Ingrid," she said, unwilling to give out her last name.

"I'm Noah," he said, and she laughed.

She sat down across from him and he told her how he had come aground on the island. He didn't hesitate telling her that while he was a carpenter by trade, he made his real money as a "black market" fisherman. The waters off the Massachusetts coastline had long been off limits for fishing in order to restore the depleted fish stock. A few daring people still went out—under cover of darkness or bad weather—and there was an unlimited and lucrative market for their catch.

Noah had been on the way home after making a delivery to a luxury hotel in the western part of the state, where the head chef was a frequent customer. Noah had lived in Gloucester, and had wanted to go back to see what was left after the wave. He seemed to grow tired at this point in his tale, and sat silent for a while. He looked around the cellar and shivered slightly. The skin on his face was beginning to heal, and he looked less disgusting, although Ingrid didn't think he would ever have been considered handsome. Manly, she supposed, in a rugged way.

"Since I got back to the coast, I've been living in a lean-to on the mainland. I was scrounging upriver one day and found the dory. Imagine! So I thought I'd try my luck fishing. Got caught in a gale, and just hunkered down under the tarp to ride it out. Fell asleep, finally, and when I woke up, the tarp and the oars were gone. Must have spent about a week driftin', gettin' carried by wind and tides, before I ended up on the rocks. Kinda wished I had died at sea then. The idea of dyin' in a dory on dry land didn't appeal to me much." He cackled hoarsely.

Cerberus was dancing around between them, unable to decide whom to pester. Ingrid patted him and hugged his neck. Comforted, the dog went over to Noah, tail wagging, eager to make a new friend.

"Meet Cerbie," Ingrid said. Then she added, "I'd like to keep my last name to myself, for now. I don't want to be found, or go back to my old life. But of course you can do as you wish, Noah. Your name fits, I must say. There you were, stranded on the rock in your little ark after the deluge. Too bad you didn't bring the animals, two by two. Some chickens and turkeys and pigs would have been good."

Noah laughed.

"There's always Cerbie," he said, smacking his lips.

Ingrid cuffed him lightly on the ear. It felt good to laugh.

CHAPTER 29

It was time for Pope Fidelis to step back and President Sheedy to come forward in his stead.

Chaos reigned. The databases on which running the country had depended were not immediately recoverable; most of his advisors had begun to think they were beyond rescue. Every state and federal agency, the market, the banks, the military, the insurance industry, the social services were either obliterated or in a state of utter confusion. People were paralyzed by fear, hopelessness, and lack of initiative. They had reached a state of total resignation and moved listlessly from place to place, unable to even devise a plan for themselves other than to vaguely tramp on and look for morsels or handouts that would keep them alive until the end of the day. Then they would search for shelter. Anything would do. A garage, a burned-out building, an empty store.

Without the structure of normal daily routines, and without anyone to tell them what to do, they languished, waiting. They did not go to work. How could they? There was no power, no transportation, and no money to create an incentive. Where were all the take-charge people, the leaders?

The trouble was that everyone was in the same boat now. Wealth, which had always meant power, had become meaningless overnight, and those used to giving orders were met with derision when trying to do so. Squatters—both the newly homeless and those who had been for generations—were taking over any cities still standing.

Most of the homeless population had been created long ago, when the welfare rolls were cut without proper provisions for those that could not, or would not, work. The government furthermore had emptied and then closed the doors of institutions holding people termed—at different times in history—*idiots, retarded, mentally handicapped,* or simply *challenged.* In the years that followed, these people had instead become *invisible,* at least as far as the government was concerned. The idea at first had been to "mainstream" them, make them do simple, menial work to support themselves, so that they would not be a burden to society. But before long they had disappeared into the shadows of humanity, into back alley cardboard dwellings that made the corrugated slums of Asia and South America look like gentrified vacation spots by comparison.

Now, however, it was *they* who owned the cities that remained, the cities that were being abandoned by the more affluent population after becoming overrun by rats and infested with disease. The garbage was not hauled away and built up into odorous, pest-ridden mountains. Store windows were no longer being boarded up; looters had already carried away all the merchandise. The cities that had escaped bombs and missiles had still been reduced to war zones, and were now echoing with gunshots and loud threats from gangs or screams by their victims.

Running water was unavailable, and the water situation had become critical everywhere. People were routinely killing each other over food and water, despite efforts to provide enough for every area. Now apathy was setting in, and instead of fighting, many were giving up, some even hoping that the coming night would be their last and that they would be carried away in their sleep.

They had gone back to the Dark Ages, the pope thought. His call to arms had failed. He had tried to spread the word with printed bulletins dropped from the air, appealing to the people to form a Volunteer Christian Army, to take charge of their neighborhoods and defend them against looters and intruders, to protect children and elderly, to root out evil. The people had taken his appeal too literally. Zealots had led his Christian soldiers on raids, beating or killing anyone caught in the smallest infraction of the law. Anarchy had set in. He bent his head in despair, ready to weep, but his supply of tears had long since dried up.

Realizing that his plan for a census was not feasible in the foreseeable future, Fidelis asked for an estimate of the loss of life. He was shocked—feeling cold and numb, as though all blood had drained out of him—when he was told that a staggering seventy-five percent of the population was believed to have been lost between the original catastrophe of the wave and the missiles, and in the ensuing continuing waves of disease and strife that had followed in their wake. And each day thousands more were dying from disease and starvation.

He wondered dully what had happened in the rest of the world. Perhaps his alter ego, President Sheedy, should try to send an emissary to arrange for a summit meeting. Send him where? Paris? London? Rome? Would there be anything left of those lovely cities, located so beautifully on the water? Their countries, too, would have been bombarded by missiles—*ours,* he thought. And would not the surviving leaders, as usual, demand that the United States come to *their* rescue and bail them out of *their* difficulties? The pope sighed. He would take a rest while the president took over. Fidelis would hide in the corner of his soul and lick his wounds. Let Sheedy, the politician, come forward to do some work for a change.

Fidelis was tired of listening to the arguments between his two selves. He was no longer able to keep them unified. Their separate convictions were driving them apart. As Fidelis, he had at first wanted to save the people, to lead them into the loving arms of the Father. When he saw the evil that lurked in the heart of man, anger had taken over. He was angry at God, of course, but unable to admit this. Instead his wrath was aimed at his fellow man. *The sins of man brought this calamity upon us.* The sinners had to be removed.

He had felt certain that, when the country had been cleansed and morality returned, they could start again with a clean slate. At first, all had seemed so clear, so simple, so beautiful. Eden restored. How could he have failed in achieving his goal, being God's own emissary?

Sheedy, his other self—seemingly a stranger now—was more pragmatic, a clever politician, and would no doubt try to use the economy and people's innate sense of greed to restore the country. *A sell-out,* Fidelis thought. But he was too tired to fight.

CHAPTER 30

It was still dark when he woke up. As happened every day, he felt angry and disappointed the moment he realized he still did not know who he was. He had been working on this puzzle continuously, ever since the day he had awakened in an unused barn, where he had slept in hay that must have been decades old and had lost all its ability to provide him with soft bedding.

He had gone through the pockets of the brown suit he was wearing and found a business card with the name Julius Prevost, above the address of a law firm, engraved in elegant lettering.

I'm a lawyer? he had thought, a little doubtfully.

When he realized that the suit he was wearing was at least four sizes too large and the pants, which were too short, only stayed up with the help of a belt, he had grown suspicious, and from then on had taken nothing for granted.

Every morning he racked his brain until his head ached, and every morning he ended up stumbling blindly along on his way. He did not know where he was going, nurturing an obsessive hope that this would be the day when his mind would clear and he would get his life back. He had been amazed to discover other wanderers who seemed equally confused and anxious. From time to time he joined groups of people and listened to them sharing tidbits of news, little by little putting together a picture of the events that had taken place.

The wave. It was the first note he had made, trying to accumulate all his memories into some sort of connect-the-dots form that might later provide a complete picture. He knew something about a wave. The mention of it had set his temples buzzing. Every day he found other items to jot down, things that seemed meaningful.

This morning he walked into a small town, *New Hope, Pop. 584*. The sign was worn and pockmarked, and the paint had peeled many seasons ago. A sleeper town serving some city nearby, by the look of it. He wondered whether the population had changed since the sign was put up. People were always on the move. "Home" was not a permanent place anymore. Where was his home? Not here, or anywhere like it. It did not have a familiar feel in any way. He looked around, scanning the street to avoid unpleasant surprises. After nasty experiences in other towns, he was cautious. In the last one he had been knocked down and then beaten when the hoodlums discovered that he carried nothing of value. This town seemed deserted at first, until he saw a group of children huddling outside a large brick building. As he approached them, they started walking up the steps, eyeing him warily.

"Excuse me," he called, waving one hand in the air.

The children hurried up the stairs and opened the door, pushing and shoving to get inside. Scared of him probably—a big, dirty man with a scruffy beard that only partially covered vivid pink scars from some forgotten event. A back alley fight? Was he just a drunken old bum? He was still dressed in the brown suit, which seemed to hang even more loosely now than when he woke up in that old barn.

He hesitated, but there seemed to be no one else about. Where were the adults? In the end he crossed the street, went up the steps, and knocked softly on the door. He heard shuffling inside, as though the children were moving away from the door and into some other part of the building. He tried the handle. The door opened easily. Inside, there was darkness and a musty, sour odor. He walked through the hallway into some sort of waiting area and continued through an open doorway into a corridor. There were doors along both sides and he opened one. An office with half a dozen desks with individual monitors and an old wall screen.

He opened each door he passed. They led to other offices, a broom closet, and a meeting room with a podium and rows of chairs. Town Hall, he guessed. He tried the last door on the opposite side of the corridor. A locker room, with a table and chairs and a sink in the corner. Doing double duty as a lunchroom. The children were all there, lined up at the back of the room against the lockers. They looked at him despondently. The largest of the boys clenched his fists.

"Excuse me," the man said again, very softly. The effort of a smile felt taut in his left cheek, pulling at a scar. "I'm looking for something to eat and some water. Do you know where I can find any?"

There was no answer, but the boy unclenched his fists.

"Where are your parents? Aren't there any grownups here?" the man tried.

The children glanced at each other uneasily, shuffling their feet a little; they looked away, anywhere—out the window, at the door behind him.

"Come on. I'll take you to them." The big boy stepped forward. He led the way out of the room, followed by the man and, at a little distance, the rest of the children.

They walked out of the building and down the street, passing rows of one-family homes all of the same design, differing only slightly in color and choice of tree on the front lawn. All the doors were closed, the windows shut. A rake lay across the sidewalk and they all stepped over it. *Simon says.* There was laundry hanging on a line, looking dry and stiff. Dingy, as though it needed to be washed again.

The boy led the way to the outskirts of town, slowing down as they neared the church, a one-story wooden structure with a cross bolted to the wall next to the entrance. The cross was pitted with rust, which had bled onto the siding underneath it. A sign on the front lawn said: Church of the Holy Shepherd. All the children stopped at the gate and the boy pointed across the fence.

"They're over there."

The man waited, but the boy would not come with him, so he went alone through the gate. He walked into the little cemetery. To the left were graves with headstones and crosses. To the right was a large field—maybe half an acre, the man estimated—where the red soil looked recently turned and no grass grew. A shovel stood in the dirt at the edge of the field. The man walked closer. Next to the shovel was a hole in the ground, a grave as yet unfilled. He walked to the edge and looked down. Then he turned around, looking toward the gate. The children were standing in a small, huddled group, looking back at him. He picked up the shovel and filled the hole as quickly as he could, throwing big red clods of dirt down into it to cover the last body.

Still maggot-ridden. Not long dead, then. He must have buried everyone else and then laid down in the hole, waiting to die, with no one left to perform the service for him. God rest your soul, gravedigger.

He pushed the shovel roughly back into the soil, fortified by the anger he felt, then realized he was exhausted and out of breath. He lumbered back toward the children, his body shaking from exertion, emotion, and lack of food.

"Are all your parents out there?" he asked, nodding back at the field.

"No. We don't live here." The little girl's face was dirty, her blond hair matted against the scalp.

"Where do you live, then?" Silence.

"It's gone, where we lived. The water took it all away." The little girl again. The man kneeled in front of her.

"How did you get here? What's your name, honey?" She looked at the other children, but no one would help her out.

"My name's Meggi. We were coming home in the bus from summer camp. Then suddenly the bus was in the water. My window was open and I crawled out. Then I tried to crawl back in..." She started crying and ran off. Two other girls followed her and tried to stop her by putting their arms around her, but she shook them off.

"She tried to go back in through the window to get her brother. We had to pull her out. We were the only ones who got away. Her brother drownded, and the driver, too. And all the other kids, except maybe some of them made it, 'cause I saw them floating off in the water. Maybe they got away and went somewheres else. But we walked and walked and then we came here, and we live here now. My name's Lans. What's yours?" The little boy, one of the youngest of the children, wouldn't stop talking once he got started. While he talked, they all walked up the street together and joined the girls.

"You can call me Julius. And what do you live on? Do you have food and water?" the man asked. Now the big boy stepped in, smiling proudly.

"Of course we do. Come on, I'll show you."

They walked across the town to the New Hope Learning Center, a cluster of buildings housing the combination school and daycare facilities of the town. They walked in through the smashed glass of the front door and the boy, who said his name was Aug, led the way down the corridor, through the cafeteria, and out into the kitchen. The pantry shelves were still stacked with a jumble of boxes of cereal and other dry staples.

"We got rid of all the bad food. Stinky, rotten stuff. But there's lots here to eat."

"What about water, something to drink?"

"We're running out of drinks. Everybody's using too much. We're trying to stop, but it's hard. There's no water coming out of the pipes, but there's water in the pool in the sports building, and we use that and mix it with milk powder for the cereal. We figure it's gotta be safe, if kids can swim in it and swallow it accident'ly, you know," he said, somewhat proudly.

The man nodded and took a quick inventory of the pantry. He pulled out a big pot and sent Aug to fill it with water then hefted a couple of sacks, handed a big tin of oil and various pieces of equipment to the children to carry, and led them outdoors. There he looked around and selected a courtyard area, where he dumped the sacks.

"Now, run out there and bring me back all the fire wood you can find, twigs and branches and anything like that. You, Meggi, take a friend and go back inside and see if you can find some paper. Look in the wastebaskets. Maybe some empty cereal boxes, anything that we can use to start a fire, okay?" Meggi nodded and took the hand of the smallest child in the group.

"Come on, Roofie," she said, tugging the little girl along. Roofie (Julius wondered if the child's name was Ruth) chattered away in her baby language, which Meggi seemed to comprehend perfectly.

"Woofie hungy, Meggi. Wan' lunth *now*!"

"I know, Roofie. We're all hungry. You'll get lunch in a minute."

The children helped peel the potatoes, which had started to sprout and soften. Julius chopped onions. They were strong and pungent, and his eyes were watering. Meggi, who had sat down next to him, looked at him apprehensively.

"Are you sad, too?" she said, putting her small hand on his arm. Julius wiped his face with his sleeve, which only made things worse. He chuckled.

"Yes, Meg, these onions can make you awfully sad." He waved one by her face, and her eyes filled quickly with tears. She laughed, and rubbed her eyes with her fists.

"I'm glad you're sad about onions," she said. Julius hugged her tightly. Little Roofie came running wanting to be in on the hugging and got a squeeze, too.

While the potatoes were boiling, he browned the onions in the big baking pan. Then he dumped the potatoes on top and stirred them around until they were golden and caramelized, and the sweet, tantalizing smell brought the children around. When they couldn't wait any longer, they reached in and ate with their hands, not stopping until the pan was wiped clean. Then Julius watched as the eleven children, their faces still shiny with grease, lay down in the grass. Meggi, like a little mother, made sure to keep Lans and Roofie next to her, and they slumbered with her as their pillow. The rest of the children slept huddled together in small groups.

As good a place as any, he thought. *I'll stay here with them. Maybe if I stop running, I'll remember.*

CHAPTER 31

Ingrid touched her ear lobe gently. The cut had healed, leaving only a tiny scar. One of her first acts on the island had been to remove the *peeper*, the Global Person Locator that had been surgically inserted into her ear lobe just after birth.

Most parents nowadays had this procedure performed on their children. That way if the children got lost or were kidnapped, they could be located instantly. It was useful in many other ways: people buried by avalanches could be rescued, and escaping prisoners could be apprehended quickly. Prisoners, however, had additional peepers implanted in their front teeth, where they were more difficult to remove. No dentist would help them. After all, an escaped criminal would certainly be actively traced, and if caught up with in the dentist's chair—well, the price to pay was just too high.

She sat, holding the tiny peeper in her hand, preparing to smash it with a rock. *No. Better to throw it in the water. Let it join all the others. More logical. A dead person couldn't destroy her own peeper.*

Who was she afraid of? With Adam dead, what difference could it make whether she was dead or alive? Who would care? Her father? Ingrid shuddered. She simply wanted to sever any connection with the mainland. What she had seen there during her infrequent forays was frightening. The pope's "Christian soldiers," rooting out all evil, indeed. Killing hungry children for stealing food. Forcing people to evacuate their homes and give up their rations to feed the "army."

How long would they remain safe on the island? They were taking precautions in the daytime, keeping a lookout toward the shore. If they wanted to be outdoors they stayed hidden behind cliffs, or went over to the seaward side of the island.

The Dogtown population was growing. Many were old residents, returning only to find the clean-scoured rock that was all that remained of the island. Most left in shock. The last person who came and stayed had arrived just a few days ago. The settlers were struggling to work out living arrangements. Some of those who stayed had built shacks on the seaward side of the island, where they couldn't be seen from the mainland. Most decided it was more comfortable on the lee side, living in the low-profile cellar homes. They worked to empty boulders out of holes and crevices large enough to live in, a task that seemed easier with the extra hands, although one group grumbled about doing "hard labor." They finally managed to get the cellars at least partially roofed over. Not winterized exactly, but winter seemed distant—and would they still be here then?

In the beginning, Ingrid had used a makeshift raft to get to the mainland. She had discovered a newly created river, which she named Wingaersheek after a beach nearby that had once been a favorite place for beachcombers like her and Grandpa Josh. The mouth of this river was just across the water from Goose Cove. She rafted far inland up the Wingaersheek, pulling herself along in the dark, and timing her trips to coincide with the incoming tides. She left the raft hidden while she went ashore and made long forays inland to check the towns, looking for food and supplies.

After Noah arrived, she enjoyed the luxury of the dory. Noah made her a pair of oars out of driftwood, and this new mode of travel cut the time needed for her visits ashore by more than half. By then there had been an emergency food distribution depot set up close to the no-man's land—still a trek that required finding safe places to stay overnight.

She had found an easily recognizable location up the river, a little bay surrounded by natural stone jetties shaped like curved arms, which she had nicknamed Embrace's Cove—a play on an old Cape Ann name, Brace's Cove, which was now submerged. With an incoming tide, she could get from Goose Cove to Embrace's Cove in a few hours. This was where she hid her dory and began to make her way on foot to the depot.

CHAPTER 32

President Sheedy was alone in the lounge at Aspen Lodge, sitting in an easy chair by the massive stone fireplace. It was getting chilly, and he had asked for a fire to be laid in.

The presidential seal was back in its place, mounted securely over the stone mantel, after having been kept in storage for years for some reason that was now forgotten. The glow from the fire played softly on the dark brown wall paneling. He was waiting for Birke and Amaral, who were coming to bring him up to date on the latest developments at Site C, where work was being done to restore satellite communications functions. They had already had partial success with the MILSTAR system, which was very old, but therefore also fairly direct and uncomplicated, and had recovered some images that were currently being studied by whatever experts they had been able to lay their hands on. They hadn't held out much hope for ever accessing the newer systems, which were tied into the centralized database at every level.

Sometimes it seemed to Sheedy that it would be faster to start from scratch. Where were all the brains who had developed these systems in the first place? Retired. Dead. Among the missing, he had been told. They had found a few. Each one was a specialist, well versed in his own area, but unable to help put all the parts of the system together. They needed someone with an understanding of the total infrastructure, someone who could draw diagrams and maps that could be followed. A Renaissance man.

It was the same wherever he turned. Every system was tied in with another: water, sewer, power, communication, transportation. You couldn't begin to fix a single one without getting stymied by the complex relationship with the others. How had they gotten into this predicament? When had they lost control? The systems had been allowed to take over and run themselves, creating links and pathways that were now totally untraceable. Of all their urgent needs, the communications system was imperative. He felt now that without SYSCOM, he could never pull the nation together. They must have a breakthrough.

Amaral walked in without knocking, followed by Birke, who looked even more agitated than usual. Sheedy sighed. The man gave him instant indigestion. Amaral handed him some of the MILSTAR images, without any comments.

Wheaton's early assessments of the military bases had been based in part on some high-altitude images captured by flight crews as they criss-crossed the country. Sheedy had seen the structural changes that the water had inflicted on the land. What the new images told him confirmed these changes, but they also showed him the destruction that had taken place since then, natural and man-made. Further earthquake activity on the West Coast, volcanic eruptions, statewide forest fires, and rivers reversing or changing course had all contributed to a vastly altered landscape. Craters from bombs and missiles pockmarked the country, giving it a moonlike appearance in the high-altitude images. The original coastline, once the most heavily populated part of the country, was well below sea level. Where the largest cities had been, eerie-looking grids could be seen through the water from a high altitude. Why had they built all their major, beautiful cities by the ocean, by the lakes, along the rivers? Simple. It was where the pilgrims had landed, and where they had situated their trading posts.

In colonial days, the water had been an instant roadway to other communities up and down the coast and along the rivers inland, while the rest of the country was vast and wild and roadless, populated by Indians and ferocious animals. Besides, people always wanted to live by the water. With the climate change over the last century and the constant heat waves, an expanse of water afforded natural cooling. Even now, fearless people were staking claims along the new coastlines and expanded lakeshores.

The president was shocked to learn that the eager fingers of the ocean had also discovered inland cities, like St. Louis. The wave had forced its way up through the country along the great Mississippi-Missouri river system, devouring cities and countryside along the way. In St. Louis, the newly constructed Vatican, some of its towers and spires and solidly built structures still rising out of the waters, glimmered tantalizingly in the sun, but would never be rescued. Further north, the bore had surged out from the Mississippi River through many lesser rivers—the Rock, the Wisconsin, and the St. Croix, for instance—and forced its way into the Great Lakes. As the water receded, the enlarged and deepened river basins had drained some of the water out of the lakes, adding it to the great inland sea. If the Vatican had been situated in Chicago, as Sheedy had wished, its golden spires would now have been gleaming, high and dry, on Lakeshore Drive. The Drive would have had to be renamed, of course, as the water had receded, leaving an extensive area of black and smelly lake bottom exposed. The city itself looked to be heavily damaged, blackened and smoking.

In the South, the Gulf of Mexico covered New Orleans, his mother's birthplace and where he had spent summer vacations with his grandparents as a child. But he had expected this, had already imagined what it would look like.

What he was not prepared for, however, was the destruction caused or initiated by man—by the citizens themselves. The interior cities that had been left intact by the deluge were now in the process of being annihilated. It was true that earthquakes and missiles had done some of the damage. But it was the result of fires that most appalled him. Fire had gutted entire cities. Even now, skyscrapers were in flames, like torches reaching for heaven. Fire smoldered and spread and destroyed the cities section by section, rampant and unimpeded. Buildings fell into each other like dominos; city block after city block crumbled. There was no way to stop the fires. Water, when there was any available, was too precious a commodity to use to put them out. He was told that most of the blazes had been started by squatters, who used fire for cooking and warmth.

He studied the photos again. It was like looking at old WWII pictures after the blitz, he thought. The missile defense system had not been able to protect them from the massive onslaught that had approached, in wave after wave, as the systems all around the world were activated. It seemed a miracle to him now that Camp David had escaped, even though he knew it must be heavily protected.

How far would they have to sink before they could turn around and start to rebuild? Was there no end to this? What would it take? What had happened to the people? Pope Fidelis' appeals and exhortations had fallen on deaf ears. Had they all lost faith? Did they feel that God had deserted them? Had they returned to some primitive stage, become heathens again? If appeals to morality and the common good had no effect, what would?

His Christian Army had failed. The soldiers themselves had turned out to be mere vigilantes and were indeed controlling the population in many areas, but for their own gain. An unholy Mafia.

Bring the military to bear on the citizens now, he thought, *and there will be civil war.* Then he remembered who he was again. Fidelis had retreated. He was President Sheedy now.

CHAPTER 33

They parted ways by the Connecticut River. Pete and Evie would keep going north toward Vermont, staying on the western side of the river, while Ariana would head east. Evie cried.

"Why don't you come with us, Ariana? What if you don't find anybody? You'll have no way to get in touch with us. I wish we could stay together. I feel like I'm losing another member of my family." Evie started crying hard again, and Pete pressed her face against his chest and stroked her hair, which had grown long and unruly.

He waved to Ariana to leave, but Evie tore loose from his hold and ran over to her, embraced her wildly, then let go.

"It's okay, Ariana. I'd go looking, too, if I thought there was a chance I'd find someone in my family. Good luck. Take care of yourself."

They were connected now only by their fingertips, and when they lost touch, ever so reluctantly, they both turned and walked in opposite directions without looking back.

Pete took Evie's hand and they walked slowly up the hill. When they got to the top they turned around, just in time to see Ariana being ferried by a scruffy-looking man across the wide river.

"She'll be fine, Evie. She's a strong lady. You'll see her again. Don't worry. Now you and I are going to look for a place to stay the night indoors. It's getting too cold to sleep under the stars."

He wondered if he was making a terrible mistake, leaving the president's wife to struggle on alone. Should he have gone with her? Was he letting the president down again? But he had his parents to think of...and Evie. Ariana had made her own choice. She was determined to disappear from public life. It would probably be easier for her without them around to remind her of it. He hoped fervently that she would locate someone in her family still alive.

CHAPTER 34

The oldest of the new Dogtown settlers was a woman of obvious means, although she arrived shoeless. "Someone needed those shoes more than I did," she explained with an unembarrassed shrug. She sat waiting patiently on a boulder in the rising dawn, after having arrived under the cover of darkness. Her clothes were dry, and she explained that someone had ferried her across in a skiff before continuing on his way south. Her bare feet were scuffed from her walk over the rocks in the dark, sandpapered to whiteness, and there were scrapes on the knuckles of her toes, but her feet were clean. On the island, not even the soles of the feet showed any dirt. There wasn't any. No dirt, no dust, not even pollen.

Ingrid walked barefoot most of the time, and the soles of her feet were callused and already as hard as shoe-leather, unlike those of the newcomer. The woman was wearing slacks and a long-sleeved shirt. A wide-brimmed hat was strapped to the small bag at her side, as though she had been preparing for a trip to Florida. Her looks were striking, with a sharply pointed widow's peak over the dark blue eyes. Her hair was black with a white streak on one side—obviously a natural aberration, since no dark roots were showing.

Ingrid brought her around to meet some of the neighbors. The newcomer had summered on the island, she said, and was distraught to find everything gone. She had lived in an apartment building inland that had burned to the ground, and had come here hoping to find her summer cottage. Remembering her own notion of locating her grandmother, Ingrid could not blame the woman for her naïve optimism.

"I think we can put you up at Granny Day's soon. They are working on her cellar hole now, and there should be room for one more person. Granny Day was the old Dogtown school mistress. Her house, which fell in long ago, was located on the edge of the moor, over that way. In the back of her house was a swamp that got named after her, the Granny Day Swamp, which had a reputation for swallowing sheep and cattle. When I was little, there was a pool in the middle of the swamp that froze over in the winter, and I went skating there sometimes. The ice was opaque and bluish. There was a group of rocks in the middle where you could sit down and rest. It's a bigger pond now, with the thickets gone, and I keep hoping to see some life there—tadpoles or damselflies, or algae, even. For some reason the wave didn't deposit any salt water there, maybe because it's pretty shallow, so the water is just sweet rainwater. I'll take you there as soon as we get you some shoes. What should we call you?"

Before the woman could answer, Ingrid went on to explain how she simply went by her first name and why. Ingrid knew she was rambling, but she was trying to put the woman at ease.

"Why don't you call me Granny, then? I always wanted to be one, but my children's careers got in the way."

Black Neil arrived one sunset, when Ingrid, Noah, and Granny were sitting on the rocks overlooking Goose Cove and the bay. It was high tide and the mainland seemed very distant, as though the island had floated out to sea. The gelid surface of the water lazily reflected the setting sun. Noah was the first to notice the disturbance in the water. Without a word, he pointed and they looked and nodded. By the time they thought of it, it was too late to conceal themselves. The swimmer was coming directly toward them and if he—it looked like a man by the way he swam, long, muscular arms stroking—had not already seen them, he would notice them if they moved. So they sat immobile, waiting for him to reach shore.

He dropped one arm at a time without creating a splash, in long, languid strokes, as though enjoying a pleasant evening swim. It was only when he tried to climb onto the rocks that they realized his exhausted state and rushed down to help.

"Oh…grateful, thank you so much… It was further than I thought," he said, heaving. They let him catch his breath then supported him on the walk to the cellar. The sun had gone down by the time they got there.

Noah quickly started a fire, even though the cellar still held the heat of the day, and gave the man some clothes to change into. The visitor fell asleep nearly instantly, remaining by the fire until morning light.

He seemed reluctant to offer his name, so Ingrid provided one: Black Neil. He was a stranger to the island, he said, looking cautiously at the faces around him, and Ingrid wondered what had brought him there. Neil's blackness was even more pronounced in the daylight, rich, nearly blue in the shadows of the deeply sculpted face. He was tall and…elegant, Ingrid thought. The way he spoke hinted at a privileged education. The purity of his features suggested that his ancestry in this country did not extend back to colonial times. He was certainly not of watered-down slave stock and was, in that, different from the original Black Neil, Cornelius Finson, who had been a freed slave and the last Dogtown resident.

"When all the other Dogtown residents died or moved down to the shore," Ingrid related, "Cornelius, or Black Neil as they called him, stayed in the old settlement. By then most of the houses had fallen in, and he lived in an old covered-over cellar hole, just like one of ours. One winter day in the year 1830 they came for him and took him to the local poorhouse, where he died a few days later, *of sheer comfort,*' it was said."

"We could use some sheer comfort," said the new Black Neil, laughing, after Ingrid told him the tale.

Two days after Black Neil arrived, a small skiff with four men pulled into the cove. There was trouble right from the start. The four newcomers secured the skiff, wedging it in a rocky cleft some way up from the water's edge, and reluctantly followed Ingrid up to the homestead. Ingrid stuck her head down into the door hole.

"We've got company," she yelled.

Noah appeared. "Granny's gone off to get water. I told her it's too heavy, but she insisted. Well, hello. I'm Noah," he said, turning to the men. They eyed him suspiciously.

Finally, one of them, a muscular, dark-haired man, took the lead and stepped forward a little. "This where you're staying?" he said, peeking down through the door hole.

"Home, sweet home."

"Any other places on the island?"

"A few. We're working on one over there." Noah pointed to a partially emptied cellar a few hundred yards away.

The men exchanged glances. "Someone told us there would be a place to stay. Guess they was mistaken."

"You are quite welcome to stay. We'll help you dig out." Noah looked at Ingrid sheepishly, worried that maybe it wasn't his place to welcome strangers, especially these strangers, onto *her* property. But Ingrid nodded in agreement.

"It's not as bad as it looks. I did most of this myself," she said with some pride, pointing to her cellar. One of the men snickered.

"Reg'lar castle, ain't it?" he said, rolling his eyes, his grin revealing missing front teeth.

Ingrid's stomach lurched. A prisoner? Were they all? Just then Black Neil appeared, carrying the water buckets, followed by Granny, who was carefully making her way between the boulders empty-handed.

"And they got theirselves a boy, too. My, my." The toothless one was grinning again.

Noah turned bright red and advanced toward the man, ready to take him on. Black Neil put down the buckets, spilling much of the water, and reached Noah's side in two quick strides. He put his hand gently on Noah's shoulder. Then he turned to the men with a placating smile.

"You must all be hungry and tired. We've got some food to share, and I'm sure you're welcome to spend the night. The island is bigger than it looks, and there are sites on the seaside that you might prefer, if you decide to stay. People have built a few shacks there, anyway. The rest of us live like this, in cellar holes."

The tension went out of the moment.

They ate what they had in silence before the four men went down to secure the skiff for the night. The granite ledges did not yet reveal the new high water lines, and Noah followed them down to make sure they pulled the boat up high enough. He returned, looking grim, without waiting for them. The men took their time coming back up. *Discussing the situation*, Ingrid guessed.

"What do you think, Noah? Will we be safe? Neil? Granny?" Ingrid looked from face to face. Uneasiness had settled on them like a cold, wet sheet. Their haven had suddenly become threatened.

"Hey, anybody down there?" A face appeared in the doorway. The four men clambered down the rough steps.

"We're gonna scout the place before it gets dark, then we'll be back. If we can shack here with you overnight, that'll do us fine. You got plenty of room here," the muscular one said, looking around. Ingrid noticed his front teeth were intact. The two they hadn't heard from kept in the background, mumbling between themselves.

When there was no response, the four backed out and scrambled up the steps. The toothless one went last, with a mock salute before he disappeared.

When the men did not return by nightfall, or by the following morning, everyone expressed a sense of relief. Maybe they had gone over a cliff in the dark and drowned. However, on the third day, they showed up, out of food. They seemed tamer, or perhaps it was just the lack of sleep.

After a concerted, weeklong effort, another cellar home was constructed—out of sight of the main compound, on the other side of the hill.

Ingrid offered the men names, guessing they wouldn't want to use their own. The muscular leader became Merry, the toothless one Grant, the other two men Johnny and Morgan, all old Dogtown names. Merry, Grant, Johnny, and Morgan moved into their cellar hole with surly reluctance.

When Ingrid next returned from the mainland with supplies, they insisted on immediately taking their share. Granny had originally taken on the task of rationing and doling out food, always putting a "tithe" aside "for a rainy day" in a large plastic tub in the corner. Now she had an uneasy feeling that some of the reserves were disappearing.

Two weeks later, Ingrid, Noah, and Granny Day woke up alarmed by the sound of voices and rapid scuffling. Someone was shouting orders.

"Stay back! Get behind those rocks!"

Noah signaled to Ingrid and Granny to keep quiet. Black Neil was nowhere to be seen. Noah crept over to the hatch and peeked out. Whatever he saw made him stiffen and hold a hand up for continued silence. Ingrid and Granny stood frozen, waiting for some new disaster to unfold. Noah retracted his head slowly from the door hatch and pressed his body against the wall underneath.

Suddenly two hands were placed on the doorjamb and a large, shaggy head appeared, obscuring the light. Noah lashed out and gripped the hands, twisting them, making the owner cry out in pain. Ingrid rushed over to help, and together they pulled the man down into the cellar hole. Noah pinned him to the floor. When the man moaned, Granny started forward, concerned for him, but Noah gave her a warning glance, lifting himself slightly off the body, letting the man draw a long, trembling breath.

"Who else is out there? How many of you?"

"There are nine of us altogether. Me and my wife and the kids. Seven boys. Please, my wife's in a bad way, she needs help. Just let me go and get her. If you don't want us here, we'll leave...as soon as she's able."

Noah slid off the man's chest, brushing the dust off the worn jacket and wrinkled trousers, embarrassed and apologetic.

"Sorry. Thought we were being attacked..."

The man got up, gingerly probing his left wrist. Granny stepped forward again, offering with a mute gesture to have a look, but the man shook his head.

"It's fine. Nothing broken."

Sudden darkness descended again, and when they looked up, seven heads ringed the hatch. The man waved feebly.

"It's okay, boys, everything's fine. Right?" he said, looking at Noah.

"Sure, fine. Come on...let's go get your wife. Ingrid, maybe you'd better come, too."

They walked down toward the cove. Halfway there they saw Black Neil, standing over the lifeless body of the woman. He shook his head regretfully.

"Sorry. She's gone."

The man sat silently by her side, stroking her hands and face, straightening her thin legs. He finally crossed her hands over her chest and bent his head, as if in prayer. The woman's eyes were closed. She seemed to have died peacefully.

The boys were allowed to see her before Noah and the man wrapped her, weighted the shroud with rocks, and put her in the dory. They disappeared from sight going around the point and continued out to sea, where they dropped her over the side.

During the night, the man moaned plaintively in his sleep and the boys huddled, sniffling and whimpering, in their corner.

The following day they began work on a new dwelling. Merry, Grant, Johnny, and Morgan refused to help.

"What? We're running a boys' camp now? And how are we going to feed all these kids? There's not enough grub as it is. Send 'em back is what I think," Grant said, pointing his thumb at the mainland.

Noah assured him they would find a way. Grant walked off, swearing mightily, and the "gang of four," as they were now being called, stayed away from the compound for the next week. Granny was forced to use up some of her precious reserves to tide them over until the next supply run.

As it turned out, there were too many islanders now for Ingrid alone to do the supply runs, and she called a meeting one evening. When the settlers had all crowded into her yard, Ingrid told them they had to divide into groups, each group being responsible for its own food and other necessities. She would take one from each group on her next run to show them how to get to the depot.

The gang of four complained the loudest, especially when Ingrid suggested that those with boats would have to share them with the rest so that every group could make one weekly trip to the mainland. Black Neil often borrowed their dory to make visits ashore. Ingrid was curious about these trips, finally deciding that it was really none of her business. Maybe he just suffered from cabin fever. Now, Neil offered to assist any group that needed help going ashore.

Since then, only one more settler had arrived. It was actually Black Neil who brought her. He had run into her on one of his forays on the mainland, he explained. Ingrid was on the way back after hiding their "rainy day" supply box among the rocks. She had gotten used to doing this before dawn to prevent anyone greedy from finding it and helping himself. It was only a matter of time, she supposed, before it was discovered. She had tried to hide it well, totally out of sight in a cave just large enough to hold her seated body. The opening was obscured by two mammoth boulders. Behind one of the boulders was a crack, allowing entrance into the cavity. It wasn't easily found, but if the gang of four became aware of its existence, they would certainly be looking for it.

After leaving the cave she never looked back, avoiding every risk of giving the hiding place away. She walked down to the water and stuck her toes in. Cold. A large, fat crab scuttled by, hiding behind a rock. Ingrid shuddered. She had seen crabs, right after she came to the island, feeding on dead human bodies. Hundreds of crabs, their legs and carapaces glistening in the sunlight that penetrated the clear water. They had been scavenging, viciously fighting each other off by flailing their long-armed claws like vultures of the sea. Noah often supplemented the islanders' diet with fish and shellfish that he had caught, but Ingrid would not touch crabs. Never again. She wouldn't even swim in the ocean. She often went swimming in the quarries, though, that were now filled with buoyant salt water. But the ocean held the dead, millions of them. Her mother was there, somewhere far away, and Adam, and Mim, and Grandmother Lil.

The sky was coloring from the east. "Rosy-fingered dawn appeared, the early born," Ingrid whispered to herself. Would she ever read Homer again?

When she started up the hill, the shape of a body separated itself from the rocky landscape. The figure was tall, covered in a gray cloak or blanket, and carrying a small bundle. The dark hair was roughly chopped off, like that of a young boy, but something in the graceful way she held her body, or the tilt of her neck, told Ingrid it was a woman. Her cheeks were hollow and her eyes withheld something, seemed to gaze inward. Yet there was an intensity there, lying in wait. *Joan of Arc,* Ingrid thought.

Later in the day, when the woman opened her bundles to reveal small bags containing tealeaves and herbs, and larger bags containing grains and flour, Ingrid laughed with delight.

"You must be Rachel Smith!" she said.

"No, my name's Ann..." the woman whispered. Her whisper had a hoarse timbre, which foreshadowed a voice that was deep and reedy.

"Some people here don't use their own names. I just gave you a name, if you want it. Rachel was one of the first settlers in Dogtown, which is where you are right now. She was a good cook, used to make johnnycake and boiled cabbage dinners. She was mostly famous for her 'dire drink,' which she made from leaves she picked in the woods. You see? So from now on, if you like, you're Rachel."

"My real name isn't Ann, anyway," the woman said, smiling weakly, as though relieved that her lie had been unnecessary.

Rachel looked around the cellar hole. Ingrid watched her, unapologetic. "This is how we live. You get used to it."

"Can I stay here with you?"

"We'll see. There are several homes. Ours is the smallest, and we'd have to enlarge it to fit another person. Granny just moved in with us recently, so there are three of us here. Then there's where the gang of four live. You don't want to stay with them. The largest home is across the way. It's also the most recent one. A widower lives there, with seven kids. We call him Luke. The children are not his own. He and his wife had been on vacation and ran into them when they rushed back toward their hometown. The boys had been out camping in the hills. Luke and his wife took them along, but there was nothing left of their town when they finally arrived there. So they set out trying to find a place for themselves and the boys, and finally showed up here. Luke's wife died the day they arrived. I don't know if you'd want to stay with them. I'm sure you'd be welcome. But the boys are a handful, and Luke's grieving for his wife."

Rachel looked away. *Everyone's grieving for someone*, Ingrid thought.

"I'll give Luke and the boys a try. Or maybe they'll give me one. I don't know what I have to offer just now."

As though Rachel's arrival had suddenly made her feel out of place in Ingrid's cellar hole, Granny made a tentative inquiry. "Wouldn't you and Noah prefer to live by yourselves, after all? Should we try and build another hole?"

Ingrid laughed. "What? Me and Noah?"

Noah gave her a long look and went off fishing.

Ingrid spent the afternoon showing Rachel around, trying to shrug off a feeling of discomfort. *Things are getting too complicated. I thought I could start over and keep my life simple. I wish I were alone again. I'm fond of Noah, but I'm not finished with Adam yet.*

Rachel was quiet, only nodding when required. After a two-hour trek over hot granite boulders, she flopped down on a ledge to rest. "Could I go and lie down for a while? I've been on the road for so long I can't even remember when I saw a roof over my head last."

Ingrid apologized and took her over to Luke's cellar. Black Neil was sitting on a ledge, keeping a lookout toward the mainland. Luke and the boys went off across island to see if they could spot Noah and the dory, while Rachel stretched out on the communal seaweed mattress that covered more than half the floor.

She tried to sleep, but had to settle for resting her tired body. Her brain continued its circular migration, ceaselessly flitting from one subject to another, in the end bringing her right back to the beginning.

CHAPTER 35

Fidelis was kneeling at the altar when Birke came in hurriedly, coughing at first to get his attention. When the pope did not react, deep in communication with his God, the senator impatiently put a hand on his shoulder.

"You are late for the meeting, sir. Please, you must come with me."

Fidelis looked up, confusion slowly replaced by irritation. "You must not interrupt my prayers, my son," he said petulantly.

"We are facing a grave emergency, Mr. President. Camp David is under attack. You are not safe—even here. We must move you immediately." Birke was sweating.

Fidelis rose, still hesitant. "Attack? Who would want to attack us?"

"The people, sir. Our own countrymen. They are desperate. And they are armed. They have already breached the outer security field, and by now they are nearing the compound. We don't have much time." He started toward the door, holding his arm out to guide the pope along.

Fidelis finally lurched forward, shuffling slightly, stiff after having knelt for what might have been hours. His memory was getting hazy.

The light outside was brilliant, the sun at its zenith. They could hear distant sounds of approaching vehicles and gunshots. Birke swore.

"Back inside, quickly!" He dragged the pope with him, bolted the door behind them, and ran toward the sanctuary. He found the hidden doorway, slid the small panel aside, and pressed the code that opened the door.

They entered a dark corridor and Birke pushed the button that shut the door behind them. He retrieved a flashlight from a niche in the wall, and pulled the trembling Fidelis along, down a set of stairs into the darkness, through the labyrinth of corridors that eventually took them to the safe room. A few people were already there and they could hear, behind them in the corridor, footsteps of others hurrying toward safety.

The safe room actually consisted of several rooms. It was a warren-like complex of cells of various sizes, separated by metal vault-like doors with steel bolt locks. They walked through two large rooms with bunk beds, barracks-style, and continued through a large meeting room that held a long table surrounded by narrow, slat-backed chairs. There was no carpeting anywhere, and the pope's shuffling footsteps echoed irritatingly on the cement floor.

Birke led Fidelis to what was referred to as "the inner sanctum," a name that now seemed particularly suitable. This small, L-shaped cell was sparsely furnished with an old army cot, a couple of folding chairs and a campaign chest that must have seen some long-dead general through a world war. It smelled musty in there, and there was no warm light to soften the jail-like ambiance, merely a bare bulb swinging from a cord.

It was the only cell in the unit that was equipped with a separate exit, which led to a secret passageway ending up somewhere outside the compound—exactly where, Birke did not know. The exit could only be used in the most acute emergency, and entering the code that opened the door would result in the automatic destruction of the entire safe room area within a matter of minutes. In this cell, he deposited the pope on the old cot that leaned on the rear wall for support.

"Sir, for now, please stay here. Try to get some rest. When everyone has arrived, I will come for you." He left quickly, without waiting for a reply—or, worse, for some unanswerable question.

Fidelis lay down slowly, first the upper body, then the legs, one at a time. He tried to get comfortable, scuttling his body around, crablike, until he faced the wall. He crouched desperately into a fetal position, but was unable to derive any solace from it. He stared at the solid cement wall, trying to look through it into the face of God.

Minerals had leached through the cement, causing great, dark stains ringed in white. Thin, dripping stalactites had formed on the roughly troweled ceiling. Suddenly he thought he saw the stalactites grow, getting fat and bulging on top, translucent like rotten onions. Then he felt them, felt them pierce his body with their needle-sharp points, injecting him with their poisonous, dripping fluid. He waited, paralyzed, for someone to come to his rescue. He was still in this position when Birke came for him.

"We are ready for you, sir, if you'll come with me."

The pope did not move. Birke thought he might have dropped off to sleep and shook him gently by the shoulder, noting with a shock how thin the man had become, the bone merely covered by a loose layer of skin. There was still no reaction.

Is he dead? Did he have a sudden stroke, or an aneurysm, like DeLong? He leaned over to see the face, which was pinched into a fearful grimace, the lips trembling, the cheeks wet with sweat—or was it tears?—the breathing in short, anguished puffs. Birke guessed he was seeing the signs of a panic attack, and swore under his breath.

"Sir, they're waiting for you at the table. There's tea made and some sandwiches, I think. You need some food. You haven't had anything since this morning. Come and break bread with us"—he thought maybe a small religious touch might help—"before we get to work. We need your help with some decisions."

Fidelis finally moved, slowly rolling over to face Birke. The pope had reached the end of his road. He had tried to split himself up and discard the part of him that was Fidelis, the part of him that was doomed, forsaken by the Lord. In desperation he had tried to fill his whole being with the personhood of the president so that there would be no shred left of the miserable failure that now lay in a heap on the cot, the old, bony carcass that God had decided not to make use of. But he was unable to complete the transition.

"You don't need *me* any longer. You need Sheedy. Go talk to Sheedy. He's the only one who can decide now. I'm too tired." He closed his eyes.

Birke thought the pope looked as though he had aged twenty years. In fact, with his eyes closed and his hands folded across his chest, he looked dead. A plan began to form in Birke's mind. Fidelis had obviously lost his sanity, gone over the edge. He had split into two separate personalities. How long would this last? This could be his chance. Now was the moment to take control. It would be easy. He already had Wheaton and Amaral in his back pocket. They were not at Camp David at the moment, but Presser was. Presser would be easy.

Fidelis, they would all agree, needed absolute seclusion in order to remain safe. Birke would be the liaison, the single lifeline. He would bring the pope his food and see to any other physical needs, as well as retrieve and pass on all communications and decisions. He would keep him in good health. The pope would be his queen bee.

Suddenly Birke heard explosions, felt them rock the ground. Fidelis looked at him like a frightened child. His lips moved, but Birke could not hear what he said. The blast had deafened him. He looked around. After a momentary hesitation, he bolted the door to the room where the others were waiting. He went over to the pope and pulled him into a standing position. The pope swayed wildly, whimpered, and tried to sit back down on the cot. Birke looked him in the eye and spoke loudly, nearly shouting, to make sure of being heard.

"We must leave. It's the only way, sir. You must pray. You must pray for our country, for our people. Close your eyes and hold on to me. Follow me. Do not stop praying even for a moment. You must get us God's help to get out of here. Do you understand?"

Fidelis nodded, his head shaking up and down as if he had been suddenly afflicted with dreadful spasms. He closed his eyes, and his lips started moving, adding to the spastic image.

Birke led him by the hand toward the door at the rear. He pulled out a small black case from his inside suit-pocket, opened it awkwardly with one hand, looked inside it briefly but with deep concentration then shoved the case back into his pocket. He studied the door before entering the secret code on the panel—rapidly, so that he would not have time for second thoughts.

It was done. A few small clicks preceded the silent, automatic sliding of the door.

He pulled his queen bee behind him into the tunnel. The door slid closed. In the total darkness, Birke realized that he had forgotten the flashlight. He grabbed the pope's hand tightly.

"Run, Your Holiness, run. Whatever you do, don't stop praying."

CHAPTER 36

"Julius, where do you want us to put these?" The children were carrying blankets that they had collected from the other houses. Julius pointed to the large double bed in the master bedroom.

"Just pile them over there. Later on we'll do up all the beds. Thanks, kids, good job." He nodded at them.

His beard had grown long, the scraggly tips reaching his chest. Aug had given him a haircut recently, a blunt chop at the neckline, and his thick hair bushed out around his head. He was wearing glasses, an old pair he had found in the last house where they had stayed. One stem was held together with tape, but he had been ecstatic at the find. He hadn't known that he—*the man he was but didn't remember*—had an eye problem until one of his contact lenses had popped out and gotten lost. Then, suddenly, he had only been able to focus with one eye closed. He had finally taken out the other lens, too, so that at least he could see properly at one distance.

Miraculously, the glasses he had found were close enough to suit his need and he treated them reverently, putting them lens-side up on the kitchen table before retiring. *Must have been some old codger*, he thought, *whoever owned them*. Nobody wore glasses anymore, except workers who used safety goggles. Contact lenses were also a thing of the past. Robotic laser surgery had corrected most vision problems. Probably his own condition had been recent, and the lenses a temporary arrangement while he waited for the surgery.

For some odd reason, he liked the way the glasses made him look. When he had first seen himself in the mirror wearing them, an old memory had flashed, but no matter how hard he tried, he could not recover it.

Throughout the fall, they had moved from house to house, using up the food and other supplies in one before moving on to the next. They had decided to live together in one house at a time, out of a need both for companionship and security. It was getting cold now, and as they moved they brought clothes and blankets along—and sometimes favorite cooking pans or items that the children had gotten attached to. Moving was becoming quite a chore.

Along the way, Julius had found some better fitting and more practical clothing, though still settling for a single change of clothes, which he kept scrupulously clean. Otherwise he abstained frugally from collecting property for himself. He recognized the need the children had for belongings, and suffered silently all the extra trips carrying these from one house to the next. At first he had thought this must mean that he had children of his own. He seemed to be a natural, as though he was used to it. He understood the children's needs without being told. Then he had changed his mind. If he had children of his own, he would remember them. He would remember the way their small hands felt in his, the look in their eyes when they were sad, their pink little tongues sticking out between their teeth when they concentrated, the way their hair got matted in their sleep, and the way they elbowed their way into his bed when they had a nightmare. You couldn't possibly forget those things.

Fall had been a season of fog and torrential rains. The downpours had kept them all indoors, sometimes getting on each other's nerves. They had collected the rain dutifully and kept the water in their main storage area up at the school, in gallon jugs. They still kept a large reserve of staples there against the day when they had used up everything in the houses, should that time come. Julius tried not to contemplate the future, feeling unequal to the challenge, not even knowing who he was.

He and the children lived from day to day and were forming a bond that he could only marvel at. The youngest, Meggi, Lans, and little Roofie, slept in his bed, snuggling against him for comfort. Aug, the oldest, tried to act older than his age, but Julius sensed his need for closeness. Whenever they were alone, Julius would put his hand around Aug's thin shoulders or sometimes give him a quick rough-and-tumble. He would not do this in front of the others, knowing it would embarrass Aug.

They lived in happy oblivion. Julius could not imagine what was going on in his country, or in the world. The notebook from his walking days still held the puzzle that he could not solve. The children were content. They had a place to live, with more than enough food and a surrogate to take the place of the parents they dimly knew they had lost forever.

Recently the rains had diminished a little and it was beginning to get cold. One morning they woke up to a hard frost. The first thought that occurred to Julius was about the latrine. He had built them an outhouse light enough to transport from yard to yard. Whenever the barrel was full, they dug a deep hole in the back of the field behind the school. Julius wheeled the barrel out and emptied it, and the older children took turns, complaining loudly and making disgusted faces while filling the hole. Now, he thought, they had better dig several holes—while the ground was still soft enough to dig—and cover them over to get them through the winter.

They would have to make sure to always keep enough food and water in the house, in case they were caught in a snowstorm. And wood to keep them warm. Most of the houses were equipped with fireplaces, having been built in an era when home fires were still permissible. Many of the fireplaces had since been blocked up and were now just a decorative folly. Some of them had electric log inserts installed in the hearth, making them impossible to use for burning wood. They had made sure, this time, to pick a house with a traditional, functional fireplace. By the look of it, it had never been used, and Julius suspiciously checked the chimney to make sure it would vent.

"Uyuth, Woofie code. Wan' bwankie. Wea' me theep?" Little Roofie, cold and wanting her blanket, was tugging at Julius' clothes, looking for a place to sleep.

"Just a minute, honey, I'll get your blanket. And then we'll have something to eat before you take a nap, okay?" Julius looked around. "When it gets really cold, we may all have to sleep in this room. We'll just bring all the mattresses in here and get rid of the furniture. It'll be like camping. It'll be fun," he said, trying to put any fear of a long, cold winter out of their minds.

"And we can sing and toast marshmallows," said Meggi, and Roofie clapped her hands.

"Muthmewowth, huwaay!" Julius laughed at Roofie's lisped effort to pronounce "marshmallows."

"No, we can't. We don't have any," said Declan, the redheaded boy who was a little contentious and liked to contradict the others.

"Well, we'll have a look-see. Maybe we can find some," Julius said. He wondered at this trait in himself, always mediating and trying to settle the little spats that came up from time to time. He was good at it, too. Was that some sort of clue to his profession? A minister maybe, or a union negotiator, or a teacher, or a bartender?

"You kids stay here and keep warm, and I'll go get some supplies. Don't leave the house until I get back," he added. He was getting too protective, he thought, as he walked down the street. The kids were safe here, and most of them were old enough to find their way around.

As he rounded the corner onto the street that led up to the school, he thought he detected a movement in the distance, near the woods behind the school. He tried holding the glasses away from his eyes a little and squinted. Whatever it was, it was gone. Maybe just a bird or a deer. They had seen deer up there before, and had contemplated hunting one for food. *With what...bow and arrow?*

He continued walking toward the school, but his footsteps had turned stealthy and he glanced around behind him, as though he was afraid of being followed.

CHAPTER 37

Rachel was coming back from one of her frequent walks. She often walked over to the seaward side of the island, where she would sit and stare out over the water. Lately the weather had been cold, and the last few days the wind had blown small, hard grains of sleet that stung her face and made her cheeks bloom like poppies. Ingrid watched her make her way down the hillside and over the stone wall that now surrounded the compound. Rachel was walking carefully, more slowly than usual. The granite was slick with ice. She was wearing the big gray cape that she had worn on the first day, over the usual loose shirt and gray sweat pants.

Shortly after Rachel had arrived, Ingrid noticed that, while she was painfully slim, her waistline was not, and as time wore on Ingrid felt sure that Rachel was pregnant. She could think of many reasons the woman might be reluctant to talk about it, but at some point she would have to. She made up her mind to take Rachel aside for a talk. After all, if it were true, Ingrid and Granny would probably have to act as midwives, unless Rachel planned to go away, savage-style, and take care of it by herself.

"You must be freezing. I have hot water going, if you'd like a cup of broth or something. Better be careful from now on or you'll get frostbite."

Ingrid lifted the hatch door just enough for them to get inside, jealously guarding whatever warmth there was. They made daily searches around the perimeter of the island to gather driftwood for their fires, and while there was never a shortage, she worried about what it would be like in the winter, if the water froze. Would they be cut off from the mainland?

Ingrid hadn't been back ashore for a long time, having shared the duty with Noah. Black Neil went across frequently, taking the dory. Ingrid still wondered why. Did he want to leave or just find out what was happening on the mainland? Once he had stayed away for several nights. But he always returned, sometimes bringing back news or some treat he had managed to scrounge. He showed a special concern for Rachel, sometimes following behind her on her walks. Maybe he had noticed Rachel's condition, too, Ingrid thought. That would make him more observant than most men. Adam certainly hadn't been as perceptive. Except in the early days of their marriage, she reluctantly admitted.

If the weather was bad, they could easily get isolated out here. Would the strait freeze over? She knew it had in the past, in very cold years. But then there had just been the narrow Annisquam River between the island and the mainland. Now there was a wide channel. *It will depend on the severity of the winter*, she thought.

Already it was colder than she felt was normal, and it was slippery down by the water's edge and hard work to gather the cold, wet wood. She put another gnarled branch on the fire and prepared two mugs of broth. They were alone, the others out on their various tasks. *No time like the present,* she thought.

"Rachel, are you feeling okay?" Ingrid didn't know whether to be direct. She handed Rachel a mug and sat down next to her.

Rachel gave her an anxious look. "You've noticed, haven't you?" It was all she said, but it was enough.

Ingrid nodded, and Rachel bent her head. When she finally looked up, a trail of tears glimmered on her cheeks. "We tried so hard. I even went to see Dr. Cadwallader in London. Then I had three miscarriages. They told me to give up. And now, suddenly, here I am. My husband didn't even know, Ingrid. I didn't want to tell him. It was so early, and something might have gone wrong again. I wish he had known, at least."

Rachel put her face on her drawn-up knees. Ingrid scooted closer and put her arm around the crying woman, holding her tightly.

"I know how you feel, Rachel. Well, that sounds presumptuous. No one ever knows what someone else feels, I guess. But I've lost my husband *and* a baby. At least you'll have your baby. You are far enough along now…"

"I'm sorry. I feel very selfish."

"I wasn't trying to make you feel guilty. I was trying to make you feel just a little less unfortunate. But you have to take very good care of yourself now. No falls on slippery rocks. Eat properly. You're too thin. We don't have a doctor here, you know, if something goes wrong. But Granny and I will help you when the time comes. You'll be fine."

Ingrid got up and wrapped a blanket around them, and together they huddled in front of the fire. The light flickered on walls that glistened coldly with moisture. The floor was covered from wall to wall with rugs and blankets and musty-smelling old clothes. Everything was damp and moldy from the constant, cold rains. They kept a stack of driftwood on hand inside to dry it out and make it burn better. The rest was kept outside in a pile that Noah kept covered with a tremendous sail that had drifted ashore one day. They had all avoided touching the sail in case it had been used as a burial shroud. But Noah had just laughed, pulling it out of the water, hauling it out as if it were a fishing net. "If a person died at sea, and there was still someone left on board to perform the burial, do you think he'd waste a sail on the dead bugger? No way."

Rachel sipped her broth. Ingrid relaxed and stared into the embers.

"Did you lose your baby in the wave?" Rachel asked.

Ingrid closed her eyes. "No. It happened long ago. I was four months pregnant. I fell down the stairs. My husband thought I did it on purpose."

"My God. Why would he think that? Oh, I'm so sorry, Ingrid. This is really personal. If you don't want to talk about it, just say so."

"It's okay. When we got married, I told him I didn't want kids for a while. I wanted to work, and us to get to know each other and create a home that kids would feel welcome in. Not necessarily in that order, but...you know. We bought a house that we loved and our life was wonderful, for a while. I didn't like my job—and that was a disappointment because it was my job that had brought us to where we were. When I told my doctor I wanted to start a family, I got pregnant almost right away. God, Rachel, I was so happy. Like you, I didn't tell my husband—I wanted to wait for the right moment. Then I fell and lost the baby." She said that last part mechanically. She had relived the fall so often it had lost all meaning, and the memory no longer kindled any emotion, only a sort of cold stiffness in her limbs.

"So you didn't tell him you were pregnant. But why would he think you'd risk your own life in a fall to lose a pregnancy when you could certainly have gone abroad for an abortion?"

"He knew I wouldn't have an abortion. We had made some agreements earlier in our marriage, and that was one."

"For religious reasons?"

"Not exactly. More because of the business he was in."

"Business? What business would that be?" Rachel asked curiously.

Ingrid sat back a little and pulled the blanket tight around her shoulders. "Rachel, I guess I can't talk about this after all."

"I'm sorry, Ingrid. Do you think we'll ever be able to talk to each other again? I mean without having to be so careful? I can't stand having to recreate myself, having a persona that's all made up. I thought anonymity was a good idea at first. I mean, none of us know each other well enough for, you know, trusting. But how do you get to know somebody who doesn't have a past?" Rachel lay back tiredly on the rumpled clothes and blankets.

We are still too numb from the disaster to feel real sorrow for what we have lost. Yet at the same time we are as sensitive as an open wound. Life has become such a brittle, tenuous thing. Do we really want to live? We have all lost our homes, our families. Our livelihoods. Our confidence, our feeling of freedom. Our joy. And what if this isn't the end? What if there is another wave? Or eternal winter? What if we were to be attacked from within or without? The fear we are living with is almost worse than what we already went through...

CHAPTER 38

It was a bitterly cold winter that followed the wet fall. The new lakes froze over, despite their salinity. On clear days their surfaces reflected the sky like blinding mirrors. In the Northeast, limbs of trees and shrubs were thickly coated with ice that tinkled like chimes in the wind. As the cold deepened and the blustery wind strengthened, branches fell, then trees, their trunks brittle from the cold. Entire frozen forests succumbed to the wind. All of nature seemed to have weakened.

The old died that winter, and the sick, and many children. In cities, the lonely and depressed panicked and threw themselves from the highest buildings still standing. Schizophrenics wandered about untreated, brushing imaginary insects off their grimy sleeves, talking incessantly to invisible listeners. The psychotic and the paranoid teamed up to terrorize the large numbers of people of limited mental capacity, who still roamed the streets unable to even contemplate fleeing to save themselves, and robbed them of anything useful or edible. These unfortunate, helpless innocents died in the alleys in large, huddled groups. Some starved, some quietly froze to death. Their bodies hardened in clusters into inseparable ice monuments waiting for the spring thaw.

People who lived down South fared no better, as the cold penetrated all the way down to the wide new gulf. There were more mouths to feed there now, after the great southerly migration, and more souls that needed housing. Darwin's theory was back at work: the survival of the fittest. There was no longer any protection for the weak in society. Townspeople barricaded themselves against the newcomers in order to preserve their homes and what little food they had left. Silent, bloody battles were fought, without generals to lead them, in muffled hand-to-hand fighting. The only sounds heard were grunts and the cracking noise of bones breaking. Those who took in the strangers fared better, ending up with smaller rations but a larger defense force.

Of the government, they knew nothing. They knew only what they could see. The perimeter of their town was the end of the world. They heard from strangers about devastation and ruin, but they hadn't seen it with their own eyes and it didn't affect them any more than the news stories they had watched in the old days on SYSCOM. There were always disasters and catastrophes. This one was no more real to them than any other. The invasion of strangers was their catastrophe, and lack of food and power. It seemed dire enough.

CHAPTER 39

"Julius, wake up. Please, Julius, Dec is sick." Aug shook Julius' arm vigorously and finally managed to wake him up.

They crept over to Declan's mattress in the corner of the room. Declan was writhing in pain and unable to stifle his moans.

"Dec, what's the matter? Where does it hurt?"

"My stomach..." He looked at Julius pleadingly before being gripped by another convulsion. Julius probed Declan's body as gently as he could.

"Aug, what did Declan have to eat at supper? Do you remember?"

"Same as I did, oaties and milk. I don't feel sick, except maybe from watching Dec."

"We'll have to wait for morning, see if he gets better. Otherwise...I don't know. You go back to sleep, Aug. I'll sit here with Dec. I may need your help tomorrow and I want you to be rested. Okay?"

Aug nodded and crept off to his mattress.

In the morning, Declan was no better. When Julius brought the boy's knee up toward his stomach, he howled.

"I think it may be his appendix," Julius whispered to Aug. "I'll have to get him to a doctor. Come outside with me."

They left the other children to watch Declan, which they promised to do, wide-eyed with anxiety. Julius went into the shed and came out leading a bike with a two-wheeled baby buggy slung behind it.

"I think I can fix this by extending the foot end of the buggy with a piece of siding, like this." He worked diligently and rigged up a makeshift, wheeled gurney. "Now, some air in the tires, and we have transportation. Aug, when you came here, do you remember passing a town or settlement that might have a clinic? If I went the way I came, it would take me at least two days before I reached people. We may not have that long."

Aug looked anxious. "There's a big town that way," he said, pointing north, "but we didn't want to go there because people were fighting, and big fires were burning." He shuddered at the memory. "Maybe you can find a doctor there. It's probably ten miles away, at least. Maybe twenty."

"That's fine, Aug, thank you. I think I can manage that. Have to try, anyway. You'll be in charge now, until I come back. I know you can handle it. After all, you got them here to start with. Meggi will help with the little guys. Just stay inside. Don't go out for any reason. Lock the door behind me. You've got enough food and firewood in the house. When you need to go to the bathroom, use the potty. Okay?"

He didn't want to mention *the man*. Aug already knew about him anyway. They had both seen him, skulking around the edge of town. He had not shown up lately, but Julius knew that Aug remembered and would be careful.

With Declan wrapped up in a cocoon of blankets and strapped securely onto the buggy, Julius took off, taking the northerly turn onto the icy highway. Drifts of snow lay like dunes across the road, and he concentrated hard on keeping the bicycle level. He didn't see the figure that was hiding among the trees, watching the curious equipage as it passed.

Once Julius was out of sight, the man turned and started walking back toward New Hope, following a route he by now knew well, toward the house with the smoke coming out of the chimney. He put his hands in his pockets and tried to whistle a tune, but his lips were too stiff with cold.

It was lunchtime before Julius, with an ominously silent Declan, arrived at the town limits. He saw people scurrying between buildings, rummaging through boxes and barrels full of trash and garbage. There were no fires to be seen now, but Julius saw enough burned-out buildings and gaping storefronts that he could imagine what had driven the children away.

He pulled over in an alley, stopping to catch his breath, which was coming out of his nose and mouth in great clouds. Declan moaned as they came to a stop. At least he was still alive. His face was white, though, and his eyes were closed. They must hurry.

Julius tried to catch the attention of a middle-aged woman who was walking toward them down the sidewalk, but she turned and ran. He got back on the bicycle and rode aimlessly toward what he felt was the center of town, past burned-out and boarded up buildings. He could tell where people lived by the frost flowers inside their windows, but when he tried knocking on a door only a hand came out, holding a gun pointed right at him. Julius hurried on.

A teenage boy came flying around a corner, hesitating when he saw Julius.

"Hey!" Julius shouted. The boy turned to run the other way. "Hey, I need help!" Julius shouted, louder. The boy's head turned as he ran. Julius stood, squeezing the bicycle between his legs, his arms spread, palms up, pleading. "We need a doctor," he yelled when the boy slowed to a halt. "Just point me to a doctor, please."

The boy came a little nearer, close enough that he didn't have to shout. "There's a doc a few blocks down that way. Hope ya got loads of cash. He won't do nothin' for nobody without cash. Good luck, man."

The boy took to his feet again, disappearing in a flash. If people were chasing the boy, he had lost them, as no one else was to be seen.

Julius sped down three blocks, and as he turned the corner he could see the shingle: *Dr. Mansell Waite.* He pulled up in front and led the bicycle onto the sidewalk.

"Hey, you can't leave that there. Get away, go on." The guard was armed and was using the butt of his gun to shoo them away. Julius put up his hands.

"I need to see the doctor. I've got a sick kid here," he said, indicating the buggy with his head.

"Got an appointment, mister?"

"It's an emergency."

"Doc doesn't take emergencies. Get lost."

"I can pay." It was a lie, but it got them inside.

Two more armed guards eyed him suspiciously. A receptionist dressed in pink sat at the immaculately neat desk. It was warm inside and the lights were on. Julius blinked. He hadn't seen electric lights for a long time. He supposed the doc was rated for some kind of emergency power.

Declan moaned loudly and started to vomit. The receptionist looked disgusted and pointed to the waiting room. There was no one else waiting. *The doctor must be with a patient in surgery*, Julius assumed. He waited five minutes then left Declan on the floor and went back out to the receptionist.

"When can we see the doctor?"

The question seemed to puzzle her. She turned her eyes to the small flip-up monitor. When she blinked, he saw that her eyelids were painted the same shade of blue as her eyes. Maybe so people wouldn't notice if she nodded off on the job, he thought.

"He'll be going to lunch next," she said.

"Lunch? What about his patients?"

"He only sees patients in the morning. You'll have to come back tomorrow." She crossed her legs and started to pick at her nail polish.

Julius leaned over the desk until his face was inches from hers. "I have a dying boy here. I can't wait until tomorrow. Go tell the doctor I'm waiting."

The guards watched, seemingly amused. The receptionist got up and knocked on the door of the surgery room. After a few moments the door opened and a short, dark-haired man appeared, looking annoyed. He wore a gray suit over an elegant silk shirt. On his feet were softly polished leather shoes. The hand that held the thin black leather portfolio was magnificently manicured, the nails gleaming rosily, edged in white.

"What's this?" he said, his nose crinkling in disgust at the sight of Julius.

"I am here with a child that needs emergency care," Julius said, hesitant, in turn, at the sight of the doctor. Could this diminutive fop be competent?

"I don't do emergencies." The doctor glanced at Declan's motionless body on the floor.

"The child will die," Julius warned.

"Not my problem. Get out of here or I'll have you removed."

Julius took a step toward him and the two guards rushed forward. Locked in their grip, he was still defiant. "I'll make you regret this someday."

The doctor laughed. "You and what army?"

"The United States Army." He didn't know what made him say it, but it gave him a great feeling of satisfaction.

The doctor laughed again, uproariously. Julius looked him steadily in the eye. The doctor blinked. *Sometimes these people run amok,* he thought. He'd better humor this poor sod. By the looks of it, the kid wouldn't survive anyway.

"There's a clinic downtown. Saint Anthony's. They take indigents," he said, nodding at the guards to let Julius go.

Julius rubbed his arms angrily then went and picked up Declan's lifeless body. He got to the door, resting Declan on his raised knee while turning the handle.

"Let me have a look at the boy," the doctor said suddenly.

Julius would never know what had caused the man's change of heart.

Dr. Waite pointed to the padded table in the surgery room. Julius walked over and put Declan down gently, stroking his golden red hair. Freckles, the source of much teasing, stood out on the boy's pale face.

"Leave him. Come back in an hour."

Reluctantly, Julius left the boy in the doctor's care, knowing he had no alternative. He went outside and got on the bicycle, riding around to try to keep warm. He passed a church and heard music. Was it Sunday?

In New Hope, Julius had started keeping track of the days to get a sense of order into their lives. Without a watch among them, they had picked a day at random to begin with, and, according to their calculations, today was Thursday. He parked the bicycle along the church wall and went inside.

It was cold in the church, but warmer than outside, with candles and bodies to give off heat. A great crowd was assembled, and, to Julius' amazement, there was a cameraman in the aisle recording the event, whatever it was. The church had an ancient pulpit of intricately carved wood, high up on the wall to the left of the altar, with a narrow stairway leading to it. Julius squinted a little to see better.

The man in the pulpit was small. Julius was able to see only the head and top of the shoulders over the pages of the open Bible. The figure was dressed in white and wore a miter edged in gold. Tufts of white hair were sticking out at the sides of his head. He was extremely thin and frail-looking, but his voice was strong. Julius thought there was something familiar about him, but he couldn't put a name to the face. Judging by the regalia, he could be the pope. Pope who? Julius couldn't remember.

***

At the end of the service and a brief, prepared homily, which he had some difficulty reading from a paper that shook in his hands, Pope Fidelis raised his arms high in the familiar blessing.

As he reached the bottom of the stairs, he was surrounded by several armed men who led him into the sacristy. A man in a tweed suit was at his elbow, giving directions to the guards before returning. Standing under the pulpit, the man held a hand up for silence.

"Dear friends, thank you for coming. We must all do what we can for our country in these troubled times. President Sheedy is extremely grateful for your continued support and contributions. We feel confident that we are coming to a turning point, and we have you good people to thank for it. Remember us in your prayers." Birke had found that Sheedy was more convincing in his pope role, but he nearly always referred to him as "the president," thereby getting the benefit of both offices.

The congregation filed out of the church into the deepening cold. It was starting to get dark. Julius hurried back to the doctor's office.

"Ruptured appendix. He'll live, though, no thanks to you. It was probably the rough ride in that vehicle of yours that caused the rupture," the doctor said with a smirk. "He'll have to stay overnight. If you took him back in that thing now, all my good work would be wasted. Come and check in the morning."

Julius didn't know whether to embrace the man or punch his self-satisfied face. He steeled himself to utter a humble "thank you," and left. Where would he go? Where could he spend the night? He remembered the pointed gun and knew he couldn't risk knocking on doors.

He wound his way back to the church, but the great, carved doors were locked. While the Church had reverted to the past in its demands of strict obedience to religious law, it had not gone back to the old tradition of leaving its doors open to serve as asylum for the needy. He walked through the graveled churchyard to the back of the building, at last finding an unlocked door that led into a basement storage area. He stumbled around in the dark, bumping into old religious statuary and dusty hymnals. In what he first thought was a closet, he found a set of stairs leading up into the back of the sacristy.

It was a little warmer up there. He groped around with his hands and feet until he found a place where he could lie down, and covered himself with a big piece of heavy cloth. Unable to fall asleep, he lay in the dark contemplating the day's events. When his thoughts arrived back to the end of the church service and the speech of the tweed-clad man, he slowed himself down, trying to concentrate. What was it the man had said? Something about President Sheedy. That wasn't the president's name. What was it?

DeLong, isn't it? No, he died. Another name appeared vaguely to Julius before disappearing just as quickly. There had been no time to connect a face to it. Who was that? *And Sheedy…what is there about that name? Of course, the speaker…the speaker who had become pope. Fidelis.* That was the man he had seen in the pulpit today.

Julius' mind was reeling with the few bits of returning memory. If Sheedy was also the president, which seemed to be what the man in the tweed suit had implied, it would mean they had a pope and a president rolled into one. Julius laughed aloud. The hollow echo of his voice reminded him where he was, and he felt suddenly tired.

He thought of Declan, and of Aug, and the children in New Hope, and wished anxiously that dawn would come so that he could go back home.

CHAPTER 40

The sound was their first warning. The wind was blowing so hard it needed all four of them to open the hatch, and as soon as they had it opened, they had to shut it again. A gale was roaring in from the ocean, dumping snow on the island.

Later in the morning, the wind seemed to quiet down, but Ingrid was familiar with the way nor'easters blew and knew that the wind would return full force without warning.

"Next high tide is mid-afternoon. That's when we'll see the worst of it. I'm afraid the wind will rip the roof off. We'll be open to the sky, Noah. Listen, do you hear the wind picking up? We should have gone ashore. Now it's too late. I'm going up the hill to see what it looks like out there." Ingrid put on several layers of clothing and tied a scarf around her head.

"I'm going with you." Noah pulled on his fisherman's sweater and a woolly black hat. His bushy red eyebrows stuck out under the hat, and the beard could serve as a neck-warmer, thick and red. Ingrid tried to hide her laughter.

Noah growled. "What's so funny? Ashamed to go out with me?"

"Oh, Noah, you're hopeless. Of course not. Come on."

They had grown closer, and Ingrid enjoyed teasing him. She was no longer afraid of hurting his feelings and, on occasion, she had secretly wished they had the cellar hole to themselves.

There's no rush, she thought. If it was meant to be, the time would present itself.

They walked as quickly and as carefully as they could over the icy hills until the ocean lay before them, writhing and white with anger. The waves were already of a terrifying height. The outer islets were easily washed over by the enormous breakers. Froth and foam was thrown into the air and carried all the way up over the island, making their faces cake up instantly with salt. Within moments, Noah's beard turned white, and their clothes stiffened. The sound of the wind and waves overpowered anything they tried to say. Finally, Ingrid made a gesture signaling that she wanted to continue on over to Lambkill. She had come to the lookout to determine the strength of the storm and to test an idea. There was something she remembered from the past that she wanted to investigate, regretful now that she hadn't thought of it before.

The narrow strait between the islands was swirling with eddies of ice-blue water, but they managed to jump the boulders across to Lambkill while the ocean suctioned the water back, preparing for the next big wave. Ingrid led the way up onto the height of land.

They were standing on the highest part of Lambkill. She had stood here with her grandfather, looking out over treetops and marshes and across the wide expanse of ocean, asking him to point to where Sweden lay. "Over there, far below the horizon."

The hill had then been known as Babson's Bird Sanctuary, with structures that had gone to ruin even before her grandfather's time. Now there was nothing left of that old bird watchers' lookout. It was simply a high knoll of bare ledge covered by a treacherous sheet of ice.

The wind coming in from the sea stung their eyes. *This is an insane idea. Total madness,* she thought. Lambkill was not as high as Dogtown, and it would take the brunt of the seas. Still, she had to satisfy herself, now that they had come this far.

Noah could only shake his head, uncomprehending, as she dragged him around, scanning the ground as they went. Finally she pointed and screamed.

"There! There's one!" She ran ahead and got down on the ground. Remnants of blacktop were visible here and there, and underneath she could see what she had come looking for. Cement. Long ago, while they were laying the road, large craters had been blasted out of the granite and cement vaults had been built under the road. They had held electric and electronic equipment, cables, utility service and water control panels that supplied the industrial park that had been located here. There had been several of these vaults, each one as large as a city bus, totally sealed and enclosed in cement and set deep into the ledge.

Now she had found one, and eagerly looked for a way in. She discovered it quickly. This one had been breached by the wave, and was filled with water and debris. Discouraged, she looked at Noah. She pointed toward Dogtown. Should they go back?

Noah shouted a question into her ear: "Are there more?" When she nodded, he shook his head.

Now that he knew what they were looking for, he gestured that they should keep at it, but go in opposite directions. They scrabbled over boulders, scraping snow and ice away from likely sites. Then Ingrid heard Noah's voice, faintly carrying over the storm, and ran toward it. Noah had found a vault, seemingly intact, its manhole entrance trapped by a boulder they would need help moving.

Losing no time, they hurried back toward the compound. When Ingrid slipped and fell down an icy slope, Noah rushed anxiously to her side and helped her up. She laughed, huffing a great cloud of steam into the frigid air between them.

Noah kept a hard grip on her arms, looking straight into her eyes, and she realized she had never looked at him like this before, intimately and close up. She had always kept things casual, just glancing at him before turning away, never really making eye contact. She was afraid that he was going to draw her in, maybe try to kiss her, but suddenly he let her go and they continued down the icy trail.

As soon as they got back to the cellars, Ingrid ran to alert Black Neil and Granny, and then continued over toward Luke and Rachel's. She thought with regret of the people living in shacks on the other side of the island. There was not enough time to get to them.

Noah went to try to convince the gang of four to come and help them. While he was away—Ingrid could imagine him arguing with that lot—she quickly prepared bags of necessities to bring along. Food, stove, clothes, a couple of pots, wood and lighters, candles, what else? She wrapped everything into big bundles. Everyone would have to carry a bundle on his back, except Rachel. As long as Rachel could manage to get herself over there, everything would be fine.

Once she was done, Ingrid gave everyone their pack and they set off, leaving bundles for Noah and the gang of four to carry. She prayed that he would be able to convince them, as without their brawn the whole plan would be in doubt. She instructed Luke to look after the boys, and Black Neil volunteered to accompany Rachel and help steady her. Would Rachel be able to get across the strait?

Ingrid suddenly felt exhausted. Her chest was hurting acutely from exertion and breathing the icy air, and she had lost all feeling in her hands and feet. She moved mechanically, steering them all toward Lambkill.

Ingrid, Luke, and the boys reached the strait and looked back for the others. She could see Granny struggling with her heavy bundle, and hoped that Black Neil and Rachel were not far behind. They left Sammy, one of the older boys, at the strait to wait for the stragglers while the rest of them jumped across and scaled the hill up toward the vault.

Luke looked out to sea and shook his head. He studied the boulder, putting his shoulder to it. The boys sat down in the lee of the gigantic rock, and then they all waited. After what seemed an eternity, Granny and Black Neil appeared, supporting Rachel, who was hanging on their shoulders.

Neil carried Rachel up the hill, her face resting on his chest, and set her down by the boulder. The boys made room in the center so that she would be the most protected. Then Luke went back down toward the strait to retrieve Sammy and the bundles they had been forced to leave behind. Ingrid kneeled next to Rachel.

"Are you okay?" she asked, shouting into Rachel's ear.

Rachel smiled faintly and mouthed an answer. "Ingrid, I think it's time."

CHAPTER 41

Pete and Evie had been on their way north for what seemed an eternity. Early on, they had encountered groups of people making their way south. Any smoke coming from chimneys now indicated homes of people who had decided to stay put. Occasionally, they walked up to a house to ask for water or some other necessity, but generally they kept to themselves. One morning they woke in an abandoned barn. Evie remained curled up, covered with an old horse blanket. They had been warm, hot even, and made love in the hay, but as soon as Pete got up she had felt the chill seeping in through the cracks in the old walls. Pete went to start the fire outside to heat water for a cup of soup. Hearing a noise he turned around and saw a man approaching. Pete turned to check for a sign of Evie, but she was still inside.

The man came closer and removed his woolen cap, and Pete started laughing.

"Patrice Demba, is that really you?"

"Nope, I'm Farmer Jones, and this here's my barn. Nice to see you, Pete." Pat grinned and clapped Pete on the back. Evie cautiously peeked out to see who Pete was talking to, and when she recognized Demba she ran out, smiling.

"Pat! Where on earth are you going? What brings you up here into the wilderness? I thought Pete was the only person I know crazy enough to want to go north." While she talked, she threw her arms vigorously around her body, clapping herself on the back trying to get warmed up. Steam was coming from her mouth as she spoke.

"Actually, Evie, I started out to meet a group a little further on. Then, a while ago, I met someone who said he thought he'd seen Pete going north in the company of two women. Guess he saw right. So, where's the other one?" he asked, looking around before turning to Pete. Pete and Evie looked at each other. Pete pursed his lips and sucked in a breath.

"Well, Evie, we've got to tell him, I guess."

Evie nodded. Pat Demba had the right to know.

"I assume you can guess who the other one is. Ariana. We tried to convince her to come with us, but she wanted to go her own way, so we parted company. I still feel guilty about that." Pete shook his head, and Evie turned away.

Demba looked at them in disbelief, waiting for the rest of the story.

"Well, where was she going?" he said finally. Pete was aware of the impatience in Demba's voice.

"Nothing much else to tell, I'm afraid. She wanted to go east to look for her brother. I think she knew she wouldn't find him, Aren lived in Boston, you know. But she had other relatives in the area, she said." Pete felt sheepish. Demba would be appalled at his lack of judgment in letting the first lady go off unaccompanied.

Demba stood looking at them silently. At last he closed his eyes and took a deep breath.

"Pete, I'm not blaming you. I know how stubborn Ariana is, believe me. I knew where her studio was, but I never told Albion. I feel guilty about that, now. She has a right to make her own decisions, of course, but still."

They sat around the fire, sharing experiences and contemplating the past and the future. Pat Demba was in the Secret Service, had covered DeLong. When disaster struck, Demba had been on assignment somewhere in the Midwest. He had been at an airport, waiting to return to Washington, when SYSCOM went down. He'd come back east with a military ground transport, but had been on foot for the last couple of weeks. Demba told them he was now part of a regional group, and even tried to recruit Pete, who listened and told him he would consider it.

In their previous discussions, Pete had always felt that Demba held a lot of information back. *Comes with being in the Secret Service, of course.* But Patrice was a curious and tight-lipped fellow, and Pete felt he always gave more than he got when he talked to Pat.

"So, where are you going? Where is this group meeting?" Pete asked.

"Oh, well, somewhere a bit further north. But I have something else to do on the way. Sure you're not interested in joining us?" he looked at Pete, who shook his head.

"I'm sure. I'm bringing Evie to meet my folks." Pete said, taking Evie's hand.

Demba smiled conspiratorially.

"Well, then. Wish you the best. Maybe we'll meet again, you never know."

As they watched Demba walk away, Pete wondered if he had just made another big mistake. But he had other responsibilities now. Evie and his folks came first.

"How much further?" Evie asked as they started out on the day's trek.

"Not long now, I promise," Pete said.

Pete had thought of Demba many times since that day, wondering if Demba had found Ariana. He also wondered about the mysterious group Demba had asked him to be part of. Sometimes he felt guilty about having said *no*, but he had pushed it aside forcefully, and he and Evie had continued on northwards. They were getting close, now.

CHAPTER 42

When the country suffered an attack of agro-terror twenty years earlier—a score of terrorists had simultaneously smeared the nostrils of animals in the largest herds in the country with a virulent strain of hoof and mouth disease—ranchers had called it the worst disaster since the extermination of the buffalo. Non-explosive warfare had become commonplace already at the turn of the century, with bio-terrorism a threat as horrendous and frightening as bombs and missiles. Terrorists had stepped up their attacks, changing their tactics frequently to elicit and encourage maximum levels of fear. Members of small terrorist cells hijacking airplanes and using them as guided missiles in suicide missions had put the country on full alert against that particular form of terror, but fanatics always found other sinister ways to instill fear, and had later chosen different avenues.

There were no terrorist attacks this year, but the deep winter with its relentless, deadbolt cold took its own toll. Famine and disease were rampant. Great herds of cattle, already starved, froze to death. There would be little or no meat for the nation.

With the spring thaw, the invasion of saltwater into the groundwater would make its real effect known, and the great farm collectives would have to leave their fields fallow for years to come.

In the deep of winter, influenza struck, reducing the human population further. In some areas of the South it was looked on as a blessing, as it staved off starvation for the survivors.

CHAPTER 43

Aug was looking out of the window when he saw *the man* coming closer. He wasn't skulking around this time, but boldly walking in the middle of the street.

Aug made the children hush and get out of sight. When the knock came on the door, they all froze. The man knocked a second time.

"Come on, kids, I know you're in there. Open the door!"

Meggi started whimpering. Her friend Lyla crept over and put her hand over Meggi's mouth.

"Sshh, Meg, he'll hear you. Ssshhh."

Meggi cried louder, and now little Roofie chimed in. Then Lans started howling. The man got bolder and tried the door handle roughly, but the door stayed shut. Aug had bolted it.

"Open up, please! It's cold out here. I'd just like to talk to you. I saw your dad leave. You need someone to look after you." The man tried the door again, throwing his weight against it, trying to break in.

They heard his footsteps as he walked around to the back of the house. The back door! Had Aug locked it? They heard the man try the door. It was locked. Then they heard the squealing sound of a window being opened.

Meggie screamed and some of the other children joined in.

"Shut up! Go hide in the bedroom and lock the door behind you!" Aug shoved the last child through the door and waited for the key to turn in the lock before he ran out into the kitchen.

The man was halfway through the window and Aug grabbed the big frying pan, planning to use it for a weapon. The man hopped down onto the floor and held up his hands in defense.

"Wait! Just wait a minute...let me talk to you. I'll stay here, and you stay there. Nobody moves, okay?"

Aug kept the pan in both hands, held high over his head, ready to strike. "Go ahead, talk. This better be good. Dad's coming right back."

"That's good because it's really your dad I want to talk to. Where's everybody else in this town?"

"They're dead." That was a mistake. "But they'll be back." That was even worse. He was too nervous. He should just let the man talk while he thought of what to do next.

The man pretended not to notice his slip-up. "Well, then, you don't mind if I stay here and wait for your dad, do you? I mean, if he's coming right back... I could use something to eat. I can see you've got some cereal there. Would it be okay with you if I helped myself to some?"

Aug's arms were trembling with fatigue. Slowly, he put the pan down.

"Go ahead. But you can't leave this room. The kids are afraid of you." Aug intended that to mean that he himself was not afraid.

The man nodded in agreement and ate some cereal right out of the box.

"We have bowls. We don't eat like animals." Aug put the pan on the stove and brought out a bowl from the cupboard. "Here."

The man took the bowl. He was tall and scrawny, with stringy, dark brown hair and the beginnings of a scruffy beard. His hands were turning a purplish red with the returning heat.

Aug knew how that felt, having had to go long distances in the cold looking for wood. He and Julius had talked about burning the furniture and the fences and sheds, but they'd save that for later, in case things got even worse. Every time he came back from his search, Aug had to endure the pain of the circulation returning to his hands and feet. Now he filled a bowl with cold water.

"Here. Put your hands in the bowl. It helps if they don't heat up too fast." It was a trick his mother had taught him a very long time ago, when he had come back from sledding with hands that were like slabs of ice inside the wet mittens.

The man put his hands in the bowl. After a minute he nodded and relief erased some of the tenseness from his face. He smelled like wood smoke and wet wool, Aug thought. His eyes were very blue, especially against the scarlet, frostbitten cheeks. Aug could tell the man wasn't wearing his own clothes. The pants were too long and the jacket too big. When he finally took his jacket off, Aug couldn't help laughing. The man was wearing a shirt and tie underneath.

"Glad to see you laugh, even if it's at my expense. I'm very fond of my shirt and tie, actually. They could use a washing, though. You don't do laundry here, I suppose?"

Aug laughed again. "'Fraid not, mister. Just our own, and we try to keep clean so we don't waste the water."

The man nodded. "What's your name, kid?"

"Aug. What's yours?"

"You can call me Jack."

After that, they sat in silence in the kitchen for a while. Aug didn't want to leave Jack alone, yet sooner or later he had to go and check on the others. Finally, he got up.

"You stay here, okay? I'll be back in a few minutes."

"Okay, boss."

"Aug."

"Aug. Okay, Aug."

"If you're tired, you can lie down on the floor."

"That's real generous of you, Aug."

Aug didn't know if Jack was being sarcastic, but decided it didn't matter and left the kitchen, closing the door behind him. The children let him in after he assured them he was alone. They were huddled against the back wall in the chilly room.

"It's okay. You can go back into the living room. The man is in the kitchen. His name is Jack. He wants to talk to Julius. I've told him he can wait there. I don't think he wants to hurt us."

At this, Meg started to sob again, and Roofie's lip trembled. Aug sighed then went over and picked her up, hugged her, and put her in his lap.

"Woofie thcared, Aug. Meggi cwy mek Woofie thad. Wan' Uyuth *now!*"

"I know you're scared and sad when Meggy cries, Roofie. Trust me, I'll take care of you. And Uyuth...I mean, Julius will be back soon."

When the children had calmed down, Aug put some wood on the fire. The room was comfortably warm, and he thought of how cold the kitchen was, especially with the door closed. But the man would have to stay there.

Of all the houses they had stayed in so far, this one was Aug's favorite. Even with the furniture taken out of the room, it was cozy in here. The walls were a nice spruce green color, and there was a picture of a ship over the mantel. There were other pictures on the walls, too, of children, and of houses with flowers around them, and even a picture of President Lincoln. Julius and Aug had covered the floor with layers of blankets and cushions. On the mantel, there were several candles that they lit, one at a time, only when it got dark.

"Wead a towy, Aug, pweath," begged Roofie. *Read a story, Aug, please.*

Hanging on one wall was a small bookshelf with old paper books, most of them children's picture books, and Julius had read aloud from them. Now Aug pulled one out and started reading to Meggi and Roofie. The other children gathered around. If they had to wait long, he'd better try to keep them occupied.

CHAPTER 44

The Provincialate of the Little Sisters of the Assumption had moved from the inner city to an old Connecticut farm many years ago. Apart from the dwellings, which were of the kind that had been added onto for generations, with wings and lean-tos sprawling across the lightly sloping hillside, there was a large stone barn, which had been diligently cleaned out by local hired hands.

This building had been turned into a nursing ward and hospice, where the good sisters cared for the indigent sick and aged with a great measure of love and patience. After the disaster, they had accepted as many patients as they could find a sleeping place for and, as time passed, most of these newcomers had either died or moved on. At least one of them, however, remained. It was a curious case, but they had been asked by the Reverend Mother to refrain from speculation and gossip and to get on with their daily work. Still, one couldn't help but wonder, thought Sister Agatha.

The patient was kept in seclusion in one of the two single rooms in the ward usually reserved for the dying, with only Mother Anne and Sister Gemma allowed to enter. And Sister Gemma would never tell; she was on the silence. The only thing they knew for certain was that the patient was a man, and this they had learned from Sister Zita in the laundry. But, yesterday, Sister Zita had more news to tell. She had been asked to launder what looked like a papal stole. What did this mean? Whispers were heard throughout the wards. *Could it be?*

Pope Fidelis tried to rest on the hard mattress. He could feel every bone in his body whenever he moved, so he tried to lie perfectly still until, agonized by stiffness, he would slowly rotate into a different position. His health had improved, and some of the time he was quite lucid. Most of the time, though, his mind wandered. Dementia was setting in. Pain made him cantankerous, and now, far from being the kind, patient and compassionate man of the past, he had become childish and demanding. He wished that irritating woman, Mother Anne, would show up. And where was Birke, for God's sake. The man was a criminal, letting him rot in here, in this cold, inhospitable asylum, where the only friendly face he saw was that of Sister Gemma, and she was not allowed to speak. He had tried to assure her that she could speak to him, her *father,* but she just shook her head, smiling sweetly. She had lovely, soft hands, though, and when she washed his body, he shuddered with pleasure, although he told her he was shivering with cold. Where was she now? The pope groaned impatiently.

The Little Sisters struggled mightily to bring their charges through the winter. Last week the influenza had reached the ward. Already, two of the oldest patients had died. They had put them in the sepulcher of the little chapel, which was too cold to use this winter, but which would keep the bodies until graves could be dug. They would usually pre-dig a number of graves for the winter, but this year there had been too many deaths, and so they were forced to keep the rest of the bodies in cold storage.

Yesterday, a new patient had been added to the ward. He was a man who frequently came to visit their secret patient, even to take him away for a day sometimes. His tweed-clad figure had become familiar to them. He was obviously a man of *importance,* and would only speak to Mother Anne. He brushed past the sisters, opening the door to his friend's room without knocking. But now, struck down with the influenza, he would not be able to visit the secluded patient. Although he had seemed to be a strong and healthy man, his condition was deteriorating rapidly. There was no longer any medication to be had, at least not for institutions caring for the poor. This was a virulent strain of flu, and sometimes people who had lived in the protected environment of wealth and extreme cleanliness were all the more prone to have a bad case.

Sister Agatha walked toward the kitchen, looking for a cup of tea. She had been on house duty, laying fires in the dining room and the great room, where most of the sisters spent the evening, taking turns to go out to do ward duty. They tried to stay in the great room as late as possible, until Mother Anne came and shooed them off to their cold dormitories. Sister Gemma was in the kitchen, sitting on a stool by the counter. Sister Martha was pouring herself a cup of tea.

"How about pouring me some while you're at it?" Sister Agatha said.

"Why would you need a cup of tea after roaming around in this warm house? You should go out to the ward. The walls are caked with ice. Oh, and that new patient is dying. Mother is with him now." Gemma was off the stool and by their side in a moment, looking great-eyed at Sister Martha.

"What? What is it you want, Gemma? If you want to see that man before he dies, you'd better hurry." Sister Gemma ran off, wimple flying.

"I wonder what she knows that we don't," said Sister Agatha.

CHAPTER 45

Julius noticed with relief the spiral of smoke coming out of the chimney. They had been gone for two days, as Declan had been too weak to travel in the sub-zero weather, and the second night they had both slept in the sacristy of the old church. Julius had worried about the cold, and wrapped himself and Declan together into a giant woolly cocoon, Julius sharing whatever bodily heat he could muster after two cold, half-starved days.

But now they were back in New Hope and everything appeared normal. The children were not to be seen and, judging by the thin coat of pristine snow covering the front yard, had not been out since yesterday. Snow had fallen during the night, creating a wondrous landscape that he had enjoyed all the way back. He knocked on the door.

"Aug! It's me. We're home!"

When no one came to the door, he leaned the bicycle against the tree, checking on Declan as he did so. The boy was fast asleep. He was pale still, but the cold had turned his cheeks red.

Julius walked over to the window and looked in. The bedroom was empty, the door to the living room closed. He continued around, checking the windows as he went. When he came to the kitchen window, he noticed the dirt and scuff marks on the windowsill. Someone had entered through the window. Aug? Had he locked himself out?

He knocked on the door, loudly now, and banged with his frozen fist on the windowpane. He tried looking in, but the windows had been covered with blankets. Then the door opened and a tall, red-faced man appeared. Julius pushed him aside roughly.

"What the hell is going on here? Who are you, and where are the kids?"

"Take it easy. The kids are fine. They're in the other room, except for the two that went to get some water. Go see for yourself."

Julius stormed through into the living room. There, in the dark, were the children, except for Aug and Derk.

If Aug felt he could leave the children, maybe things are not too bad, Julius thought. *Assuming, of course, that he's still alive.*

"You kids okay? Has this man been bad to you?"

The children first nodded, then shook their heads. "He was cold. He's been staying in the kitchen. He came here to see you." Meggi explained the situation succinctly, Julius thought. She was a smart little girl.

"How long has Aug been gone?"

"About ten minutes, I think, or half an hour."

Why did he even ask? Children had no real sense of time. Suddenly, he remembered Declan. He rushed out through the front door and reappeared in a moment, carrying the still sleeping boy. The children looked at him anxiously.

"Is he 'live?" Lans asked, looking serious.

"He'll be just fine, Lans. He's sleeping. Hopefully, he'll be able to sleep a lot today. It'll help him get well faster. We'll just put him here and keep him warm. In a little while I'll have to wake him up and give him something to eat. Meanwhile, let's try to be quiet so he doesn't wake up too soon. Now, you all stay here and watch Dec while I go and talk to the man."

Julius got up, walked out into the kitchen, and closed the door behind him. The man was sitting at the table, drinking a cup of coffee. Aug must have supplied him with hot water. Julius went to make himself a cup. The coffee jar, which had been half-full when he left, was nearly empty. Julius swore.

"We ration things here. I drink one cup in the morning and one at night. You've used up at least a month's worth of coffee in two days."

"Sorry. It's been cold. I haven't seen coffee for months."

Julius went over to the table and sat down. He brought a box of cereal, which he ate dry, pouring some powdered milk into his coffee.

"What is it you want?" When he received no answer, he looked up to find the man studying him intently. When Julius caught him, he looked away briefly.

"Sorry. What do I want? I was looking for a place to stay. Not for myself, for some other people," he said quietly, turning again to study Julius'face.

"What kind of people?" Julius wondered.

"Just people. They've lost their homes. Lots of people are looking for places to stay. I'm scouting for an organization that helps place people, find safe homes for them."

"Sounds very noble. What organization is this?" Julius sounded doubtful.

"Doesn't matter. There are plenty of them. Point is, this town could handle a lot of people, the man said, waving his arm expansively in a circle.

Julius stuck his chin out.

"Not really. We are using things up quickly. There would be lots of problems: water, bathrooms, fire wood. We take care of ourselves, do a lot of scrounging," he said obstinately.

"What makes you think other people wouldn't be happy to scrounge and take care of themselves? There are lots of homes here. There are plenty of trees in the woods over there that could be chopped down to burn, and snow to melt for water. You think you're the only one in this country using latrines? And we have runners that would bring food."

"Runners?"

"We're tied in with the food distribution centers. A runner, the guy who delivers the stuff, would bring supplies to this community, enough for the number of people who live here. Food, necessities. It's free from the government, as long as it lasts. Our people are sort of a public delivery service. The government needs the National Guard now to keep the uprisings under control. We are all volunteers. All you have to do to receive supplies is get organized." He paused. "Our group specializes in people who need to stay hidden." He gave Julius an odd look, which Julius either ignored or did not notice.

"What do we have to do?" Julius asked.

"Nothing. In fact, since you don't own this town, you can't stop it from happening. I'll be leaving in a little while, and later on this week you'll have new neighbors," the man said, matter-of-factly.

"And you'll be one of them?" Julius was losing his temper. Things had been under control until now, he thought. He resented this intruder, bringing change into the relative order he had created for himself and the children.

"I move around. Maybe I'll be here for a few days, get things set up. Then I have to move on."

"What's your name?" Julius asked tersely.

"I told the kids to call me Jack."

"But that's not your name, is it?"

"What's yours?" Jack retorted, without answering Julius' question.

"Julius."

"And is that really *your* name?" Jack asked, a tentative smile playing in his eyes.

Julius grimaced. "What kind of people will you bring? Will my kids be safe?"

"Probably safer than they are now. I'm not bringing murderers and thieves, if that's what's worrying you."

Julius finished his coffee in thoughtful silence. "I've got to check on Declan. He's recovering from surgery. He'll have a rough couple of days, with some pain, I expect. He needs something to eat and I suppose the other kids do, too." Jack nodded, and Julius got up and went into the living room. He gestured to Jack to follow and pointed to a cushion by the fireplace.

"Get warmed up a bit before you go."

"What's that? Here's your hat, what's your hurry?" Jack asked with a short laugh.

Jack gratefully sank down on the pillow and rubbed his hands in front of the fire. Julius studied him from the other side of the room. Jack didn't look quite so threatening now that they had talked. After a visit to a barber, he would probably turn out to be a handsome man, and younger than he now appeared. He sounded educated. Maybe he could educate Julius.

"Who's the president of this country?"

Jack laughed, then understood that the question had been asked seriously. "You mean you really don't know? How long have you been living here?"

"I don't know. Since after, you know, the wave," Julius said, vaguely.

"Sheedy. Former speaker of the house. Or Pope Fidelis, if you prefer."

"*Former* speaker?"

"Well, he couldn't be all three, could he? Although, strictly speaking, he still is. Of course, there's the little fact that there's no more House. Everyone who was in Washington is swimming with the fishes. Most of the rest of the senators and congressmen were lost in the Camp David attack, except Sheedy and Birke. The attack was carried out by the militia. All brawn and no brain. People call Sheedy 'the president in hiding.' He appears now and then, according to bulletins we get, reporting on the 'progress' the country is making. Reads prepared statements. They've got him stashed with the nuns. From what I understand, he's out to lunch. If they dress him in a suit, he thinks he's the president; if they put his robes on, he's the pope. I mean, he *literally thinks* he's two separate people. Senator Birke's running the country, to the extent anyone can right now, and we suspect he's running Sheedy, too."

"What happened to the vice president?" Julius asked. Jack gave Julius another quizzical look, leaning forward slightly as if to adjust to a more comfortable position.

"You mean the *former* vice president? Albion? Died in a plane crash the night of the wave."

Julius felt sudden pain rushing through his body. Wild, screeching noise seared his brain. He stared at Jack, who was watching him closely.

"God."

"What is it, Julius?" Jack asked.

As quickly as it had come, the moment of terror passed for Julius, as though it had been a bad dream that he could not remember on awakening, and he sighed.

"I don't know, Jack. Some kind of nightmare. Must have been the wave. You see, I've lost my memory. Probably that night. That's why I decided to stay here with the kids, until I remember. It seemed safe here, like you say. The kids aren't really mine, of course. They're orphans. I help them and they help me. They keep me sane."

"What *do* you remember? Anything? Are you married?"

Julius shrugged and pointed to his wedding ring, a wide, gold band. It was loose now, could almost fall off. He must have lost a lot of weight.

"Just a date. No names."

"What's the date?" Jack asked.

"July 20, 2040."

"You've been married ten years. What's your wife's name?"

"Won't work, Jack. Trying to remember will just give me a terrific headache. Believe me, I try all the time."

Jack nodded. The wedding date may be enough, if it was as he thought. And if it *was* as he thought, his plans would have to change.

CHAPTER 46

Pete and Evie had arrived at the McPherson cabin in the middle of the night, with the dew reflecting the full moon and sprinkling little moonbeam starlets across the countryside. It was too cold and wet to even dream of sleeping outside, and Pete quietly tried the door. It was locked, so they had to knock. After a few minutes, it opened just a crack.

"It's me...Pete." Now it was thrown wide, and robed arms reached out, pulled him inside, into the darkness, and enveloped him into a fierce embrace.

"Pete, oh, thank God! We thought we'd never see you again! Hey, Matt, look who's here!" the old woman shouted, turning toward the interior of the cabin. Grumbling noises and the shuffling sound of slippers preceded the gruff voice.

"Christly, what's goin' on heah?"

"Dad, Luce, this is Evie." Pete pulled Evie in behind him. Luce had just managed to light a candle, with trembling hands, and held it up in front of the visitors. Matt, trying to wrap himself in a flannel robe, stepped into the circle of light.

"Well, ah'll be dahned." Dark brown eyes peered out at them under a wild tiara of untamed hair.

"Dad! Your hair turned white!"

"You don't say. You look pretty stahtlin' yourself."

Pete knew he'd lost weight, making him even bonier than before, and his black hair had grown long. Evie wanted to trim it, but Pete said he wanted to look like a back-woods man. He was quite successful, Evie thought. With the beard and the lumber jacket, he looked a perfect, if skinny, Paul Bunyan.

"Well, Jeezum Crow, shut the doa!" Matt said.

Luce scuttled ahead toward the kitchen, and they followed her and the light. She put the candle on the large, round table and put the kettle on the old stove, stirring the embers and adding a log. Pulling a tin out of the cupboard, she put a few generous scoops of grounds into the kettle. When the water boiled up, she stirred the brew vigorously before putting it aside to settle.

"Not real coffee, of course. Just chicory. We dug the roots in the fall and roasted them. We sure got enough chicory around here." Luce poured.

Matt and Luce still lived pretty much as Pete remembered they always had. Matt—a born Yankee, with the accent still to prove it—was a *survivalist,* a throwback to early pioneer days. Pete wondered how his mother, delicate as a houseplant, was doing in her neat, modern condo apartment in Salt Lake City. *If* Salt Lake City still existed.

Matt chuckled at the sight of the beef jerky that Pete had saved and now reverently placed on the table.

"Tomorrer ah'll take you down the cellah. We got a stash down theah. Moose, deah. You like juhky? We got it. And we got eggs from the chickens. We don't eat the chickens, though. Tough old bihds, they ah. Roostah's getting ole and mean, too. Maybe we'll eat *him,* soon. Cock-o-wing, you know."

Luce giggled and sipped on her drink. Then she reached over and placed her arm around Evie's shoulders and gave a good squeeze.

"You two must be tired. You best sleep in the living room; your old bedroom is too cold, Pete, being closed off for the winter. In the morning we'll open it up and ready it for you. That is...you are staying for awhile, aren't you?"

"Thanks, Luce. We'd hoped to, at least for now. If it's not too much trouble."

"Family's no trouble," Matt said. "We already have a bahn-full of strangahs. Now *that's* trouble. As much as we want to do all we can to help, theah's a limit. Some of these folks won't do for themselves. They think of us as hosts, as though this is a hoo-tel and we ah' supposed to feed them and keep them wahm and comf'table and entertained. And now we've just been told there's maw of them comin'. We could use some help cleanin' out the stables. Only place left to put people now. We had to put the hawse down befaw Christmas."

"Not old Hiram?"

"Ay-uh." Matt nodded, his face crimped with bitterness.

Hiram had been old and sway-backed already when Pete was last at the farm. Matt had kept him for sentimental reasons, letting him serve out his retirement in the hillside meadow beyond the barn. When Pete last saw Hiram, the horse had been standing in the shade of an old birch, nuzzling tender blades of grass. His large, gentle frame, with the deeply curved back, had been outlined by the sun, a white aureole around the golden mane and the warm russet body.

"We were fawced to, so that we could provide food for our *guests*. I shot him befaw they tried their own way of butcherin'." Matt's voice was filled with hostility. "*We* didn't eat any..." he shuddered. "Buried what was left out in the field, just befaw the ground froze. Else the cay-otes would have hawned in, too. It's the same all around, Pete. Cattle's all gone 'round heah, 'ceptin' the five cows, but I s'pose they'll be next. We still got a cuppla pigs, 'nuff to see us with bacon through the wintah, I guess. We been invaded. O' cahse, we'll see what they say when theah's no milk and no cahves in the spring. Who knows what it's like elsewheah? Do you? Is this the bad of it, or is it wuhse wheah you come from?"

"Worse. From what we hear, and I've been in touch with some of my people who have good information, people are dying from cold, starvation, flu, typhoid, and some unspeakable diseases you've never heard of. Then there's murder and mayhem, cannibalism, and looting. Bands of thugs are intercepting food deliveries. There's no medicine to be had any more, even for medical centers. Unless, of course, you are willing to barter with the drug lords. You'd have to be prepared to offer everything you own. Money has lost its value, but is being hoarded by a small, elite group of people who seem to think it'll come back in style when they form our next leadership."

"These people of yaws that you seem to trust, they wouldn't be the ones who keep sendin' folks heah for us to take cah of?"

"Well, no, not directly, anyway. You know there's no government. With Albion gone..." Pete suddenly slumped in his chair. The weight of the loss—not of *the president,* but of *his friend*—hit him with surprising force. Ever since he looked into Albion's eyes and lied to him on the White House lawn, Pete had suppressed his feelings, first of guilt, then sorrow. Now they overwhelmed him and he sobbed helplessly, his thin chest heaving.

Matt got up and got a towel from the kitchen. "Heah, son. Wipe yaw face. It's been rough for all of us. I can only imagine how you must feel, bein' so close to it."

Pete nodded. As he calmed down, he took up where he left off. It felt good to talk. He had avoided talking to Evie about it, thinking it might make them both too depressed to go on. Talking about it now helped him see clearly just what they had been through and where they stood.

"Sheedy's holed up with the religious folks in some mountain aerie and now, without Birke to steer him in politics, the man just raves. Birke died of the influenza, I heard," Pete continued. Our fear now is that Sheedy will be manipulated by a horde of extremists from within the Church. 'The New Inquisition,' our people call them. I've been trying to locate legitimate members of the government, but there are hopelessly few left. We've tried to gather a lower echelon of people, state-level types, but it doesn't look very promising. At that level, they all follow the leader. They're all willing to 'stand up strong with Sheedy.' Misguided patriots. It's almost better to leave those sleeping dogs lie. If the whole world weren't in the same straits, which we have to assume it is, we could be overrun in a day. We just have to remember that other countries may still have their leadership intact, and may be more efficient in restoring order and military power. If we live through the winter, we'd better start checking the skies."

"You think they'd invade?"

"Wouldn't be the first time in history."

"Look at that…your Evie's gone to sleep. You two must be dead tahd. We'll talk some maw in the mawnin', Pete. It's good to have you back. Maybe you can help me with these guys who keep bringin' us people. They ah' stoppin' by soon, they said. Promised they'd give us some supplahs if we could take in maw people, but I don't trust 'em. We've done all the supplahin' so fah."

CHAPTER 47

When Noah finally arrived at the top of Lambkill with the gang of four, the whole group got to work trying to heave the boulder out of the way. The howling wind tore at their clothes, and their faces turned red from cold and exertion. The task proved impossible. They could not budge it.

"We need levers," Noah said.

Desperate, they spread out over the ice-covered hills and looked around, but nothing useful could be found. Suddenly, Black Neil, who had disappeared over the highest ridge, came back into view. He was waving wildly, signaling for them to come to him. He had found another vault, intact, with the manhole cover accessible. When they reached him, he was trying to pry it open, but it seemed to be frozen in place.

"Maybe if we heated some water and poured it on?" Granny shouted. Her long scarf flapped in the wind, like a red pennant.

Noah shook his head. "You couldn't keep a stove lit in this wind," he yelled back.

They looked at each other anxiously. Now they were worse off than if they had stayed in the cellar holes. The tide had come up and they would not be able to cross the strait to get back to Dogtown. Rachel certainly couldn't. And soon there would be the storm surge, and they all risked getting swept into the sea by a rogue wave.

"Whose brilliant idea was this?" Grant roared as he stepped forward, crossing his arms and casting an intimidating glance at Noah. Ingrid felt her stomach muscles tighten.

Merry pushed Grant aside. "Hold on, let me have a go," he shouted into the wind, which seemed to be strengthening by the moment. He inspected the cover. "Aha, thought so. It's locked."

He was talking to himself then raised his voice as he turned to Ingrid. "Used to work with these buggers. Got some of your kitchen gear handy? Let me see if there's something I can use."

Ingrid, hearing enough to understand what was needed, checked the bundles and found the bag of clanging kitchen tools. Merry picked through them until he found a ladle with a hollow handle, which he banged into shape against the ledge. Moments later, he had unlocked the cover and managed to lift it away. They all closed in on him now, anxious to get down into the hole, out of the searing, sleeting wind, and started piling inside, steadying themselves on whatever they could grab on the way down.

The inside was colder than an icebox. In the dark it looked smaller than they expected, with pipes, cables, and metal panels covering the walls, and larger pipes criss-crossing the floor. They shuddered and trembled and cried, and swore and fought for space, tripping over the obstacles. The wind and sleet came pouring in through the manhole opening, and as soon as they had lit the lanterns and the small glow-heater, which they had reserved for a dire emergency, Noah pulled the cover closed.

"You have to leave space for air—this place must be pretty airtight, and we'll get poisoned otherwise," said Ingrid.

Noah pulled the cover back just enough to form a slim crescent, through which the wind whistled shrilly. Ingrid returned to the far corner, where she had left Rachel and

Granny. Rachel's contractions were coming every few minutes now. She was writhing in pain on the bundle of clothes and blankets Ingrid had seized.

Granny looked at Ingrid. "We'll need hot water."

"Cold may have to do. Let's hang a curtain across here. We can tie it onto these pipes. Use that dirty blanket. We'll need the clean ones." They screened off a small section of the vault.

"Noah, could you get the stove going? Try to heat some water."

"Hell, we need the water for drinking. And where are all the blankets? It's damn cold in here." Grant was tugging at the screen.

Black Neil looked at him from across the small space. "Sit down and shut up. This place will warm up soon. We've got enough bodies in here to heat Hades. When the water boils, we can all have some soup. Leave the women alone, or you'll find yourself on the outside. Noah, how about if we try to collect some of that sleet coming in? I don't know how long this storm will last, but Grant's right about one thing. We'll need extra water."

He came over, steered Grant out of the way, and looked around the screen at Rachel. "How is she doing? Coming close, isn't she?"

Ingrid nodded. She couldn't speak for the panic rising in her. Fear of being inadequate was tightening her chest. Rachel was probably in her mid-forties, and this was to be her firstborn. Even with qualified care, complications might arise. And Granny, despite her name, had no more experience than she did.

"I think I'd better get out of these clothes." Rachel's hoarse whisper brought them back to reality, and they started preparing in earnest.

With the women tied up in the birthing process, the boys were left motherless again. They sat silent, listening to the moans and cries of pain coming from behind the curtain—shuffling their feet, sniveling, wiping runny noses on their sleeves. Luke, who had been a lost soul and an ineffective father-figure ever since the death of his wife, made an effort at pulling himself together.

"How about some of those campfire songs, boys? Just quietly, though. They might cheer her up, you know. Maybe they'll distract her a little...from the pain, I mean."

The boys huddled close together and, with voices trembling from fear and cold, started singing. After a while they began to warm up and put a little more emotion into their performance. They had forgotten how much they missed music, which they had listened to around the clock—even in school, if they got away with it.

They stopped to eat some hot soup, but started up again as soon as they were finished. Luke sang along in a ponderous, churchy voice. Noah also joined in, humming loudly when he didn't know the words.

"Don't you kids know any sailor songs?" Noah asked when the boys began to run out of ideas. And so it happened that Rachel's child was born to the tune of "The Land of Libertie," sung with a great deal of feeling, especially the last lines:

"I hope time will come agi when our comrades all we'll see,
And once more we'll live together in love and unitie."

The voices overpowered the feeble cries until the last note. Then the boys fell silent, and they all waited. Finally, Ingrid appeared from behind the curtain.

"It's a little boy, and he's fine. You can go on singing," she said, before disappearing again.

The boys, relieved, sang on, repeating some of their earlier repertoire, a mixture of simple folk tunes and camp songs.

Ingrid closed her eyes and cut the cord, after tying a piece of clean string around it. Then she handed the baby to Granny to clean and wrap.

"Quick, quick, wrap him as fast as you can. We'll wash him better when it gets warm in here. Now, Rachel, you have to push again. I know you're tired, but you won't feel better until the afterbirth is out. Then you can sleep, I promise."

"Bring me the baby first, Ingrid," she said.

Ingrid turned around to Granny, who handed her the tight little bundle. She laid him across the new mother's chest.

Rachel spit on her fingers and touched the baby's head. "I name you Cricket," she said, barely audibly.

As Ingrid handed the newest Dogtown settler back to Granny, Rachel started her final contractions.

CHAPTER 48

Matt, Pete, and Evie spent the morning mucking out the old stable. After putting Hiram down, which had left the stable empty, Matt had cleaned out the stalls, so it wasn't too bad, Evie thought. She had been in a pigsty once, and had been expecting the worst. Some of the folks who lived in the barn came over to watch.

"Now, do you see that, Willie? That's what real farmers do. That's a pitchfork that the man is using. And on the wall there, you can see the reins, and a thing called a 'bit' that they put in the horse's mouth so they can steer him. Is it too smelly for you, dear? Let's go see what's for lunch today, shall we?" The mother took her children and ambled back over to the barn.

A couple of teenage boys came over instead and climbed up on the wall that separated the stalls so that they could watch without being in the way. Pete looked up at them, grinning.

"How'd you like to give us a hand?"

The boys stared at him before climbing down and taking off, snickering. At the door one of them turned around. "Thought you'd get some free labor, didn't ya?" They turned and ran down the lane toward the fields.

Pete looked at Matt, incredulous. "I see what you mean, Dad. When I was their age, I would have given anything to help out on a farm. And I had to grow up in the city! I wish you'd had this farm then. Think of all I would have missed!"

Matt shook his head. "Funny thing, lahf. Just the week befaw the wave, ah said to Luce, *'Think what that boy would have missed if he'd grown up heah on the fahm. Wohking with the president, bein' on top of the wohld.'* Wouldn't trade places, but it's been the raht thing for you, hasn't it, Pete? Luce agreed with me. You know, she's mahty prahd of you, though she's ahwys wishin' she'd had a chance to get to know you better. Well, maybe now's the tahm."

They spread clean straw thickly in the stalls. It was impossible to completely get rid of what Matt called the "bucolic aromar," but that's the way it was. Keeping the place warm would be the biggest problem. In the barn, they had the old furnace that would burn anything, and there was plenty of wood and trash that could be used for fuel. The stable was newer, and had been heated with electricity, with a generator for backup. With no fuel for the generator, they had to depend on wind power.

Farms were allowed a certain amount of solar and wind power that did not have to be fed into the grid, but the small windmill was already inadequate for lighting the barn and running the pump in the well. Matt had never considered solar power, finding the hi-tech look objectionable. He liked the timeless view of the little farm buildings nestled in the grove of trees, and kept cars and anything that looked modern hidden in the outbuildings. Luce hand milked the cows, and they used pitch forks to feed and buckets to water the animals. If electricity and a generator hadn't come with the farm, he would have done without. Now he felt they had also been a serious drawback since he had become dependent on them and neglected the care and upkeep that would have kept the buildings warm and draft-free.

They worked on sealing the walls and windows as well as they could, to keep the cold out. "Maybe we could build a brick oven against the back wall, heah. Quite safe, ah think, as long as folks keep the place clean and the strawr well away from it. Got plenty of bricks from that old chimmeny we took down last yeah. How about some suppah, and then we'll see 'boat it?"

They went back to the house and had a meal that consisted of bread and translucently thin slices of smoked venison, swallowed down with home brewed beer, which tasted rich and yeasty.

"This meal would have cost a small fortune in Washington, you know," Pete said, playfully licking the foam off the edge of the glass. Evie swallowed hard and got up to help Luce clear the table.

Pete looked at Matt. "God, I forgot. Can you believe it? For a moment I actually forgot."

"That's okay, son. You need to fahget while your body heals up. Then, ah believe you've got some wohk to do. Yes, sah."

"What do you mean?"

"What you said last night. Tryin' to get good people togethah. You ah *one* of them, ahn't you? As much as we'd like you to stay, you can't hide heah fo'evah. The fahm won't stay like this for long. These people will take it away from us… it's been happenin' all around heah. Unless you find us some leadehs, we'll have a revolution."

"It's already started, Dad. It's just a matter of time."

"Then you know yaw duty. Rest up for a while, then awf with you."

Later in the afternoon, they returned to the stable and built the brick oven, venting it through the stone wall. They filled the oven with heated rocks, and covered it with a tarp to help it cure. In a couple of days, when the grout was dry, they would test it. They went to bed early, weary from a long day's work.

***

Winter came in hard and Pete and Evie dug in, feeling safe and comfortable and at home. Pete became more and more reluctant to break away. They were fine here. Why couldn't they all become survivalists and live out their lives on the farm? It could be idyllic.

He didn't miss his bachelor pad in Washington. True, the neighborhood had been nice. The building itself had lacked charm but had been safe, with an around-the-clock security guard and every inch monitored. That's one of the things he'd hated, the monitoring. He used to wave and say "hello" to all the hidden cameras, which intruded even into the bedroom. *Now,* he thought, *maybe those cameras are filming fishes, like sequences from a submerged Titanic.* Evie's place had been a relief from this, had given him precious moments of privacy that he still remembered wistfully.

Pete knew he was dreaming. His father was right; he was needed elsewhere.

***

Late one night, Matt stuck his uncombed head in the door. "Pete," he whispered, "wake up. We got comp'ny."

The *organization men* had arrived. Pete pulled on his clothes and woke Evie before he joined the group in the living room. Evie got dressed and went to sit in the kitchen with Luce.

"What's going on in there, Luce?" Evie asked, looking around to see what she could do to help. Luce had already gotten breakfast going. Evie smelled bread baking.

"Usually, the men come to prepare us for the next onslaught of people needing a place to stay. You'd think we were the only farm left in Vermont." Luce flipped pancakes and stirred some rashers while she talked.

"Why don't you let me do that," Evie said, putting her arm around Luce's back, "and you sit down and have a cup of coffee? Looks like you've been up half the night already."

Luce nodded gratefully, and handed Evie the spatula. The pancake stack grew as they waited for the meeting to end.

"So, Evie, are you and Pete talking about the future yet? You know, life will go on. You can always stay here, if it comes to that."

"Thanks, Luce. Right now, I think that's what Pete would want to do, and I'd be very happy here. But I have a feeling that he needs to go back and help with whatever needs to be done, even though I can't imagine what it might be. I love Pete, and I'd be happy to be with him wherever he chose to go, if he wants me. Especially since it won't mean going back to Washington. I don't think I could stand that." She shuddered, added another stack of pancakes to the platter and transferred some crispy bacon to the large mound on the back burner.

"Come on now, Evie, sit down and rest. They'll be a while, I'm sure."

***

Pete sipped on his coffee while trying to get the kinks out of his back. His hands were red and raw from working in the cold, but he was finally beginning to get used to hard manual labor.

He sat back and listened to the conversation. The men looked like a group of itinerant farm workers, he thought.

"I see you got the stable all set up. Looks good, Matt. You put a lot of work into it. It'll be appreciated, you know that. It's folks like you who are keeping the nation alive right now."

Matt nodded. "Got a helpah now...my son, Pete. He's only heah faw a spell, though. Pete, this is Lobo. He's headin' up this group."

Pete nodded in greeting. Lobo looked at him a fraction longer than an ordinary first meeting required, Pete thought, as though taking his measure.

"Yes, we knew he was on the way here. Our runners have a jungle telegraph and relay messages back and forth. We keep in touch all across the country this way, although some of the news gets to be pretty old before it gets to us. But we did hear about Pete."

"From Patrice Demba?" Pete asked.

Lobo nodded. "Pat is with our group, but we lost contact a while back. Happens a lot, communications being what they are." Then, turning to Matt, he continued. "There's been a change of plan, Matt. The people we had assigned to you have been taken elsewhere. We have chosen another group for you."

"I shoah hope we ahn't gettin' any maw of these genteel types, Lobo. I've had just about enough of 'em. I don't mind sharin' my place with truly homeless people, you know that. But theah must be some really needy folk out theah who ahn't afraid of gettin' theah hands dihty with a little bit of wohk. We ah too old to take cah of all these people like they was payin' guests."

"This group is different, Matt. And Pete is part of the equation, so I hope he'll stick around for a while. I can't tell you any more, other than we'll be back with them by the end of the week, if all goes well. We need Pete's help with something he may be the only one who can do." He looked at Pete, waiting for a response.

"I don't know what to tell you. I'll be here certainly more than a few days longer. If whatever it is turns out to be is something I can do, I'll consider it. Satisfied?"

Lobo nodded.

Now the men joined Luce and Evie in the kitchen, where they got treated to as good a breakfast as they had probably seen since they were last at the farm. They started out before dawn, reluctantly leaving the warmth of the cabin. Their breaths trailed behind them in wisps that remained for a while, like contrails, in the frigid air.

It was still dark; the winter sun had barely tinged the horizon. Pete and Evie stood and watched as the far hills were slowly tipped in miserly pink. It would be a cold day. The people in the barn were not awake yet and would remain huddled under their blankets well into the day.

"Let's put something warmer on. I'd like to take a stroll around the farm. It's Sunday, after all, so we should be able to take some time off."

Evie nodded. She felt that she was beginning to recover from the loss of her family. She realized she had spent a lot of time sleeping lately, and felt guilty. She wasn't the only one who had suffered a loss. In fact, she was lucky, she thought, having Pete and his family around her and living in comfort.

Pete gave her a quick hug, looking forward to taking her around. With all the work to be done they hadn't had much time for each other, which he regretted. He knew where he wanted to take her: down the lane toward the paddock. He wanted to show her the view of the fields and the valley beyond that he had often called up in his mind when life in Washington got too complicated and stressful. Later on, he would tell her about the meeting, even though he was still not clear about what was going to come of it. What had they meant by him being "part of the equation," for instance?

CHAPTER 49

Sister Gemma stormed into Mother Anne's office.

"I'm getting out of here! I don't care where I'm going! I'm leaving, today, now…"

"Sister Gemma! Get a hold of yourself. You are forgetting your vow of silence!"

"Silence, you say? The Holy Father in there released me from it! He gave me permission to speak, so I will! That man is no Holy Father, take it from me!"

Sister Gemma had walked up to the desk, and now she slammed her fist down hard, setting pens and paper clips flying. Mother Anne picked up her Bible, whether for her own protection or to protect the book from harm, she couldn't have said.

"Sister Gemma, you must calm yourself. You have permission to speak. Please sit down. Here, have a glass of water."

"I don't want any of your water, and I am not going to calm down! That beast in there just attacked me! Look!"

Mother Anne suddenly noticed the state of Sister Gemma's robe, which dragged behind her, ripped. Also, Sister Gemma's blond hair was peeking out under her wimple, and the simple silver cross she always wore was missing.

"Why, Sister…" Mother Anne swished around the desk with unaccustomed speed, nearly tripping over the little needlepoint footstool by her chair. She led Sister Gemma by the hand over to the inglenook, where a small fire was burning.

"Let's sit down and you tell me everything that happened, Sister Gemma. I promise I will not interrupt, and you will not be punished for telling the truth."

A group of the sisters had gathered around the kitchen table, white-faced and anxious. What could have happened to Sister Gemma to make her fly into Mother's office in such a state, half undressed? And swearing and talking under her breath, when she was under vow? What monstrous event had taken place?

Ever since that man Birke died, they had sensed an ominous change in their secluded patient. Food was sent back to the kitchen with plates smashed; Sister Zita was complaining about the amount and state of the laundry. Who was that in there? They did not dare to discuss what they all guessed, for how could it possibly be true, especially now, after this shocking turnout? They sipped their tea, which had gone tepid.

Finally, Mother came out of her office. Her face was stern and she looked taller than usual. Her back was straight and she carried her head awfully high. She looked almost proud, they thought. She came over to the table and scanned their faces.

"Something very serious has happened here. We will not discuss it just now—I must speak to Father Theodore first. Meanwhile, Sister Gemma will need someone to care for her, as she has had a fright and is ill. You must not *speak* to her. That could be very harmful. She must have silence, and kindness, and lots of care. Sister Agatha, will you take the first turn? Sister Martha can relieve you later. We are expecting Father

Theodore, Father Ambrose, and a few others later. When they arrive, please show them directly to my office *without a word of what has happened here.* Is that understood?"

They all nodded, and Sister Agatha left her now cold cup of tea to follow Mother Anne to where Sister Gemma was resting.

CHAPTER 50

Declan saw them first.

"Julius! Who are all those people? Is that them, the ones Jack was talking about?"

Declan was sitting on a chair by the window, wrapped in a warm blanket. He was feeling much better now, but they were still careful with him and all looked after him. They put up with his usual mischief and teasing, brought him treats, and made sure he was warm and comfortable. Roofie sang for him, songs she made up that had no melody and might as well have been in Chinese for all anyone could understand of the lyrics. Dec seemed to enjoy them, though, and sometimes started laughing so hard that Julius got a little worried and had to ask Roofie to stop singing. Soon Dec might get spoiled, Julius thought, but he would let it go on a little longer.

Julius walked over to the window and looked out. He was not happy. He expected this would be the people who were going to move into town and be their neighbors. Everything would change now. He had come to enjoy his life with the children, the daily routines and tasks. The feeling of being responsible, and living up to it, of being trusted and loved, and loving in return. He sighed. It was selfish, he realized. The need must be great all over the country, if Jack was right. He didn't feel ready to face that reality. Yet they would have to accept these newcomers, whoever they were.

He bent down so that his head was next to Declan's and looked out. It was getting dark outside, and with the light from the fireplace reflecting in the window, it was hard to see. But Declan was right; there was a group of people out there, coming down the snowy hillside. Their dark mass stood out against the snow like a giant inkblot. *Why, there must be dozens of them.*

"Well, Dec, I guess that must be them. I better go see if we can offer them something to eat, what do you think? They'll be hungry, I'm sure."

"And cold, Julius. And their houses will be cold, too. Maybe we can give them some wood?" Declan looked at Julius with serious eyes.

"You bet, Dec. That's the spirit, all right. We'll share." Julius smiled. Declan looked relieved.

"Meggi, Aug, come and help me in the kitchen. We've got company!" Derk and Lans joined them, and helped get plates and silverware out, while Roofie did her best to be under foot.

"How many, Julius?" Lans asked.

"Oh, it looks like maybe twenty or thirty. Oops, watch out, Roofie, I don't want to step on you."

"But, Julius, we don't have that many plates!" Lans said.

"They'll have to take turns, then, and use bowls and mugs. Or else we'll go and raid the kitchen in the house next door. They had lots of dishes, remember? I think I'll make a pot of soup. That'll be quick and it's the only thing we can make lots of right now. Aug, we need water. Do we have some in the bucket in the mudroom? We'll have to bring in another bucket from the shed to thaw for the morning. Okay?"

Aug went through the living room and hallway to the mudroom, and just as he hefted the bucket, using both hands, there was a loud knock on the door. He put the bucket down. Should he get Julius?

"Who's there?" he asked timidly.

"It's me, Jack! That you, Aug? Open up. It's cold out here!"

Aug smiled and opened the door. Jack pushed it wide open, nearly turning the bucket over, and stepped inside, stomping his feet and clapping his snowy mittens together.

"Careful, don't spill the water! That's your supper," Aug said.

"That the best you can do? We're very hungry." Jack laughed and picked up the bucket.

Aug led the way to the kitchen, and by the time the whole group had entered, there wasn't even enough room for everyone to sit. Julius carried the big kettle into the living room and hung it on the hook over the fire, while Jack and a few of the newcomers went to get wood and laid in fires in the neighboring houses.

Aug looked around at the people. They hadn't seen strangers for months and it was fun to look at their faces and hear them talk. Suddenly he noticed something odd. They were all men. He walked over and whispered to Julius, who turned around, frowning slightly. Then he looked at Aug.

"Maybe their families will come later. Maybe they want to make everything ready before they bring the kids, and the mothers have to stay and take care of them until then," he said quietly. Aug nodded. But Julius was worried, too. Aug had been right. It seemed odd.

He had trusted Jack. But what did he really know about him? On the other hand, what could they possibly want with him or the children? There was certainly enough space here for them all.

CHAPTER 51

What remained of the great central river systems lay frozen, along with the new inland sea, giving the illusion of a country again united into one large and solid continent. The spring thaw was still in the future, the undreamed future. People slept like animals, lightly, just below the surface of awareness. They could not afford to dream, to get transported away from the dangers that might face them in the night. They were simply trying to survive the winter.

Every common cold was a battle, without medicine and sufficient food and often without heat. Any illness beyond a cold was now life-threatening. Food distribution had slowed to a trickle, and each region had to ration its reserves as best it could. Regional self-sufficiency had been a notion of the long ago past. Since then each area had developed a specialty of its own to export to other parts of the country. Now some lucky regions were overstocked with grains, while others were left with heaps of rotten vegetables, yet others with carcasses of spoiled and inedible meat. If the food processing industry had kept running by altering its processes, for instance using some of the ancient ways to preserve meat by salting and drying, they could have had enough food for years, especially considering the drastic decrease in population. However, in the aftermath of the disaster, the people—numbed by shock—had looked to the government to organize their salvation, and now it was too late.

A year ago there had been untold wealth and prosperity in their land; science and medicine had made them comfortable and safe, with the promise of long, healthy lives. Like well-mannered and contented children, they had come to depend on their government to rule every aspect of their lives. But when catastrophe struck, the leadership—the framework of their society—had been the first victim. And now what was left of it was in tatters, like remnants of a cobweb wafting in the wind.

CHAPTER 52

"It must be Friday," Ingrid said.

The Dogtowners had survived the worst of the storm. The wind had abated during the night, and Ingrid and Noah climbed out of the vault at dawn to take a look around. At first they had been unable to open the cover, which had become iced over during the night, and they had been gripped by a sense of panic. When they finally forced their way out, they saw a landscape totally unlike what they had left behind. The islands had frozen together and were covered with waist-high snow, which would be deeper in the clefts and gullies. From what they could see around the edges of the island, Ingrid guessed that the channel to the mainland would be completely frozen over.

"Do you think there's anything left of the supplies?" she asked.

Noah shook his head doubtfully. They stood close together, and Ingrid leaned toward him and put her head on his shoulder. Noah snuck his arm around her back to pull her closer, and they watched as a frigid white sun, like a disk of ice, rose out of the water.

They had slept huddled next to each other in the vault, with Ingrid trying to overcome her final fear of his closeness. Noah had covered them with an old woolen blanket, which gave them a modicum of privacy. Whispering, he told her of himself and of growing up on the island. Ingrid allowed him to go on and tell her of his life, something she had so far made excuses to avoid. She still felt she couldn't face learning all the little details about him—dreaded the intimacy, one step leading irrevocably to the next until the trap would shut again.

She had tried to keep her body from touching his, getting cramps in her back and legs as a result, and squirming uncomfortably. Noah whispered on. He had been married, he said, but his wife had left him years ago; she hadn't minded the money he was making, just the absence of her accustomed social life. Noah had always been a loner, liked to sail or go blueberry picking, and had never cared less about partying or going into the city for an evening. Ingrid began feeling drowsy and relaxed a little, letting her hip rest against his.

When Noah finally grew quiet, she haltingly began her own tale—reluctant at first, before the dam burst and words and memories flooded out of her and she told him of her life with Adam, trying to explain her mixed feelings over losing him. Trying to sort them out for herself, really. It seemed easier now, lying thigh to thigh with Noah, feeling warm and drowsy.

He reached across and rolled her up against him, and if they had been alone, she knew it might not have ended there. As it was, they both slept fitfully. Ingrid had gotten used to his presence and been grateful for the spiritual comfort it had given. Now, the closeness of his body had become a source of physical heat, as well.

A cold wind brought her back to reality. Noah bent down and scooped up some snow and squeezed it into a ball. He tossed it down the slope and it slid, pinging, hitting ledges and boulders like a marble in a pinball machine.

"I'll try to make it over to the compound later to check on things," he said.

They returned down into the bunker. The smell of humanity was getting strong to the point of being unpleasant, and they both gagged slightly. Rachel had recovered quite well, to Ingrid's amazement, and was trying to nurse the baby, who snuffled fussily. The gang of four was sleeping soundly in the corner they had staked out. The others were awake and in various states of trying to clean themselves and get a hot drink.

Ingrid and Noah shared a cup of tea, after which she and Granny checked on Rachel and the baby. Keeping Cricket dry had been a problem until Granny gave up her silk scarves, of which she had brought a miraculous number and which dried quickly.

"Are we moving back to the cellar holes?" Sammy wanted to know. He and Levi were brothers, Ingrid had learned, and more helpful and talkative than the other boys. No doubt being in this cramped space was becoming hard on the boys, and the eagerness to leave showed in their eyes.

"Soon. I'll take a walk over to check things out first," Noah said.

Merry stirred in his malodorous lair. "We're going with ya," he growled.

The rest of the gang started grunting and rolling over, a preamble to what would come next: complaints about the lack of space and food. *The sooner we move back, the better,* Ingrid thought.

Noah looked unhappy, but resigned himself quietly to taking them along. Luke also volunteered to come, knowing that Noah could use his help. It would make things easier on Ingrid and Rachel to have the gang out of the way.

As soon as everyone had finished their ablutions and had their rations of sustenance, Noah, Luke, and the gang took off. Ingrid gave Noah a quick peck on the cheek, which he returned by giving her a hot kiss square on the mouth, with an impish glint in his eye.

Rachel nodded appreciatively. "Aha," she said.

After Noah and the others left, Black Neil went on a cleaning rampage. He emptied the night bucket and returned it to the corner. They had used some of the drinking water to wash the baby's diapers, so he tended to melting snow next.

By noon everyone except Rachel and Cricket had been outside to get some fresh air, even though another snow flurry struck, creating a whiteout for nearly an hour. When Noah had not returned by mid afternoon, Ingrid began to fret. Finally Black Neil agreed to go and see what caused the delay.

"They're probably just digging out. I can imagine the scene over there," he said, trying to calm her fears. He bundled up and left, with the sun now receding toward the west and the mainland.

Ingrid went back down into the vault and released the baby from Rachel's grip, which was strong even though she was fast asleep. Little Cricket was contented and snoozing, but Ingrid rocked him nevertheless, a process that soothed her and made her forget her worry. It was therefore an even greater shock when Black Neil came down the ladder and sat down next to her, looking grave.

"Ingrid, I have some very bad news," he said. She thought she knew even before he said it what the news would be.

"Noah," she said, trying not to breathe, or scream.

Black Neil shook his head. "No, Luke. I don't know what happened, Ingrid. I found him on the ice. He might have fallen and hit his head, or..." He did not continue.

"And Noah and the others?"

"I couldn't find Noah. From what I could tell, he'd been working on our cellar hole then gone over to see how Luke was doing. From there I followed his footprints over to the gang of four's place. There were too many footprints to deal with after that, and I don't know what happened. Noah and the gang are all missing. The skiff, too. I don't know if the gang took it, or if it disappeared in the storm. Same with the supplies. Nothing's left. Noah's dory is still there, jammed between the rocks. Cracked. Would be useless in the water. The whole compound is a disaster. We would not have survived if we had stayed there."

Small consolation, now. Ingrid felt a black hollow opening up inside her. "Oh, Luke. Dear Luke," she moaned. "And please, God, don't let anything have happened to Noah."

Black Neil put a hand on her shoulder firmly. She nodded. She could not afford to break down now. They must act fast, or they would all perish. She knew what they must do, what they should have done in the first place. Leave the island.

CHAPTER 53

When Father Ambrose and Father Theodore entered, followed by a phalanx of black-robed clergy, a hush fell over the Great Room. The Little Sisters busied themselves with carrying dishes to the kitchen and wiping the table, lining up the rows of books on the shelves, and a general straightening of the furniture. Father Ambrose, used to receiving a friendlier greeting from the sisters, stood still for a moment and observed them. Father Theodore made an effort at a smile, trying to look patient and kindly. A sharp crease down each cheek served to give him a look of determination and fortitude, and perhaps a touch of something else, not cruelty exactly, but something close to it—intolerance, impatience with human weakness.

Cardinal Theodore Helmsman from St. Louis had always insisted on being addressed simply as Father Theodore. He wanted to appear modest and humble, and expended a lot of thought and effort on this. Unlike Fidelis, a good and kind man only suffering from an unexpected little vanity with his carefully chosen wardrobe, Father Theodore wore the plainest of garb. He rarely donned the scarlet zucchetto, the cardinal's skullcap, preferring to use the black one of the common priest. Only for liturgical celebrations or other official functions would he wear the required vestments of a cardinal bishop. He had a habit, when he was alone, of rubbing at the edges of his sleeves to make them slightly frayed, and would never wear anything that was in any way adorned or decorated. He would not be transported in a limousine or other fancy vehicle, preferring to be driven by a lowly staff member in a rented PTV.

Finally Father Ambrose nodded to Father Theodore, and they proceeded to Mother Anne's office. Once the door had shut behind them, with that marvelous *clunk* of the solid, heavy oak, the sisters sat down again, looking anxiously at each other.

After a short while, Mother Anne appeared in the doorway, asking that tea be brought. Sister Agatha got up and hurried to the kitchen to prepare it.

The sister returned quickly with a tray that held their finest china cups and a teapot covered with a brocade cozy. She stood poised to knock on the door, but her knuckles stopped in midair. She could hear the voice of Mother Anne, just barely, through the thick door, and remained frozen to the spot, lowering her raised hand to help support the tray. She leaned forward a fraction. Mother's voice sounded distraught.

"But, Father Theodore..."

"Mother Anne, I know this must be difficult for you. But what you tell us is unthinkable. The Holy Father is surely blameless. And Sister Gemma has a long history, if memory serves, of trouble. 'Rebellious,' I remember you called her. 'Refuses to obey, uses improper language.' You thought her vow of silence would help. Obviously it did not. Perhaps it added to her feeling of repression and her spiritedness took other forms. And then she broke her vow, did she not? She spoke to you herself, and told these terrible lies..."

"But, Father Theodore, the Holy Father himself gave her permission to speak..."

"If that is true, he did it out of kindness and compassion, no doubt. And look how Sister Gemma repaid him! You must understand we cannot take *her* word for what happened against that of our Holy Father! That *she* seduced *him* is quite without a doubt. She must be restrained, made to repent, and removed from here, so that she does not spread this contagion. This must all remain between us, despite her grave sin against the Holy Father. A scandal in the Church is unthinkable. As for Sister Gemma, I have a place that will serve…"

Sister Agatha suddenly sprang into action, knocked on the door, and entered Mother Anne's office without waiting for permission. She came back out a moment later and shut the door gently behind her before hastily giving a wave to the sisters to follow her to the kitchen. She related what she had heard.

"I know the place Father Theodore is talking about. Sister Gemma must not be sent there. It's worse than a prison, and she'd never see the light of day again. We have to get her out of here, and not waste a moment doing it. Sister Luke, please get some clothes from the chest in the ward, whatever you think she might need. Just stuff them into a pillowcase so it looks like a pillow. Then bring it to Sister Gemma's room. Sister Zita, come with me, we will run ahead and prepare Sister Gemma. Sister Martha, you stay here. If they come out, you must delay them. As soon as they open the door, tell Reverend Mother that they all must go out to the ward on some emergency. Father Ambrose will respond, I know him. Just make something up while you wait! Come, Sister Zita!"

Sister Zita and Sister Agatha ran down the hall toward the room where Mother Anne had left Sister Gemma, and where embers from a small fire were still glowing. Sister Martha remained seated in the Great Room, paralyzed by anxiety, waiting for the Reverend Mother's door to swing open. She could think of nothing to say; no plan would form in her mind.

When Father Ambrose's bony hand finally opened the door, and Mother Anne and the priests emerged, Sister Martha rushed forward and grasped Mother Anne's hands.

"Reverend Mother, please come to the ward! They need you! There is a problem in the private room, and since Sister Gemma isn't here…" She didn't need to continue. Mother Anne and her companions were already rushing off toward the ward.

Just as Mother Anne, Father Ambrose and Father Theodore were running across the muddy yard, Sister Gemma was disappearing down the country lane on the other side of the main house. Sister Agatha followed her to the gate, where she remained, watching Sister Gemma disappear into the mist. Then she quickly ran back into the house, where she told the sisters to disperse and stay out of sight.

Sister Agatha went out to the chapel and immersed herself in prayer. She kneeled on the cold stone floor in front of the altar, wondering how long she would need to pray to make up for her deceit.

While her spirit took flight into the chilly, dark corners of the chapel, Father Ambrose and Father Theodore faced a challenge of their own after Mother Anne had graciously left them and their retinue alone to visit the Holy Father, so that they might speak with him in privacy.

CHAPTER 54

Jack and Julius trudged through the snow up to the school. Jack wanted to see where the supplies of food and water were stored. He had returned to New Hope with a plan, and now he faced the task of putting it into action. He sensed it was not going to be easy.

It was too cold to talk outside, so he waited. A brittle layer of ice coated the snow, and their boots sent sharp little ice flakes tinkling down the slope as they made their way up toward the school. The moon shimmered through the frost-covered trees, lighting their way. They never used flashlights unless they had to. Conserving had become second nature. As they went inside, however, Jack pulled a torch out of his backpack to light their way. Julius pointed out the various areas where supplies were stored. He knew they would lose some due to the cold; in fact, they had already dumped many burst containers. The cafeteria had turned into a walk-in freezer, he thought. They stopped at the back door before returning to the entrance the way they had come.

"It's a beautiful night," Jack said. Julius nodded. "Julius, we need your help," Jack continued, deciding it was time to bite the bullet. "We are looking for people like you, resourceful, practical. We have a project going that we would like you to join. It means your leaving this place, though, and coming with us." He studied Julius for his reaction.

Julius shook his head. "Jack, you know I can't leave. The kids, they need me. They don't have anybody else. Besides, you know my predicament. How can I help you when I can't even help myself?"

"We'll take care of the kids. I brought a lot of very good people with me tonight. Some of them will come with us, and some will stay here with the kids. I knew you would worry about them. Also, another group is coming tomorrow, women and children. Your kids won't suffer, I promise. We need you, Julius."

"Sorry, Jack, no go. I won't leave these kids. They've already lost everything once. I can do more good here than anywhere else, of that I'm sure," Julius said with finality and started toward the door.

Jack had expected something like this, and sighed. "Then how about if the kids come along?" he asked.

"Are you crazy? They'd freeze to death out there. Where are you going, anyway?"

"Too far to walk, Julius. We've got transportation this time. The kids would be perfectly safe, and the place we're going to is no worse than this. Maybe better, really. They've got plenty of food and beds, and better heating than you have here."

Julius did not answer. He opened the door and stepped outside. The moon was going down, and they started down the hill into the approaching darkness. Julius knew his way in the dark. Jack stumbled along blindly behind him, worrying about the outcome of his plan.

When they got near the house, Julius turned toward him. "Okay, Jack. If what you say is on the level, and my kids will be safe, we'll come with you. But I won't leave them stranded somewhere. Wherever I go, they go. Deal? When do we have to leave?"

Jack answered urgently, while hurrying toward the house before Julius could change his mind. "Tonight. Vehicles are waiting up on the main road. Take as little as possible—just have the kids dress warm. You know, have them put on all the clothes they want to bring along so they don't have anything to carry, otherwise there won't be enough room. I hadn't figured on bringing the kids, you know."

Jack was relieved at the turn of events, but anxious at the same time. He had set something in motion that was taking on a life of its own.

He hoped everything would be accepted at the other end—and that he hadn't figured wrong.

CHAPTER 55

Fidelis was standing with his back to them as they entered. He turned around at the sound of the door.

Birke had procured a number of vestments for the pope of the simple but refined kind he preferred, but today Fidelis was wearing the white suit of his own design that he had worn when he fled Camp David. Over his shoulders he had draped a white stole decorated with garlands of brilliant red flowers. Sister Gemma had spent a month embroidering it for him when he first arrived here. His head was bare, and the white hair lay matted against his scalp. He lifted his arms in a reflex greeting, which made him lose his balance and topple sideways into a chair. Father Ambrose rushed forward to help.

"Are you ill, Holy Father?" he asked anxiously.

Fidelis looked at him, confused, and mumbled incoherently. Father Theodore, watching with narrowed eyes, suddenly understood clearly what was going on, what had been going on all along with Birke in command. Birke had insisted that Pope Fidelis was too frail to meet with any large assembly—except, of course, for prayer or a brief speech—and all matters had been handled via Birke, who presumably had the pope's full attention behind closed doors. Well, Birke was gone now, and somehow they had to carry on.

The Pope's current state could be explained away, but only *if necessary*—*if* word somehow got out about Sister Gemma's disgraceful and shocking behavior, for instance, a behavior which Father Theodore privately began to doubt at this very moment. He wondered how much the other sisters knew. Sister Gemma had to be removed—now even more urgently. She must have a great deal to say that she had never been able to divulge while she was under a vow of silence. And the Church must not be tainted by even so much as a rumor.

The pedophilia scandal earlier in the century had implicated priests and the bishops who protected them; this one would implicate the pope himself. The pope, a fornicator! If they were to take over leadership, the Catholic Church could not afford a scandal, especially one of Borgia-like proportions.

Father Theodore had to work swiftly. He would pick up where Birke had left off, only his agenda would be different. Unlike Birke's, Father Theodore's ambitions were not purely political. He had been on the short list with Father Sheedy, and had felt cheated when this *political opportunist,* as he had thought of Sheedy at the time, had made pope. Well, Birke and Fidelis had both taught him their lessons. Now, he would apply what he had learned.

"Holy Father, let us pray," he said and fell to his knees.

Father Ambrose and the others followed his example immediately and together they prayed, led by Fidelis, his voice as loud and clear as a child's.

CHAPTER 56

The Dogtowners waited for dead low tide before starting out across the ice. That way they did not have to be afraid of falling through at the edge, where the ice was slushy and thin at high tide. Instead, they had to maneuver across great blocks of ice, which posed a different problem when they tried to bring out the dory that was loaded to the gills with their belongings.

They were like explorers trying to cross the North Pole, Ingrid thought, as they were scaling the tall ice blocks that had been pushed up all along the shore. But they managed, and once they got the boat over the last hump, they loaded Rachel and the baby into it as well before pulling it along behind them like a sled. On the other side of the great strait lay the mainland. Without vegetation or houses, the prospect was of a vast, blinding, sloping wilderness, snow-covered and unrecognizable. One hillock after another, blanketed in white.

Ingrid had been shocked at the state of their cellar home. The roof had blown off, as she had predicted, and whatever hadn't been sucked out by the gale winds was frozen down by ice too hard to hack through. Nothing to do but leave everything behind. The supply hideout had been ransacked, assuming there had been anything to find. Once they left the compound, Ingrid did not look back. This time she had no wish to return. Ever.

Black Neil had walked up to the high point and looked down to where the shacks had been. They were gone, and he had not been able to see any movement. Ingrid, Rachel and Cricket, Black Neil, Granny, and the boys were the only survivors. Where was Noah? Was his body hidden somewhere in a crevasse of snow and ice? Was he dead, too??

She had hurried along the icy slope, looking for him. Then she had slipped and fallen between two large boulders, and pulling herself up she had noticed something on the lower edge of one of the rocks. Bending down to see better she saw... letters. There were *letters* carved into the rock. The rock was upside down, but she was able to read part of it: *"Never try..."* She remembered the rest. NEVER TRY/NEVER WIN. It was one of Babson's rocks. Ingrid knew what it meant: she had to try to get the boys to safety.

As they made their way across the strait, Ingrid thought of Luke and the boys, and their sad arrival. Luke and his wife had given their lives for the little rag-tag band that now trudged behind her across the ice, some still sniveling and crying at the loss of a man who had become like a father to them. Ingrid bent and patted Cerbie, who was running around trying to herd them all. He was obviously glad to be out and roaming around again.

When Ingrid surreptitiously looked around for Luke's body, Black Neil moved closer to her, adjusting his rope so he would still be effective in pulling the dory.

"Luke's gone, Ingrid. Buried at sea, like a sailor." He didn't go into an explanation.

After determining that Luke was dead, he had gone up and cut a piece out of the sail Noah had used to cover the wood, and which had been frozen to the ground except for a piece that had been flapping in the wind. He had wrapped the body and a large boulder in it, turning it into the shroud Noah had adamantly denied that it was, and pushed the body as close to the open water as he dared to go. Then he had given it a hard shove. The open water was black; the ice near the edge was pale green and slushy and gave way as the body neared it it, and Luke had slid into the water without so much as a splash,

When they were a little more than halfway across the channel, they heard a loud crack, as from thunder or rifle fire. They looked around, terrified. Even Cerberus started whining. Were they under attack, or was the ice breaking up? Ingrid couldn't help laughing.

"It's nothing to be afraid of, kids. We used to go skating on the lakes in Sweden when I was a kid and sometimes you'd be right out in the middle and the ice would start booming and cracking. It's just expanding and contracting. It's okay…it won't open up," she said, looking reassuringly at the boys and Granny, who seemed the most anxious.

They made it safely across and continued up the Wingaersheek River. They ate on the move, wanting to get as far inland as possible before dark. As they got away from the ocean, the river ice got thicker, and they felt more confident. The going was slower than Ingrid had hoped. She remembered her day trips up the river in the dory. On foot, and dragging the dory behind them, it was taking an eternity. It was time to start thinking about leaving the dory behind. That meant they all had to carry the supplies they would need to survive.

Close to nightfall, they saw a shack up along the bank and a column of rising smoke. The shack was roughly patched together out of whatever had been at hand, pieces of board and old blankets, it looked like. Black Neil held up a hand for silence and signaled for them to stop. He motioned for everyone to pull over behind an outcropping of snow-covered boulders while he went ahead to check. Before leaving, he gave Ingrid a long look, which she had interpreted a thousand ways before he made his way back.

"The place is deserted. Whoever was there left their campfire not too long ago. They didn't leave anything else behind, so we don't know if they plan to return. Could be the gang, of course. Then again, it could be anybody. We'll have to take a chance. It's getting dark." He stood waiting, pounding his hands together to keep the circulation going.

They were all willing to try, exhausted and cold and drawn to the campfire. Cricket was crying weakly, and Ingrid worried about him and Rachel.

They crept toward the shack quietly, and when they reached it and found no one around, Ingrid quickly added some of their precious driftwood to the fire to keep it from going out. Black Neil melted snow and they had luxurious amounts of broth and tea; after a while, their frozen limbs began to thaw.

The islanders had come ashore, and while they were all relieved to have escaped, they could not imagine what awaited them now. Where could they possibly go? Ingrid had a plan, which she now shared with Black Neil.

CHAPTER 57

The drone of the vehicles quickly put the children of New Hope to sleep. Aug had looked at the army transport vans, big-eyed, impressed. "Wow, AT-17s...are we going in them?"

Jack had nodded, hustling them all inside quickly before the heat dissipated. The armored vans were dark green, and both of them had the Red Cross emblem on the sides and roof. They were designed to be multi-fuel capable and were currently running on the government supply of gazene, a mixture of petroleum and biofuel. The military were using up all the old fuels they could lay their hands on, now, saving the highest grade for aircraft. The stockpiled fuel cells for ground transportation were reserved, kept at strategic locations, for more important eventualities.

They drove without stopping through the night and into dawn. Abandoned vehicles, under humps of snow, still littered the side of the highway, the electric recharge depots abandoned. The world was like the garden of Sleeping Beauty, thought Julius, who, because of the children, had been steeped in fairy tales of late. Everything had stopped. Would the prince ever turn up? And where was Sleeping Beauty herself? Was it Meggi, sleeping in his lap? He bent his head down and gave her a peck on the cheek. She didn't wake up. No, it wasn't Meggi. Or else, *he* wasn't the prince.

Except for brief stops to let the children relieve themselves among groves of snow-laden trees, they continued through most of the day. They nibbled from the bag of snacks Julius had brought. In the middle of the afternoon, the first van driver stopped. The road in front of them was totally blocked. Probably by vehicles—it was hard to judge from the shape of the mountain of snow. There was no way to detour around it, the roadsides were too thickly forested.

After a brief conference with the second driver, they decided they had to retrace their steps. They checked the maps and selected an alternate route. By evening they were entering a mountainous region, and the children covered their ears, feeling the change of pressure.

"Ouch, we need some chewing gum," Aug said. There was none, but Julius said chewing on a cookie was just as good, or pinching your nose while swallowing. The children decided the cookie worked better and dipped into the bag for more. Julius indulged them, and soon they were sated and fell asleep, one by one.

Jack was in the first van with the men he had picked to come along, and Julius and the children were the only passengers in the second van. The driver sat in the front cab, separated from them by a metal wall with a bulletproof window. Julius finally joined the children and nodded off, sleeping fitfully. In moments of semi-awareness, he worried. Had he made a terrible mistake? What if they forced him to join their roaming gang? Then he would still be leaving the children, and in a new, strange place. No, he would never agree to it. Satisfied with this decision, he fell asleep again.

***

Julius woke up when jostled by the two boys sitting next to him. Meggi nearly bounced off his lap onto Roofie and Lans, who were sleeping in a bundle on the floor. He put Meggi down next to them and crawled forward to look through the window. Dawn had come and gone and an early morning mist was rising from the snow, but he could see rough terrain rising ahead of them. They were going up a steep mountain road.

When they reached the top, the road wound down the other side toward a set of buildings. They turned into the yard and waited. The children woke up and rubbed their eyes. Through the window, Julius saw Jack get out and go inside one of the buildings. After a moment he came back out and waved to the drivers to cut the engines. They had arrived. They all piled out of the vans, the men and the children, and started moving toward the building where Jack stood waiting, hurrying them along.

Inside, everyone was awake. Evie was in the kitchen, helping Matt and Luce get some breakfast together. Pete sat in a dark corner of the living room, observing the newcomers. The children were a surprise—he hadn't expected them, and such a large number of men. But maybe some of them would continue on from here.

Looking over the faces of the men, Pete did not understand what his assignment might be. A bunch of bearded young guardsmen, and another bearded man, too old to be in the guard, unless he was an officer. But, no, he didn't have the look. Jack pointed them toward the kitchen, and, once they had all gone through, he joined Pete.

"Well?" Jack said, studying Pete's face closely..

"Well, what?" Pete replied.

Jack shook his head in disappointment. He had hoped Pete would see what he had. Maybe it was too dark in here. Maybe it was the beard. Maybe if he heard the voice.

"Come on. I need some coffee, bad. We'll talk later," he said, trying to make light of it.

They joined the others in the kitchen and stood along the wall, since every seat had been taken. Pete watched the children voraciously dig into the mounds of scrambled eggs and strips of smoked meat. The bearded old man watched over them like a mother hen, pouring them drinks and passing them more food. He bent over the little girl with the blond hair, and she whispered something to him. He laughed, a soft, rumbling laugh.

Pete swore softly under his breath and looked over at Jack. Jack nodded. His face did not betray the jubilation he felt. He motioned to Pete to come with him.

They went into the small study behind the living room, next to Pete's bedroom, where they lit the hurricane lamp and sat down by the worktable.

"Where'd you find him? And what the heck is he doing, camping out with a bunch of kids?" Pete asked. Frustration and disbelief showed in the way he hissed between clenched teeth.

"Pete, he doesn't know who he is. He's got amnesia. Best I can figure, he survived the plane crash somehow. No doubt with a serious concussion, judging from the cuts and scars on his head. How he found his way to where I ran into him, God knows."

Pete shook his head. The succession of events ran through his mind, culminating in this unbelievable and surreal meeting with the president. How could they possibly resolve this?

"This is incredible. What next? I'm no psychiatrist, but you can't confront an amnesiac with who he is, right? So, how do we wake him up? Maybe if we give him a shave and a haircut and put him in front of a mirror? If we can't bring him back, he's no better than Sheedy, who hasn't spoken in front of an audience except to say a prayer. Even then, they have to lead him away afterwards, I hear. We don't need *another* lunatic to take control."

He shook his head again. "I have an idea. I'll have Evie offer to do some barbering. Albion was real fond of Evie. Maybe he'll recognize her. Her voice, at least. She looks different from the way she used to, but, then, we all do."

When they returned to the kitchen, Luce had already tucked all the children into bed, and Matt was busy piling blankets and cushions around the floor of the cabin for the men to sleep on. Julius was bedded down on the couch. Three of the smallest children had crept over and were now sleeping draped across him like a lumpy quilt. The long journey, with the constant worrying about the children, had taken its toll, and Julius was fast asleep and snoring, open-mouthed.

Pete walked over and looked at him closely. No question in his mind now, even though the man had lost a lot of weight and aged considerably. But with the trauma he must have gone through, how safe would it be to pull him out of it? Then Pete remembered Ariana. *Oh, my God,* he thought, *Evie was right. We should have made Ariana come with us. How can we find her now? If she's even alive. So many have died. And with her bouts of depression. Well, one thing at a time. But we can't mention her unless we know for sure that she's alive. I must warn Evie.*

CHAPTER 58

"We have an opportunity, my dear brothers, to return our people to a simpler time. To a life of serving Christ, a life where the law of the Lord is the law of the land. Our people have been shown that all the money and excess materials they had gathered cannot stay them now in the face of calamity. But we have no less than the people did who started this country over four hundred years ago. And we have no less than Jesus Christ did, over two thousand years ago. We will begin here, today, and we will go afield and teach the people to start over. We will seek out those who are pure in their goodness, and make them our new leaders. We will shun the cities, which are like Sodom and Gomorrah, where temptation to greed and evil lurks. We will go back to the land, and we will forswear all the technology and materialism that brought us to the brink of annihilation."

Father Theodore paused, taking a sip of water from the small, chipped cup he kept on the pulpit. The church was filled with clergy gathered from near and far, and from all branches of religion. He felt generous in this inclusion of the others since it was obvious to him that the Vatican could make it on its own. But there was an enormous amount to be done, and this way they would all share the burden. Anyway, it was only an illusion, a sleight of hand. He had other plans for *later*.

In fact, he had been laying the groundwork for years, and now he would let fate—*no, God's own dramatic gesture*—help him play his hand. For the moment, he would simply see to it that there was a hierarchy, and that the Vatican remained the dominating force. Eventually, all citizens would be brought under one Church; it was time for the Jews and the Muslims and all the other little sideshows to relinquish their hopes for equal but separate status and join the "mainstream"—time, in other words, for a *State Church.*

Unity was imperative. This was the United States, not the Middle East, Ireland, Asia, or any other part of the world perennially divided and torn apart by religious strife. Pope Fidelis would continue on as the titular head, for now. The pope was still living with the Little Sisters of the Assumption, but in a securely locked room in a wing of the main house, where he was tended to by the Reverend Mother herself and two elderly sisters. *No more young beauties for the old goat,* Father Theodore thought. But he needed to keep Fidelis alive until he could maneuver himself into a position of such strength that he would be invincible.

It was the only logical solution. And it was perfectly simple, really. The elected government was no more. Communications, utilities, and the media all were still in utter disarray. The military was a headless force without the Pentagon. The crumbled cities were abandoned, the countryside homes overcrowded and under constant threat from roving gangs of hoodlums. Evil lurked everywhere. The only nationwide infrastructure left intact was the Church. It was in the churches all over the country that the future was being debated, and where it would be decided.

Local churches had picked up the slack in every area of human need: education, health, food distribution. They had devised a postal system that relayed mail from parish to parish, a modern-day Pony Express. They had taken on crime and punishment, providing both judge and jury. As soon as it became evident that schools would not be reopened, conscientious people in small pocket areas had begun home-schooling their children. The Church had recognized the need—indeed, the opportunity—for restarting education, and quickly begun to arrange for elementary school to be taught in all areas of the country. Thus, all schools were now parochial, and vouchers were as obsolete as World War II ration cards.

The curriculum included religion, of course. Each school day started with prayer. Morals and ethics were what the children needed, what the country needed, and the school children learned through Bible study and rote indoctrination of moral principles. School was taught in spare rooms on church property, Masonic and other brotherhood halls, even abandoned school buildings, if they could be made safe and comfortable. The nunny-bunnies, as the teaching nuns had been nicknamed a century ago, were back in business. And without access to books, the Bible would be their Reader.

The Church had, of course, taken on health care. Hospitals had become mausoleums filled with the remnants of technology: advanced scientific appliances, diagnostic equipment, laser and radiation labs, robotic surgeries—all now useless without sufficient power and skilled labor. Churches opened medical clinics, often in the rectory or some unused function hall, for the most primary medical needs only. They could handle the setting of bones, delivery of babies, and providing hospice care. Cancer, heart disease, and other grave illnesses had to go untreated. It was all according to God's plan.

Under Father Theodore's astute and watchful eye, the Church developed a bartering system between area communities. For now, food was the main trade. Eventually, he hoped, the system would cover the whole country, resulting in waves of goods being traded and giving each area a more balanced availability of products. The Little Sisters already had quite a larder, but it was not to be wasted on generals or other officials who fancied themselves important. Such people had to be made to understand that the clergy itself was living in poverty. Their food supplies were for the sick and the poor, and all the work the Church was doing came out of its reserves of Goodness and Justice.

Crime was rampant. For many, it was simply a way to survive. It was a sensitive issue, and one where religious ethics and morality came up against constitutional law. A case could be made, temporarily, for the special circumstance of a national emergency, but it was still a matter that caused great debate. Rifts of serious magnitude could open up unless it was handled properly and with authority. Father Theodore knew he was capable of the kind of authority that would be needed. *There's a dearth of leadership left in the country, and the people will want to be led by someone they trust, someone above reproach. Someone like me.*

Father Theodore looked out over his audience. They were hanging on his every word, he thought, just waiting for him to guide them, lead them, and save them. They did not know—any more than he did—that his heart had long since turned to stone and the sin of pride had altered his conscience so that truth had become a malleable thing, and could be hidden or exposed according to what he determined was expedient.

CHAPTER 59

As soon as dusk began to fall, the Dogtown settlers—who were now becoming inlanders—started looking for shelter for the night. They were far away from the no-man's land now, and the hillsides were forested. They had been on the move for nearly three weeks, and in a day or two they would run out of supplies. But they ate full rations at every meal, trying to remain optimistic. It was better to eat and stay healthy than to starve themselves slowly, they reasoned.

They had to find a safe place to spend the night. Luck was with them again. Cerberus started dancing and yipping, and Black Neil went to investigate. Cerbie had found a well-trampled path in the snow, which led to a lean-to that had obviously been used by other passing travelers. Someone had even generously left a candle and a few scrawny logs inside. They piled in and huddled together for warmth, as they had done every night. At first they were too tired to think about food. Black Neil set a fire going outside, as close to the opening as he dared. The flames licked the walls of the hut, but the wood was frozen and only hissed as the ice slowly thawed. The fir branches that formed the roof were covered with heavy snow, which began to steam and drip as the heat rose. Once the group had rested and thawed a bit, they began to sense their hunger pains and got up.

"We're down to the last of the dried fish, folks. Tomorrow we have to find food. I figure we have another week or so until we get to Bennington. Then, if my house still stands, we'll have shelter. Can we make it?" Ingrid looked around at the weathered faces encircling the fire.

Heads nodded, but not enthusiastically. Granny was exhausted. Even Ingrid and Black Neil were tired. Rachel and the baby were miraculously doing well, the baby thriving and Rachel looking healthy—getting extra rations had certainly helped. The boys were boys and could normally have gone on forever, but sadness and hopelessness had begun to take a toll on them, and Ingrid could feel a mounting rebellion against this eternal march.

After they left the no-man's land, they had continued along the snow-covered highway. Ingrid hoped that things would become more civilized as they moved west. So far, whenever they had tried to enter a small town along the way, they had been met by gun-toting militia who hadn't even bothered to listen to their requests for food. Turned away, the group had continued their march.

In the morning they moved along again, each in private thought. Ingrid had given up hope of ever seeing Noah again. She tried not to think of what might have happened to him, but the grim possibilities presented themselves in images before her, over and over. She tried to shake them off, grunting and stomping her feet angrily.

"Still thinking of Noah?" Granny asked.

"Trying not to, Granny," Ingrid said.

"We all miss him. He's probably fine, you know."

"I don't know, Granny. That's just it. It's the not knowing. If I knew, one way or the other, I could deal with it." She thought of Adam then. *Adam and Noah. They're both dead. And so will we be if we can't get hold of some food. Bennington is still a long way off. Without new supplies, we'll never make it there. What a stupid idea. And now I'm responsible for the lives of all these people.*

Cricket, who was well bundled into a makeshift little hammock that hung in a sling around Rachel's neck, started to cry, and his mother opened her coat and nursed him as they walked. Soon they would have to stop and heat water for broth. The last of Rachel's tealeaves were gone and she, especially—who was nursing—had to be careful not to get dehydrated. Suddenly, Levi sat down in the snow beside the path.

"What's the matter Levi?" Ingrid asked, nearly bumping into the other boys, who had stopped short.

"I'm tired of walking. Why can't we stay where we are? Why do we have to walk so far?" He threw his pack down beside him. "I miss Luke. Why did he have to go and die? Why does everybody have to die? Are we going to die, too?"

Sammy sat down beside Levi, and one by one the other boys joined them. The revolt had begun. Ingrid looked at Granny, who had lagged behind all day. Would she agree with the boys? Black Neil had put down his pack, taking the opportunity to rest. Rachel took Cricket from her breast and put the baby's thumb in his mouth instead. She was stricken with guilt and remorse. The boys had just begun to accept her as yet another surrogate mother when Cricket was born. Since then, she had been too preoccupied with the baby to pay much attention to them, and hadn't noticed that they were floundering. How could she have missed it, especially after Luke's death? She stepped forward and sat down in the snow next to Levi.

"Boy, I'm tired, too," she said. She put her arm around Levi briefly and squeezed his shoulder. "You know, if you boys weren't here, we would never have gotten this far. I appreciate you helping me carry my stuff. I bet Granny could use some extra help, too. You think you could divide some of her things between you? And I was wondering...do you remember how you sang for me while Cricket was being born? That was a great help. It almost made me forget about the pain. Do you think that maybe you could sing while we march? It would make time pass faster. We don't really have that far to go, and we are a lot better off than if we had stayed on the island. If we all pull together, we can make it. What do you say?" She reached over and patted Sammy's shoulder.

The boys got up, and Rachel held out her arms for them to help pull her up. Cricket, who had just nodded off, opened his eyes at the jolt. He looked up to find his mother in her usual place and, satisfied, went right back to sleep.

Sammy and Levi jostled some of their friends a bit, laughing, feeling better after Rachel's encouragement. Troy and Jamo, the two oldest boys, joined them in the lead. It was always hard to start walking again after a rest, and they trudged along stiffly at first, but soon they were off at a gallop.

"Hey, boys, us old people can't keep up with you...wait up!" Rachel called to them.

As they reached the top of an incline, a sign appeared: Greenfield, 5 miles. The boys cheered. They were getting close to the home stretch. Another sixty miles and they'd be in Bennington.

Sixty miles. But those are sixty miles through the mountains. And we are still in the grip of winter, Ingrid thought. She let them have their moment of joy, though.

Sammy started to sing "One More River to Cross," and everyone except Ingrid joined in.

*"Old Noah he built himself an ark,
There's one more river to cross…"*
Ingrid's throat tightened at the memory of Noah.
*"Chickens and turkeys and pigs,
There's one more river to cross…"*

CHAPTER 60

Amaral was studying some of the latest MILSTAR images. Wheaton had brought them earlier in the day, and later they were to helo over together to meet with Sheedy's new "aide," Father Theodore.

Birke was bad enough, but at least he was a pol, and you could talk to the man. I don't trust the religious. They have an agenda, I know it—I just can't figure out exactly what it is, he thought.

Amaral turned back to the image. The MILSTAR ground equipment had suffered serious damage in the Camp David attack, but being a relatively simple system, it had been promptly repaired and had proved to be of some use in providing at least rudimentary information.

If I had looked at this without knowing, I would have thought it showed the last Ice Age, Amaral thought. Snow capped the top half of the earth's landmasses, extending far down over the continents. Due to this voluminous white blanket, it was hard to distinguish the shorelines on the northern hemisphere. He took a deep breath and studied the other continents, paying special attention to Europe, Asia, and northern Africa. New Palestine, fought for so bitterly, was but a sliver of land. Were Arabs and Jews still cohabiting Jerusalem, which had nearly been turned to rubble before the peace agreement? The agreement had in the end been pushed for and brokered largely by other Arab states that had advanced in worldliness and greed, and lost the flame and desire for *jihad*.

Amaral still had a hard time adjusting to the new continental outlines. *At least we don't seem to be under threat from other nations— yet,* he thought. *But what do we really know? And what if this is actually the beginning of a new Ice Age?* He shuddered at the thought, even sitting right beside a blazing fire. He had yet to locate someone with sufficient credibility to give him an expert prognosis. He had listened to excitable doomsayers and serious scientists with grave voices, who had offered a wide range of prospects, none of them cheerful.

They had taken over a farm outside Thurmont, initially to be near Camp David. Now it didn't seem to matter what they were near. There was no central government—they were the closest thing to it. Thurmont was at least an area known to them all, and the familiarity of the Catoctin Mountains lent a semblance of comfort and security.

Wheaton returned a few hours later and they proceeded to the helo pad. The trip to Sheedy's "headquarters" in Connecticut would take an hour or so, and Amaral hoped the nuns would put on a good dinner and give them a heated room. The sisters tended to be a bit frugal, and he had dressed warmly, just in case.

When they arrived, Father Theodore was waiting for them in the small room set aside for their meetings. A few slim twigs glowed in the fireplace. Father Theodore sat at the desk, wearing his usual worn and frayed cassock. He had on a sweater underneath, a fact he tried to hide by keeping his hands on his lap to keep the woolen sleeves from showing. However, the extra bulk gave him away and Amaral, behind Wheaton's back, sniffed his contempt.

Wheaton put the folder on the desk, and Father Theodore grasped it and slid it onto his lap. He nodded for them to take a seat, and they pulled two stiff-backed chairs up to the desk. Mother Anne walked in with a tray of tea and three very small sandwiches— thinly sliced bread with a paper-thin slice of cheese and no spread. Amaral sighed, a fact noted by Mother Anne.

"We must conserve in order to use our resources to help save our patients, Admiral." She turned and swished out of the room without giving him a chance to respond.

Mother Anne had no illusions about Father Theodore. He was a pompous man, and thought himself godlike. The fact that he was obviously rising in power frightened her. She had seen signs of what his wrath could do. Therefore, she had not been helpful when it came to looking for Sister Gemma. On the contrary, Mother Anne had taken care of matters in her own way, sending Sister Agatha after the fleeing Gemma to make sure that the poor girl made it to a safe place. She trusted only herself now, and the Little Sisters.

Of the clergy, the only one left that she had any respect for was Father Ambrose, but unfortunately he was too humble— maybe even weak—to stand up for what he believed in. For Father Theodore, she felt only deep contempt. She knew that he would sneak out into the kitchen and help himself to extra food. Still, being intensely pacifistic, she despised the military more and would not give any special privileges to them. *Especially to officers,* she thought, gliding quietly down the corridor toward the kitchen, where a more generous meal was being prepared for the sick and indigent out in the ward.

In the office, Father Theodore pushed the small plate of sandwiches toward his guests.

"You must be famished. Please, have mine," he said.

You unctuous hypocrite, Amaral thought. *I bet you eat well enough when you are alone.*

CHAPTER 61

Evie agreed to perform the barbering on Julius. Now all they had to do was get Julius to agree.

"No, thank you," he said when Jack tried to cajole him. "The kids might not recognize me. They're comfortable with the way I look. So am I."

"How about just a little trim, sir? The hair. Just the ends. It wouldn't alter the way you look that much, but it might improve the kids' morale to see you neatened up."

"I suppose," Julius said reluctantly.

Evie was called for, and she arrived with a big pair of scissors.

"What are those for? Sheep shearing?" Julius asked.

"No, sir, but they're good and sharp," she laughed.

"No need to call me 'sir.' Just call me Julius," he said. "And I don't want anything drastic done, now. Just a little trim, like Jack said." Julius was showing, with a chopping motion of his hand, just about where he wanted the hair to end. Evie took a mirror down from the wall and made him hold it.

"There. Now if you think I'm being too rash, you can stop me," she said.

Julius watched her in the mirror while she combed the knots out of his hair. He suddenly felt worried that his hair might smell. It had been a couple of weeks since he washed it. She seemed oblivious enough and started snipping away.

"Do you live here?" he asked.

"No, sir, I'm from, ah, further south," she said. She couldn't make herself say "Washington." Pete should have discussed suitable topics with her, she thought.

"I don't remember where I'm from," Julius said, "or who I am."

"That must be hard. Although sometimes I wish I didn't remember, either," she said.

"Lost your family?" he guessed.

"Yes."

"Husband?"

"No. I'm not married. My boyfriend and I came here after... you know."

"The wave."

"Yes."

"Can you tell me about the wave?"

She stopped snipping. Then she shook her head. "I don't think so. Sorry, sir."

"Were you in the military?"

"No, why?" she asked.

"You keep calling me 'sir.'"

"I'll try not to, if it bothers you."

"Jack did, too. But I guess he's a military man."

"Jack? I don't think so."

"Must be just plain respect for an elder, then," Julius said.

"Oh, now, I don't think you're that old. If you'd let me shave that beard off..."

He turned around, looking sternly at her. "I said *no shave.*"

She nodded anxiously. "Of course, sir. I wouldn't. I was just joking."

"There you go again, calling me 'sir.' Is your boyfriend a military man?"

"No…" She was going to add, *but he works for the government.* She stopped herself just in time.

Evie was sorry now that she had agreed to do this. "How's that? Did I leave enough of your handsome mane? You can still put it up in a ponytail, if you want to. I'd really like to give you a proper haircut. Why don't you talk to your kids and leave it up to them? They could even come and watch me do it. And I'd be glad to give them haircuts, too. It's what I used to do for a living."

Julius picked up the mirror and looked into it. He twisted his neck, trying to see the back of his head. When he looked at Evie in the mirror, she tilted her head sideways and winked. Julius slowly put the mirror down.

"Evie," he said.

CHAPTER 62

It was Sunday, and people who were lucky enough to live in safe and remote rural communities put on their warmest clothes and walked to church. Some went on horseback. Here and there, people had even dragged out old carriages and sleighs that had been stored in their barns for generations. It made the ride to church almost a festive occasion. They were at least as well off as the pioneers had been, they had to admit.

In church, nothing had changed. The stained glass windows still drew the eyes of the children, and candles flickered and guttered in the draft. People sat close together, and soon their body heat dispelled the chill air.

Mourning of departed family members had ceased. Even out here, in the relative safety of the countryside, they had all lost so many that it no longer mattered. They understood now how the early settlers had been able to withstand the loss of all those young children. Only the living counted. Every Sunday, clergymen read the rolls of members of the congregation who had perished during the week. The dead were interred in large, communal graves, trenches that had been dug before the frost. Hymns were sung and prayers said, but there was no outward display of grief.

Spring was working its way up through the South. The cherry trees would have been blooming in Washington, D.C. Those dear old trees, given to the country by the Japanese such a long time ago, would never bloom again. But far inside the new coastline, too far for the wave to have reached, the edges of the woods were bursting with sturdy dogtooth violets, and slender white anemones bobbled in the wind. On the hillsides, laurel and rhododendron buds were plumping up.

Cardinal Helmsman—Father Theodore had at last decided that the weight of this title would benefit him more than his previous image of modesty and humility in his bid for leadership—sat alone in his study. He was working on ways to come to terms with crime, which was marching forward in a wave as powerful as the one that had struck their coastline, and if unchecked would soon destroy the spirit of the nation. It was going to be a sweeping work that would be printed and eventually dispersed countrywide.

The cardinal had decided that this would be one avenue by which he would gain control. The nuns could handle education. The sick and dying—well, that was up to God, wasn't it? But to bring crime under control—that was a task Cardinal Theodore Helmsman had chosen for himself, and thereby he meant to reap his reward. He would use the Bible as his guide. An eye for an eye. *And, who knows?* he thought philosophically. *Maybe the uncompromising, radical arm of Islam*—which had spawned the terrorist movements they had never managed to completely eliminate—*has something to teach us, after all.*

Even Generalissimo Franco's "Catholic Nationalism," a name hissed by the outraged, had a positive ring in the Cardinal's ear. Why not? Where had the laws and constitutions created by Western man taken them? Laws that diligently protected the rights of the criminal and let the victim become twice victimized? Laws that furthermore had permitted abominations such as pornography, homosexuality, abortion, euthanasia, and adultery, to name just a few. Were these laws superior to God's? No! Man had nearly destroyed all the earth—and himself in the process—thinking himself omnipotent.

The thrill of privilege rushed through his veins. He felt he had been chosen to make a new beginning. The slate was almost clean now, and he would make certain that this time, God would prevail.

CHAPTER 63

It was when he went down among the rocks to check on the dory that Noah had spied the gang of four, far out on the ice. They were running and sliding, pulling the overloaded skiff behind them. Unchecked anger tore at him. If they were getting away with all the provisions, the rest of the group would not stand much of a chance.

Inspecting the cracked dory, he knew it would never ride the waves again. Noah didn't bother trying to salvage anything from the cellar. The jumble of bedding and boxes were eerily suspended in the thick sheet of ice that covered everything in the hole. Luke was nowhere to be seen, and Noah shouted his name in the brisk wind until his lungs began to hurt. When at last he found Luke's thin, bludgeoned body lying face-down behind the woodpile, he looked back out across the bay. The men were still visible, closing in on the mainland. He had to go after them. The skiff had been loaded, and he guessed that meant they had located the reserve food stores. Noah knew that he had to leave Luke where he was. No more harm could come to him now.

Noah had followed their trail all afternoon. By evening he realized they had eluded him. He swore, rested for an hour then returned to the island. Arriving just before dawn he knew, as soon as he noticed the dory gone, that everyone else had left, too. Where would they have gone? He went back to the cellar hole, and there he found a cardboard box stuffed with a cache of crackers, soup cubes, and some dried fish. And a note. *Noah— Going home. If you are alive, please follow.*

Exhausted, he had wanted nothing more than to lie down, but knew he could not afford to sleep. Luke's body was gone, probably thanks to Black Neil, he assumed. He had also noticed that the ice was thinning near the shore, and without a skiff he might not make it back to the mainland by morning. If he hurried, maybe he could catch up with Ingrid and her little band. They were his lifeline now, the only people that mattered. And whatever was between Ingrid and him still had to be played out. They were not finished yet. At least *he* wasn't.

He had set out again, following the same path. After a week he had caught up with the gang of four. They had managed to steal some bottles of whisky and drunk themselves silly. While they were lolling about inebriated, the militia or some local vigilantes had caught up with them, and whoever hadn't died of the gunshot wounds had frozen to death.

Noah hoped Ingrid and her companions had gone by a different route and missed seeing the frozen bodies. Someone had been by, but only to grab whatever food and other useful items the gang had carried with them. Noah thought it unlikely that it would have been Ingrid. She would have covered the bodies of her ex-neighbors, at least.

Noah rationed his meager food supply to last him for the trek. Traveling alone, without the encumbrances of youth or old age, he must have passed the others somewhere along the way, because he arrived in Bennington before them. He had no difficulty recognizing the place from Ingrid's description: the wrap-around porch, the little park across the road, the tall maples lining the street.

He entered the house through the front door, which was unlocked. Remnants of old barricades were scattered on the floor inside. A terrible stench emanated from the dark interior, but he walked on anyway. There was no furniture left, only piles of rubbish and dirty clothing. He picked his way through what had been the living room and into the kitchen. The marble counters were encrusted with remnants of food and grime that had first dried, then frozen. There was not a clean surface anywhere, but the stench did not originate here.

He left the kitchen by another door and found a set of stairs that led to the second floor. As he walked up the steps, the smell got stronger, and he was tempted to go back down and leave, just wander back out into the crisp, clean winter air. Instead, he hurried his steps and arrived at the landing. He opened the first door he came to, and a gush of warm and nauseating air met him. Embers were still glowing faintly in a fireplace in the room, and on the floor in front lay the source of the stench. The man was dead, had obviously been dead for some time. The woman, who was lying curled up next to him with her hand on his chest, seemed to be staring at the ceiling. Noah covered his face with his sleeve, kneeled next to her, and touched her face. Still warm. He felt for a pulse, but found none. *She may have been alive when I walked into the house,* he thought.

Swallowing hard—thinking it was a good thing there was no food in his gut—he hauled the surprisingly light, emaciated bodies outside, after wrapping them up in the blankets they had died on. Then he looked around for a place to deposit them and found a garage where they would freeze and keep until it thawed. It was the best he could do.

After that he went back upstairs and opened the windows in the bedroom, leaving them open to let the cold air temper the smell. Then he continued his tour of the house. He was anxious to wash his hands, but there was no water. There were no towels, either, or toilet paper, and no alcohol or disinfectant in the vanity. The medicine cabinet was empty except for a half-full bottle of bright pink nail polish. He thought of Ingrid then, tried to imagine her standing there with one foot on the toilet seat, painting her toenails. He shook his head, trying to force himself back to reality. There was a note taped to the bathroom mirror, which he took down and read twice. He turned it over and read what was on the back. About to put it into his pocket, he changed his mind and reluctantly stuck it back up.

When he got back out into the yard, he bent down and scrubbed his hands vigorously with snow. The snow was granular and made him aware that winter had lost its grip. Noah longed for spring, as though it would bring back with it the life he had loved, along with the dogtooth violets and johnny-jump-ups. He suddenly felt that it never would—for him, anyway.

He made a small, smoky fire and heated water in the tin cup he carried on a string from his belt. When the water started sizzling around the edge, he dropped a soup cube into it. The cube instantly expanded into some sort of wormy-looking noodles and bits of synthetic vegetables that floated to the top. He had a few cubes left—then he would be out of food. He drank the broth quickly before it cooled. The warmth made him feel a little better, and he walked back inside.

He went through all the rooms to collect the rubbish and garbage, dragged it out through the back door, and covered it with snow. Then he opened the door to the basement, but when he saw that it was filled with rubbish, too, all the way up to the top of the stairs, he just closed the door tightly. The wood he left stacked inside the front door, in case someone wanted to make a fire. He cleaned the kitchen as well as could be done, scraping the filth off the floor and counters with his jack knife. There was nothing he could do about the large stain on the bedroom floor. He hoped the smell would abate, with the source removed.

When the house was as good as he felt he could make it, he left. He did not look back, just disappeared among the stately trees that lined the street. A large, starved dog, his fur matted and dirty, followed at a distance. Later on, after he had crossed a ridge, made a wide circle around the outskirts of the town, and was striking out toward the north, the dog was still following behind, stopping now and then to sniff his footprints.

CHAPTER 64

When Julius recognized Evie, she started to cry. Not quietly, with small, dainty sobs and tears trickling down her cheeks. She howled like a little girl abandoned in the street by her mother, without holding back or caring if anyone was watching.

Julius remained in his chair at first, taken aback by her keening and convulsive sobbing. Then he recovered and got up, retrieved the towel that fell from his lap, and pulled Evie to him until her face was against chest. She clung to him, and he patted her curly red hair clumsily. The smell of his shirt, which he had worn now for days without washing and which was permeated with the odor of smoky fires, cooking, traveling, sweating, sleeping, and cuddling grimy children, gave her such a perverse sense of comfort that she had to laugh. She took the towel from him and wiped her face with it.

"I'm sorry, Mr. President," she said, suddenly unable to stop laughing.

When she got herself under control, she noticed that he was quiet and very still, as though waiting to say something. She thought she knew what it was.

"I don't know where she is, sir," she whispered. She didn't dare to say it any louder, and wished she had said it better. "We haven't had any contact with...people who might know."

"Pete said she had gone ahead..." he mumbled.

Her heart ached for him. If she could only tell him what she knew. But it might make it worse later—if they were to find out that Ariana had died since they parted. They shouldn't have let her go. She was on the verge of tears again when Pete stepped into the room.

"Well, Julius, that's a little better," he said with an approving nod.

"That's Mr. President to you, son."

Pete looked dumbly from one to the other.

"Did you tell him?" he asked Evie.

"She did not. She just gave me one of her charming winks and I came flying through a black hole. I'm beginning to think I want to go back to where I was, though." He paused for a moment. "Pete, Evie tells me you don't know where Ariana is. I thought you, of all people, would know." It was as close to an accusation as he would come. Pete had been like a son to him, and now Albion felt disappointed, even betrayed.

Pete was torn, but decided to stick to his original decision—only he wouldn't lie again, not to this man.

"I'm sorry, sir. We had to get you to safety. I know it may seem wrong now, but I felt then that it was the right thing to do." He was sure Albion would detest him and probably discard him after this.

"Has anyone looked for her?"

"Mr. President...there really is no way, in the current circumstances, to look for anyone. Unless you send out an army of people to look, physically look, I mean. But we have small groups, like the one here with us that can send out runners to ferret out information. Maybe we can discover something. We will do our best to find her, sir." He tried to sound sincere without appearing overly confident.

Albion nodded. The thought of losing Ariana was more than he could bear. He knew that the inability to face this loss must have caused his subconscious to fight against coming out of the amnesia. He would have to suppress it consciously now in order to function. The whole world was in mourning. If he gave in to grief now, he would not have the strength to do what he must: step back into the presidency.

"Pete, you're going to have to bring me up to date on all that has happened. I know more than I thought a few minutes ago, when I woke up. Some things that I didn't comprehend at the time—when I was Julius—are getting clear now, but my mind is reeling a bit. Can we sit down somewhere and talk?"

Pete was relieved, but he knew that Albion had not forgiven him. Unless they found Ariana, he probably never would. But at least he was the president again, and Pete would do what he could to help.

"We should bring a few of the others in on this, sir," Pete said eagerly. "There are people here who know firsthand about situations that I am not up on. Like Jack, who recognized you in the first place."

"I don't know whether to be grateful to him or not. But I'm sure you're right, Pete. Let's make it a small group, though, to start with. I need to go one step at a time, so I can process things. I don't want to be barraged with information. Okay?"

Pete agreed. He would ask only Jack and Lobo.

"Do you mind if I let the rest of them know? That you are alive, I mean... The only people who know are Jack and the three of us."

"Let's wait until we have had our little session. I want you to tell me who all these people are who have gathered here, and what their roles are. It's not that I'm ungrateful, but I'd like to be ahead of any decisions and activities from now on."

Pete felt an astounding sense of relief. Albion was taking charge.

CHAPTER 65

Wheaton and Amaral had again been summoned to Cardinal Helmsman's side. They were no longer fooled by the pretense that Helmsman was just an aide to Sheedy. It was quite apparent to them now that Sheedy had entered the shadowlands of dementia and was merely a puppet, with Helmsman holding the strings. As much as they had detested Birke, he had been a puppeteer more to their liking. Now things had definitively taken a turn for the worse.

Sheedy, up until his unlikely step into the presidential office, had behind him a long political career of responsible and dogged effort on behalf of the people, and was considered always to have been honest and above-board, no matter one's political affiliation. As Pope Fidelis, he had been a good and caring shepherd until his recent descent into the nightmare he must now be living in. Helmsman—well, that was another story. Torquemada and Bernardo Gui rolled into one, judging by the tactics of his incipient inquisition. Rumors about his ruthlessness abounded. Furthermore, the man was a sinister liar, able to inveigle other clerics into cabals where secrecy was the constant password. Amaral was familiar with the existence of an inner circle that was becoming known as The New Inquisition. There was more than pride hiding behind that austere and humble façade.

The military—with Wheaton and Amaral generally thought of as its leadership—was seriously considering a coup. And with the knowledge that there was no legitimacy left to the presidency, their plans were coming to a head.

As they entered, Cardinal Helmsman looked up briefly and gestured for them to be seated. Then he ignored them and returned to what he had been occupied with. He was hammering out the final details of his work on crime, oblivious to any possibility of mutiny. *Let those puffed-up turkeys wait. Teach them a little humility,* he thought.

He took a sip of water from the cup on his desk, hoping it would cover up any odor of his lunch, which had included hard-boiled eggs and slices of heavenly smoked ham that he had filched from a tray meant for the ward. When he looked up, Wheaton and Amaral sat stiffly, staring straight ahead. They were not keeping up a conversation even between themselves, which unnerved him slightly, and he coughed.

"Admiral, Colonel, thank you for waiting. We called you here today because we feel we are not being sufficiently kept up-to-date on events. We need to work out a more efficient way of communicating, I'm afraid, and we have made some plans to make this possible."

Amaral noticed Helmsman's use of the royal "we" and stifled a chuckle.

"We must regroup and place the entire government leadership in one central area, which will include a White House, if I may use that term loosely, and the military-industrial complex, such as it is. We have found such a place, and now we need to speedily—and with complete cooperation between the branches of government—put the plan into operation. I have made a number of copies of the plan, which of course has to be kept strictly classified until carried out. If you gentlemen would be so kind as to take these," he pointed to a cardboard file box, which he had pulled out from behind the desk, "and deliver the folders to the individual named on the front of each one, we believe our move could take place very soon. There is a different timetable in each one; however, the first entry on each list is the date of a general meeting to coordinate the move. And now I'm afraid I'm expected by President Sheedy, who wished me to report to him as soon as I had delivered the information to you."

The cardinal rose and ushered Wheaton and Amaral to the door in rather unceremonious fashion, hoping to cut any questions or objections off before they were voiced.

The colonel and the admiral walked in silence down the corridor, carrying the cardboard box between them by the rough holes cut in the sides. When they reached their vehicle, they put the box in the front seat with the driver and sat down in the back, pulling the window to the driver's compartment closed.

"That's it, don't you think?" Wheaton asked.

"Yes. Let's go back and have a meeting with the boys. I think the time has come. You know, I never imagined there would be a military coup in this country. I thought that was just a third world thing. In the past, I would have been incensed at the mere suggestion, but now I see no other way. It shouldn't be too hard. After all, where are the people or the nations of the world who might object? I would say we can just announce it, and it will be done. Helmsman has no constitutional claim on the leadership, and Sheedy—well, worst case, *we* could become the string-pullers. But I don't see it coming to that." Amaral sat back into the hard leather seat.

They drove back looking out over a greening countryside. Later, when they got back to headquarters, they would take the folders out of the box and laugh at the cardinal's master plans.

CHAPTER 66

"How about Monticello?" Evie asked. "I've always wanted to go there. That is, if it's still there, of course…"

Pete and Albion looked at each other.

"Pete? It's not a bad idea…I like it. The kids would like it."

They all knew by now that Albion wouldn't go anywhere without the kids. This had caused some consternation at first, but they had gotten used to the idea.

Once Julius had fully resumed his old identity, he asked Evie to finish the barbering job. He had studied his scruffy self in the mirror a final time, wearing the glasses. *I look like Grandfather,* he had thought, elated to feel bits of memory returning.

Evie had given him a proper shave and haircut. When he walked out into the kitchen, the children had barely looked at him, as if he were a stranger that they didn't need to pay attention to. As soon as he spoke, Aug had turned around and looked at him, gaping. He had gotten out of his chair and come right up to Albion, squinted, and reached up to touch his scar.

"What happened to you there, Julius? Is that why you grew a beard?"

Albion had chuckled, and Aug had looked at him again.

"You don't look like yourself anymore, Julius. You look sort of like…the President," he had said, and Albion threw his head back and laughed.

The children had been speechless when they found out that Julius was, indeed, the president—except for Roofie, who had remained unimpressed. "Uyuth, whea'th you heah? Wead me a towy, pwease!" *Julius, where's your hair? Read me a story, please.* And then Julius had explained about the haircut, put Roofie on his lap, and read her a story.

Now they were seated on the porch, well dressed against the cold, watching the children romp in the snow. The little farm in Brattleboro was idyllic, but far away from where he knew they had to be.

The new White House had to be in a more central location. He wished he could get inside the brains of the earliest presidents. Their life and times were in so many ways similar to the present, and when Evie mentioned Monticello, it seemed an apt choice.

"See what you can find out, Pete. Talk to Jack, he seems to have gotten around. I always knew you were a smart girl, Evie. I'm glad Pete brought you. I told him to, you know." He fell silent, remembering.

Pete got up quickly. "I'll see if I can find Jack."

In the previous two days, Albion had met with as many of the group as he could handle. He had quickly come to realize that they were exactly the kind of people he would need. They had all come forward voluntarily, simply in the spirit of trying to do what was right, without expecting pay or favors. It was a unique and hardworking group of men and women, and he felt they would form the core of his government. He already thought of them as his "cabinet," and he hoped most of them would stay on if it turned out that he could reclaim the office.

Pete returned shortly with Jack. "Monticello? In the hands of the National Guard. Wheaton decided early on to have the

Guard protect as many national monuments and buildings of irreplaceable historical value as possible. Many of the sites were destroyed, of course. But Monticello would be a good possibility. That is, if you can get the Guard to move out... they've been living in a five-star hotel, you might say."

They all laughed.

"We could send a flier to scout it out, without setting down, of course. I think it's better if we surprise them, and if it looks good, we could bring you there with a small group. The rest of us—whoever you decide you need—would follow. I would think the Guard could remain with you in a protective capacity, at least temporarily, until we get the Secret Service on it. I've already sent out for Patrice Demba, if he can be found. Pete said he met Pat on his way here, but that was a long time ago," Jack continued.

Pete felt a small shockwave at the mention of Demba. He had told Patrice that Ariana was alive, and if they found him again, Pete hoped Demba wouldn't spill the beans before they could warn him. He made a mental note to talk to Jack about it. Then Jack would make one more person who would know about Ariana. Pete felt that, despite his resolution to be honest, he was again being trapped in a web of lies.

CHAPTER 67

Ingrid recognized the airport tower. Nothing else was as she remembered. At least there was no militia to greet them here, and she soon understood why. Most of the homes had been burned or ransacked, and the town did not look inhabited.

She walked up her street. The bare, black branches of the maple trees still reached for the sky. In the fall, they would again fly their shocking colors, no matter who was here to see. Now the town was drawn as in a Currier and Ives winter scene, with snowdrifts still mercifully covering some of the destruction. Up close, her neighbor's house was a black, burned-out shell. She had to steel herself in order to walk beyond the great privet hedge that she and Adam had planted to shield their garden from view.

Now she could see the wrap-around porch. *The swing is gone,* was the first thing she noticed. Most of the clapboard had been ripped off, along with the gingerbread fretwork, but the house looked fairly intact otherwise.

She led the way onto the porch. The door was unlocked and stood ajar. There she lost her nerve, and asked Black Neil to enter first.

When she followed, what she saw numbed her. She didn't know what she had expected—everything to be the same? Had she thought she would be walking into her well-ordered living room and neat kitchen? There was nothing left. Even the space seemed different without their belongings.

She stood immobile. The boys started running around and up the stairs. It was the first time they had been inside a house since they had left their own before the wave, and they were squealing like pigs, choosing places for themselves and their backpacks.

Ingrid walked through the rooms, touching door handles and woodwork wherever she passed, searching for the familiar, longing for a feeling of homecoming to overwhelm her, but nothing happened. The den was pitch-dark and smelled heavily of mold. Her once beloved kitchen belonged in a slum. The basement had been used as a dump, and was filled all the way up to the top with trash, as though people had simply opened the door and tossed things down the stairs.

She walked upstairs to the bedroom. It was empty, and there was a great black stain on the floor. Someone had left the window wide open, and the floorboards underneath it were starting to warp, but she didn't bother to close it. The room strangely did not cause her more pain than any of the others. She closed her eyes to envision it the way it had been, with the great four-poster bed they had bought at an auction, and the blue and white rag rugs her mother had made. Adam did not appear in her vision, and she sighed and left the room.

She wanted to *feel* something. She wished she could sit down and listen to the old opera voices, which often had triggered her emotions in the old days. Anything would be better than this numbness.

Dusk had set in by the time she walked into the bathroom, and in the dark she nearly missed the note on the mirror. She had already stepped out through the doorway—taken aback at the sight of the overstuffed toilet and the soiled floor—and it was as she was turning around that her peripheral vision caught it. She remembered having left Adam a note before she left the house for that last time. Maybe that was it. Still, she stepped carefully back in over the grimy tiles until she could reach out and remove the piece of paper. She brought it with her out into the stairwell and over to the little round, leaded window that shed a faint light onto the stairs.

I am alive. Are you? I will look for you here when I can. Don't try to find me. I move around a lot. Did you find my message on your Litkit? If you should see this note and decide to leave again, put a message here. Adam.

Her heart lurched and she squeezed the note into her hand. Her wish for a return of emotion, of *feeling* something again, was being granted, but now she wasn't sure that she wanted it. Her first thought was of Noah. That made her feel guilty and terrified, suddenly not knowing whether she was relieved or sorry to find that Adam was alive. Now Noah seemed to be rapidly slipping away, sailing right out of her life the way he had sailed into it. Was Noah alive? At that moment, the thought of having to choose did not occur to her. Thoughts tumbled helplessly about in her brain, looking for a place to settle. A noise made her turn around. Rachel was coming up the stairs.

"We've got everything we need except food, I think. Neil has been scouting around the neighborhood with no luck. The boys are hungry, of course. Too bad we didn't save a little something for our first supper here." She looked at Ingrid. "You look like you've seen a ghost. I'm sorry. It must be a nightmare coming into your home and finding it like this."

She put her arm around Ingrid's shoulder. Ingrid opened her hand and passed the note to Rachel, who uncrumpled it and read it.

"So...he is alive. At least you may be able to tell him. Whatever it is. Everything. The truth about losing the baby. About Noah, if you want to. You can set the record straight, Ingrid. What does he mean about the message?" She passed the note back and Ingrid stuffed it into her pocket without noticing an address that was scribbled on the back.

Before she could answer, the boys came clomping up the stairs. Rachel held on to Cricket tightly, as if she was afraid one of the boys might knock the baby out of her hands.

Ingrid smiled. *Not a chance,* she thought. *Rachel would have them all falling down the stairs like candlepins.* She shushed the boys, pointing to the sleeping baby, and she and Rachel wandered back downstairs.

Granny Day was in the kitchen, using snowballs to clean the countertops, and Sammy and Troy were helping clean the floor.

"Somebody was here not long ago I think, doing some cleaning. There's a whole pile of rubbish out back. The boys found it when they were hauling the trash out of the basement. There was snow on top of it, but somebody had shoveled it on. You can see where they scraped it up in the yard. Remember it snowed a few days ago? Whoever did it was here after that." Granny scrubbed away vigorously until the marble gleamed the way Ingrid remembered it.

Must have been Adam, she thought. *We probably just missed him.*

"Has anybody seen Black Neil?" Ingrid asked, trying to change her train of thought.

"Still out looking for food, I guess," Rachel said.

Black Neil had hovered around Rachel as though he was her personal guardian ever since they left the island. Had he fallen for her? Rachel didn't seem to have noticed, but, then, she was so preoccupied with Cricket. Rachel had also made sure to give the boys a lot of mothering lately, and they now followed her around like happy little ducklings.

The fact that Black Neil had disappeared must mean he thought they were safe there. Ingrid felt secure enough, especially since the town seemed deserted. Besides, she was in her own house. She realized she was beginning to get comfortable with that feeling. It reminded her now of the early days, before the new appliances and furniture had arrived, while they had still been living frugally and working on creating a home here. Later, as they were able to make improvements, they had kept some of the old appliances and put them in the basement for extra summer storage, to hold soda and…

"I'll be right back," she said, breathless, hurrying toward the cellar stairs.

Once downstairs, she felt her way in the dark. It still had the sour smell of the rubbish that the boys had just removed. She stubbed her toe on one of the paint cans that Adam had insisted on keeping "for touchups," and then her outstretched hand felt the door of the old refrigerator.

CHAPTER 68

They sat in the hoverjet, looking out over unfamiliar territory. Albion saw a large lake in the distance. Rising out of the water like surreal, avant-garde islands were in fact the upper parts of the dome and cooling tower of a nuclear power plant. When they came closer, they could see a small boat tied up to the tower. The jet was coming in quite low, and when they flew over the boat they saw that the two men in it were fishing. The men turned their heads, looking anxiously up at the plane.

"Do you think they are catching anything?" asked Aug, who sat in the window seat next to the president.

Albion had insisted on taking Aug along with him. The other children would follow behind later. Evie had promised to take good care of them.

Albion had felt reluctant to fly as he stepped into the jet. It made him think back on that last, fateful trip, and he had suddenly had a vision of the co-pilot jabbing a needle into his arm. *He probably saved my life,* he thought with a wry smile.

This time he had made sure Pete was along in the jet. McPherson was now seated behind Aug, intently following their progress on a map. Jack had remained behind and was planning to personally go in search of Patrice Demba.

"Doesn't look like it. Maybe the water's too deep for angling." *Maybe everything in the lake is dead...and maybe the fishermen will soon be, too*, the president thought, filing the image away for later. He would not forget the men in the boat and the possibility of radioactive leakage in the area.

They were leaving Pennsylvania behind. They had seen villages and known from the smoke rising out of the chimneys that they were inhabited. The cities they flew over—those that had not been turned into craters—had a different kind of smoke: sooty, billowy clouds from the continuing fires in buildings and back alleys. They had seen bands of people running in the streets, some shooting at the plane. Their weapons had not been powerful enough to reach them, but the pilot had nevertheless ascended to be out of reach. Albion had been informed that the militia had acquired large supplies of laser and other heavy-duty weapons, therefore he assumed that these shooters were just gangs of hoodlums.

The small jet used as Air Force One had been flying over mountains most of the way, across Vermont and New York, and was just entering Maryland airspace. They could already see the unfamiliar new coastline, even though they were not at a high altitude, and Albion sensed that soon they would be flying over Washington, D.C. He looked down searchingly, wondering where Ariana had been when the wave struck. When he saw, through the water below, ghostly grid lines of streets and the rubble of buildings that remained along the coast, he closed his eyes. It was too painful.

It wasn't Pete's fault, of course. Albion knew how difficult his wife had been about letting people know of her whereabouts, whether she went to the studio or just drove around aimlessly. The Secret Service men assigned to her were always frustrated, and Albion himself had asked her to be more reasonable. "Let them know about the studio," he'd said. "They'll just make sure it's safe and leave you alone." But Ariana had stubbornly refused to have her hiding place monitored.

He knew there had been suggestions among the staff that she was having an affair. Albion had never questioned his wife's feelings for him, and knew that she put up with being first lady only because she knew there would be an end to it. She had felt trapped, though, and now he felt guilty for having tried to prevent her from living free and untethered, the way her spirit had required. They had never argued about it, but she had become so silent that it had frightened him.

As a senator's wife, she'd had more privacy and had never balked at working with troubled youngsters and performing the various other duties that political wives had to put up with, as long as there was time enough for her art work at the end of the day. Since they had moved into the White House, their relationship, which had always been warm and full of bantering and friendly disagreements about both private and public issues—Ariana was rebelliously and warmheartedly liberal—had been put on hold. The bedroom had been an exception. Now he thought guiltily that maybe this had stilled *his* needs, but what about hers? Ariana was a romantic— not the wine-and-roses type, but intimate communication and spiritual closeness were important to her, and without those she had begun to withdraw into her shell. He had been confident that things would return to normal once his term ended.

Albion remembered her standing by the bedroom window in the West Wing, looking out at the yellow roses that bloomed below. She had remained turned away from him as he left the bedroom. That was the last time he saw her. Albion felt himself getting choked up and turned to look out the window.

The ground rose again as they entered the Virginia Piedmont. They were flying over Shenandoah National Park, with the sun low in the sky. The mountains lay blue and undulating to their right, the sky purple and pink beyond them. Aug had fallen asleep, and Albion left him alone until the co-pilot came and told them they were only a few minutes away from landing. Then the President shook Aug gently by the shoulder, and they all looked down into the graying countryside.

There it was. The Grove, the Roundabouts, and, at the top—with the sun still hitting the roof and the surrounding tree tops, turning them pink and gold—Monticello itself.

The pilot set the craft down on the West Lawn, and suddenly they were surrounded.

CHAPTER 69

It was like a three-ring circus, thought Sister Zita. The sisters all knew by now that it was the pope who had been residing in their midst, and that the pope had been the cause of Sister Gemma's flight.

Now Fidelis, dressed in one of Mother Anne's robes with Sister Gemma's flower-embroidered stole around his shoulders and his white hair long and flowing, was dancing around wildly with Father Ambrose in the Reverend Mother's office. Father Ambrose was red in the face and stared anxiously around him, trying to avoid tripping over chairs and lamps. He was making a desperate effort to force the Holy Father to release his grip, but Fidelis' hands were clamped solidly around his.

Sister Zita fled down the hall toward the kitchen to alert the others and to find Reverend Mother. Father Theodore—Cardinal Helmsman, as he wanted to be called now—was chasing after the pope, trying to grasp him from behind without success. Finally, the cardinal stepped aside, breathing heavily.

"Let us pray!" he shouted, sounding for all the world like one of those evangelical preachers he disdained.

Fidelis hesitated for a moment, which was just enough to allow Father Ambrose to kneel down in front of him, ready for prayer.

"The Lord is my shepherd," the cardinal began in his granular, pedantic voice.

Fidelis, suddenly vigilant again, took over the prayer and led them with bell-like clarity.

He looks like a painting by El Greco, Father Ambrose thought, *emaciated, the bony face lit from within—or like a pious child grown prematurely old, looking up at his God in adoration.*

When he came to the end of the prayer, Fidelis simply fainted onto the floor very gracefully, falling almost without a sound. His face was set in a soft smile, his cheeks were a high pink from the dancing, and his right hand grasped the flowered stole.

The cardinal and Father Ambrose knelt at the side of the pope. The cardinal put his hands together and closed his eyes, his lips moving silently. When Fidelis did not immediately come to, Father Ambrose gently shook the Holy Father by the shoulder. Fidelis' eyes remained closed. Ambrose felt for a pulse, but found none.

"I'm afraid he is gone," he said, stunned, and crossed himself.

The cardinal opened his eyes wide. He sat silent for a moment before leaning over to close the pope's eyes.

Father Ambrose got up hastily and left the cardinal to perform the rites over Fidelis. Ambrose could not even make himself stay and watch. *How sweet must your feeling of triumph be now, my dear cardinal,* he thought.

On his way out he nearly collided with Mother Anne and Sister Zita, who had been standing in the doorway watching and now came forward to kneel at the side of the dead pope.

Once outside the room, Father Ambrose felt regret at having left the fallen old man. He winced with a sudden jolt of pain when he thought of the pontiff's legacy. All those years of exceptional and loving work on behalf of the oppressed and the poor had lately been overshadowed by Fidelis' own human frailty, and then this lamentable descent into madness. But Fidelis was safe now with the Father, who would give him his due.

As he walked down the corridor, Father Ambrose remembered Colonel Wheaton and General Amaral, who were expected shortly. *Now it begins,* he thought. He wondered what his own role would be. Where would he stand? Would he force himself to stand with the cardinal? Which side was God on?

Father Ambrose wondered whether Wheaton and Amaral were aware that the cardinal had already begun his campaign of terror, or what Helmsman himself called "the Crusade for Justice." Father Ambrose had personally seen proof of it. He closed his eyes in dread when he remembered a scene that was mercilessly burned into his mind. A jeering crowd surrounding a prisoner—an adulterer, someone had told him—in a town square. The chant. "Jus-*tice,* jus-*tice.*" Then the stones. They had all been eager to cast the first stone.

CHAPTER 70

Ingrid opened the door of the old refrigerator. In the dark, she couldn't see into it, so she waved her hand inside to feel if it was empty. She cried out after getting her palm gashed by broken glass. The liquids had frozen and burst the bottles and jars. The plastic bottles had cracked or popped their caps. The only unbroken containers were dispensers of mustard and ketchup and other condiments, which had simply gone bad after the power had gone off.

Disappointed, she sat down on the bottom step and cried. When she ran out of self-pity, she got up and looked around in the dim light from the stairwell. She found a rag on Adam's tool bench and wrapped her hand with it before climbing the stairs back up to the kitchen.

"Well, Granny, there's no food in the house, and we didn't pass any nearby emergency depots that I noticed. What are we going to do? We can at least keep the fires going and spend the night. We'll have to rig up a potty in the garage. Where are Neil and Rachel?"

"They took the boys on a tour of the neighborhood, looking for anything useful or edible, I suppose. I told them to all stick together. Not that I had to—Neil watches out for Rachel and she for the boys. Quite a little family, really."

"I've noticed, too. I hope they come back before it gets dark. Why don't you take a rest, Granny? Go sit by the fire in the living room. I had one more idea while I was down in the basement feeling sorry for myself. I'm going out, but I won't be long."

Granny Day nodded and gratefully wiped her frozen hands on her shirt. She was cold and hungry, and so tired. Maybe this would be the end of her road. She didn't think she would be able to set out again from here. No, this would be her last stand.

Ingrid went out by the back door and looked into the garage. She closed the door quickly, nearly crying out. They'd have to find another place for a makeshift outhouse.

She walked through the backyard and across several of her neighbors' yards. Their houses had been burned, or trashed and left open to the elements, and were useless even as shelters. Whatever the reason, her house still stood. Maybe the people living in it had been able to defend themselves. Although the two poor souls in the garage hadn't looked strong enough to fight anyone off.

When she got to the end of the block, she crossed the street and went in behind another house that was still reasonably intact. She remembered the people who had lived there. Emma Rose had taught at the school with Ingrid. Her husband, Mick, had been in the army, a tall, wiry fellow with a crew cut. Brusque and a little unfriendly, Ingrid had thought. Emma had been happy to have Ingrid over for coffee at times when her husband was away, but when he was home, they had rarely appeared to entertain or socialize.

However, Ingrid remembered coming over once and finding Mick in the backyard with a few friends who were helping him on a project. Mick had nodded at her, but had not introduced her to his friends, and she had gone inside to look for Emma, who was apologetic. She wouldn't have time for coffee after all. Mick had come home unexpectedly, and now Emma had to fix lunch for the guys who were helping them construct a bomb shelter. They were all taking turns to help each other, and today it was Mick's turn.

Bunkers and bomb shelters had been popular at various times in the past to hold people and food in case of emergency, especially among members of the military. Ingrid had tried to hide her feelings on the matter; she remembered thinking that this was a preposterous idea from another age that only paranoid and fearful people would act on.

Later, Emma had showed her the entrance to the underground bunker. Now Ingrid walked into the back of the empty garage and opened the door to the closet. She removed the piece of linoleum covering the floor. There was the hatch door. She pulled at the large brass ring, and the heavy, metal door squeaked open. Slowly, she made her way down the hatchway ladder and into the musty space below, brushing spiderwebs from her face.

Staring into the murk, she had to wait for the streaks of dust in the air to settle before she could see anything. The solid concrete walls held shelves, heavily draped with cobwebs and a thick layer of gray dust. Her hands trembled as she brushed the cobwebs away. Underneath she found layer upon layer of cans. Many had burst, but some were intact. They had food and water here that would last them for a while.

Thank you, Mick, she thought. *I hope you are well. Someday I'll repay you for this, and apologize for thinking you were paranoid. Emma, I hope you are safe.* What could have happened to them that they left all this behind? Ingrid knew that there were additional spaces down here—rooms branching off, with mattresses and shelves loaded with books, a dry toilet, and even a generator, she remembered. Well, if they decided to stay, this place would come in handy. Right now she was ecstatic to be able to bring some food to her starving clan.

CHAPTER 71

The guardsmen did not recognize Pete McPherson when he stepped out of the plane, and he was instantly surrounded at gunpoint. Albion rapidly followed him out, as if to protect him from harm, and was quickly subjected to the same treatment. It was Aug that saved them from whatever dreadful accident might have taken place. He jumped down the ramp and ran up to the guards, shouting, "Don't shoot the president!"

The great tumult that followed finally ceased, and the president was led—under heavy guard, as if an attack on him was suddenly expected—up the stairs of the West Portico and into the parlor. The rest of the weary travelers followed, allowed to walk freely and without guns pointed at them.

The guards placed themselves along the walls and at the doors, arms at the ready, while the president and his motley entourage sat down in the various sofas and chairs placed haphazardly around the room. The president selected the Campeachy chair that he knew had once been a favorite of President Jefferson's because, according to Jefferson, "age, its infirmities and frequent illnesses have rendered indulgences in that easy kind of chair truly acceptable." Albion couldn't have agreed more. The atmosphere in the room, however, was still tense.

"I guess we should have called ahead," Albion stage-whispered to Pete.

There was only a brief wait before two officers, a colonel and a sergeant major, burst into the room, causing a stiffening in the stance of the guards, and Aug to rush to Albion's side. Albion put a calming hand on the boy's shoulder. He nodded to the officers and waved them forward.

"Pull up a chair. I think we need to have rather a long chat, so could you provide us with something to eat while we talk? Nothing fancy. A roast beef sandwich would do for me. Cheeseburger for the boy here. What about you, Pete? Enchiladas?"

Consternation clouded the faces of the officers, and Albion laughed. "Just a joke, fellas. Whatever you can rustle up will do us fine."

Relieved, the colonel—the younger of the two and looking far too young to be a colonel—signaled for one of the guards and gave him a brief order. The sergeant major pulled up a chair, lighter but somewhat higher than the president's. He hunched down into it, as though embarrassed to tower over Albion, who seemed oblivious to the officer's predicament.

"I'm Sergeant Major Findlay, Mr. President. You cannot imagine my relief at seeing you here, alive…"

"Well, now, Sergeant Major, I am happy to be here as well, and later we can swap stories. For now, let's pass on the small talk. The country waits. I would like to talk to the brigadier, if he is here. I need to go right to the top. I don't want to have to go over the same thing twice—there's too much ground to cover," Albion said.

Findlay stared at his shoes before replying. "I'm afraid I'm it, sir. Lieutenant General Sweeney and Brigadier General MacIntosh were both at a funeral in Washington. I believe you were there as well. They didn't make it back. Several of our other officers were there, too. Colonel Parker, here," he nodded toward the young officer, who was instructing some of the guards to set up tables and chairs for dining, "has been very recently, ah... promoted, sir. I needed to replace some of the officers I lost. However, we haven't had the ability to promote anyone to the top, yet. Nobody here with the authority, you see."

"Of course. Now that you mention it, I remember seeing MacIntosh in the cathedral, along with a large number of other officers. I suppose we must have lost quite a number, then?"

"Yes, unfortunately. I do know that Colonel Joseph Wheaton of the Air Force and Rear Admiral Charles Amaral are alive and very active. I have a list in my office of the high-ranking military officers we have been able to ascertain as being alive, sir. If you'd like, I'll send Parker to get it."

"That would be helpful. In the meantime, if we could get word to the colonel and admiral that I would like them to join me here immediately—send my plane for them, if necessary. You'll have to help me understand later about our capacity for communication and mobility."

Findlay nodded and gave quick instructions to Colonel Parker. Then food appeared, platters of steaming meats and vegetables giving off such an aroma that everyone groaned, and there was a rush to the table.

CHAPTER 72

Cardinal Helmsman had learned from grave mistakes that other ambitious churchmen had made in the past. *Never delegate anything important*—someone else will reap the benefit. *Never be the one to pass on sensitive or potentially scandalous information*—you will reap the blame if it comes to light that you knew of it. *Never share power*—sharing it will bleed you dry. *Never let people know what your plans are*—or they will know when they are being manipulated.

He had worked diligently and secretly, long before the wave, using the Church's funds and swaying power to infiltrate and influence the political and legal arenas in anticipation of the day when people would realize that the Church was the preeminent power. The Church—God's representative on earth—was better suited to guide them than their pitifully inadequate Constitution and law books. What he was now about to do went against all the clever practices he had learned. It was a calculated risk, and he knew it.

The cardinal closed his eyes in concentration so that he could recall with certainty who had been present when Fidelis was stricken. Father Ambrose. Sister Zita. Mother Anne. He must speak to them immediately. He would leave Father Ambrose for last, fearing that the women would be more likely to immediately go and share the news with the rest of the nuns and—God help him—with the people in the ward.

The cardinal hurried his steps down the hall, soft-shoeing his way by Father Ambrose's door before entering the Great Room. It was nearly suppertime, and most of the sisters were busy in the kitchen. Conveniently enough, Mother Anne and Sister Zita were alone in the room, so absorbed in their own conversation that they did not notice his approach. The Reverend Mother was holding one of Sister Zita's hands in hers. The young nun was crying openly, and Mother Anne was consoling her, stroking the tears from her cheek.

"The Holy Father is at peace now, Zita," Mother Anne said. "His sins are forgiven. We must remember the good man he was all his life. What happened here was a sin, certainly, but the father had lost his faculties and was not in his right mind, and God will know that."

"But, Mother, what about poor Sister Gemma? Did she also sin?"

Cardinal Helmsman made his presence known by coughing slightly and making his steps heard on the mosaic tile floor. He smiled, sadly and benignly at the same time, to show them that he also mourned Fidelis, yet retained the strength needed to lead and carry on.

"Mother Anne, I am here to discuss something of great import with you—and with Sister Zita as well, since she was also present when the Holy Father was borne away to eternal life. We are living in very difficult times, and we must do everything we can to bring our country back from the brink of disaster.

"If the people were suddenly to find out that the world's greatest religious leader now has died, it would plunge them into deep sorrow. And if they found out that he also was the president, and that the country is now truly without a leader, it could cause grave fear and confusion, and lead to unimaginable disaster. Therefore, we must, for the moment, keep this to ourselves, at least until the Church leaders have been informed and the process to replace the Holy Father has begun."

Mother Anne studied the cardinal. She did not trust him, did not like this secrecy, and yet it seemed to make sense. She nodded thoughtfully.

"Then I must gather the sisters together, before they have a chance to speak to anyone else," she said. "Sister Zita, please go and call them here. Make sure everyone is present."

It had been that easy. No one had yet been out to the wards with the news, and the sisters had readily agreed to his request. He had not needed to go into any great detail of the effect the news would have on the people; the Little Sisters could easily imagine it, and had seen enough confusion and suffering during the past year to do anything to avoid creating more.

When the sisters went back to their duties, Cardinal Helmsman proceeded to Father Ambrose's room. Father Ambrose was lying prone on the floor with his arms outstretched. Well, he had always been somewhat of a hysteric, Helmsman thought.

"Father Ambrose, we must talk."

CHAPTER 73

When Pete had finished telling Jack about the first lady—about Ariana getting out of Washington alive and traveling with them until they separated at the Connecticut River all those months ago—Jack stared at him unbelievingly.

"And you didn't tell Albion?"

Pete had explained his fears, and Jack had reluctantly agreed that it made sense. Pete also mentioned that he had told Demba about Ariana, and that if Jack found Demba he must warn him not to say anything to the president until they'd had a chance to search for her.

Jack took one of the vehicles and a relief driver and set out in search of Demba, a search that had now taken on new importance. Demba had always been thorough, never liked loose ends. Maybe he had followed up on Pete's lead and looked for the first lady himself.

He decided to start the search from where Pete had last seen Demba, and took off along the highway southward through the hills from Brattleboro toward Massachusetts. It now seemed that an eternity had passed since he arrived at the farm with Julius and his swarm of children, but when Jack saw the tracks from their convoy on the highway, he remembered it had only been a few days. It hadn't snowed in the interim, and driving was comfortable. Up in the mountains the trees were still weighed down with snow, but already as they descended into the upper valleys, the snow was melting and the streams that ran along the road were swollen. He prayed not to run into flooded roadways, knowing the mountainous terrain would make it hard, even with this vehicle, to go off-road and find an alternate route.

They drove non-stop, taking turns at the wheel and eating on the go. It was eerily still, and if there were people living anywhere around, they kept themselves hidden. A soft rain began to fall, adding to the melting ice and snow on the roadway and causing great ruts that Raymo seemed to take as a personal challenge as they careened downhill at breakneck speed.

As they reached lower-lying areas the fields and meadows were lush and verdant, the trees were dressed in their early spring greenery, and they saw several small groups of deer in the distance. It wasn't until they were nearing the Massachusetts border that they saw a human being. The man was plodding north along the highway, accompanied by a bedraggled-looking dog. The driver glanced at Jack, who shook his head.

"No, don't stop. He's going north, anyway. Can't risk being hijacked now. Just keep going."

He looked out at the man as they passed him. The dog, which trotted a little distance behind him, was lean and mangy, and he limped slightly as he loped along. At least he was alive. Most people weren't willing to share food with their own pets these days; some even ate them when they got desperate enough. Jack shuddered.

As the vehicle passed the dog, it raised its head and looked up at them. Jack grabbed at the door handle.

"Stop! Raymo, God Almighty, stop the van..." he said hoarsely.

He barely waited for the vehicle to come to a halt before he was out the door, stumbling in the muddy gravel by the side of the road. The dog turned around and came bounding toward him and nearly knocked him over, barking and putting his great forepaws on Jack's chest. He knelt and buried his face in the dog's stiff and smelly fur.

"Oh, Boru, you great stinky beast, you're alive!" he said.

The man had stopped up ahead and was watching curiously. Slowly, he edged toward them. The dog let out a low growl and the man hesitated and stopped. Jack patted the dog.

"It's all right, Boru. Good boy." Jack turned to the man. "Where did you find him?" he asked.

"He found me is more like it, and he's been following me ever since. Is he your dog?" He didn't really want to know, but he had to ask.

"He sure is. Haven't seen him since the wave. Thought he was dead."

"And you said his name was Boru? Brian Boru?"

"Yes," said Jack, surprised. He looked up at the man, who had remained standing a few yards away.

"Then you must be Adam," the man said.

"How on earth would you know that?" Jack said, rapidly getting up from his kneeling position beside the dog. Boru whined anxiously.

"It's a long story."

"Let's get in the van, where it's warm. Sorry you're not going in our direction or we could give you a ride."

"As a matter of fact, I *was* going in your direction. And I'll be glad to accept the ride."

"You'd better hop in, then, and explain. By the way, name's Jack now, if you don't mind."

The man nodded.

Jack got back up into the front seat, letting the man and the dog climb into the back. Boru tried eagerly to squeeze into the front with Jack, and finally managed to claw and pull himself through. Jack pushed him onto the floor at his feet; the dog seemed happy there and started to scratch himself vigorously.

"Let's go, Raymo. Guess we've got passengers," Jack said then turned toward the back seat. "So, tell me who you are, and how you come to be here."

Noah sighed, studying Jack's face carefully. So, this was Ingrid's husband.

"Name's Noah. Don't quite know how to tell you the rest. Where are you going, by the way?"

"I'm looking for a lady," Jack said.

"Well, there may be one waiting for you at your house," Noah said.

CHAPTER 74

The leather-bound book was titled, in gold leaf script surrounded by heavily curlicued ornamentations, *THE CITIES OF THE ROSARY*. It held the cardinal's intricate plans for the future layout of his realm: maps, raw architectural sketches, pages with in-depth descriptions of cities to be built according to his specifications.

After the title page and a brief introduction came the map section, the first being a topographical one that showed the country approximately as it now was, at least according to the latest information provided to him by the military. Around the heartland, which held sketchily drawn outlines of the new lake areas, lay his proposed cities, forming a great necklace. The cities were connected to each other by roads—the cities being the beads in the rosary, the roads the chain that held them together. Within the circle formed by the rosary, the land would hold all they needed, and outside the circle—well, he would deal with that later.

Some of the cities were already named: Pater Noster, Annunciation, Visitation, Resurrection, Assumption, Coronation, Crown of Thorns. He had scribbled the names in ink in his tight, scratchy hand next to the circles on the map.

The architectural sketches were beautifully colored. This was the original set of his plans, from which his minions had drawn a small number of copies in black and white, later to be distributed to serve as guidelines in the actual planning and construction of the cities. One of the cardinal's underlings, a young deacon who had a talent for art, had been asked by Helmsman to add some watercolor to the original set. The deacon had joyously performed the task, and the images of the cities were transformed into jewels of light and shadow. Then these *illuminations,* as the cardinal thought of them, had been bound in leather.

Each city centered on a cathedral forming both the spiritual and the social core. The multi-spired edifice towered high into the sky, before sprawling out into block after block of architecture that resembled, perhaps, wings of eagles or capes of clergy—or great waves, with the cathedral as a rock rising out of the sea. The interior of the structure got more secular as it went outward from the sanctuary itself, beginning with small individual chapels, prayer walks, and student ministry centers, and eventually branching out into convention centers, libraries, museums, concert halls, malls and food courts, fitness centers, skating rinks, youth centers, cinemas, even parks with ponds and waterfalls under great glass domes.

Directly connected to the Grand Cathedral Center by arched and glassed-in walkways were the city apartment blocks. These were crowned by rooftop conservatories that housed restaurants, botanic gardens, and observatories. On the ground between the buildings were safely contained and domed atrium courtyards with year-round swimming pools and play areas for children, as well as seating areas and small convenience kiosks where snacks and appropriate literature and magazines could be bought.

There were walk-in medical and dental clinics in the malls, and every sector of the city had its own elementary school, run by the church. The secondary schools and colleges were situated outside a ring-road on the perimeter of the apartment blocks, along with major hospitals and large office complexes; beyond them were water parks, zoos, lakes planted with fish to encourage father-and-son outings, ball parks, and other destinations for relaxation.

Outside of the city limits—well, here the cardinal's plans were still in the formative stage. Somehow, factories, power plants, and military installations, along with people who were not acceptable in the Cities of the Rosary—criminals and the insane, for example, or those who refused to conform to the requirements of a new society—all would have to be accommodated out there.

Each city was entirely self-sufficient. There was nothing that could not be had within the city walls. Religion, education, culture, relaxation. Jobs for all. A completely safe and stress-free environment, a controlled and protected setting for people looking for security and peace of mind. A safe road would connect the cities so that the inhabitants could visit relatives or vacation in a secure place—away from home, yet unthreatening in its familiarity, and totally safe.

The cathedral itself was the key, of course. The sanctuary alone was designed to hold at least 10,000 people, and would be open around the clock. There would be frequent services and other religious events going on continuously. In the classrooms there would be Bible study, pat-the-Bible classes for infants, Sunday school, counseling for the elderly or the terminally ill—the list went on.

The ecumenical meta-Church had been a great mistake, Cardinal Helmsman thought wearily. Allowing other branches of religion to join with the Catholic Church had watered down its doctrines and tenets. Always, there had been some minor adjustment, some allowance to be made, and some interpretation to be tweaked. Some word to be left out. Some practice to be condoned. That would now end. The Church would go back to where it had been, become pure and pristine again. The people who were to live in the Cities of the Rosary would have to be in communion with the one true God, and with each other. They would have to be like-minded people, sharing the same morals and values, having the same dream. A homogeneous society. They would again be *"one nation, indivisible, under God."* To live in the Cities of the Rosary, people would have to be avowed members of the Church, and their children would have to be brought up in the faith.

Putting the leather volume down and returning his thoughts to the present, the cardinal felt it was regrettable that Father Ambrose had disagreed with him on the issue of secrecy about Fidelis' death. Who would have guessed that this nervous little twit would suddenly use a tone of voice like that and go against him? After that, of course, the cardinal had been forced to transfer him to a safe place. Father Ambrose had been transported to a secure facility—in fact, the very one that Cardinal Helmsman had planned to send Sister Gemma to, had she not disappeared.

It still made him uneasy to think of her out there, on the loose somewhere. But he had not lost faith that she would be found. He had a large enough network of similarly minded bishops and priests, steeped in his own conservative mode of thinking and ready to return the Church to its true self, and they all had an ear to the ground. Besides, Sister Gemma did not yet know of Fidelis' death.

CHAPTER 75

Sister Gemma was weeding the herb garden. Early in the morning, when the herbs were their most fragrant, she had harvested several large basketfuls before hanging the bunches to dry from the rafters in the shed. Lovage, sweet woodruff, sage and tarragon, bergamot and rosemary. The lavender was just beginning to bloom and, later in the week, when they were in full flower, she would pluck the stems and put a small bunch in her bureau drawer and a few sprigs under her pillow. She would wait on the basil until it got bushier, and let the dill go to seed for the crowns they would use in pickling. Thyme and savory, which flourished all season, was in plentiful supply in the kitchen already, kept along with a wide choice of other culinary herbs in small, well-marked canisters. Still, Sister Gemma preferred going out daily for fresh herbs to use in salads and to dress up platters.

The sun was hot on her back, and weeding was getting harder as the sun baked the soil. Sister Gemma stood and arched her back, and worked the kinks out by rolling her shoulders and flexing her arms like a chicken trying to fly. Her garb no longer hid her condition, but it didn't matter here. The only person who would care was Mother Odilia, and Mother Odilia was blind. Sister Gemma had seemed a godsend to her, since Sister Eustace, who had been Mother Odilia's only fully capable helper, had broken her hip and lay useless in her small room on the second floor. The rest of the staff was recruited from among the residents, a group of severely mentally handicapped adults. *When my time comes, the blind and the incompetent will tend me,* Sister Gemma thought. But Mother Anne had promised to see if she could spare Sister Zita temporarily.

Sister Gemma pushed the wheelbarrow over to the compost and dumped out the weeds. Indifferently, she passed stands of rue, tansy, and feverfew, the mayapple that was now wilted, its little yellow fruit hanging from the stem, and bushy pokeweed plants with juicy, inky berries that grew next to the shed. They no longer tempted her. The ability of these and other plants to cause spontaneous abortion had been known by pregnant women and their midwives for hundreds of years. There had been moments early on when Sister Gemma, who was well read in herb lore, had been painfully aware of their presence. It had taken Mother Anne to set her back on the right path.

When she fled, Mother Anne had sent Sister Agatha to intercept her and bring her to this house, where she would be safe—simply because it was such an unlikely place to look, and so remote. Mother had come to visit herself to make sure that Gemma was safe, and had quickly realized her situation.

Mother Anne had also guessed at Sister Gemma's state of mind and immediately understood the torture she must be going through. Without once alluding to the possibility of ending the pregnancy, she had started talking about the child: "Every child is a blessing." The first time Mother Anne had mentioned Fidelis, however, Sister Gemma had run from the room.

Since then, with Mother Anne's continued help, Gemma had accepted her state. She had gradually restored within herself the image of Fidelis in his earlier days, a man she had admired and, yes, *loved,* before he lost his mind and sinned so gravely against his God and against her. She would tell the child of the kind of man he had been then. Of course, she could never tell the child who its father really was. But that was still far in the future. At the moment she had to stay hidden here, and at some later time, when she was ready and the child could travel, they would have to find a home for themselves.

Mother Anne was due for a visit within the week and might have something to tell her by then. She had promised to help find a place for them. When Sister Gemma left here, she would no longer be *Sister* Gemma. She would have to enter the world again, and right now that thought scared her more than anything.

CHAPTER 76

Ingrid shivered. She had been sitting in the waning light, blindly watching the swaths of rain that swept across the yard and washed away the last of the snow.

Rachel stuck her head out the door, the baby dangling in his usual little hammock that hung suspended from his mother's neck. Cricket was getting better at holding his head up, which gave Rachel free hands to work in the kitchen and to give hugs to her "other children." The boys, in turn, had become remarkably cooperative and helpful, and nearly tripped over each other keeping the place picked up.

"I've been looking for you! Why are you sitting out here in the cold? We have a nice fire going inside, and something that smells pretty good and looks like chili—it's potluck, though, because the labels have fallen off the cans. Won't you come in and have some?"

Ingrid didn't appear to hear her, and Rachel stepped outside. When the sharp wind struck his face, Cricket started crying, and Ingrid suddenly turned her head.

"Oh, sorry." She picked up the Litkit and shoved it into the pocket of her jacket.

"Did you listen to it yet?" Rachel asked.

Ingrid nodded. She had played it over and over, long minutes filled with Adam's voice. For two days she had hesitated, unable to touch the message icon. What could he have had to tell her back then, before he went to New York, before they knew of the wave, before they were torn from each other, before each believed the other to be dead?

Now that she had listened to it, she realized that she no longer knew her husband. He had become a stranger to her. His voice alone was familiar, almost like a touch, and had made her shiver even before the cold had chilled her to the bone. Adam had seemed to enter her body physically through the tiny earphone. She had pulled it out of her ear so that the sound couldn't touch her, and only slowly and with closed eyes had she been able to get used to his voice—the familiar cadence, the timbre, the closeness of it, as if she and Adam were lying side by side in the bedroom. When she was finally able to listen to what he actually *said*, she could hardly believe it. She had known that something had been going on, but this? It seemed too unbelievable.

Adam's voice had started quietly, growing stronger as he spoke: "I am not really working for TB&M. In fact, I haven't for a long time. I've been working for the government, looking into a number of illegal activities—bribery, extortion, jury tampering...infiltrating the media, spreading false information...vote buying...things I can't tell you here..."

Ingrid wondered at the tape. Why couldn't Adam have told her about his new job before? What was so secret that he couldn't tell her? She had sensed, way back then, that there was something wrong. So why hadn't she just asked him? Because she had been afraid that he'd been involved in something shady, maybe even illegal. Why couldn't he simply have told her he had a government job, and that there were things he wasn't allowed to talk about? They were married, after all.

Maybe, she thought, *it was because I wasn't there to listen. I was so involved in my own work and my own problems.* But she refused to blame herself, especially when she realized that in all of the six minutes that she had listened to over and over, and now knew by heart, there wasn't a single personal sentiment—no "I miss you," no "I'm sorry," not even a "take care of Boru." Certainly no "I love you." Just a litany listing the trials of his secret life, an almost proud recital of the lonely life he had led away from her, removed from her, as time went on, both physically and spiritually. Of course, had he actually told her all this back then, maybe she would have thought it too fantastic to be true. Now, anything was possible; nothing seemed too fantastic.

Rachel had gone back inside. Ingrid remained sitting on the porch deck, leaning against the clapboard wall. She looked up at the hooks that had held the porch swing and closed her eyes. They had sat there, a young couple dreaming of the future, and Adam had laughed when she said she looked forward to them sitting there in their old age and remembering the past.

She thought suddenly that she heard the bark of a dog—such a familiar bark, but it couldn't possibly be…and yet, when she opened her eyes, it *was*. Boru, a sad-looking and shaggy thing, bounded up the porch steps. Then she heard a noise from the street, and when she looked up, Adam was briskly rounding the privet hedge, and behind him, Noah.

CHAPTER 77

President Albion walked around in the cabinet, part of the private suite of rooms that Jefferson had referred to as his "sanctum sanctorum." (Albion compared it in his mind to the "inner sanctum" down in the bunker at Camp David, and decided he liked Jefferson's version better). The suite also included the library, which was called the *book room;* the greenhouse; and the bedroom, and he had moved into the rooms with great delight. The cabinet had been Jefferson's office, and held some of his favorite furnishings and gadgets.

The president was waiting for Amaral, who was to arrive with the result of an important inquiry. Albion had met with Wheaton and Amaral two weeks earlier, at which time they had informed him that the military had been perched on the brink of a coup. Before the shock of this announcement had had time to subside, they had described their last meeting with Cardinal Helmsman, and showed Albion the contents of the files they had been given. After going through them—reading about the new White House-Pentagon Complex and the Cities of the Rosary—Albion had raved for half an hour before giving in to exhausted laughter.

Later in the meeting he had charged Wheaton and Amaral with the duty of trying to make physical contact with some of the allies in the rest of the world, any leaders left in Europa naturally being the primary prospects. Amaral had promised to go along on the flight personally, even at the risk of being shot out of the sky.

Albion sat down in the revolving chair by the revolving tabletop desk, which kept everything within arm's reach. In the room was also a revolving bookstand, which could hold up to five reference books at once, tilted at different angles. *Jefferson liked his conveniences,* the president thought. The room was painted oyster white, and adjoined the bedroom via a passage and also through the alcove bed, which was open to both sides. On the wall at the foot end of the bed hung a small, framed photograph of a painting: the outline of a cheek, the tip of a nose, and the shell of an ear with the peculiar little chubby earlobe that was so familiar to him.

He agonized again over his loss, as if it were fresh. The photo was a gift from Evie, who had carried it with her in her wallet. *Ariana must have shared the secret of her studio with her,* Albion thought without rancor. He had wanted to ask Evie about it—had she ever been there?—but each time he had choked up, unable to bear the thought of listening, of even speaking his wife's name.

He gave the chair a spin with a shove of his stockinged feet the way a child would, and then, dizzy and a little embarrassed with himself, got up and paced impatiently back and forth.

The children had arrived last week and were spending time with Evie outside, under the watchful eye of the National Guard. It was getting crowded at Monticello, with all the rooms traditionally used for bedrooms or guestrooms already occupied, and the book room and dining room being turned into bunkrooms at night. Pete and Evie had made a makeshift home in the book room.

The south piazza, or greenhouse room, was a bit chilly at night but a lovely place in the daytime. That's where Albion now turned his step. All he had to do was walk out the cabinet door and through the hallway that also led to the book room, then turn right into the glass-enclosed area. He had already had a table and some comfortable chairs borrowed from the tea room and placed on the tile floor.

Evie and the children had picked bouquets of flowers—columbine, wild geranium, rose campion, Virginia bluebell, prairie flax, and the large white peonies whose somnolent fragrance made the president feel drowsy. They had set them about the room so that the appearance of a greenhouse was complete. Outside the door the fringe tree was blooming, with its peculiar flowers that looked like old men's beards hung out to dry.

When Amaral appeared two hours later, he could see Albion through the glass-paneled door, asleep in his chair. He cleared his throat audibly before knocking and when the president snapped awake, he walked in. Albion was instantly alert, and looked up at the admiral questioningly.

Amaral stepped closer and waited for the president to sit up. "Well?"

"We've made contact," Amaral said with a satisfied smile.

CHAPTER 78

Cardinal Helmsman stood in front of the two men, who were dressed in simple black cassocks and who had arrived suddenly and unexpectedly—and with the worst news imaginable.

Still, he listened to them with a mere frown, stifling his more violent reaction until he was alone. When he finally calmed down enough to face his secretary, he ordered dinner to be laid in his room. He was not about to face Mother Anne and her circle of dutifully smiling nuns around the dining table, especially if they had heard rumors of Albion's sudden resurrection. *The indignity of it.* Just when he felt he had the assurance of the papacy sufficiently in hand to have a call issued for a conclave of cardinals to cast their vote.

Time was of the essence. It had been nearly three weeks since Fidelis' death, and the conclave should by rule begin fifteen or, at the most, twenty days after the pope's death. But, then, the cardinals had not yet been informed that Fidelis had died. Cardinal Helmsman had been on the verge of making the announcement—after having kept the pope in a coffin in the back of the ice room in the butchery—when the news about Albion arrived.

Now he would have to use whatever means he could in order for his plan to work. He must immediately call the College of Cardinals here, and keep them isolated from the outside world until after the conclave. And Mother Anne must be warned to keep the sisters from communicating *in any way* while they brought meals or otherwise came into contact with their illustrious guests. He could not afford to have any slip-ups now.

Helmsman rang for his secretary again, impatient for some food and anxious to get his plan moving. The secretary nodded eagerly that he had understood and hurried out of the room on his important errand. He had surmised some time ago that Fidelis was dead, and understood immediately what the gathering of the cardinals signified. *And what it might mean to him.* He might soon be the pope's private secretary!

Mother Anne herself arrived at the door with the meagerly laid out dinner tray. The cardinal searched her face for evidence that she knew anything, but her usual placid façade betrayed nothing.

The cardinal gestured for her to enter. "I have something to discuss that will affect you rather imminently. Won't you come in and join me in a small glass of sherry?"

Mother Anne stared at him. Had the man lost his mind? She set the tray down on the desk and watched him take out a half-full bottle of Amontillado from the cupboard behind the desk.

"A gift from a friend. Nothing special, of course. But it will do. Now, Mother Anne, I will come right to the point. I have just dispatched my secretary on an errand. A large number of cardinals and bishops are about to gather here, and as soon as all are present, we will inform them of the death of the Holy Father and hold a funeral.

"After the novemdialis, the College of Cardinals will go into seclusion here for a conclave, which will hopefully produce a new leader within a very short time. The country needs vigorous leadership, and we must help provide it. I hope this will not be too much of a hardship— I will naturally inform our guests of the restrictions we must live under, and request whatever additional food and other materials that can be procured to replace the stores of the Little Sisters of the Assumption."

The cardinal poured a small amount of sherry into two glasses and set one down on the desk within reach of Mother Anne. He stoppered the bottle and put it back into the cupboard before gesturing for her to take a seat, and then sat down himself. He took a sip and sat back, closing his eyes as if to concentrate his thoughts. Mother Anne reluctantly picked up her glass. When the cardinal opened his eyes and looked at her, she took a tiny sip and then put the glass back down. The cardinal cleared his throat and continued his one-sided "discussion."

"I know you will instruct the sisters in their duties, and here I must again emphasize the importance of silence," the cardinal continued. *"Silence prevents lies.* You must remind them that we are doing all we can in order to protect our countrymen from unspeakable sadness and paralyzing fear, and that soon, hopefully very soon, there will be cause for gladness—when a new Holy Father is elected."

You grave-robbing hypocrite! You are nothing but a scheming megalomaniac, thought Mother Anne, while at the same time helplessly nodding her assent.

If only Father Ambrose were here. Is it possible that the cardinal put him where Sister Agatha said he wanted to put Sister Gemma? I must ask Sister Agatha where that is. Not that poor Father Ambrose would be able to stand up to the cardinal, but perhaps he might know someone who could.

CHAPTER 79

The convoy had finally arrived at Monticello and was making its way up from Thoroughfare Gap, crossing the four great Roundabouts with their allées of mulberry and honey locust. Spring had busted out all over—in fact, this far south it was already early summer—and on the long trip toward their destination, they had driven through a veritable botanical garden of blooming shrubs and tender blossoms wafting in the wind along the roadsides.

Fortunately, baffle fences along the highway had shielded them from seeing much else: the hundreds of miles of burnt-out cities, ugly factory structures, and Gaza strips of closed-down shopping malls that abutted the road. It was like driving with horse blinders on, the driver thought. The flickering of the fences made him drowsy, and he had kept a bag of snacks handy to help him stay awake.

There were four vehicles, each filled to the last seat. They had been stopped at the gate, naturally, and after long and involved negotiations and careful searches of each vehicle, had been let through, escorted by several vehicles before and after. After they had crossed the third Roundabout Road the convoy slowed, and here they were stopped by a fresh set of guards.

Slowly, the vehicles were finally permitted to continue, at walking speed only, and soon they could see the great pillars of the east portico. The vehicles were unloaded of people one at a time, and the travelers were escorted into the entrance hall. They collected on the grass-green floor cloth, looking like a tour group waiting for a guide, and after a short while a guide of sorts did come along, and showed them through the house and right outside again onto the west Lawn.

A game of softball was in progress, the teams consisting of children of all ages, with a few guardsmen acting as referees. At the sound of the approaching visitors, the umpire turned around and removed his facemask. He smiled broadly at the sight of Jack and looked beyond him to the others, who were still spilling out through the door.

"Glad to see you, Jack! That's quite an entourage you're bringing. I hope you don't expect us to put you all up for the night!"

"Actually, Mr. President, yes, I do. But, first, we're ravenous. I hope you've got a fast food chef hiding in the scullery." Jack stopped talking when he noticed that Albion's attention had again shifted to the other newcomers.

Jack turned around and saw Rachel, who had just come through the door carrying the baby, surrounded by her clan of boys. Black Neil was right at her elbow, guiding her out onto the lawn. She walked forward slowly, smiling at the boys and hugging Cricket a little nervously. She didn't stop until she stood right in front of Albion, who was standing very still.

"Hello, Ben," she said. "Nice glasses."

Albion's face crumpled as he stumbled forward and pulled her to him. He stood and held her tightly for a long moment, and finally she had to gently push him away, so that the baby could breathe. The boys huddled around her anxiously, and she reached out and enfolded as many of them as she could at once.

Black Neil—whom Jack knew as Demba, and who had followed the first lady and, once he found her, made it his duty to keep her safe—kept the boys back while the president embraced his wife. Now he smiled encouragingly at them and ushered them forward.

"These are my boys, Ben," she said, "and yours, too, of course," she added.

The president nodded and turned around. He gestured to the children on the lawn, who were still holding their positions, waiting for the game to resume. They came running and surrounded him.

"And these are my children, Ariana. And yours, too, of course," he said, with the low, rumbling laugh that she had remembered with such longing and sadness when she thought he was dead.

Little Roofie peeked out from behind Albion's leg. "I biggah! I big geal now. I not baby, Uyuth," she proclaimed, looking at Albion, who nodded.

"You sure are a big girl," Ariana said. "What's your name?"

"Woofie...I Woofie," she said and pointed to her own chest.

Albion laughed and picked Roofie up. "And in case you were wondering, Ariana, I'm *Uyuth*. I'll explain that one later. Well, I know you always wanted children, but isn't this going a little overboard? A total of nineteen, if I'm counting right. As you can see, I don't have any babies to contribute, though."

"Let me introduce you, then. This is Benjamin Jiminy Cricket Albion...'Cricket' for short," Ariana said, looking at him steadily. She had enjoyed calling her husband Jiminy in private, after he had insisted it was a nickname for Benjamin. Now she enjoyed seeing the shock on his face. "We sure have a lot of hungry mouths to feed. Can we manage, do you think?" she asked.

"Well, we can always send out for pizza," Albion said.

CHAPTER 80

When people in thousands of communities—isolated from each other and the world—found themselves alive in the spring sunshine, they began to feel ashamed. They realized that they were still, miraculously, alive. Slowly, some of them began to pull themselves together and form groups. The members of each group sat down and talked about what they could do. At a minimum, they could clean up in their own backyard, tear down burned-out buildings and repair others, and see to it that there was food and water for everyone.

Then the groups started to delegate someone to go out in search of other groups, and to find out anything they could about the status of their country outside of their own little perimeter. The delegates from the small groups got together in ever widening circles and selected regional delegates and sent them in search of remnants of a government. It was quickly established that Washington was off the map, and that even Camp David was no more.

However, as the circle grew wider, the delegates began to hear rumors. *The president had died in a plane crash. Pope Fidelis had taken over as president, but had disappeared, and might also be dead. Some sort of power struggle was taking place between factions of people grasping for the leadership.* Details were scarce, however, and the delegates—riding on horseback, streaking out like so many Paul Reveres—began to despair.

It was in the churches that they found most of their information, and they came to realize that the Church had begun to take on a leadership role. It was comforting, they thought, to see a large and well-supplied food depot outside each church, where people stood patiently waiting in line for staples. One of the buildings near the church always sported a red cross so that people would know where to bring the sick. Less comforting to watch was the punishment of criminals that was carried out in public. The delegates shared all that they saw and compared their experiences with what others had learned in the rest of the country.

One day, one of the regional delegates, a man named Soul Trayne, ran into another rider, whom he at first mistook for a delegate. As soon as he started to question the man, he found himself grilled in turn. Rather than stay in the saddle, exposed to the noonday sun, the two finally dismounted and sat down in the shade. The delegate introduced himself. He was used to the raised eyebrow his name caused.

"Used to sing. City boy then. Now I'm a country boy. Don't feel much like singin' anyway. How about yourself?" he asked. *Quiet type,* he thought. *Won't get much information out of him.*

"Name's Lobo. I'm out looking for general information, same as you. You say there are more delegates like yourself? I'm sort of a delegate, too, but not quite like you. I think if we got my group together with your group, maybe between us we could come up with enough information to get a good picture. How'd you like to come and meet my guys?"

"Sure. Could use a change, anyway. Don't think I was ever meant to be a cowboy, though. Is it far?"

"Two days' ride. Have to make a stop that's a little bit out of our way, but on the other hand it may yield some interesting information. We should get there by nightfall, and hopefully they'll treat us to supper."

They mounted and rode off. Soul tried to keep pace with Lobo, who was a seasoned rider. As the day wore on, great blue thunderclouds appeared, and a wind came up and whipped the branches of the trees. Lobo turned around and waved Soul along, a little impatient at being slowed down.

"Not far now. If we hurry, maybe we'll beat the rain..." he shouted.

Soul nodded and adjusted himself delicately in the saddle before letting his heels give the horse some encouragement. Lobo streaked ahead, soon a blur in the distance. Soul followed at a bouncing gallop, knowing he'd be paying for it all night.

Just before the rain began to come down in cascades and sheets that swept across the landscape, lashing the ground and turning the roads into rivers, Soul saw a farmhouse up ahead, which made his spirits rise.

Sister Gemma let them in and they followed her, still dripping wet, into the dining room, where Mother Odilia and Mother Anne were seated by a large, rectangular table. They were accompanied by a group of loud and rowdy people of various ages, who laughed and talked with their mouths full and banged on the table for seconds. They ate a simple but tasty dinner amid the clamor, and then the noisy group clattered off toward the kitchen, carrying with it the dirty dishes and leaving behind a somewhat deafening silence.

"Now, then, Lobo," said Mother Anne. "Tell us all the news."

"They found the first lady..."

"Praise God!"

"...and she is now with the president at Monticello. Apparently, their family has grown, also—a baby of their own and eighteen orphans!"

Mother Anne looked startled. Sister Gemma was demurely looking down at the floor. She was growing her own family, and suddenly felt a surge of joy. She smiled, a stealthy Mona Lisa smile that did not go unnoticed by Mother Anne.

"And what news do you have for *us*, Mother Anne?" Lobo asked.

Mother Anne returned her attentions to Lobo. "Father Ambrose is coming around slowly. If you hadn't gotten him out when you did, it would probably have been too late. You may visit him when we bring him his tea, but you must keep it short. He is still very weak. I have some other news for you that you may find more pressing, if not ominous. The Holy Father is dead—we just had the funeral—and the Provincialate is presently hosting a conclave to elect a successor. Of course, you know what my fear is. Cardinal Helmsman made sure to call the cardinals together into seclusion before the news that President Albion is still alive had reached them, and presumably the cardinal is the only one who knows. The sisters and I were all sworn to secrecy, for the good of Church and country."

Mother Anne bitterly regretted having agreed to the cardinal's request for secrecy, seeing what it had led to. She clenched her fists in her lap under the table, still angry at having been used,

"I'm not sure any longer what he is trying to do," she continued. "I suspected at first that he was trying to 'inherit' the presidency from the Holy Father by having himself elected pope—and you know, Lobo, that he has managed to arrange it so that this will happen—but now, with President Albion alive, this seems unlikely."

Soul listened with knitted eyebrows to what Lobo and Mother Anne had to say. The amount of news that he had just absorbed today was staggering. The president was alive! The business about the pope he found less interesting, except that there seemed to be something threatening about it.

Lobo, who had listened intently to Mother Anne, stood and began to walk about in some agitation. "I need to see Father Ambrose. I need to see him immediately. I promise not to keep him long. Could you show me to him now, please?"

Mother Anne nodded and got up. Lobo turned to Soul.

"Wait here, Soul. Won't be long. But we may have to change our plans and continue on tonight. Are you up to it?"

Soul sighed deeply, made a face, and nodded.

CHAPTER 81

The white smoke rose in the stillness of the countryside, with no one there to pay any attention to it. A new pope had been elected. The supreme pontiff was to be known as Pope Peter Universalis—*Peter* after the first pope, *Universalis* to signify the width as well as the depth of his power as head of the universal Church.

The conclave had come together to cast their ballots in the chapel of the Provincialate of the Little Sisters of the Assumption, which was the only place large enough to hold them all at one time. However, it was a small chapel and there were not enough seats for them all, and so they had taken turns sitting in the pews and milling around.

The stained glass windows were old and unsophisticated, thick bits of colored, heavily leaded glass with the images outlined in black, depicting saints and parables. Colored specks of light flickered on the walls and floor and on the faces of the cardinals, throwing blue and purple and red and yellow glints on their old, pink skin. There was still a smell of death in the chapel, even though the dead bodies that had been stored there had been removed for burial some time ago.

The cabalistic and secretive members of the cardinal's New Inquisition had, after all, not been strong enough to make the two-thirds vote on the first ballot, and on the second day, they still had not been successful.

Cardinal Helmsman was seething inwardly. If they had only stayed with the old method of voting by acclamation, he thought, the vote for him would probably have carried. Intimidation was a supremely efficient tool. With everyone casting a secret ballot, people could betray you in a heartbeat. However, with great effort, he had managed to convey an image of patience and forbearance.

After three days without result, a day of prayer and discussion had been called. Cardinal Helmsman had used every available opportunity to instill a general anxiety in those he suspected were voting against him. He had done this by talking quietly to each of them individually of the urgency of the situation in the country—*no, the world*—and how important it was for the Church to be at the very forefront of the New World Order. There was no time to be lost. Whoever was to be elected, they all needed to act immediately and in concert to lead the faithful out of the dark valley.

On the following day, a great thunderstorm came down the valley, along with torrents of rain. The downpour turned the placid stream, which wound its way down from mountains and along the lower end of the wards, into a raging river. It was enough of a sign to many of the cardinals, and at the very next ballot Theodore Cardinal Helmsman was elected.

The ballots were burned in the small fireplace in the sacristy, and now Pope Peter Universalis stood calmly and humbly in the shadows at the back of the chapel instead of presumptuously up at the altar. He raised one hand in blessing and bowed his head in graceful acknowledgment and assent, and thus the conclave was ended.

The cardinals made individual acts of homage and obedience before filing out of the chapel, leaving him finally alone, and he knelt—with something that felt to him like true gratitude—in front of the crucifix.

CHAPTER 82

"Mr. President, the French ambassador has suggested that we might include two of our satellites in their next Ariane rocket. The launch is planned for the end of the month. That would mean we could get a basic telecom system going. We could try to negotiate with Eurospace to add a few more later in the year. Unfortunately, our own launching pads are either gone or too heavily damaged, and it will be some time before we are up and ready. Arianespace's base outside Paris was destroyed, but they have several functioning launching spots elsewhere."

"Excellent, Jack. Once we get communications back up, we can engage the people. I believe they are waiting anxiously for us."

"Sir, if I could ask you a favor…could you please call me Adam? Otherwise I might revert to calling you Julius, which could be a bit embarrassing. Jack was a name I took to hide my identity. I don't think I'll need it anymore. I'd be glad to explain…"

"You don't have to, Adam. I've trusted you all along, haven't I? Besides, Lobo told me you've supplied them with a great deal of information, which I suspect will come in handy in the near future. Now, I've only known you as Jack, so I'll have to get used to calling you Adam. The children still call me Julius sometimes, and then they remember and get embarrassed, not knowing what to call me. They'll hopefully learn to call me

Dad. Whenever they're ready, of course. Most of the young ones already do. They forget more quickly, I guess." The president checked his watch. "Have we heard from Demba yet?"

"He should return soon. I sent the helo for him at the prearranged place and time, and I'm assuming he'll be there to catch his ride. Hopefully he can fill in some of the blank spots. We knew where Lobo was meeting with the group, and Demba should return with a lot of information."

"Fine, certainly hope so. Now...I've been meaning to talk to you about something else. How would you like to do some work abroad? Ambassadorship in a Euro country of your choice? We could use someone like you, Jack—eh, sorry, Adam—a dedicated workaholic type with some diplomatic ability." Albion studied the younger man's face and guessed that he was about to be turned down.

Adam did not answer immediately. He looked across the desk at the president, but without seeing him. During the recent months he had come to realize how working for the government had taken over his life, become a compulsion. What Adam had learned— the discovery that had led him to contact Washington, and what he had meant to tell Ingrid in person—was that while TB&M was officially part of the district attorney's team, the firm was also connected to the Church through a clandestine extension of the local archdiocese.

When Adam informed the government official—he had flown to Washington and gone directly to the office of a senator—he had been referred and quickly recruited to his job as a government spy. During the years that had passed since that day, he had found that the district attorney's office and the firm had been helpful in covering up and disguising a host of immoral and unethical activities engaged in by the archdiocese. In fact, he had found ties leading even further up through the hierarchy, right into the heart of the Vatican itself.

The firm had also actively gone after any legal cases that involved moral and religious disparity with the law, to further the political causes of the religious right. In his dealings with the archdiocese, Adam had made a list of politicians who contributed to, as well as benefited from, these activities.

Adam had been so preoccupied with the job that his private life had ceased to exist. While officially going after and representing cases for TB&M and at the same time meticulously charting and passing on information to the government on the unlawful practices of the firm, there had been little time for Ingrid.

He had always meant to explain to her what he was doing, and had justified the delay by telling himself that it was safer for her if she didn't know. Little by little he had become so immersed in the daunting and nerve-wracking tasks that he hadn't noticed that they were drifting apart. In thinking back, what puzzled him a little was that Ingrid hadn't spoken up, hadn't insisted on equal time. But, he thought guiltily, he had been too busy to pay attention. And maybe she had been too upset and distracted after losing the baby—women reacted differently to an event like that than men did.

He remembered having been angry when it happened, and even blaming her somehow for the accident. She had been withdrawn afterwards, he remembered and he had thrown himself ever deeper into his work. When he finally got around to trying to tell her everything, the message he had left on her Litkit had simply been meant as a first step, a way to lead up to sitting down with her and explain. But then the wave had struck. *What incredible timing,* he thought. And now it seemed that she had found someone else.

"Thank you, Mr. President. I am honored. But I have some unfinished personal business at home to take care of," he said with a short laugh.

"I'll keep the offer open, Adam," the president said.

CHAPTER 83

A flutter of red and purple silk announced the arrival of the bishop of St. Louis, as the pope was still to be known until a new Vatican City could be established. He was accompanied by a number of his staunchest supporters among the bishops and cardinals.

The purple bishops swirled and mingled with the red cardinals, creating an impressive pageant weaving its way through the halls and rooms. The pope wore white. He had achieved his goal, and while the show of modesty and humility had served him well, he would now move forward into his new role with the dignity he was entitled to. He had bestowed on each of his companions a new pallium—the circular band of white wool, marked with six crosses and with front and back pendants—which they now wore about the neck. The pallia had been fabricated by the Little Sisters of the Assumption from the wool of two lambs blessed by Pope Fidelis on the feast of St. Agnes.

Once inside the door, Pope Peter Universalis had removed the long, silken, green cope, the mantle he had worn during the journey, and draped it over the outstretched arms of some minor servant (Evie, as it happened), who had hung it in the back of the room on a convenient pair of antlers. Now the pope stood, as if by chance, in a shaft of sunlight that glinted on his white zucchetto and threw a cascading iridescence over his pristinely white cassock. His hawk-like face was as severe as ever and set in a stern frown, the lines down each cheek exaggerated by the sharp light. He had gained some weight around the middle, which only served to give him additional stature. The Holy Father, annoyed at being kept waiting, clasped his hands and tapped his thumbs together impatiently.

At length, the door opened and the president ambled in, followed by Pete McPherson. Albion was casually dressed in rumpled pants and a checkered short-sleeved shirt that he hadn't bothered to tuck in. The press secretary, likewise, was jacketless, but somewhat neater in appearance. The gathered churchmen were appalled by this discourteous reception, but waited quietly for whatever was to come next.

The president had decided to leave the rest of his own entourage—including Adam, who would be leaving for Bennington before the end of the evening—in the dining room, where the guests were to be taken first. Thereafter they would proceed to the meeting room: the parlor. The parlor was the largest room in the house, and Albion had realized with a sigh of disappointment that it would not be large enough for future needs. He had come to love Monticello, to feel at home here, but they would need to move into larger quarters soon.

The president glanced over the colorful assembly, finishing by making brief eye contact with the pope before smiling and opening his arms wide to greet everyone in the room.

"Welcome all, to our temporary White House. Won't you join us in the dining room, where we have prepared a small meal for you? You must be hungry after your long trip. After that, we can talk."

He walked ahead of them as he spoke, opened the door, and led them through the hall and into the dining room. Pete waited until all of them had filed into the hall before following. The room had been set up with a long row of tables and chairs. At each seat was a small collection of plates holding bread, salad, cold sliced meats arranged with pickles and olives, and a tall glass of water.

"As you see, nothing fancy. The salad comes from our garden. The greatest luxury in front of you is the water. It is from a spring not far from here, and is brought to us daily."

After a brief blessing of the food they were about to eat, the room filled with the blended communal sound of hushed mumbling, slurping and chewing, clinking of silverware, and the rustle of silk sleeves. It reminded the president of sitting under the great blooming linden tree outside the west wing of the old White House, where thousands of bees had hummed and buzzed as they gathered the sweet nectar, creating a single sound that had no beginning and no end.

When the last fork had been put down, a pivoting serving door with shelves slowly revolved to reveal cups of steaming coffee. The president himself got up and served his guests.

"And now, let's move into the parlor. Bring your cups and glasses if you would like refills of coffee or water."

Pete offered to carry the pope's cup and glass, but the Holy Father shook his head. "We are not used to such excesses these days."

The parlor had not been rearranged, and the president suggested that everyone take a seat wherever they liked and offered to help drag chairs and couches around to place people where they wanted to sit. The pope immediately gravitated toward the Campeachy chair—the most throne-like—which addled Albion somewhat, as that had by now become *his* seat. He noticed Pete glancing at him, no doubt to catch his reaction, and started whistling tunelessly while pulling up a low, overstuffed club chair that he sank into with a contented sigh. Pete hid a grin by turning his back to the president, and got roped into dragging a large sleeping sofa toward the circle of prelates all waiting for an advantageous seat.

Small tables were placed in the center to hold cups and glasses and carafes of water, and a large coffee urn was wheeled in on a castered table from the dining room and left by the bust of Jefferson, next to the window overlooking the west lawn. The president rose and offered to pour coffee, but as there were no takers, he poured one for himself. He did not go back to his seat, but rested his elbow on the stand of the bust, giving Jefferson a smile and the slightest of bows. Then he turned to the pope.

"Well, Your Holiness, here we are," he said, using the unavoidable address, even though it seemed to stick in his craw.

"You have found yourself quite luxurious accommodations," suggested the pope, "considering the state of our nation and the situations most of our citizens find themselves in."

"Yes, indeed, we are very fortunate. The National Guard has performed an invaluable service in protecting our national heritage places, and we were certainly grateful to be able to occupy this venerable house for a while. However, as you can see, it is too small to serve as a permanent White House, and we are currently looking for a more suitable place. If anyone has a suggestion, we will add it to the list of possibilities."

"Perhaps we are getting a little ahead of ourselves," the Pope said.

"What do you mean, Your Holiness?"

"Well, there is another issue that needs to be settled first, namely the presidency itself," the pope answered. A hush settled over the parlor, where a certain amount of whispering and moving about had been taking place. *Here it comes,* Albion thought.

"Surely there is nothing unsettled about the presidency. Am I not standing here before you, occupying that role?"

"For the moment, I suppose. However, that may soon change." The pope shifted in his chair, stretching himself slightly to gain an inch or two in height, and putting his arms languidly on the green velvet armrests.

The president turned away from Jefferson's bust and walked across the floor, coming to a stop in front of the pope. "And how is that to happen?" he asked, taking a sip of coffee and casually keeping the other hand in his pocket.

"Impeachment proceedings are under way," said the Pope, leaving his elbows on the armrest but placing one hand on top of the other in front of his chest.

"Impeachment proceedings? On what grounds?"

"Several. Firstly, the citizens of our country were not warned of the disaster that was about to befall them. Millions died as a result. Your culpability is as enormous as it is obvious. Then the country languished for months while you were in hiding. It has been suggested that you suffered from amnesia, which seems a convenient excuse. If it is indeed true, we have yet another reason for questioning your ability to serve." The president had stepped closer to the pope's chair, so that His Holiness now had to look up at him and was beginning to squirm.

"And while these proceedings were going on, who would lead the country?" the president asked.

The pope stood, but the president did not back off, and an angry blush was creeping up the pontiff's neck. "I would. Standing here before you, *I* am, in fact, the president," the pope said.

At this declaration, bedlam erupted in the room. The pope took the opportunity to step sideways, away from Albion's breath, which smelled like bitter coffee, and took up a position in the middle of the floor before raising his hands for silence.

"Let me clarify, so that there will be no misunderstanding. Moments before my predecessor Pope Fidelis died, he named me, in his office as president, as his vice president. Therefore, at his death, *I* became the president. There is no question anywhere in the country that Pope Fidelis, *as President Sheedy*, was the legitimate president during the many months after the deluge, having been next in line as the speaker of the house. Therefore, in the constitutional order of presidential succession, I became the president."

All of this sounded tantalizingly true, even to Pope Peter Universalis himself—except, of course, for the small part about Fidelis having named him vice president, which had never happened. That was simply a little white lie *for the benefit of the country*. It was his great good fortune, the pope thought, that Albion had yet had to name a vice president of his own before all of this happened.

Albion glanced at Adam and Pete, who were both trying to signal to him not to make any comment. The president looked around the room, casting his eyes over the faces of the bishops and cardinals, who seemed nearly as surprised as he by the pope's declaration. Albion realized that they had not known what was coming. They had not guessed that Cardinal Helmsman had been wrestling his way into this position, had used and manipulated everyone around him, including, no doubt, poor Fidelis, to grasp both the power and the glory. For the moment, the president knew that he had to break this meeting off.

"I think this is a good time to finish our talk for the evening. It has been a long and exhausting day for all of you, I'm sure. We have made overnight sleeping arrangements for you at Mulberry Row, and Pete will now show you out to our vehicles, which will take you there. In each room you will find a basket of fruit and cheese, as well as some soap and towels. In the morning you will be picked up and brought back here for breakfast. I'm sure we'll have more to discuss at that time. Until then, may I wish you a comfortable stay."

The reconstruction of Mulberry Row included the log cabins that had been used as the plantation's slave quarters. The cabins had been outfitted with sleeping cots and simple wooden furniture—hardly "comfortable," but, then, these people were apparently used to living simply, the president thought. He left the room without waiting for a response from the pope, and Pete McPherson began to usher the guests out. The pope, who was frowning with dismay and irritation, gathered his skirts angrily and swished by Pete, who was holding the door.

"I will need my cope," he said testily.

Pete nodded and turned to one of the guardsmen. "Think you could go and get the pope's cape? It should still be hanging in the entrance hall on one of those elk antlers in the corner."

The guard smiled. "Sure thing. I'll bring it right out to him."

CHAPTER 84

Adam sat with Lobo and Soul Trayne, sharing information. Demba would be back in Monticello by now to brief the president.

Adam had hitched a ride with a group of guardsmen on their way up toward the Canadian border, and as soon as he had finished reporting to Lobo, he planned to head for Bennington.

On their way up, they had driven through a succession of severe thunderstorms, with downpours that had washed out the mountain road in several places. From where they now sat in the small mountainside chalet, they could see another thunderstorm rolling in. Early summer had been unbearably hot and humid, with frequent afternoon lightning storms. Adam was watching the buildup of thunderheads, a billowing purple mass expanding at eye speed. Streaks of lightning flashed in the distance, and the rumble echoed against the mountainsides. Shafts of rain extended from the clouds across the valley, and the rain approached in swirling curtains that reminded him of the aurora borealis he had seen in Sweden the year he and Ingrid were married.

Soul coughed, waking Adam out of a reverie. What had they been talking about? Politics. Lobo was still trying to locate members of government. Soul had been helpful, repeating what he had learned from other regional delegates. Lobo kept careful notes and was able to add the names of a couple of congressmen and senators still alive to his list. Then Adam had described the meeting that had taken place between the president and the pope, causing Lobo to shake his head in utter disbelief.

"I had a few minutes with Father Ambrose. Helmsman—the pope, I mean—had him put away, you know. Don't know why...must have been trying to hide something, I suppose. Anyway, Father Ambrose is still very weak, although they tell me he is improving, and I hope to have another chat with him on my way back down," Lobo said.

Adam gave Lobo a distressed look. "I'm coming with you. There's something I need to ask him." He sighed. There would be no going back to Bennington now.

CHAPTER 85

The children came running into the bedroom. One by one they took aim and jumped up onto the bed where the president and first lady were sleeping, then rolled across it and finally slid off the other side as though it were a piece of gym equipment.

Meggi pushed Lans and Roofie over, before she herself laughingly rolled across the by now heaving mound. They woke Cricket, who had been sleeping in his laundry basket crib on the cabinet side, and the baby joined his voice to the squealing and shrieking of the other eighteen children.

Ariana slid out of bed and barely avoided being pummeled by Declan, the redhead with the Irish temperament who, she had quickly learned, was always getting into trouble. She bent down and picked up the baby, amazed at her husband's ability to sleep through this daily ritual. When all the children had made it across, the president opened one eye and yawned.

"Last one to the breakfast table is a rotten egg!" he said as he slipped out of bed.

Since the children had to make their way across the alcove again before following him, the president had a good head start. Ariana walked through the passageway with Cricket. They would be the rotten eggs, as usual. (Roofie would jump up and down, yelling, "You'we a wotten e-egg !")

The president, still in his pajamas, ran quickly through the entrance hall, past the parlor and into the dining room, where some of the guardsmen were still asleep on their cots. Moments later, the cots had been put away and the president and a few of the children—according to a preset schedule that was posted on the bedroom wall—had gone downstairs to the kitchen to make breakfast. Lunch and dinner were prepared by the guardsmen's kitchen crew, but breakfast was the president's specialty.

After breakfast the children played outside, under guard. Ben and Ariana refilled their coffee cups and went to sit in the greenhouse, where they could watch their clan.

"Looks like a schoolyard," Ariana said. She had already taken on the role of teacher, bringing the children into the book room, where they studied maps and globes and old books and began to learn about the event that had changed everything. They had to start somewhere, and this was something they were all curious about.

The memory of it still caused them a great deal of anxiety, and Ariana thought it would be good for them to work through it together. Evie had joined her in the class room, and sometimes they grouped the children by age to teach at a level each would understand. The youngest ones, Lans and Roofie, seemed to have an easier time adjusting, but the future would tell what traumatic memories might still be hiding within.

The president and his wife sat watching the children in silence while Ariana nursed Cricket. The day would be busy, as was every day now. Pete had left a note listing the meetings that were scheduled, and at the bottom he had added, as though it had been an afterthought, "wedding."

"Look at this, Ben. Did Pete think we'd forget?" Ariana laughed.

She had impishly given Pete and Evie a deadline for getting married if they wanted to continue living together in the president's mansion, and the wedding day had finally dawned. They were to be married late in the afternoon on the west lawn, in the shade of two great tulip poplars. The winding flower border of the Roundabout was in profuse and determined bloom, and would make a lovely and fragrant backdrop. But before then, a heavy schedule awaited the president.

A soft knock on the door announced Pete, who stuck his head in apologetically. "Sorry to disturb you, sir, but there's been a small change in the schedule. Adam returned late last night and wants to see you first thing—he's still asleep, though, so you've got a few minutes yet. He said to let you know the other thing's been taken care of."

"Adam's back? I thought he was on his way to Bennington?"

"I'm not clear on why he's back, sir. He didn't go into it last night. I'm on my way now to wake him up. Will you be here or in the cabinet?"

"Thanks, Pete. I'll stay here until he's ready. Tell him to bring his coffee and join us out here, and then we'll go on into the cabinet."

Ariana waited until Pete was gone before asking what "the other thing" was that had been taken care of.

"It's supposed to be a surprise. Oh, well, I guess I'll tell you. I told Adam to arrange for a helo to bring Matt and Luce here for the wedding. Pete thinks it was to pick up Lobo."

Ariana got up and put Cricket down in his basket before giving her husband a hug. "You're such a romantic," she said, and started unbuttoning his shirt. The president was beginning to respond to her amorous advances just as Adam walked in.

"I thought you were still asleep," said Albion, reluctantly turning away from his wife.

"What, with that racket outside? Can't you control your kids, Julius?" Adam said.

"That's Mr. President to you, *Jack*," Albion said.

"Sorry. Too tired. As soon as I pass on my information, I'm finding a quiet spot to put this weary body down."

"Come on. I'll get you some coffee. Meet me in the cabinet, Adam."

Ariana remained in the greenhouse, lounging comfortably with Cricket back on her lap. She turned around at the soft sound of Meggi tiptoeing into the room, with her constant shadow, little Roofie, right behind her. Ariana gestured for the girls to come closer, and Meggi advanced shyly. Roofie walked around the room before climbing up on a chair to look out the window. Outside a ballgame was in progress. Suddenly she jumped down and ran back toward the door.

"Woofie pway baw, too, wiw Aug an' Dec an' Lanth an' Thammy," *Roofie play ball, too, with Aug and Dec and Lans and Sammy,* she shouted, and was gone.

Meggi stood looking at the baby for a while.

"Would you like to hold him?" Ariana asked. Meggi took a step backward and shook her head vigorously. "He's your little brother now, you know," Ariana said.

Meggi looked at her, wide-eyed. "I used to have a little brother," she said.

"Does Cricket remind you of him?"

Meggi shook her head then started to cry. "I don't remember what he looked like," she said between sobs.

Ariana put the baby back in his basket and took Meggi onto her lap instead. "I have an idea, Meggi. Maybe we can try to draw a picture of him to make you remember."

She went and got a pad of paper and a box of pastels and sat down next to Meggi. She made a quick sketch of a child's head, basing the features and shape of the face on Meggi's, but keeping them vague and baby-like. She had noticed that children simplify the recognition process and accept a reasonable look-alike. She gave the child the same wavy blond hair and large blue eyes as Meggi.

"Does this look like him?" she asked.

Meggi shook her head. After looking at the picture some more, she picked up a dark brown crayon. "His face is this color," she said.

Ariana took the crayon and changed the skin color then continued and made the eyes brown and the hair dark.

Meggi nodded happily. "That's him! That's my brother, Ebben!" Then she started crying again. Ariana held her until the sobs began to subside. "Will I be *adapted*, too, like Ebben?"

Ariana couldn't help laughing. "Yes, Meggi, and you'll have a lot of adopted brothers and sisters from now on."

Meggi nodded, a happy smile crossing the little face still swollen from crying.

***

When Albion walked into the cabinet, he found Adam asleep, his legs hanging over the side of the red leather loveseat that Ariana had ordered dragged into the room so that she would have a comfortable place to nurse Cricket. Albion checked the time and reluctantly shook Adam awake.

"My apologies, Adam. You'll have to catch up on your sleep after we finish. I'm expecting a papal delegation later this morning. What do you have for me that's so important you came all the way back here? I know how anxious you were to get home. I hope this won't harm your chances…"

"Que sera, sera, as they say. In order to assess the importance of *my* news, I'd love to hear what the judgment here has been regarding the legality of the pope's declaration, since I left before the second session took place. Without access to my law library, and, well…unfortunately I don't carry a copy of the Constitution on me."

"Let me fill you in, Adam. Pete, bless him, remembers his early training well, and was the one to point out the obvious—that while Sheedy may have named Helmsman as vice president, the nomination had not been confirmed by Congress. Of course, the pope had an immediate answer to that: He had already sounded the waters and insisted that his confirmation is assured. Thanks partly to you, we know he's had a large network of loyal underlings out there working diligently on his behalf. He may have a better list than we do of who's left in the Congress and Senate. He mentioned a few names I hadn't heard from our sources. And if he has initiated impeachment proceedings, it may become a tangled web. People may find it easy to believe the pope, after all that's happened. And if there's anger over the fact that there was no warning about the wave…well, I personally wouldn't blame them. Think of how many lives could have been saved…"

"Mr. President…sir. Blaming yourself won't do anyone any good. You must be aware of what this man would do to our country. You must stop him, sir."

"But how, Adam? By force? You of all people know how deep the Church's network goes. If he has access to it, can we fight it?"

"We may not have to, sir."

CHAPTER 86

Ingrid watched as Noah sanded the planking smooth. He was working on a new dory, and after steaming the wood so that it would curve gracefully, he had shaped it into the narrow, sylphic form she remembered from their many trips between the island and the mainland. Next he would paint it buttery yellow with dark green trim, using Adam's leftover paints.

Noah missed the sea. Ingrid could tell by the way he scanned the horizon when they were out walking along the wide fields that bordered the west side of the town. He would vent his bottled-up frustration by kicking at rocks, slapping the heads off tall weeds, or by sighing deeply at the sight of a leaf dancing across a puddle. She wished she could help him, wished that she could suggest going back to the seashore, but she didn't want to see the sea again, not yet.

Watching him work, she ached for his touch, jealous of the wood he was caressing and smoothing so lovingly. Was it too late for them now? Would it have made a difference if they had established that final bond and made love before she found out that Adam was alive? When Adam and Noah rounded the hedge together, would it have given Noah the advantage if he and Ingrid had been lovers? Would she have reached out to him in front of Adam and touched him in the way lovers touch?

The fact that she and Adam knew each other in the biblical sense and had made love for years had not given Adam an advantage at that moment. Of course, in the last few years, especially since her miscarriage, that bond had loosened. Severed, if truth be told, and she realized with vague surprise that she could not remember the last time they had made love. They had each retreated to their own half of the bed, rarely crossing the imaginary line drawn in the center. She had been filled with a mixture of resentment and relief over his constant absences, a feeling of deepening alienation upon his returns, and puzzlement over the change in him. The silence between them had often been uncomfortable, yet neither had been able to break it. The circles they walked in to avoid touching had grown ever wider. Where was the idealistic young man she had met and fallen in love with? The man that had slept next to her in the last few years was a stranger. Sometimes after he had fallen asleep, she would study his face, had even touched him, tracing his features with feather-light fingers to see if it would rekindle the feelings she had for him when they first became lovers.

When Adam rounded the privet hedge, a flame of disappointment—a feeling that the game was up and no happiness would be hers—had singed her. Somehow, it had removed both Noah and Adam from her future sphere. Each had excluded the possibility of the other.

It had only taken moments for Adam to catch on. Noah's shyness, his avoidance of going near Ingrid, or even looking at her, had been clues so obvious that Adam had sensed something was going on. So both Adam and Noah had avoided her—and each other. And then, the moment Adam caught sight of Black Neil, his priorities had suddenly changed anyway.

Black Neil had led him into the house, which had been overrun with children, and out to the kitchen, where he had introduced Adam to Rachel. *The first lady.* It still seemed unbelievable to Ingrid that she hadn't recognized Ariana Albion. She would never forget the shriek that had come out of her kitchen, followed by Rachel's running into the living room, looking wildly around her. She had been carrying Cricket aloft, precariously balanced on her outstretched hands, and when she caught sight of Ingrid, she had charged at her and embraced her with such force that the three of them fell to the floor. Fortunately, Cricket had landed on top of Ingrid.

"He's alive, Ingrid, alive!" Rachel had shouted. For a confused moment, Ingrid had thought she meant Cricket, until Rachel had said, laughing, "No, silly—my husband, the president!"

A few hours later, Adam and Ariana and the all the children had somehow managed to pile into Adam's vehicle, and they started on their long trek to reunite with the president. Adam had cast one last look at Ingrid. He had looked tired and haggard, but she had not been able to read anything into that look.

Black Neil—or Demba, his real name as Ingrid had learned—had set off in a different direction for a separate rendezvous. All that remained of the new Dogtown settlers was Granny Day and the two who now had to sort out their unfinished affair: Ingrid and Noah.

Ingrid had explained as well as she could to Granny what the situation was. Granny had listened carefully and without comment. Finally, she had said, "Well, dear, it's up to you now. I won't try to influence you one way or another. If you feel like talking about it, I'm here." But Ingrid knew how fond Granny was of Noah, and it made it all the harder to remain open to all possibilities.

It would be so easy to choose Noah. He loved her, quite obviously; he was funny and easygoing and she enjoyed his touch enough to know that they would get pleasure out of their physical relationship. She had already opened herself to him to such an extent that it seemed the final bridge was insignificant and could be crossed in a heartbeat. And yet, there remained the fact that she once had made a commitment to Adam that she had thought was for life. Why had Adam returned? To fulfill that same commitment? After all the loveless years they had spent together, was there anything left to preserve? Did he still feel something for her? Ingrid herself didn't seem to be able to feel anything at the moment.

She had, maybe wishfully, convinced herself that Adam was dead. Was this in order to justify falling in love with Noah? And now that Adam was alive...no, she couldn't make sense of it. Her head ached right along with her heart.

Granny Day came out on the porch and called to them that there was food waiting on the table, and Ingrid felt guilty for forgetting the time of day. Noah came over, put his arm around her, and led her toward the stairs.

"The dory's ready. Now all I have to do is wait for her to dry and then get her launched. Of course, there's the slight problem of the distance from here to the sea. But I'll figure something out. Then, sweet lady, I'm off for the seashore." He looked at her searchingly, but didn't ask her to come with him. Was he too proud, or had he lost hope when Adam appeared?

CHAPTER 87

The papal delegation—the hard-core nucleus of the New Inquisition, the cream of the crop of the St. Louis curia—was delivered promptly, and the president sat waiting for them in the dining room.

The table had been set up for a formal conference, without tablecloth and with water carafes and glasses placed within arm's reach of all present. Their last meeting had ended badly, with the pope and his large retinue leaving triumphant yet angered that the president still had refused to admit defeat. Today's delegates arrived carrying large black briefcases. *Witnesses for the prosecution,* Albion thought, *prepared to hang the defendant.*

The ecclesiastic dignitaries seated themselves, taking time to smooth out their creased silk cassocks, patting their hair into place, and adjusting their skullcaps. The president waited and watched patiently while the group settled.

"Welcome, Cardinal Drysdale," he started, continuing down the line to greet each cardinal by name. "I hope today will mark the end of the impasse we found ourselves at after our last meeting."

In the barely perceptible pause before the president continued, Cardinal Drysdale took the opportunity to speak. "We certainly hope so, Mr. Albion," he started (Albion didn't fail to notice that the cardinal had avoided calling him "Mr. President"), "since President Helmsman is eager to lead the country out of its current state of chaos. The president has a very complex set of plans for rebuilding the country that we need to embark on as quickly as possible so that we may lead the world into the future." As he bored his steel gray eyes into Albion's, there was a general hum of agreement from the other cardinals.

"Perhaps we are getting a little ahead of ourselves, Cardinal," said the president, exactly mimicking the pope's words from the previous meeting.

"And what is that supposed to mean?" The cardinal stood, no doubt to appear more intimidating. He was a broad-framed man, although he had begun to cave in to old age. The shoulders sloped gently, and the spine was beginning to bend, as though the head was too heavy for the neck to hold up. He tried to hold himself erect as he glared at Albion.

"It means, to start with, that I don't accept His Holiness as president. I am fully prepared to wait for Congress to convene and vote on his confirmation, should that turn out to be the appropriate action. In the meantime—and until you have succeeded in impeaching me and removing me from office—I am still the president. My impeachment would obviously have to precede His Holiness' confirmation. While we are waiting for these steps to be taken, we should certainly, as you say, embark on our plans to rebuild the country. I have studied His Holiness' extensive proposals, and I am afraid that we have very different priorities. I have prepared an outline of my own plans—with the cooperation of staff from many of our national agencies as well as members of my own cabinet—which I will make public in a few weeks."

Cardinal Drysdale had remained standing, and his back had stiffened. He lifted his chin defiantly as he began to reply.

"I must warn you that the impeachment process is underway *as we speak,* and from polls taken there is no doubt that by tomorrow you will be impeached. From there to removal from office is but a very small step. President Helmsman, who rightfully claimed that title, is currently in the Midwest meeting with a gathering of powerful leaders. As soon as the hearings end tomorrow, he expects the cloud of confusion regarding the presidency to be dispelled, and he will then announce the location that he has selected for the new White House." The cardinal sat again, apparently exhausted by the effort.

"And I am afraid that His Holiness is again moving too fast. We have someone present here today who would like to address you." The president made a signal to the guard by the door, and as the door opened, an emaciated figure appeared, supported by Pete and Adam. They led him, step by shuffling step, until he was able to sit down at the table.

"Father Ambrose, please accept my thanks for your willingness to help," the president said. He then turned to the delegation. "For those who may not be personally familiar with him, this is Father Ambrose, formerly a close associate of Pope Peter's. I must ask that you listen to what he has to say without interruptions or questions. Father Ambrose will remain at the White House as our guest during his recuperation, and any questions you have will be answered as soon as he is physically able. Father Ambrose, I will only trouble you today to repeat the statement you made to me earlier. I asked you then if you were present at Pope Fidelis' death. Please tell me your answer again."

Father Ambrose tried to stand, but Pete whispered to him that he should remain seated. The cleric, ashen from illness and exhaustion, cleared his throat carefully.

"I was present when the Holy Father died," he said simply.

"And before he died, did he speak...to make confession, to pray, anything? Did he have any last words to say to the world?"

"No. The Holy Father suddenly collapsed and fell unconscious. He never regained consciousness." Father Ambrose spoke in a near whisper, and the cardinals had to lean forward to hear him.

"Is it possible that the Holy Father made some important announcement to Cardinal Helmsman *before* his sudden attack?"

"Mr. President, the Holy Father had long been removed from his senses. Dementia. Senator Birke hid this fact and used the pope to gain power until the senator himself died of the influenza. I am sorry to say that Cardinal Helmsman continued in the senator's footsteps, and hid the Holy Father's condition, and even his death, from all but those who took care of him at the Provincialate. Cardinal Helmsman has...for many years... been..." Father Ambrose's voice was trailing, and his hands shook against the table. It made a rustling sound, as though his skin was made of tissue paper. He leaned back into the chair, unable to sit up straight.

"Father, thank you. We must not tire you further today. We are very grateful for the information you have given, information that I know must have caused you a great deal of pain to divulge. Mr. McPherson will take you back to your room, where I hope you will be able to rest comfortably until dinner." The President signaled for Pete and Adam, who helped the old prelate through the door and then simply picked up his thin body and carried him to his bed.

The delegates sat in shocked silence. Seated around the table were the Vatican's most ruthless and powerful leaders, who ordinarily would stop at nothing to expand the size and strengthen the power of the Church. In Pope Peter Universalis, they had seen a new messiah. Wasn't it marvelous that there were twelve of them? They were the new apostles, gathered around the messiah to spread the gospel again, and to see to it that humanity listened, this time.

They had seen the signs. The second flood had arrived to punish the sinners who had brought the world to the brink of ruin. Ruin, redemption, and resurrection. The three "R"s of the Christian faith. They were also men who had lost their faith a long time ago, although they didn't know it. They simply never thought about it. Power corrupts, and they had been corrupted. Only very occasionally did they look for or take notice of signs from God. The wave had been a sign. The volcanic eruptions and apocalyptic missile attacks. The great thunderstorm that had raged when they were preparing to elect the pope had convinced the conclave that God was speaking to them. Now they wondered, *Why would God have told us to elect Cardinal Helmsman?* Would God believe that the means justify the end?

In their lifetime of service to the Church, they had all done expedient and sometimes even criminal things: hiding facts that would cause scandals; buying their way out of lawsuits; catering to the rich simply to accumulate wealth for the Church; and neglecting the poor and defenseless by insisting that the Church had insufficient liquid assets to help them. They had thought *(hadn't they?)* that whatever they did, they did for the Church. If their collection boxes overflowed, it was *the Church* that prospered. (Of course, in wealthy parishes, the clergy also ate well.) If cardinals became powerful and influential, the power went *to the Church*. (Of course, a cardinal's accommodations and mode of travel would also improve.)

They all knew very well that Cardinal Helmsman had been *one of them,* a man driven by the need for power, and a man with a great record of achieving his goals. Father Ambrose's aborted hint of Helmsman's previous transgressions hadn't surprised or shocked them in the least. Father Ambrose was obviously a stickler for the minutiae, an idealist who did not understand that accommodations must be made in order for the vast amoeba that was the Church to be able to continue its growth—until it had absorbed everything and covered the earth. One had to smooth the way—for the organism was now so large and cumbersome that its own sheer weight slowed it down—squash any obstacles, break off any thorns that might pierce its skin. A certain amount of ruthless pragmatism was necessary.

That the pope would lie about the dying words of Pope Fidelis in order to climb the papal throne as a step to the presidency was, however, beyond even their imagination. That was blasphemy, sacrilege. Maybe the thunderstorm had been an indication of God's wrath, not His approval.

Cardinal Drysdale pushed his chair back and stood again, a little shakily. He looked around the table at the rest of the *apostles* as if to assess their combined strength, but with the news of the weakened messiah, they looked withered. He turned to the president—*our Pontius Pilate,* he thought wearily—and spoke in a voice that was hoarse and barely audible.

"Perhaps we all need some time to consider how to proceed from here. May I ask to confer privately with my brothers? The information we have just been given, if verifiable..."

"Mother Anne and the Sisters of the Provincialate were deposed in front of witnesses along with Father Ambrose," inserted the president.

"Then we have a situation that requires a great deal of thought."

"Unfortunate for you, isn't it, that there is no impeachment process to remove a pope. You are stuck with him until the end of his days, unless, of course, he should choose to resign. Unlikely, if I have read him correctly."

Cardinal Drysdale was fading rapidly, and the president decided to relent. "You may use this room for your conference. I have other meetings, which I will hold in my private office. Let us know if you need anything—food or drink, or a place to rest."

Albion got up and gestured to the members of his own staff to leave with him so that the papal delegation would have complete privacy. *They will need more than privacy to sort this out,* he thought.

***

Later, as Albion sat in a meeting with Amaral, he received a handwritten message from Cardinal Drysdale:

Dear Mr. President,

The present situation requires that we leave immediately. Our intentions are to send a messenger to the Congress, presently meeting outside Philadelphia, to put a hold on the hearings before a premature vote is taken. Despite the fact that our delegates were not unanimous in all matters, you have my assurance that I will do my utmost to convince our people to let this matter rest until a properly elected and assembled Congress can look into the matter fully. In the meantime, we will recommend that you shall remain as president.

With prayers for your continual safety, and with special regards to Father Ambrose.

Cardinal Ewan Drysdale

CHAPTER 88

The helo that dropped Matt and Luce on the west lawn (Pete and Evie had been sent down to Mulberry Grove on a contrived errand) picked up a passenger and left as quickly as it had come.

"Nahs fahmland," Matt said, looking around. "But whea's the bahn? I thawt this was a wohkin' fahm?" Luce took him by the arm and steered him toward the house, where Aug stood and waved them on.

Albion had arranged for Adam to get flown back to the Bennington heliport to make up for time lost. "Good luck, son," the president said, briefly interrupting a meeting when Adam showed his face in the cabinet passageway.

As the helo took off and turned northeastward toward Maryland and Pennsylvania, the president met with Amaral.

"I would like to have you as my vice president, Doug. Would you accept the nomination?" Albion asked.

Amaral couldn't help laughing. "This is much easier than a coup," he said. Then he became serious. "Of course, sir. I would be honored."

"I'll give your name to the Congress for confirmation, then," Albion said.

Amaral had just reported that their lists of surviving congressmen and senators had been adjusted upward after they had received information from Lobo and a handful of the regional delegates. They now had thirty-two congressmen and seventeen senators confirmed alive, and the process of information-gathering was continuing. Assuming the satellite launch was successful, they might have sufficient communications ability to organize an election come November.

***

By the time the wedding party was gathering under the tulip poplars, Adam was crossing the border between Connecticut and Massachusetts. The sun was making its way westward, and the sky became a giant peach, tinged with pink and orange.

At Monticello, the president picked up the first lady for the ceremony. "Several power plants ready to go. We're starting to print new currency. We're rebuilding Camp David—apparently, a few of the cabins still stand. Ah, let's see…the White House is moving to Charleston, West Virginia, which apparently escaped virtually unscathed. Great capitol building there, bigger than the one in Washington, and you'll love the governor's mansion, which we hope to wrest from the guv and turn into a home for us. What else? Oh, Amaral said yes. That's it, I think…not bad for a day's work."

"I'll miss this place," was the only thing she said.

The president laughed. "I knew that's exactly what you were going to say. However, I can promise you a bed with a little more privacy…"

Next, they picked up their nineteen children and led them out to the Roundabout. They all walked along the winding path, at a decorous pace to start with, until Meggi and Roofie and Lans caught sight of balloons and ribbons flying. The next moment a bedlam of children took a shortcut across the lawn to join the burgeoning party.

Balloons were immediately severed from clusters and handed to the younger children, who ran around happily until music was suddenly heard and the children were waved back. Matt and Luce appeared and were quickly surrounded by children with wildly bobbing balloons to accompany the bridal party down the path.

***

While Pete and Evie were exchanging vows, Adam was walking across the tarmac. He could see the grove of trees that surrounded the little town of Bennington, and followed the path he had always taken when the shuttle or airport limo was not scheduled to leave immediately. It was only a half-hour walk, or a twenty-minute jog if it rained.

As he walked, he thought about the future. Would the president be able to hold onto his position? Would they ever return to some kind of normalcy, now that a government seemed to be forming? Would the world be the same or forever changed? What would his own role be—would he take the president up on his offer and accept a position in Europa?

When he caught sight of the maples that grew along their street, he realized that during the long walk he had not once thought of Ingrid.

As he rounded the privet hedge, a strange equipage was making its way across the lawn. A bicycle was towing a small yellow boat perched on a homemade trailer. The trailer rolled on wheels robbed from other bikes and wobbled like a prairie schooner. Noah, his red hair in a flurry around his head and the beard bushing out in front, waved at Adam as he neared, but didn't slow down. The bike swerved ominously as it hit the gravel and Adam gave it a steadying push out toward the road.

"I'll be back in a couple of weeks, Ingrid," Noah called out as he left the yard. "You've got one chance, Adam..." he wheezed as he disappeared down the street between the tall sugar maples.

When Adam turned back toward the house, he saw Ingrid sitting in the old porch swing, which Noah had found and resurrected. He walked up the steps and sat down next to her, pushing off with his feet to set the swing going. He could see that she had been crying, which didn't help. At last he rested his arm around her back—gently, so that she didn't feel trapped. When Ingrid squirmed he removed his arm.

As Ingrid listened to Adam's long and involved explanations of his life in the past years, she began to feel a strange relief. She and Adam were no longer who they had been when they married. They had started to recreate themselves during his long absences, and now all they had in common were pleasant memories of their early days. She was grateful for those memories, but they were not enough. Adam had a different future than the one she envisioned, going down a road that he had started on years ago. His future would include more long absences in a role he alone had chosen. It was an important role, she realized, but it did not offer a life that she wanted to share.

Ingrid knew already what she wanted to do. On their way to Bennington, she had heard the distant voices of children whenever they got near a community. There would be a great need of teachers now, and she would be one of them. And Noah, if he came back, was a man of all trades. Carpenter and fisherman, weren't they revered old trades?

She told him as gently as she could, and while Adam felt an initial stab of jealousy, it was strangely mingled with relief. He was free, and his blood began to pulsate faster at the thought of being part of setting up a new government. The president needed him, as Ingrid did not.

What was likely to become a part of Ingrid's future had disappeared through the garden gate a little while ago. Adam remembered, with a last twinge of envy, Noah's last defiant call to Ingrid, and he rose and caressed her cheek.

"Two weeks, the man said. Bet he'll be back before then," he said with a slight smile.

CHAPTER 89

The climate was still undergoing a great change. The traditional weather pattern they had been used to, which had been unpredictable enough, would not return, and it would be several years before the earth's climate would stabilize.

Furthermore, there was no telling what might still happen at the South Pole. They had learned from satellite photos that Antarctica was absorbing moisture and growing ice sheets again, and tossing its lacy petticoat around coquettishly, but no one knew what might happen there in another season—maybe more breakoffs, or new ice melt. The continent still held a vast amount of ice; if the global climate changed sufficiently, might it not all melt? They had to plan for the possibility of a continually rising sea.

Neither the old standby arsenal nor the newer weapons—the Apokalyps missile and the highly sophisticated Zetaquake fibrillator—nor a myriad other attack or defense systems had served to save any nation. What nature had not managed to destroy, man had done his very best to finish. It was unlikely, however, that the realization would forge a warm and permanent bond between nations. Competition was in the nature of man, far stronger than the will to cooperate for the common good. The formerly great countries were striving hard to be great again. The old alliances were reformed at a rapid pace, following the same groupings as always. In all countries, the religious pointed out what they thought was obvious—that God had spoken to the world—which was met with the same response as always: *Man was created with a free will, and would exercise it.*

The global population explosion that had led to famine, disease, and war was no longer a critical problem, at least for the foreseeable future. In fact, some of the countries where overpopulation had caused the greatest hardship now had the opposite problem, and waves of immigrants would flow in the reverse direction.

The world clock had been set back by 200 years. Would it go forward again at an accelerated rate? Would man learn from his mistakes? In his hubris, would he not simply decide to replace what he had lost? He would not have to invent a thing, just reproduce the world he remembered, cashing in on past knowledge.

Man—at once selfish and altruistic, thoughtless and clever, innocent and full of sin—would once more avail himself of the earth, defend his territories and freedoms, and when nature struck him down again, plead with or rail against his God. The cycles would repeat, endlessly; empires would rise and fall and rise again, triumphant; new civilizations would appear like phoenixes out of the ashes, until ashes were all that remained.

For the present, it would be remembered that the sea that lapped the new shores could not be trusted. It might suddenly make another claim on the land. Meanwhile, the rains would fall and cleanse the earth, and then the sun would shine and there would be a bow in the cloud.

ABOUT THE AUTHOR

Gunilla Caulfield was born and educated in Stockholm, Sweden, before immigrating to the United States. After ten years as an art dealer in Boston she moved to Rockport, Massachusetts, where she served as reference librarian at the Rockport Public Library. Along with husband Thomas and a steadily growing clan, she divides her time between Rockport, Massachusetts, and Bridgton, Maine.

Another novel by the author is in process, and future publications include sequels to "Murder on Bearskin Neck," with Annie Quitnot as sleuth, and a book of Christmas stories.

Made in the USA
Charleston, SC
07 August 2010